Boots had had his tonsils out, and on Sunday Chinese Lady – which is what the Adams family called their Ma – and Lizzy came to see him in hospital.

'Can he eat yet?' asked Lizzy.

'What I've been able to partake of so far, is hardly keeping my body and soul together.'

'Hark at him,' said Lizzy, 'can't he yap? I tell yer what we brought yer, Boots. Apples.'

'Apples! Apples!'

'Do yer good,' said Lizzy.

There was a boy on the other side of the ward staring at Lizzy. A rather handsome young man with a nice smile. Lizzy began to blush.

'He's lookin' at me,' she said, flustered. 'He keeps lookin' at me.'

'Only at the hole in your stocking,' said Boots, getting his own back for the apples.

When they'd gone Nurse Wharton came and plumped up the pillows.

'Aren't you lucky to have a nice mother and pretty sister?' she said.

'We're in pawn,' said Boots.

'Well, you're not the only family, so don't brag about it.'

They weren't the only family in pawn, not in Walworth. But they were the only family that had a daughter as nice as Lizzy. And the next time Lizzy came she was wearing her Sunday best and she didn't have a hole in her stocking, and she looked across the ward to see if the young man had come again.

and published by Corgi Books

DOWN LAMBETH WAY

Mary Jane Staples

CORGI BOOKS

DOWN LAMBETH WAY
A CORGI BOOK : 0 552 13299 3

First publication in Great Britain

PRINTING HISTORY
Corgi edition published 1988
Corgi edition reprinted 1988
Corgi edition reprinted 1989
Corgi edition reprinted 1990
Corgi edition reprinted 1991 (twice)
Corgi edition reprinted 1992
Corgi edition reprinted 1995
Corgi edition reprinted 1997

Corgi Books are published by Transworld Publishers Ltd,
61–63 Uxbridge Road, London W5 5SA,
in Australia by Transworld Publishers (Australia) Pty Ltd,
15–25 Helles Avenue, Moorebank, NSW 2170,
and in New Zealand by Transworld Publishers (NZ) Ltd,
3 William Pickering Drive, Albany, Auckland.

Printed and bound in Great Britain by
Cox & Wyman Ltd, Reading, Berkshire.

TO THE FAMILY

CHAPTER ONE

Chinese Lady came to see me on Sunday afternoon in Guy's Hospital, and brought my sister Lizzy with her. Chinese Lady was my mother, she having almond eyes and having taken in washing for a few years before getting a cleaning job at the town hall. She had been friendly with Mr Wong Fu of the Chinese Laundry off the Old Kent Road, and they still stopped for a chat if they met in the street, although that didn't happen too often, because Mr Wong Fu was rarely seen outside clouds of steam.

'Can Boots talk yet?' asked thirteen-year-old Lizzy, as she and Chinese Lady sat down at my bedside.

'I don't know, you better ask him,' said Chinese Lady, who didn't mind being called that by her children. She thought the Chinese were the most polite and civilised of all peoples.

'Can you talk?' Lizzy asked me.

'Of course I can talk,' I said.

'Pity,' said Lizzy, 'we was hopin' you'd lost some of yer yap.'

'Lizzy, Lizzy,' said Chinese Lady, who was looking as she liked to look on Sundays, properly reverent in her black widow's weeds, 'don't talk so unfeelin' to your brother when he's just been operated on.'

'It's only his tonsils,' said Lizzy, 'it's not like they've took his leg off like they did with Mr Tiddle.'

'Mr Tibble,' said Chinese Lady with asperity. She rarely got cross, but she was often severe. 'If you're goin' to be like that, you can go outside.'

'When you get round to asking how I am,' I said, 'I'm still poorly.'

'Can he eat yet?' asked Lizzy.

'I don't know, what a question,' said Chinese Lady. 'Can you eat yet, Boots?'

Why everyone called me Boots would have been a downright mystery if Chinese Lady hadn't told me that her cousin, our Aunt Victoria, had knitted me some blue bootees when I was an infant, and that she used to come and visit and say, 'Who's a ducky blue boots, then, who's our pretty boots?'

'What I've been able to partake of so far,' I said, 'is hardly keeping my body and soul together.'

'Hark at him,' said Lizzy, 'can't he yap? It's that education of his what's doin' it. Boots, shall I tell yer what we brought yer? Apples.'

'Apples? Apples?'

'Do yer good,' said Lizzy.

'Stop it, Lizzy,' said Chinese Lady, looking around to see if anyone was lying next door to death. Everyone in the surgical ward had visitors, who were all talking away over the heads of even the most parlous cases.

'How am I going to eat apples, just tell me that, go on, tell me,' I said. 'When I swallow, it's like I'm sawing my own head off.'

'You'll be all right,' said Chinese Lady, giving my pillows a motherly beating. 'You're a bit wan, but that can't be helped, and Matron said you bled very healthy.'

'I brought it all up in the night,' I said.

'What, all yer blood?' said Lizzy.

'Well, it wasn't custard. How could it have been? I hadn't had any custard, I hadn't had anything except the operation. When your throat's bleeding while you're asleep, it all goes down into your stomach, and when your stomach's full up—'

'Benevolent hommeridge, that's what it's called,' said Chinese Lady, 'but don't worry, I seen Matron before we come to your bedside, and she said you'll be coming out Wednesday.'

'If I don't choke,' I said. 'Fancy bringing apples, with me in my condition.'

'Sammy got 'em for yer down the Lane,' said Lizzy. 'Here y'ar.' She handed me a brown paper bag. I opened it and saw a bunch of black grapes. Lizzy's giggle was a silent one. Chinese Lady wouldn't have stood for a loud giggle, not in a hospital, and especially not on a Sunday.

'You Lizzy,' I said, 'I think I'll tell me fellow patients how that dog ran off with your drawers in Aunt Victoria's garden.'

Lizzy blushed crimson. In the bed on my left, Mr Clark, who'd broken both legs falling off his corporation water cart, gave her a wink. Lizzy went redder.

'Boots, you shouldn't say things like that,' said Chinese Lady, 'it's downright vulgarising.'

'Lucky they weren't the ones she was wearing,' I said, 'or the dog would've run off with her as well.'

Mr Clark chortled. His placid wife, who was visiting him, smiled peaceably.

'Oh, you an' yer yap,' muttered Lizzy.

'Still, she looks nice on Sundays, our Lizzy,' I said to Mr Clark.

'Young peach, that's what she is,' said Mr Clark, who had a cradle over his legs.

Lizzy did look nice. Her dark brown hair, as glossy as a horse chestnut, was topped by her Sunday hat of yellow straw, banded by red ribbon, and her white Sunday frock was waisted by a red sash. In 1912, sashes and ribbons were all the thing, especially on Sundays. Lizzy, with her brunette colouring, had a picture postcard look most Sundays. She was a good cricketer too.

'Boots, you get well now,' said Chinese Lady, 'then you'll be home Wednesday and back to school Monday week. You don't want to miss no more lessons than you can help.'

'Have a grape,' I said, and offered the bag. Chinese Lady and her one and only daughter accepted, and Mr Clark and his wife also took one each. Lizzy ate hers succulently. I ate one cautiously, and my throat went raw and fiery as I swallowed. 'Where are Sammy and Tommy?' I asked.

Sammy was nine, Tommy was eleven, and they were my brothers.

'Up the park,' said Lizzy, taking another grape. A wicked look entered her eyes. 'Em'ly's been askin' after you.'

'Oh, not her,' I said. 'Tell her I passed away.'

'Now don't you say things like that,' said Chinese Lady, shocked, 'it's provokin' Providence. And don't make faces or you'll get struck.'

'Might be an improvement,' said Lizzy. 'Em'ly was awful burdened the day you come here. Her mum didn't like the look of her tea leaves.'

'My throat hurts,' I said, 'I can't talk any more, especially about Emily Castle.'

'You ought to 'ave 'eard 'er,' said Lizzy. There was a hole in one of her black stockings, camouflaged by a touch of Cherry Blossom boot polish. ' "Oh, he won't die, will he? Oh, he won't die, will he?" '

'Lizzy, stop that,' said Chinese Lady.

'But she kept saying it,' said Lizzy. ' "Oh, he won't die, will he?" She's a bit fanciful, 'aving an aunt who's always under the doctor.'

'I'd be under him myself,' said Chinese Lady, 'only I haven't got time.'

'What'll I tell Em'ly?' asked Lizzy.

'Tell her I'm composing myself for a peaceful end,' I said.

Mr Clark chuckled and said, 'You're a one, you are.'

'Boots, didn't I tell you not to say things like that?' said Chinese Lady worriedly.

'He can't 'elp it, Mum,' said Lizzy, 'it's 'is posh schooling.'

'Everything all right?' Nurse Wharton stopped to enquire. Chinese Lady smiled respectfully.

'He's comin' on a treat,' she said, 'he's enjoying some nice grapes.'

'Lizzy is, you mean,' I said.

'Are you Lizzy?' asked Nurse Wharton of my skin and blister.

'Yes,' said Lizzy, suddenly shy in the face of uniformed authority.

'When we were at our Aunt Victoria's last year,' I said, 'a dog ran off with her—'

Lizzy clapped her hand over my mouth.

'He wants a clip,' said Chinese Lady, 'only what with his operation and not being able to swaller proper, he'll have to wait.'

'Oh, we can turn him over and smack his bottom,' said Nurse Wharton cheerfully. 'That won't affect his operation. Shall I do it for you?'

Chinese Lady looked uncertain. Lizzy looked bucked.

'Well, he's a good boy most of the time,' said Chinese Lady.

'All right, Mrs Adams,' said Nurse Wharton, 'but call me if you change your mind.'

She swished away.

'You 'aven't said proper what I'm to tell Em'ly,' said Lizzy.

Emily Castle was the girl next door. At thirteen, she was the same age as Lizzy, and her best friend. How Lizzy stood her, I didn't know. She was a skinny-legged terror. Small boys ran indoors when they saw her coming, and she could hack splinters off big boys. Her mum called her a pet, and her dad was proud of her.

'Why'd you have to tell her anything?' I asked.

''Cos she'll ask, that's why,' said Lizzy. 'She'll be on the doorstep as soon as me an' Mum get back. "Oh, he's not dead, is he?" That's what she'll say. "Oh, he's not dead, is he?" What'll I tell her?'

'What she wants to hear, I suppose. That I've passed on.'

'There you go again,' said Chinese Lady agitatedly. 'Yes, you can smirk, my lad, but saying things like that when you just been operated on, well, you could wake up smirkin' on the other side of your face.'

'Now, Mum, don't go on,' I said, 'people are looking.'

Chinese Lady went a little pink and hid herself under the brim of her black straw hat. Of all things, people looking was the worst.

'Mr Finch is comin' to see yer tomorrer,' said Lizzy.

11

Mr Finch was our lodger. Everyone in Walworth had a lodger, if possible. Lodgers helped with the rent. A lodger was like an uncle to some families, and a worry to others. Mr Finch had lodged with us for five years and wasn't a worry to anyone. He was a river pilot operating out of London docks, after having worked in the naval dockyard at Portsmouth and been a merchant seaman before that. He had a very nice way of talking to people, sounding quite educated, and the ladies respected him very much. His hours of work were irregular, due to tides and so on, but he always looked spruce coming or going, and never failed to lift his hat or his peaked cap to any lady he knew, even including Mrs Percival. Mrs Percival was a great big drunk of a woman, who spent a lot of time being taken to court and being fined or getting seven days for brawling with men outside pubs at closing times. She was always nearly sending some man or other to hospital. I say nearly because all the men refused to go. They had their pride, the working men of Walworth, and weren't going to let any hospital know it was a woman who'd done them over. It made Mrs Percival mad that they wouldn't go, because her declared aim was to put every man in England in hospital. Her husband had run off to Australia with her sister years ago, and she'd had it in for men ever since.

'I'll be happy to see Mr Finch,' I said. 'Are we still hard up?' I whispered.

'Mum's had to pawn Grandma's tea service,' said Lizzy.

'I'll have a relapse, I will,' I said.

'Why?' said Lizzy. 'Grandma left her tea service to Mum, not you.'

'Anyway,' said Chinese Lady, 'it helped to buy you a nice pair of secondhand shoes good as new down the Lane.' East Street market was always called the Lane. 'They look nice, they're for school and to make up for your operation. I'll get the tea service redeemed soon as your monthly school grant comes through.' Chinese Lady being a widow, I received a grant of ten shillings a month to help see me through secondary school. She had an Army

12

widow's pension herself, our dad having gone to a hero's death on the Northwest Frontier in India in 1906. The Army had sent her his medals, and she'd written to ask if she could have two shillings a week more on her pension instead, as she had four children to find food for and they couldn't eat medals. She received a very kind reply, which took four long paragraphs to say no. So she framed the medals with a photograph of our dad in his uniform, and kept it on the parlour mantelpiece, and neighbours said how proud she must have been of him. Chinese Lady said she'd have been a lot prouder if he'd had the sense not to get his head blown off. The pension wasn't much, and she had to go out to work charring six mornings a week at the town hall, leaving home at a quarter to six and coming back about half-past nine. They paid her eleven shillings a week.

'We ought to hold Grandma's tea service more dear than to put it in pawn,' I said.

'Crikey, listen to you,' said Lizzy, 'you sound like—' She stopped. She blushed under her hat. A boy was eyeing her from a bedside opposite, where he sat with his mother visiting his father, who'd had his appendix out. He looked about seventeen, and as if he came from somewhere like Denmark Hill, where people had a bit more than we did in Walworth. There were some nice streets off Denmark Hill, except they were called roads or avenues, and the houses all had gardens. The boy wore a grey suit, with a collar and tie, and he had a frank smile for our Lizzy. Well, Lizzy really did look nice in her Sunday frock, which was a cast-off from Cousin Vi, Aunt Victoria's only child.

The boy got up and strolled over. Lizzy went violently pink.

'Hello,' he said to me, 'what're you in for?'

'Tonsils,' I said.

'Crippling,' he said. He had a cheerful and vigorous look, well-brushed hair as darkly brown as Lizzy's, and a lot of self-confidence. Our Lizzy had quite a bit of her own, but it seemed to have drained into her polished Sunday

13

boots at the moment. 'Hello,' said the boy to Chinese Lady.

'Good afternoon, pleased to meet you,' said Chinese Lady.

'Are you his sister?' asked the boy of Lizzy's hat. Her hat was all he could see of her, because she had her head bent. She gulped.

'Yes, she's my sister,' I said. 'Her name's Eliza.'

Lizzy shot me a fierce look. She hated the name Eliza, and frequently took Chinese Lady to task for burdening her with it.

'I'm Ned,' said the boy. 'Eliza's pretty nice, don't you think?'

Lizzy gave him a quick upward glance. He smiled at her. Her blush got worse.

'Cheek,' she muttered.

'Pardon?' said Ned.

'She said how'd you do,' I said.

'No, I didn't,' breathed Lizzy.

'Well, I've got to buzz now and meet some friends,' said Ned. 'I've seen my dad's operation. Looks a treat. I'm bringing him some books tomorrow evening. He likes Rider Haggard. D'you fancy a book or two?' he asked me.

'Thanks, I've got books,' I said, 'what I'm after is something I can eat.'

'Mr Finch, our lodger, is comin' to see him tomorrer evening,' said Chinese Lady. Being a motherly woman, she was engagingly irrelevant at times.

'He'll get Irish stew tomorrow,' said Ned, 'they always serve that on Mondays. I had my tonsils out here several years ago.'

'Well, fancy that,' muttered Lizzy to her feet.

'Will they do dumplings with the stew?' asked Chinese Lady. 'Boots likes dumplings.'

'Me too,' said Ned. 'Well, see you all again, I hope.'

'Pleased to have met you, I'm sure,' said Chinese Lady, and Ned smiled, gave Lizzy's hat another glance, called goodbye to his mother and father, and left.

'Cheek,' said Lizzy again.

'What's got into you?' asked Chinese Lady.

'He was lookin', that's what,' said Lizzy, who seemed irrationally pink.

'Only at the hole in your stocking,' I said.

'Oh, it don't show, do it?' said Lizzy in dismay.

It did. The hole was out of true with the spot of blacking on her shin. Lizzy was plainly mortified.

'Lizzy, you should of let me darn it before you put it on,' said Chinese Lady.

'No wonder he was standin' there lookin',' said Lizzy furiously. 'That's what he was doin', lookin' an' grinnin'.' She essayed a glance at Ned's parents. They gave her a smile. She blushed again. 'Oh, all boys are grinnin' lumps,' she breathed. She seemed very put out.

'We'll get the tea service out of pawn when I come home,' I said.

'We got to have a bit of money,' said Chinese Lady defensively. 'You got to stay at school, Boots, and pass your exams and get a nice job in a bank. We got to find money somewhere, and we won't have nothing extra coming in till Lizzy leaves school when she's fourteen and finds work.'

'We'll go to Australia,' I said.

'Don't talk senseless,' said Chinese Lady.

'We're goin' to do an Empire Day pageant at our school,' said Lizzy, worrying her dress to keep the stocking hole covered.

'Well, we'll go to the farthest corner of the Empire, that's what,' I said, feeling depressed about our poverty. 'As soon as I'm out, Lizzy, we'll take Chinese Lady to Australia House and help her fill in forms.'

'Crickey, listen to him, Mum,' said Lizzy, 'anybody'd think he was sir and we was only muck.'

'Well, he only had his operation Friday,' said Chinese Lady, 'we got to make allowances, lovey.'

A bell rang and Nurse Wharton reappeared.

'Time's up,' she called, clapping her hands, and visitors made preparations to leave.

'We got to go now, Boots,' said Chinese Lady, and gave my hand a pat. 'Get better now, and I'll come Wednesday to fetch you home.'

'I might have a fatal turn in the night,' I said.

'Can't you have it now?' said Lizzy. 'Then Mum'll know she won't have to fetch you.'

'Ain't she a corker?' said Mr Clark.

'She needs her ears boxed, saying a thing like that,' said Chinese Lady, 'they're as bad as each other, the pair of them.'

'I'll tell Em'ly you're goin' to live,' said Lizzy.

When they'd gone, Nurse Wharton came and plumped up the pillows that Chinese Lady had tidied up.

'Aren't you lucky, having such a nice mother and pretty sister?' she said.

'We're in pawn,' I said.

'You're not the only family, so don't brag about it. Sit up more, it'll perk you. Tea's coming round in a minute, and you can try some bread and butter.'

'Thank you kindly, nurse,' I said, 'but if I pass on before it arrives, Mr Clark can have it.'

'My, my, aren't we droll today?' said Nurse Wharton, who smelled like a fascinating mixture of lavender and antiseptic. 'Well, we'll try to see it arrives before you leave us. You don't want to arrive hungry at the pearly gates. They might already have had their tea up there.'

'Play yer draughts, Boots?' said Mr Clark.

'All right,' I said.

Nurse Wharton set the board up for us on a chair between the beds, then buzzed around giving what for to patients who were looking slipshod and untidy. When tea was served I tried some bread and butter and fruit cake, and as it all went down without actually killing me, I decided to live.

CHAPTER TWO

Next morning I felt considerably better and ate a plateful of sugared porridge. A postcard arrived, with a fluffy yellow chick on the front and an accompanying poem.

'*Easter comes but once a year*
To fill our hearts with hope and cheer
Christ is risen as our Saviour
Praise the Lord and love thy neighbour.'

On the back was a pencilled message beneath the green halfpenny stamp.

'*I do hope you'll get better yours faithly Emily Castle from next door.*'

'Who's it from?' asked Nurse Wharton.

'Just a neighbour.'

'Nurse, me legs itch,' said Mr Clark.

'I'll tell Sister,' said Nurse Wharton, 'she'll tell Matron, Matron will tell Mr Lancaster, the surgeon, and everyone will be thrilled.'

'You're a comfort, you are,' said Mr Clark.

'Have you been?' Nurse Wharton asked me.

'Been?'

'Yes, before I came on duty. You know.'

'Oh, that. Yes, I've been, thank you kindly, nurse.'

'Good. I'm happy for you.' Nurse Wharton ruffled my hair.

'Can I have a bottle, nurse?' cried someone in need, at which Mr Clark broke into song.

'*Oh, I went for a wee on a train up to Crewe,*
And the train it was swaying like old howjerdo,
And I didn't know how I could aim my wee straight,
So I just shut me eyes and left it to fate.'

17

'Very funny,' said Nurse Wharton, after the hysteria had subsided. 'Surgical is always full of comedians. Any more songs like that, Mr Clark, and I'll call Sister Hardy.'

'Kiss me, Hardy,' I said.

'What was that?' she asked severely.

'It was what Nelson said at the battle of Trafalgar.' I never liked my school learning to miss out on an audience. 'You know, when he was dying and saying his last words to Captain Hardy. "Kiss me, Hardy," he said.'

'That reminds me,' said Mr Clark, and broke into poetry.

'*Oh, it was Christmas Day on the troopship,*
And the soldiers was eatin' dry bread,
There wasn't no Christmas pudding,
'*Cos the sergeant had done what they said.*'

Nurse Wharton rushed out.

'Where's she gorn, where's me bottle?' cried the patient in need.

Nurse Wharton returned with a flushed face and a glass full of thick liquid.

'Mr Clark, your medicine,' she said.

'Is that for me itch?' asked Mr Clark.

'For your general condition. Drink it down, every drop.'

'Kiss me, 'Ardy,' said Mr Clark.

'Nurse, me bottle,' begged the urgent case. She brought him one. Beneath the bedclothes, he used it. 'Gawd 'elp us,' he said, 'talk about the relief of Mafeking.'

Mr Finch, our lodger, arrived during the evening, when a short visiting time was allowed. Mr Finch was a man in his early forties. He was tall, fair-haired, with pleasant features, healthy colouring and grey eyes that lit up when he smiled. It seemed to give him a twinkle at times. He wore nice suits, some dark blue and some dark grey, which he took good care of and in which he always looked spruce. He also had his river pilot's uniform, with a peaked cap. He went to the Turkish baths twice a week. He equated cleanliness with godliness. The family all bathed

18

once a week in our scullery, in our big tin tub. Mr Finch's lodging was a living-room and a bedroom. He paid Chinese Lady six shillings a week. The rent for the house was twelve shillings a week, so Chinese Lady had to find the other six.

Reaching my bedside, Mr Finch gave me his hearty seafaring smile and said, 'Well, well, so here we are, Boots.'

'It's very kind of you to come, Mr Finch,' I said, 'and who's that behind you?'

'Your sister thought she'd like to come too,' he said, and Lizzy edged into view.

'It was in case you was passin' away,' she said. 'Our mum thought I ought to see yer once more before yer went.'

Mr Finch laughed. Nurse Addison looked. Nurse Addison, who had come on duty after Nurse Wharton had left at six, was crisp and pretty. Nurse Wharton was smiling and companionable. I was in love with Nurse Wharton. Her starched bosom was thrilling whenever she leaned to plump up my pillows.

Mr Somers, the appendix patient and the father of the boy whom Lizzy had accused of looking yesterday, gave my sister a wave and a smile.

'Good evenin', sir,' said Lizzy.

'Good evening, young lady,' said Mr Somers.

Lizzy seemed unusually smart for a weekday. Lizzy had four outfits. An old darned pinafore school frock, a serviceable frock if she wanted to change when she came home from school, her Sunday frock, and also for Sundays, a very pretty white blouse and a dark blue skirt. She was wearing the blouse and skirt now, and her Sunday boater sat on her chestnut hair. She looked so pretty I didn't mind anyone knowing she was my sister.

'You didn't have to dress up for me, Lizzy,' I said.

'I'm not dressed up,' said Lizzy.

Mr Finch drew up two chairs and he and Lizzy sat down.

'Well, Boots,' he smiled, 'how are we today?'

19

'We're improving, thank you, Mr Finch,' I said. 'Lizzy's in her Sunday best.'

'Lovely,' said Mr Finch, who had a warm affection for her.

'It's not me Sunday best,' said Lizzy.

'She's got a hole in her stocking,' I said.

'Oh, I ain't!' whispered Lizzy in a panic, and lifted her skirt to examine her black stockings. 'There, I ain't.'

'That's it, show everyone,' I said. 'She'll be my death, you know,' I said to Mr Finch, and the twinkling light entered his eyes. He and Lizzy were on quite loving terms. Lizzy ironed his handkerchiefs for him. Chinese Lady did his washing for him for sixpence. He was almost like one of the family, and Lizzy sometimes said she wouldn't mind him for a dad, except that Chinese Lady declared she had enough on her plate without taking on a new husband, especially as our real dad had only been gone six years. It would be like being unfaithful to him. Lizzy had said what did she mean, unfaithful? Chinese Lady had said never you mind.

'Boots,' said Mr Finch, 'as you came bravely through your ordeal, I couldn't do less than – let me see, where is it?' He patted his pockets. 'Yes, here it is.' He fished out a huge half-pound slab of Cadbury's milk chocolate.

'All that?' I said. At fifteen, I had a great liking for milk chocolate. 'Upon my soul, you are kind, Mr Finch.'

Mr Finch laughed.

'Listen to 'im,' said Lizzy.

'It's true it's been nearly life and death for me,' I said, 'but this much chocolate? Well, I can hardly find words, Mr Finch—'

'He's orf,' said Lizzy.

'Ain't he a caution?' said Mr Clark from the next bed.

'Oh, he's always talkin' like a pound of best plums,' said Lizzy, 'it's 'is second'ry schoolin' what's doing it.'

'Who'd like some chocolate?' I asked. I unwrapped the slab and broke off a section. I passed it across to Mr Clark, who accepted it with pleasure.

'A real sport, you are, Boots,' he said.

'Have a piece, Lizzy?' I said, breaking off another section.

'No, it's yourn,' said Lizzy, but eyed it wistfully. I pushed it into her hand, and Mr Finch smiled. I offered him a piece.

'Just one square,' he said, 'to please your giving heart. Thank you, Boots.'

Lizzy's eyes closed in rapture as she placed a square of chocolate in her mouth to let it linger and melt. A tall boy walked briskly in, carrying a couple of books.

'Hello,' he said, smiling at us all, and made for the bedside of Mr Somers, his dad.

Lizzy, opening her eyes, moved her chair so that Mr Finch partly hid her. She was rosy. Rosy? Lizzy? I gave her a look. And Ned, although talking to his dad, seemed to be trying to glance round corners to make more of the little he could see of her.

'Bleedin' cheek,' breathed Lizzy. That was a bit strong for Lizzy and would have earned her a rare old talking-to from our mum.

'Lizzy's being looked at,' I said to Mr Finch.

'I'm not surprised,' he said. 'Lizzy's the prettiest girl in London. Woe betide Philistines who dispute it. I'll chop their heads off. My Aunt Trudy always says boys are made of salt and vinegar, and girls of peppermint cream.'

Mr Finch frequently quoted his Aunt Gertrude, who lived somewhere in Kent and had looked after him when he was orphaned and before he went to sea. They wrote to each other, and once a year, on his summer holidays, he went to stay with her. His aunt was his memory book, and he was obviously fond of her.

Ned was looking again, and Lizzy was trying not to notice. Nurse Addison, passing by, said to me, 'Bobby Adams, you can get up first thing tomorrow.'

'What, and walk about?' I said.

'Up, up,' she said as she went on her way. 'Tomorrow. Up, up.'

21

'That means you'll be coming home on Wednesday, as your mother said,' smiled Mr Finch.

Lizzy took a quick peek at Ned. Ned caught the peek and gave her a smile. Lizzy blushed like a red sunset.

'Is that you, Eliza?' called Ned. 'I wasn't sure if you were there or not.'

'Oh, would yer believe,' gasped Lizzy, 'he's even talkin' to me now and he don't even know me, not properly he don't.'

'Talking isn't allowed without an introduction?' said Mr Finch gravely.

'Oh, lor',' breathed Lizzy, for Ned was coming over, leaving his father with his nose in a book.

'Good evening, sir,' said Ned to Mr Finch, 'your son's better, I hope?'

Lizzy had a gulping fit. Mr Finch smiled.

'Unfortunately, I can't claim the honour of being his father,' he said. 'His father, I'm afraid, died on one of the Empire's many battlefields.'

'Oh, sorry,' said Ned, 'that's my big foot.'

'That's all right,' I said, 'we show a brave face, don't we, Lizzy?'

'I'm sure it's very brave,' said Ned, 'but I don't think I've seen your sister's yet.'

'Cheek,' breathed Lizzy, who had her head bent low.

'Pardon?' said Ned. 'Did you say something, Eliza?'

Lizzy was scarlet. Lizzy was actually shy. It had never been known before. She could be sensitive, but never shy.

'Not many people call her Eliza,' said Mr Finch.

'Can't think why,' said Ned. 'I like Eliza. You must be the lodger. I remember now, you were mentioned. I'm Ned Somers. How'd you do, Eliza?'

'How'd' yer do, I'm sure,' said Lizzy to the glass of water on my bedside locker.

'I'll tell you when Eliza did put a brave face on things, Ned,' I said, 'and that was when we were at our Aunt Victoria's and a dog ran off with—'

'Oh, stop him!' gasped Lizzy.

22

'With her shoes,' I said.

'Well, worse things can happen at sea,' said Ned.

'Better things too,' said Lizzy to her feet, 'like some brothers falling overboard.'

'Have my chair, Ned,' said Mr Finch, 'while I talk to your father.' Our lodger was always ready to be friendly. On this occasion, I think, he was ready to be accommodating and give Ned a clear field with Lizzy. Ned was obviously taken with her. She went rigid as he sat down beside her.

'Where do you two live?' he asked.

I told him precisely where, and we had a chat. His own home was in Herne Hill, an area considered posh enough to attract people who worked in Government offices. Ned was nearly eighteen and had attended Wilson's grammar school near Camberwell. He had not long started a job in Great Tower Street with a firm of wine and sherry importers. The firm had very good connections with City business houses and West End hotels. I mentioned we sometimes had a bottle of port at Christmas. Ned said yes, you could get a good port for half a crown, but his firm dealt mainly with Spanish sherries.

'I'm nobody at the moment,' he went on, 'I just move bottles about, hump cases and wash glasses. They're always tasting the stuff. But they say there are prospects for someone bright. How bright, you may ask, and the answer is am I just a hopeful lemon? What're you going to do when you leave school, Boots?'

'I'm at West Square. I've got another year to go. My mother hopes it'll fit me for banking.'

Lizzy gave me a pitying look. I had a talent for sounding important, and had accordingly been appointed a prefect in advance of other hopefuls.

'Banking?' said Ned. 'High finance?'

'I'll start at the bottom, of course,' I said.

'Well, even the Rothschilds did,' said Ned. 'My old man started right at the bottom, as a grocer's errand boy in Peckham, but he's got his own shop in Herne Hill now.'

'Mr Finch, our lodger, says life is a ladder, that perseverance will take you up and sloth will drag you down, but that most people stay where they first set foot on it.'

'I don't think you'll find any sloth in high finance,' said Ned, and Lizzy, sitting stiffly beside him, obviously couldn't believe this was a conversation. Ned glanced at her, and she at once became stiffer. 'You're not saying much, Eliza.'

'Oh, I'm only here to make sure Boots ain't passin' on,' said Lizzy.

'Mr Finch could have made sure all by himself,' I said.

'Well, I come as well,' said Lizzy. 'In Christian pity,' she added.

'Christian pity's got a lot to be said for it,' remarked Ned solemnly. 'By the way, why'd you call him Boots?'

'I don't know, I'm sure,' said Lizzy haughtily. 'I wasn't born when they give 'im that label, was I?'

Ned laughed. That made Lizzy haughtier, and she sat up so straight that her snowy white blouse showed she was beginning to grow.

'Eliza, I think you're fun,' he said, and Lizzy blushed yet again.

The bell rang and Nurse Addison requested the evening visitors to depart. Mr Finch returned to collect Lizzy and take her home. Ned said goodbye to us.

'Oh, and good luck, Boots,' he said, 'I might pop in on my bike one day when I'm passing.'

As he left, I wondered if he'd pop in to enquire after my defunct tonsils or to afflict Lizzy with more blushes. Lizzy with a rosy red look was the eighth wonder of the world.

'A very nice young man,' said Mr Finch, 'and with a future, if his father is right. Boots, I shall now have the pleasure of escorting your sister home. On a tram. We'll look forward to seeing you on Wednesday.'

'Mr Finch, many thanks for the chocolate,' I said.

'A pleasure,' said Mr Finch.

'Come along, come along,' chirruped Nurse Addison.

'At once, nurse,' said Mr Finch. 'Keep a caring eye on Boots.'

'Boots? Boots?' she said.

'That's me,' I said.

'Nonsense,' said Nurse Addison, 'you're Bobby Adams, not a chemist's shop.'

CHAPTER THREE

Chinese Lady arrived on Wednesday afternoon to fetch me. At fifteen, I was hardly an infant, and was an inch taller than she was. I could have managed to get home by myself, I said.

'No, you couldn't,' she said, 'you're only just out of your sickbed. You might come over faint on your way home. Anyway, I've got to see the Lady Almoner.'

Nurse Wharton escorted us, and on the way advised Chinese Lady I'd been a fairly good patient.

'Well, I hope he has,' said Chinese Lady, 'seeing he's my only eldest son and all. I wouldn't like to think he'd been a trouble.'

'Just a little droll at times,' said Nurse Wharton, taking us briskly along corridors.

'I hope that doesn't mean he's been disrespectful or saucy. It would make his dad turn in his grave.'

Since our dad had been literally blown to bits by cannon-firing Pathans, I didn't think he'd do any turning.

Nurse Wharton halted outside the Lady Almoner's office, knocked on the door, opened it, ushered us in and gave me an encouraging pat before disappearing from my life for ever. The Lady Almoner proved a kind and understanding woman, a great relief to Chinese Lady, who could get agitated if authority showed a stern face. She explained what money came in from her pension and her charring work, and that there wasn't very much to spare.

'Oh, yes,' said kind authority, 'you're an Army widow – I'm so sorry. Well, you need not pay anything, Mrs Adams.'

'Oh, I want to pay something,' said Chinese Lady. 'I

mean, there was the operation and all the food he must have ate.'

'I hardly ate anything,' I said. 'Well, not until yesterday.'

'We got to give the hospital something,' said Chinese Lady.

'You need not,' said the Lady Almoner gently.

'Well, two shillings?' said Chinese Lady, digging into her purse and coming up with a shilling and two sixpences.

'A shilling will do,' said the Lady Almoner.

'I don't mind one an' six.'

'That's very good of you, Mrs Adams.'

'It's a volunt'ry contribution,' said Chinese Lady proudly. Everyone was familiar with hospital posters appealing for voluntary contributions. The Lady Almoner, who, with her small staff, was a major force in the running of the hospital's administration, smiled warm-heartedly.

'Thank you very much, Mrs Adams. Now, you know what to do about Bobby?'

'See he goes to the doctor's next Monday.'

'He'll probably get a tonic. Goodbye now – and goodbye, Bobby.'

'Thank you kindly,' I said, 'it's been a pleasure.'

Outside the hospital, Chinese Lady said, 'We better get a tram home. You can't walk while you're still weak.'

'How much money have we got?' I asked, feeling pale in the fresh air.

'Well, I got eightpence and the sixpence from the two shillings for the hospital, and that's not countin' the gas money.' Gas money was the little store of pennies kept in a Fry's cocoa tin for the meter.

'We can't count that, anyway. What we've got is one and tuppence.'

'Well, we had to pay the hospital something, Boots. They done a nice operation on you. Dr McManus said your tonsils was pickin' up every germ going.'

'We'll walk and save the fare,' I said. 'It's only down to the Elephant and Castle, and along Walworth Road.'

'Well, if you're sure,' she said. 'Oh, your school grant's

27

been paid in and we can draw some of it. We'll have a nice high tea this evening. I got some cold rock salmon this morning from the fried fish shop, five pieces for tuppence. We'll heat it up with fried potatoes and bread and butter.'

The fried fish shop in Walworth Road sold leftovers from the previous night's frying when it opened at noon, and Chinese Lady must have been first in the queue if she managed to get five pieces. We wouldn't actually have bread and butter, of course. Bread and marge. But Chinese Lady never said bread and marge. She didn't like that kind of thing to slip out in front of neighbours.

We walked down Borough High Street. We were all used to lots of walking to save tram fares, and Chinese Lady bought Blakey's world-famous metal brads for us to hammer into the soles and heels of our boots and shoes, to slow down wear on the leather. We were lucky, really, that our mum and dad had examined priorities early on in their married life. Food, clothes and rent were the top priorities, in that order, and after our dad had gone, Chinese Lady made no change. In some Walworth families the top priorities were beer, grub and a bit of rent on account. Some kids in some families took turns to wear what boots were available.

Chinese Lady could be reckless when she had silver in her purse, and come back from shopping with several good secondhand clothing bargains, and then find she had to pawn something to buy tomorrow's dinner, although she was never reckless enough to buy new clothes, not when the secondhand clothes stalls sometimes had stuff that looked nearly new. Nor could she resist a food bargain, such as a dozen cracked eggs for sixpence from the Maypole Dairy, even if that meant going into the baker's to get two loaves on tick.

She walked beside me in a very upright way, her handbag in her shopping bag. Except on Sundays, she never went anywhere without her shopping bag, whether she was going shopping or not. She felt incomplete without it. Moreover, it gave the neighbours the impression she was always financially equipped to make purchases.

She was rather thin, and nearly always dressed in black as a mark of respect for our blown-to-bits dad. She had a nice, kind face that sometimes looked careworn, and people often said what lovely big brown eyes she had. No one said they were almond eyes, like Chinese ladies had. That was because people respected her and didn't want to suggest her mother had fallen for a Chinese gentleman. There were some faded sepia photographs of her and our dad in a veneered casket with a curved lid and satin lining, and they showed she hadn't been thin then. She was now, but she still had a motherly bosom and carried it proudly, as if it signified she was a woman nature had blessed. On spotting flat-chested Mrs Dobney in the street, she had once said, 'Oh, poor woman.' Mrs Dobney was quite young, and Chinese Lady obviously felt it was a sad thing for a married woman only in her twenties not to have a proud bosom.

Her black straw hat was rarely off her dark brown hair. She put it on first thing in the mornings when she went to her work, and mostly kept it on for the rest of the day. She believed a lady could only claim elegance when she had her hat on. She had a second hat. This was also black, but not as well-worn as her weekday one, and she kept it for Sundays. She had worn it once on a weekday, when she took us to the ABC teashop for a cup of tea for herself, and a currant bun each for us. It happened when I was awarded my secondary school grant, and we all sat stiff with awe, except her. She waved one gloved hand about like an upper-class lady. It must have impressed the waitress, because she addressed her as Madam.

We reached the Elephant and Castle, and crossed to Walworth Road by subway.

'We can go to the post office,' said Chinese Lady, 'and you can draw two an' six out of your grant, and I'll send Tommy to the pawn to get the tea service out.'

'How much did you pawn it for?'

'Two shillings. There'll only be a penny int'rest, Boots, so there'll be fivepence change. Of course, you could draw three shillings, if you like.'

'No, I couldn't. Two and six a week is our drawing. With one and sevenpence in your purse, we can easily last until your Friday wages.'

'I think our Lizzy ought to have some new plimsolls and stockings. They got good plimsolls fourpence a pair down the Lane, and stockings almost as good as new.'

'Just some plimsolls,' I said.

'I s'pose we shouldn't be squand'rous, but Lizzy could do with nice stockings now she's growing. She's never had new ones since she come out of socks a year ago. What she's got is all darned.' Chinese Lady bridled as a big woman bore down on her and almost forced her off the pavement before barging on. 'Some people. I don't know, they wasn't like that when your dad an' me was walkin' out. Lizzy wants to look nice now she's growing. I bought them nearly new shoes for you, so's we wouldn't be ashamed of how you look going to school. You don't want to be ashamed of Lizzy, do you? You don't want her to look darned and ragged, do you?'

'She didn't look darned and ragged when she came to the hospital with Mr Finch on Monday to see if I was dead or not, she looked—'

'Oh, you wicked boy!' Chinese Lady's skirts rustled angrily. She swept along amid the pedestrian traffic. 'Fancy saying a terrible thing like that about your own sister.'

'I didn't say it, she did.'

'Lizzy's a loving girl, that's why she went to see you again. I don't know what gets into you sometimes.'

'Mr Finch says it's all related to the mystery of our individual souls.'

'Mr Finch says a lot of things like that, him havin' been all round the world, but you're not out of school yet and you can still get your ears boxed. I got some obstrep'rous children, I have. Goodness knows what you'll all get up to when I go.'

'Go? Go where?'

'When I pass on,' said Chinese Lady darkly.

30

'Now, Mum, don't talk about passing on. We've already had Dad do that.'

'Not on purpose, just a bit careless, like. Your education's not meant for you to give me any lip, it's for you to get a nice safe job in a bank when you mertricerlate. Your dad wouldn't want you standin' on street corners because you learned more about answering back than about your lessons. Lizzy says you talk very stuck-up at times.'

'No, I don't—'

'There you go, contradictin' me.' Chinese Lady gave me a severe look, then said, 'You feeling all right, Boots? You look a bit peaky. Never mind, we'll soon be home and I'll make you a nice cup of tea. We'll just go to the post office first. We ought to have Grandma's service out for Sunday – Miss Chivers is comin' to tea.'

We were passing Southwark Town Hall, Chinese Lady's place of work, and she walked very proudly, knowing she did a good cleaning job there.

'It's always nice to have Miss Chivers to tea,' I said.

Miss Elsie Chivers lived in our street with her widowed mother, who never went out because she said she was an invalid. We called her the Witch. She had a beaky nose, jutting chin, glinting eyes, and hands that looked like claws in black mittens. She rarely let her thirty-year-old daughter out of her sight, except to go to her daily work at the Admiralty. They never had anyone visit. Especially, they never had men visit. Miss Chivers was never even allowed to go for a Sunday walk to Ruskin Park, as many people did in the summer. She was a slave to the Witch. But she was the nicest of persons, quiet and shy and gentle. She was allowed just one concession. She was permitted to come to us for Sunday tea once a month, as long as she didn't stay later than eight o'clock. After tea, she often played our piano. Our dad had bought it for thirty bob when we were young. Lots of families had pianos, left by Victorian grandparents. Ours wanted tuning, and Chinese Lady said we'd have it done as soon as we could afford it. A piano had no priority except as a medium of family entertainment. Miss Chivers never mentioned it wanted tuning. She played it very well. Music hall songs were part of her repertoire, and we'd all gather round and sing. Chinese Lady had quite a nice voice, and her favourite was 'Soldiers of the Queen' by Leslie Sarony. That was because of our heroic if careless dad, of course.

I drew half a crown from my post office savings book, used for my grant. Then we made our way to Browning Street, with its working-men's club on the corner, where the unemployed stood hopefully about. We walked down Browning Street until we reached Caulfield Place, where we lived. It was a cul-de-sac, with twelve terraced houses on one side, and six houses and two factories on the other. The cul-de-sac was formed by the rear wall of St John's Church School, attended by Lizzy, Sammy and Tommy. One factory was a drug mills, which gave off pungent, spicy smells, and a man whose clothes and beard looked yellow roared the kids off if they poked their noses in. The other factory was a printing works. Street cricket was played with the wicket chalked on a blank wall. It wasn't allowed, so the kids had to watch out for bobbies on their beat in Browning Street. Also, residents said cricket hooligans broke windows. That couldn't happen if you used a ball made of rags and bound tightly with string, but it could if someone produced a rubber ball. Anyone with a rubber ball was entitled to pick the sides, to go in first and to stretch the rules a bit. Lizzy was good with the bat shaped out of wood. She was a natural walloper of a ball, with a fine eye, but couldn't bowl to save her life. Being a girl, she always wanted to, of course, and the kids could have a wearying time trying to get the ball off her.

Arriving home, Chinese Lady pulled the latchcord depending from the letterbox. The door opened and we went in. There was a six-foot-wide passage, with the parlour door on the left and a rickety hallstand on the right. The passage reached to the stairs, where it turned left and straightened out as a narrower passage to the kitchen. On the left was Chinese Lady's bedroom, which she shared with Lizzy. Farther down, on the right and under the stairs, was a cupboard in which we kept jumbled junk. There was a step down to the kitchen, which served as our living-room, and through the kitchen was a door opening onto a scullery of whitewashed brick. The scullery contained a sink, a gas oven, a wringer, a copper, a big tin bath hanging from a huge hook and pots and pans hanging from other hooks. All the pots and pans were black iron, and each bore steadfast witness to Victorian durability.

The kitchen had a coal range with an oven. In the winter, when the range was glowing, Chinese Lady would put a rice pudding in the oven and leave it there for hours. Succulent rice puddings, with a deep brown skin to them, were a feature of her cooking when the days were cold. Coal was expensive, a shilling a hundred-weight, but counted as a winter priority, and Chinese Lady sank deep into pawn to keep the kitchen warm and cosy. Sammy supplied the firewood, scrounging broken fruit crates from the market and selling them to our mum for a penny.

The passage, stairs and all the rooms, except the scullery, had linoleum-covered floors. The kitchen lino was very cracked, and Chinese Lady was always saying that as soon as our ship came in, we'd have new lino everywhere. There were several upright chairs, all old and none of them matching, and an ancient deal-topped table that opened up by use of a winder so that a leaf could be inserted. In the bay window overlooking the paved back yard stood a nineteenth-century sewing-machine, which when closed I used as a table for my homework. In the yard was the timber coalshed and the outside lav. The indoor lav was upstairs.

To one side of the kitchen range, in a wide recess, stood a huge old dresser with drawers and cupboards. Cups hung from shelf hooks, and saucers, plates and dishes stood on the shelves. The mantelpiece above the range was covered with an old purple velvet overlay from which some bobbles dangled and some had gone missing. The wallpaper, dark with age and smoke, still managed to show its rose pattern. There were tears and dents. We pasted back little hanging bits from time to time, and the wallpaper seemed grateful to be tidy-looking again, but only for a while. Chinese Lady kept on to the landlord's rent collector about new wallpaper. The rent collector would come in, take a look, and then say you don't know when you're well off, it's still good for ten more years.

A thick wall divided our back yard from next door's. The crowded nature of houses and yards kept Monday's washing hanging limply on some occasions, and the sooty content of the air on a completely windless day could gradually make clean white look very grey. This upset Lizzy far more than Chinese Lady, for whereas Chinese Lady was philosophical, Lizzy was fastidious. Even in her shabbiest clothes, Lizzy liked to feel her garments were clean.

The outside lav was used by Sammy, Tommy and me, although it could be cruelly perishing in winter. The upstairs lav was used by Chinese Lady, Lizzy and Mr Finch. In the outside lav was a hook from which dangled a wad of torn-up squares of newspaper, and there was also a little wire rack containing two books, *Tarzan of the Apes* and *Tom Sawyer*. Chinese Lady wasn't too keen on books in a lav. She said they kept people occupying the place for far too long, and that sometimes she didn't know if Sammy was still reading or had died in there. She didn't like to think of anyone getting seriously ill in a lav, because how could a responsible family give them first aid through a bolted door? Sammy had recently been told not to use the bolt. Sammy didn't mind. At nine, he wasn't old enough to demand unconditional privacy or sensitive enough to plead for it.

'Lizzy an' the kids'll be home from school in a minute,' said Chinese Lady, entering the scullery, 'so I'll put the kettle on now and make a nice pot of tea.'

'I'll put the cups and saucers out, then sit down for a while,' I said. The walk home had found me out.

'Yes, all right,' she called from the scullery, 'I expect

you're a bit done up, and you probably feel depressed, like. It's what most people feel when they're just out of hospital. Still, a nice cup of tea'll cheer you up.'

A nice cup of tea was the cure for all ills in Walworth. I heard water splashing into our iron kettle, which was another antique. But Chinese Lady refused to replace it with a tin kettle, which would get its bottom burned off in no time. I said the iron kettle was all right on the kitchen range, where it could murmur away all day in winter, but we'd use far less gas with a tin kettle in the summer. I attempted a scientific explanation, but Chinese Lady said don't try that lark on, she wasn't going to waste money buying any tin kettle.

I put out cups, saucers and sugar bowl. The deal table was covered with what had once been a dark blue Army blanket, something our dad had brought home in his kitbag. Chinese Lady asked how much the Army had charged for it. Our dad said it was a free one he'd found lying about unused. Chinese Lady said what criminal untidiness. She stitched a hem all round it and it made a permanent cover for the kitchen table. It was frequently put into the Monday wash, but never wore out.

I went to the parlour to make use of an armchair. As I entered, someone pulled the latchcord of the front door. I poked my head out of the parlour and saw a girl on the step. She had a thin body, thin legs, thin face and a great mass of tangled, untidy auburn hair. Her mother never seemed to brush it or clean it, and it was a certainty she never gave it any attention herself.

'Oh, you're home,' she said, and her breath hissed. She had eyes as green as a cat's. Standing on the doorstep, she was all jerky legs within jigging skirts. She never seemed able to stand still, and her sharp elbows were constantly poking. She was the Caulfield Place terror. Emily Castle could black a kid's eye before he opened his mouth. Her mother would say placidly, 'Now, you Em'ly.' Her father would say, 'Ain't our Em a caution?'

I once overheard the nearest her mother ever got to a critical examination of her irrepressible daughter.

'Em, what you been and gone and done to Jimmy 'Iggins?'

'Nothink.'

'Mrs 'Iggins 'as been round, givin' me an earful, so yer must of done something.'

'Didn't do nothink.'

'Now, love, you must of done a bit more than nothing.'

'Didn't.'

'Mrs 'Iggins said 'e come 'ome with a bleedin' nose.'

'Me foot slipped.'

'Up in the air? Now 'ow could yer foot slip that 'igh?'

'He fell on it.'

'Lor' love yer, Em'ly, you're that fanciful. 'Is nose fell on yer foot?'

'Well, 'e pulled me clothes up.'

'Oh, and you wearin' them pretty drawers of yourn, the—'

'They ain't pretty.'

'They was when I bought 'em for yer. Oh, would yer believe, that young Jimmy 'Iggins pulling yer clothes up, and 'is mum comin' round—'

'They're ragged an' they ain't been mended.'

'What's not?'

'Me drawers.'

'Well, I'll buy yer some more.'

Emily eyed me now from the doorway. Her great big nosy green eyes always looked as if they were seeing more than was visible.

'Yer back safe an' sound, then,' she said.

'Yes, hard luck.'

'Can I come in?' she asked.

'No,' I said.

So she came in, with a hop and a skip, and closed the door. She stood against the passage wall, scratching her left leg with her right foot. Her school clothes looked a mess. Her eyes darted about before coming to rest on my long trousers. I'd gone into long trousers when I was fourteen. It was a school regulation. Emily seemed slightly in awe of them.

'Was it awful?' she asked, pulling at her tangled hair. Not requiring any answer, she went on, 'It must of been paralytic.' She got that word from her dad, a council navvy who went to work with straps around his trousers, just above the knees, to keep sewer mice from running all the way up. 'I mean, all them knives cuttin' you open – everythink must of been red with yer blood. Mum says most people pass on very painful after they're operated on, only the doctors never let on. She says it would ruin their business if they did. She'll be that relieved yer come back alive. Me dad said we wasn't to worry, he said you'd never depart this life until you'd recited *Amlet*, he said we'd all get an invite to yer deathbed to listen to it. Me dad likes yer a lot, Boots. He don't like everyone, but he likes you. Did yer get our card? Mum said—'

'Yes, I got your card, thank you. It's the first one I've received in the middle of an operation.'

'Oh, yer do talk grand,' she said, eyes darting again and her feet jigging about. 'Mum said she 'oped the card would reach yer in time, as she didn't like the look of 'er tea leaves the day you went in. She did it with three cups, and it come out fateful each time. Did yer meet anyone nice in the 'ospital?'

'I don't know, do I? I couldn't see through all the blood.'

'Oh, crikey,' gasped Emily, 'it must of been like rivers. Still, yer all right now, ain't yer?' She rubbed her back on the passage wallpaper, and her shapeless school dress went up and down with her body. 'Mum said anyone who gets out of 'ospital and lives to tell the tale is few an' far between.'

'Is that you, Em'ly Castle?' called Chinese Lady.

'Yes, Mrs Adams, I'm only just standin' and talkin'.'

'Well, see you don't knock the hallstand over while you're only talking.' Chinese Lady's voice came from the kitchen. 'You're home a bit early from school, aren't you?'

'I run all the way,' said Emily, and did a long jump from the hallstand to the doormat.

'Run all the way?' Chinese Lady appeared at the kitchen door. 'What for? Is your mother ill?'

'I dunno, Mrs Adams, I ain't seen 'er yet, I come straight in 'ere to see if Boots was all right.'

'D'you want a cup of tea?' asked Chinese Lady.

'No, she can't stop,' I said, 'she's got to see if her mum's ill or not.'

'No, I ain't,' said Emily, and dashed down the passage, leapt the one step and propelled herself into the kitchen. I heard cups and saucers rattle. I heard her say, 'Oops, I near done meself in then – yer table come up and 'it me, Mrs Adams.'

'You got six left legs, Em'ly, that's your trouble,' said Chinese Lady, then called to tell me the kettle was beginning to boil.

'A tin one would have boiled ages ago,' I called back.

I heard her say, 'We're not havin' no tin kettle in this house.'

Lizzy came in then. Sammy and Tommy wouldn't be far behind.

'Oh, back from the dead, are yer?' she said. She was in the pinafore frock she always wore for school. It was shabby, but tidy and clean. Lizzy was particular about her appearance. Even in the shabbiest clothes she still managed to look neat. And she was sensible in accepting cast-offs from Cousin Vi. They always looked better on her than on Vi, even if they were long past their best.

'Emily's here,' I said. Emily and Lizzy were bosom friends, both thirteen and both attending St John's Church School. It seemed an odd friendship to me, with Emily so slipshod and loud, and Lizzy so fastidious. 'Tell Mum I'll have my cup of tea in the parlour.'

'The parlour?' said Lizzy, her hair thick, wavy and shining. 'It's not Sunday.'

Allowing for exceptional occasions, the parlour was used only on Sundays, Bank Holiday evenings and Christmastime.

'I'm just out of hospital, I'm treating myself to an armchair.'

'Well, no one's going to – 'ere, you kids!'

Tommy and Sammy had burst in. Eleven-year-old Tommy had mousy hair, a sturdy frame and a willing spirit. Nine-year-old Sammy had dark hair, wiry legs and a covetous soul. He tried never to do anything without getting paid for it. Tommy was equable, Sammy was lippy. Their blue shorts were patched, their grey jerseys darned, their knees grubby.

'Yer back, Boots,' said Sammy.

''Ad a good time, 'ave yer?' said Tommy. 'What's fer tea, Lizzy?'

'How do I know?' said Lizzy.

'I'm starvin',' said Tommy. 'Would yer do us a slice of bread an' drippin'?'

'Oh, all right, then,' said Lizzy, 'I'll do yer both a slice.'

'Yer wasn't cut in 'alf, Boots, was yer?' said Sammy.

'Well, if I had been, I'd be standing here in two pieces, wouldn't I?' I said. 'Tommy, Chinese Lady wants you to get Grandma's tea service out of pawn. You can eat your bread and dripping on the way. Sammy can go with you and help you carry it.'

'Crikey, you're gettin' real bossy, you are,' said Lizzy, and went into the kitchen with the kids. I heard Sammy give a yell. Emily the terror had jumped him.

I heard Chinese Lady say, 'Em'ly, stop that now. Behave yourself.'

'Yes, Mrs Adams,' said Emily. Chinese Lady seemed the only person able to take the steam out of Emily. 'I'll carry Boots's tea to 'im, if yer like. Wasn't it a godsend, Mrs Adams, that 'e come out alive? Mum said 'ospitals is such fateful places.'

'Well, Guy's Hospital is all sanit'ry and caring,' said Chinese Lady. 'Your mum must mean them workhouse institutions.'

I sat down in the parlour. The leather armchairs and sofa had horsehair stuffing, which could make them feel a bit prickly. The leaves of a huge aspidistra tickled the net curtains of the bay window. The old upright piano stood against a wall, a fireguard stood in the hearth, and an iron poker lay on the brass fender. We did own a brass companion set, but it spent its time in and out of pawn, and it was in at the moment. And a glass-fronted china cabinet was empty of Grandma's tea service. The wallpaper was ancient, but in better condition than that in the kitchen. On the piano was a framed photograph of our mum and dad, with our mum sporting a feathered hat and our dad a moustache.

Emily came in with my cup of tea.

''Ere y'ar, Boots,' she said. Half of it was in the saucer.

'You've left some in the cup,' I said.

'Gertcher,' said Emily, and aimed a larky punch. It caught my shoulder. The cup fell over in the saucer, and warm tea cascaded over my trousers. 'Oh, cripes,' breathed Emily, and backed off.

'I don't care if they do hang me,' I said, 'I'm going to murder yer.'

'Em'ly!' Chinese Lady called. 'Your tea's getting cold.'

'Comin', Mrs Adams,' cooed Emily, and escaped by taking a flying leap. On her way back to the kitchen, I heard her coo some more. 'Boots 'as been an' upset 'is tea, Mrs Adams, it's gorn all over 'is long trousers.'

CHAPTER FOUR

I was fully recovered by Friday, and on Sunday morning went to church with Lizzy. Sammy said he couldn't because his Sunday boots were too cracked. I said he only needed to smarten them up with some Cherry Blossom boot polish, but he scarpered off the moment I turned my back. And Tommy went off to Camberwell at the request of Chinese Lady. He was to call on Aunt Victoria, who was given to bursts of family generosity and spells of acid criticism. Sometimes when she visited, she bestowed kind kisses and a penny each for pocket money. At other times, she'd be sour and crusty. She often said what a godsend it was that she hadn't got four kids to put up with. Chinese Lady would say that having four was a great comfort to a woman, which was a dig at the fact that Aunt Victoria only had Vi. Vi's dad, our Uncle Tom, had a steady job at the local gasworks, so Vi didn't have to go short of things like most kids. She wore good clothes, and whenever Aunt Victoria was feeling family-minded she would offer to let Lizzy have one or two things Vi had grown tired of. Sometimes there might be a nice vest and petticoat, or a frock. On Lizzy's behalf, Chinese Lady would accept everything that was offered. On her own behalf, Lizzy would accept the things she knew would fit and turn down those that didn't. She knew what the kids would sing about any girl wearing clothes obviously not her size.

'*Where did yer get them togs?*
You're a cheeky baby,
We know where yer got 'em from,
Off some fat old lady.'

Aunt Victoria hadn't offered anything for six or seven

months, so when she wrote asking Chinese Lady to send one of the kids along to collect some things, Tommy willingly offered to go on Sunday morning.

Lizzy and I walked to church with Mr Finch, he clad in a dark grey suit and trilby hat, dispensing his brand of philosophy on the way.

'One should spare some time for worship. We should all believe in some kind of God. Such belief gives us humility, Boots. And humility is good for us, Lizzy.'

'But can poor people afford it, Mr Finch, that's what I'd like to know,' said Lizzy. 'Our mum has an 'ard job keepin' the wolf from the door, and a lot of humility might let it in.'

'Your mother, Lizzy, is an exceptional woman. No wolf will reach your larder.' Mr Finch chuckled. 'Any wolf that did would soon wish itself elsewhere. Your mother will see you all grow up to enjoy our green and pleasant land.'

'It ain't green round here,' said Lizzy, 'not till you get to Ruskin Park. I ain't seen no green besides that, except Peckham Rye an' Brockwell Park, an' you need to pay a tram fare to get to them.'

'Mr Finch is speaking generally,' I said. 'There's lots of green land outside London.'

'I ain't seen it,' said Lizzy.

'Well, we will when our ship comes home,' I said.

'It's a long time comin',' said Lizzy, 'it's probably got sunk.'

'No, no,' said Mr Finch, 'our own ships of fortune never get sunk, Lizzy, although they can take a long time to arrive.'

'Ours don't know where the port is,' said Lizzy. With bitter relish she added, 'Em'ly's catching us up.'

'God forfend,' I said.

'God whatter?' said Lizzy.

'Too late,' I said, for Emily was with us. There was a bruising wallop in the middle of my back and the sound of shoes clacking on the pavement. Emily jigged into jerky shape and scattered us. Her pink Sunday frock was already a mess, her mass of hair all over the place under a

42

boater with a brim that looked as if the mice had been nibbling it. You had to watch the Walworth mice. They scampered around as if they owned more of the place than you did. Lizzy hated them. Chinese Lady made war on them. Sammy caught them and tormented them, getting his own back on the vermin for the way they frightened his sister, and then handing them over to Mrs Castle's great fat tabby cat, which swallowed them at a gulp.

'Good morning, Emily,' said Mr Finch pleasantly.

''Ello, Mr Finch – can I come in church with you, Boots?'

'Not if I can help it.'

'Boots, Boots,' said Mr Finch gently.

'Don't want to, anyway,' said Emily, and put her arm through Lizzy's. We reached St John's Church in Larcom Street, next to the church school, and the forecourt was full of kids waiting until the last minute before going in. Some boys advanced on Lizzy. She eyed them distantly. Lizzy considered boys daft and mucky, and was yet to be convinced that God was responsible for them. Watching her becoming a shadow of her usual self in the presence of Ned Somers at the hospital had been almost mortifying. I didn't like any boy to think my sister was a quivering halfwit.

'Watcher, Lizzy.'

'Where'd yer get yer lid, Lizzy?'

Lizzy's lid was a Sunday hat of white straw, bought by Chinese Lady for a penny in the market and lovingly refurbished. It was fixed to Lizzy's chestnut hair with one of our mum's bead-headed hatpins. Her white Sunday frock, with a pink sash, was sweet, and although her shoes were a little cracked, they shone with Cherry Blossom.

'Give over,' she said amid a closing group of boys. Emily kicked an ankle as she was elbowed aside. Mr Finch, giving the young people a smile, made his way into the church with an acquaintance. He always came to church with us, but left us to our intemperate friends on arrival. The bell was ringing, summoning its Walworth parishioners, and

43

women in their desperate Sunday best and men in shiny Sunday suits were responding to the call. Every worthwhile activity centred around the church, which sponsored Crusader groups for boys and girls, a pioneer Scout troop for boys, a Brigade company for girls, Pleasant Tuesday Afternoons for women, the Sunday school and a Christmas bazaar in St John's Institute.

The boys crowding Lizzy had Emily in a fury. She pushed and shoved, a boy stuck out a leg and she fell over with a scream. I picked her up, for which kind assistance she kicked my shin.

'Boots'll do yer now, Em,' said a boy.

''E nearly didn't come out, yer know,' said Emily.

'Didn't come out where?'

'They cut 'im up in 'ospital till 'e was all over blood,' said Emily. 'Nearly went to 'is death, didn't yer, Boots? The day 'e come out 'e was only 'alf alive, so 'e went and poured tea all over 'is togs, didn't yer, Boots?'

Girls shrieked. Boys hooted.

'Adams!' The verger, in the church doorway, was pointing a finger. 'Adams, into church at once. And all you other boys and girls.'

In church, I sat with trousered friends, and Lizzy sat with frocked friends in the pew behind. We sang the hymns. We liked hymns. We suffered the sermon with silent groans, although there wasn't a nicer man of God than our vicar. Midway through his sermon, a hard pea struck the back of my neck. I turned. Emily had her eyes turned soulfully up to God's rafters, her pea-shooter out of sight. I gave her a growling look.

The sermon over, we sang the final hymn, then received the vicar's blessing. Another pea hit the back of my neck. I wondered how long Emily Castle had on this earth before she became a strangled corpse.

When we came out, Mr Finch dealt kindly but efficiently with the deadly menace.

'You go on with Lizzy, Boots,' he said. 'I'll walk with Emily. I want to help her become a lady.'

44

'I don't wanner be no lady,' said Emily.

'You're too modest, Emily,' said Mr Finch. 'I'll help you take the first steps while we walk as far as the public house. Then you can go on home.'

'Oh cripes,' muttered Emily.

'Splendid,' said Mr Finch.

After Sunday church he followed the custom of other men by taking a glass of ale in the pub in Browning Street. He drank very modestly for a river pilot. Sometimes he came home with a small bottle of nourishing stout for Chinese Lady to enjoy with her Sunday dinner. In return, she usually invited him to join us. He rarely accepted. He was almost like one of the family in many ways, but avoided too intrusive a role. He never entered the kitchen without knocking, or failed to thank Chinese Lady for doing his weekly washing. She respected him. He had kitchen facilities in his living-room, and most of the time he prepared his own food.

With Mr Finch and Emily behind us, Lizzy and I walked home.

'That's a scream,' said Lizzy, 'Mr Finch tryin' to talk Em'ly into being a lady, and her with all that messed-up hair. I never seen such a mop.'

Lizzy had a very clean and pretty look all over. Also, she took after Chinese Lady in the way she walked, carrying herself upright.

Five minutes after we got home, Tommy arrived back from Aunt Victoria's with a brown paper parcel. Chinese Lady unwrapped it. Aunt Victoria had done Lizzy proud with a sky-blue frock, a grey skirt, a cream blouse, a winceyette nightdress and some cotton stockings. Everything looked in good condition.

'Bless us,' said Tommy, taking off our mum, 'the Lord's been good to yer, Lizzy.' He picked up the nightdress and held it against himself. 'Ain't it fancy?' he said.

Lizzy flared up.

'Leave that be,' she said, 'it ain't fer you to put yer grubby 'ands on.'

'Lizzy, Lizzy, do speak more proper,' said Chinese Lady, who occasionally went on about proper and improper. 'Don't keep saying ain't. You and Boots is both growing up, you should both speak a bit nice.'

'Just because 'e sounds like Lord Muck don't mean I got to,' said Lizzy, 'and I don't want that nightdress, not now Tommy's near wiped 'is nose on it.'

That was typical of Lizzy's fastidiousness.

'Bleedin' blimey,' said Tommy, 'I ain't—'

Chinese Lady boxed his ears. Tommy rocked and Lizzy looked uncomfortable.

'Well, I don't know,' said Chinese Lady, more sad than angry, 'I just don't know. Language like that, and on a Sunday too.'

'It ain't fair,' said Tommy. 'Crikey, I been all the way to Camberwell an' back, an' all I get for it is a wallop.'

Lizzy ran round the table and gave him a hug and cuddle.

'Sorry, Tommy,' she said, 'I'll 'ave the nightdress, honest.'

'Well, fank goodness that's settled,' said Sammy, 'I was gettin' noises in me ears.'

'They're all nice things,' said Chinese Lady, examining the frock. 'They're not what we can afford till our ship comes home.'

'We're poor, we are,' said Tommy.

'But honest,' I said.

'Well,' said Chinese Lady firmly, while the aroma of the Sunday roast invaded the kitchen, 'being poor but honest means we'll all reach heaven long before the rich and sinful. Your dad always said the rich and sinful'll have to do hundreds of years of hard labour in the devil's inferno before they can knock on the pearly gates.'

''Undreds of years?' said Tommy. 'Crikey, I ain't ever going to be rich an' sinful, just rich.'

'I wouldn't mind being a bit sinful,' said Sammy, 'if it got me rich quicker.'

'We won't have silly talk,' said Chinese Lady.

46

'Can I 'ave a rock cake, Mum?' asked Sammy.

'You can in five minutes when I take them out of the oven,' said Chinese Lady, and held the sky-blue frock up against Lizzy. 'There, that's going to make you look so pretty, lovey. Oh, I baked a cake as well. We got Miss Chivers coming to tea, remember.'

CHAPTER FIVE

Sunday tea was at five. Miss Chivers arrived at quarter to. She wore a brown frock with a white collar, and her light brown hair was finished off with thick buns. Her glasses were on. She needed glasses to help her with her clerical work at the Admiralty, and for knitting and for seeing clearly. The Witch made her wear them always. When Miss Chivers left the house to go to her work each morning, nearly always the Witch would call to her from her bedroom window. 'Elsie,' she'd screech, 'you got your glasses on?' 'Yes, Mother,' Miss Chivers would say. Everyone knew it was all to do with the Witch's determination to make her daughter look unattractive to men.

When I was ten and leader of the street gang, which we called the Dread Seven, we discussed whether there was a way of accidentally burning the Witch to a cinder on bonfire night, November 5th. The trouble was, you couldn't light bonfires in the street, not without the local bobby coming along to put it out and to clip a few ears. But there was always one at Peckham Rye. Lizzy and Emily, co-opted female members of the gang and eight years old at the time, suggested putting the Witch into a coal sack and carrying her to the Rye. Yes, but how were we to load her onto the bonfire? Emily said to chuck her on, still in the sack. She said everyone would be chucking something on, so the whole Dread Seven could chuck the Witch on. The Dread Seven all voted in favour, except me. I was keen, but had reservations. However, when bonfire night arrived, there was no sign of the Dread Seven. We'd all funked it, and so had our co-opted females. It knocked the stuffing out of the gang, so we formed another one and left Emily

48

and Lizzy out. That provoked Emily. She knocked on the door of every house in the Place and informed the grown-ups that I was the leader of a gang that was going to cut off the tails of their family cats. A policeman came to our house the following day, took hold of my ear and said, 'What's all this we hear about you torturing cats? You'd better come along with me, my lad.' Chinese Lady straightened things out with the law, and later with Mrs Castle, and Mrs Castle said, 'Oh, that Em of mine, no wonder 'er dad calls 'er a caution.' She and Mr Castle never did anything about Emily at any time.

Miss Chivers stood up to the harassing ordeal of being the Witch's daughter, and she stood up well. Her air of gentle, uncomplaining tolerance was very much admired. She was a wonderfully calm-looking woman, with a softly handsome face and soft, myopic brown eyes. Her voice was soft too, soft and quiet. Everyone said that thirty years of being the Witch's daughter could have given her a bowed and haggard look, but no, she always had a nice, quiet smile for everyone and a straight back. She never talked about the harridan, and whenever Chinese Lady asked her how her mother was, she'd always say, 'Oh, just about the same.' Nothing more. What the same was, everyone knew. Chronic.

'Come in, Miss Chivers,' I said, having opened the door to her knock.

'Thank you, Boots,' she said, almost shyly, 'it's so nice of your family to put up with me so often.' She stepped in, removed her glasses and put them in her handbag. That uncovered her long thick lashes and brought the soft, myopic look to her eyes. I took her into the parlour, where the family was assembled. Everyone was in Sunday clothes, and Tommy and Sammy had given their cracked boots a shine. And Lizzy had brushed our mum's hair and wound it around her head in a very fetching fashion. The round mahogany parlour table was laid for tea, the aspidistra leaves had been bathed and the piano dusted. Sammy had also been dusted – and polished as well. Even his knees shone. He and Tommy came to their feet as Miss Chivers entered. It was all a familiar ritual in honour of our monthly guest.

'Good afternoon, Miss Chivers,' chorused the family.

'Hello,' smiled Miss Chivers, gently peering. 'My, you do look handsome, Sammy.'

'I been washed, would yer believe,' said Sammy. 'All over, nearly,' he added darkly, 'and after I washed this mornin' already.'

'Oh, they haven't been wasted exercises,' said Miss Chivers, seating herself, 'you're shining, Sammy. How are you, Mrs Adams?'

'Worn out washing Sammy nearly all over,' said Chinese Lady.

'Sammy's a pickle?' smiled Miss Chivers.

'Been a pickle all his life,' said Chinese Lady.

'We've spent years trying to get him back in the jar,' I said.

'Wouldn't be no use if we did get 'im back,' said Tommy, ''e'd only pop out again.'

'And how are you, Lizzy?' asked Miss Chivers.

'I'm lovely, thank you, Miss Chivers,' said Lizzy demurely.

'Yes, I can see you are,' smiled Miss Chivers, gently peering again.

'How is your poor mother?' asked Chinese Lady.

'Oh, just about the same,' said Miss Chivers. 'Aren't you going to sit down, Boots?'

'Oh, Boots likes to stand about lookin' manly when you come,' said Lizzy mischievously.

'I'm on my feet,' I said, 'because I'm about to go and put the kettle on.'

I put the kettle on. We sat down to tea minutes later, pride of place on the table given to the huge glazed brown teapot and its earthenware stand in front of Chinese Lady. Lizzy offered the plate of bread and butter to Miss Chivers. The bread and butter was for the grown-ups. Chinese Lady always forked out for butter when Miss Chivers came to tea, buying two ounces from the Maypole. There was bread and marge on another plate for Lizzy, me and the kids. Someone knocked on the parlour door.

'Come in,' called Chinese Lady, and Mr Finch showed himself.

'Ah, I'm disturbing you,' he said.

'Of course you aren't,' said Chinese Lady. 'Won't you join us? We've only just sat down.'

'How very kind of you,' said Mr Finch, and smiled warmly. 'Thank you, Mrs Adams – and good afternoon, Miss Chivers.'

'Good afternoon, Mr Finch,' said Miss Chivers, lowering her eyes.

Mr Finch cheerfully took a vacant chair between Lizzy and me, and we all tried to look innocently bland. We were all in on this other ritual. Chinese Lady said it was best to do it this way, so as not to cause any trouble. The fact was that whenever Miss Chivers came to tea, Mr Finch made a well-timed appearance that resulted in him joining us. He was never officially invited, as Miss Chivers was. He simply appeared and was asked to sit down with us. That meant Miss Chivers could truthfully assure her mother beforehand that only she had been invited. The Witch would have fallen off her broomstick in a screaming fit if she'd thought her daughter was going to come into social contact with a man, and without her glasses on. It didn't matter that the neighbours knew Mr Finch always joined us. No one in the Place would tell the hag anything unless she clawed their eyes out.

'Bread an' butter, Mr Finch?' said Lizzy, offering the special plate.

'Thank you, Lizzy,' he said, and took a slice. 'What a pleasure to share your Sunday repast, and to find you here too, Miss Chivers.' A little flush disturbed Miss Chivers's clear complexion. 'How are you?'

'Very well, thank you, Mr Finch,' she said, cutting her bread and butter and keeping her eyes on it.

'A lovely day for the time of the year,' said Mr Finch,

always able to be commonplace as well as interesting. It was late April, and Easter had been and gone, and so had the *Titanic*. That had been a shock to people, and a sadness to Mr Finch, he having been a seaman.

'Yes, lovely,' murmured Miss Chivers, eating her bread and butter shyly and delicately. Sammy and Tommy were gobbling, hurrying to get at the jam. Chinese Lady required us all to eat two slices of bread and marge before having jam on the rest. There were two new jars of jam on the table, as well as a dish of rock cakes, a seed cake, a Madeira cake from Hall's, the bakers of Walworth Road, and a Swiss roll. No wonder Chinese Lady never knew where the money went to. Most of it went on food. She deplored the hungry look of some kids, and she'd sell the clothes off her back to keep that look off our faces. She had once asked Mr Cooley, the pawnbroker, if she could pawn the piano.

'Now, have a heart, Mrs Adams, where can I put a pianner?'

'Oh, we'll mind it for you,' said Chinese Lady hopefully.

'Very kind of you, I'm sure, Mrs Adams, but no, I can't offer for any pianner. I'll loan you a few bob for your ring.'

'That's me wedding ring.'

'Well, you're a widder now.'

Chinese Lady stalked out, dragging me with her.

'Can I 'ave some jam now, Mum?' asked Sammy.

'Yes, now you can, lovey,' said Chinese Lady, and dished him a large spoonful.

'I wanted the uvver, the strawb'ry,' said Sammy.

'Well, you got raspb'ry, you can have strawb'ry next.'

'May I try the raspberry?' asked Mr Finch.

Miss Chivers softly asked for some of the same. Mr Finch passed her the jar, his kind smile putting the little flush on her face again. Chinese Lady had two reasons for bringing Miss Chivers and Mr Finch together at Sunday tea. To allow Miss Chivers the kind of male company the Witch denied her, and to indulge her matchmaking hope that Miss Chivers and Mr Finch might elope and live happily ever after. She didn't say so, of course, but Lizzy and I knew. Chinese Lady was an open book to us, and she had every good woman's wish to promote romantic attachments. That Mr Finch had a warm regard for Miss Chivers was obvious. That Miss Chivers found him a kind and tactful man was also obvious. Lizzy liked the way he treated Miss Chivers. She said he didn't paw her or breathe heavily over her. She said he was very nice to her. She said that with all Miss Chivers had to put up with from the Witch, she must think Mr Finch was like a bit of manly heaven.

Lizzy was listening as Mr Finch and Miss Chivers conversed over the table, Mr Finch lending an agreeable note to the talk, and Miss Chivers being softly earnest. They were talking about H.G. Wells and his novel, *The War of the Worlds*.

'I thought it powerful,' said Mr Finch, whose years of sailing the mighty oceans had made him wise and worldly.

'Almost frightening,' said Miss Chivers. 'And a warning, didn't you think so?' She put the question shyly, as if she hoped it would not offend him. Mr Finch gave thought to his reply.

'A warning?' he said. 'Yes, perhaps you're right, Miss Chivers, a warning to our own world about our warlords.'

'It's such a dangerous world, even now,' said Miss Chivers, giving him food for more thought.

'One hopes we're all becoming more civilised,' said Mr Finch, who might have said our lady guest was far too charming to allow herself to worry about the imaginative mind of H.G. Wells. But he never did say things like that to her.

'There are so many countries with big armies,' said Miss Chivers, gently cutting a slice of Madeira cake on her plate.

'Our Empire will look after things,' said Mr Finch with cheerful confidence.

'But we have a very small army ourselves,' said Miss Chivers, 'although, thankfully, we do have a large navy.' She would know that, of course, working as she did at the

Admiralty. She added in a shy little rush, 'Oh, I'm sorry, Mrs Adams, we shouldn't be talking like this over such a nice tea.'

'Or in front of the children,' I said, finding her fascinating.

Mr Finch laughed.

'Boots is an engaging boy, isn't he, Miss Chivers?' he said.

Miss Chivers gave me her soft, myopic smile.

'Oh, everyone likes Boots,' she said.

'Don't you mind that he's stuck-up?' said Lizzy.

'Lizzy!' Chinese Lady was shocked. 'Don't you dare talk like that in front of guests. Boots isn't stuck-up.'

'Well, 'e is a bit,' said Tommy.

'I'll clout you,' I said. 'Not in front of our guests, of course, but later.'

'Garn,' said Tommy, 'I'll bite yer leg off.'

'An' I'll bite 'is uvver one,' said Sammy.

Miss Chivers put a hand to her mouth, smothering a little burst of laughter. Mr. Finch roared.

'What a family I've got,' said Chinese Lady, refilling teacups.

'Mrs Adams, you've a fine family, very fine,' said Mr Finch, 'and boys will be boys.'

'Yes, but what sort of boys?' said Chinese Lady.

'Ones that bite their bruvver's legs orf,' said Sammy.

Miss Chivers laughed in soft delight.

'I've a good mind not to let you have no more cake, Sammy,' said Chinese Lady.

'I ain't done nothink,' said Sammy.

'I wish you'd speak more proper,' said Chinese Lady.

'Whaffor?' asked Sammy.

'Well, you see, Sammy,' said Mr Finch, 'English is a wonderful language and deserves our full attention. My Aunt Trudy was a tweaker of the ear whenever I was careless in my articulation. There, that's a beautiful word itself, articulation.'

'Wassit mean?' asked Sammy, mouth full of rock cake.

'Speakin' proper, I expect,' said Chinese Lady.

'Quite right, Mrs Adams,' said Mr Finch.

'I like carpentry best,' said Tommy, 'and 'ammering nails.'

'Hammering,' I said.

'Yus, 'ammering,' said Tommy.

'Tommy,' I said, 'say I hit the elephant house with a hammer.'

'Oh, the poor elephants,' said Miss Chivers.

'I ain't gonner say it,' said Tommy, 'I'm 'avin' cake.'

'Boots, leave off,' said Lizzy.

She and I, with Tommy and Sammy, cleared the table when tea was over and washed up in the scullery sink, using a kettleful of hot water and lots of soda crystals. Sammy said he'd dry up *and* put the china away if he could have a penny.

'Nothing doing,' I said.

'It's a fag, 'anging cups up and everythink,' said Sammy.

'Leave off,' said Lizzy, 'we're not made of money.'

Actually, Sammy didn't mind doing any kind of job as long as he was paid for it. He and Tommy got a penny each pocket money from Chinese Lady, and Lizzy and I got tuppence each, but we all had to earn it by doing jobs in the home or running errands. Sammy augmented his income by knocking on neighbours' doors and offering to run any required errands for a penny, or for a halfpenny if it was only to Ashford's, the sweetshop in Browning Street which also stocked a few groceries. Sammy had initiative, and at nine was already looking ahead.

When the washing-up was done and we were all assembled in the parlour again, Miss Chivers consented in her shy way to play the piano. We all gathered round. She sat in one of the chairs. The piano stool had long since found its way into pawn and never been redeemed. Miss Chivers looked charming at the piano, her soft brown dress draping her quite elegantly and showing she had a bosom which Chinese Lady no doubt thought hadn't been given a chance to be put to its proper use yet.

Miss Chivers played from an old music book, Mr Finch turning the pages for her. The parlour echoed to the sound of the tinkling keys, and no one said the piano needed tuning. She played bits from Brahms and Chopin, the bits that were well-known and rated as popular music. Then, without the aid of music, she began to play what we really liked, music hall songs. She didn't forget to start off with Chinese Lady's favourite, 'Soldiers of the Queen'. Our dad had gone off to the Boer War to the tune of that song, when I was very young and Lizzy was an infant. When he came back he looked the colour of brown beetroot, and when Tommy was born nine months later, he looked the same colour.

We all sang 'Soldiers of the Queen', Chinese Lady with misty eyes, of course.

When Miss Chivers finally closed the piano lid, there was a sharp knock on the front door. Miss Chivers looked startled. Chinese Lady looked worried. Had the Witch heard the singing, had she heard Mr Finch's voice, and had she tottered along to put a curse on Mr Finch and give her daughter a screeching piece of her haglike mind? But then the latchcord was pulled to open the front door, jigging feet clipped the passage lino and Emily, who treated our house much as if it had been her own, put her tangled hair and thin, peaky face into the parlour.

'Oh, hello,' she said. 'Oh, you're 'avin' a party. Oh, hello, Miss Chivers, 'ow's yer dear mother?'

Emily was honey-thick at times.

'D'you want a rock cake?' said Chinese Lady, obviously thinking of sweetening the minx. Emily thought no more of the Witch than anyone did, but she was the one person who, in a fit of traitorous delinquency, might just knock up the harridan and tell her that Mr Finch had been at our Sunday tea party, and that she'd seen him actually standing next to her daughter.

'Oh, thank yer, Mrs Adams,' gushed Emily, 'we only 'ad bread pudden ourselves.'

'I like bread pudden,' said Tommy.

'There's two rock cakes left,' said Chinese Lady.

'I'll eat 'em up for yer, Mrs Adams,' said Emily.

To get her out of the way, I said, 'Come on, then, I'll lead you to them.'

She followed me to the kitchen, giving me a playful shove from behind as I reached the single step down, and of course I almost fell flat on my face. Her playful shoves were like hammer blows.

'Gotcher,' she giggled.

'Not quite,' I said. I took her into the kitchen, got the cake tin out of the larder and gave her the rock cakes. She crunched into the crisp casing of one. 'Well?' I said.

'Ta,' she said through crumbs, and her green eyes cast me a sly glance. 'I ain't gonner tell,' she said.

'I should hope not. You'd get lynched.'

'You can give us a kiss, if yer like,' she said, standing on one foot and eyeing the second rock cake.

'I'll give you a smacking, that'll do you a lot more good.'

'Oh, yer don't arf sound grown up sometimes,' she said.

'Eat your other rock cake.'

'Don't want it. Full up with bread pudden. I've a good mind, yer know, I've a good mind to tell on yer family.'

'No, you haven't. You're too nice. You're horrible, but you're too nice, all the same.'

She wasn't nice at all. She was a spoiled, trying little vixen. But one had to sacrifice the truth sometimes.

Emily looked down at her feet and jerked them about.

'Oh, I won't tell, Boots, honest I won't,' she said. 'Mum's just been sayin' I'm goin' to be pretty when I'm older, she says me face 'as got just the right bone stature for being very pretty when I'm grown up.'

'I think she means structure,' I said. And there it was, as I realised years later. There it was, the reason why Emily was the eternal irritant as a girl. It was her resentfully instinctive kick against whoever was responsible for her being thin, peaky and plain, and everybody was responsible. And it was the one way she could command attention, even the angry attention of those she irritated. Her best friend was Lizzy, and Lizzy was pretty. Emily clung to Lizzy's side at times, perhaps to identify herself with her prettiness. Lizzy drew boys, and so Emily shared the attention. 'Well, off you go, then,' I said, 'your mum's probably wondering where her pretty girl's got to.'

'I told 'er I was comin' in 'ere. Can I stay, Boots, can I join yer party?'

'All right,' I said.

Emily laughed stridently and punched me. But I took her into the parlour and she spent the time being quite good, sitting next to Lizzy. Lizzy was always nice to Emily. Perhaps Lizzy understood her even then.

Miss Chivers departed at two minutes to eight in order to appear before the Witch on the dot. She thanked Chinese Lady earnestly for her hospitality, and she brought a sixpence out of her handbag, gave it to me and asked me very sweetly to share it with the others.

'Thank you most kindly, Miss Chivers,' I said, 'it's been a pleasure to have you.'

'Oh, thank you at our most kindest, Miss Chivers,' said Lizzy, taking me off, 'it's been divine.'

Miss Chivers smiled tenderly in her regard for our Lizzy.

'You're such fun, Lizzy,' she said.

'Goodbye, Miss Chivers,' said Chinese Lady, 'and do come again Sunday four weeks, won't you?'

'Thank you, Mrs Adams, I'de love to,' said Miss Chivers. 'Goodbye, Mr Finch.'

'Goodbye, Miss Chivers,' said Mr Finch.

She avoided his warm and friendly glance, and I saw her to the front door.

'It's nice of you to come so often,' I said, 'but you're sure it's not boring for you?'

'Oh, no, Boots, no, you must never think that,' she said in a soft rush. 'It's – it's – ' She hesitated, then went on. 'It's like being in the land of the living. You needn't say anything. I know you understand.'

She put her glasses on and went, walking in her flowing way, her brown dress softly whispering.

The parlour table being clear, Mr Finch played Snap with us until nine-thirty, when Emily went home and Sammy and Tommy went up to bed. Chinese Lady then made a pot of tea, and Mr Finch stayed on for a cup. Departing up to his rooms, he did not go without saying how grateful he was to be allowed such happy contact with the family.

'An' such convenient socialising with Miss Chivers,' murmured Lizzy, after he had disappeared.

'Well, it's nice for both of them,' said Chinese Lady, picking up some socks of Sammy's that needed darning, 'and it's a shame they can't properly romanticise.'

'You're not going to darn on a Sunday evening, are you?' I asked.

'Sammy needs 'em for school tomorrow,' she said.

Taking her off, I said, 'Well, I won't have it, and I don't know what that Sammy's coming to, always making holes in his socks.'

'Listen to him,' said Lizzy. 'You're gettin' to be a sore trial to the whole fam'ly, you are, Boots. The sooner you're in 'igh finance bankin' like that boy talked about –' She stopped. 'Oh, him,' she muttered, 'you and him are two of a kind.'

'Back to school for you tomorrer, Boots,' said Chinese Lady.

CHAPTER SIX

'Adams!'

A small piece of white chalk struck my head. I looked up from my browsing. Mr Horton, our art master, had me in his gimlet sights.

'Sir?'

'I'm sorry to have woken you up,' said Mr Horton, who had had several water colours exhibited. 'It's a pleasure to have you back, my boy, but you're coming it a bit, aren't you, nodding off so soon?'

'I was in deep thought, sir.'

'Ah,' said Mr Horton in an expectant way, and a titter ran round the class, like it did sometimes in a magistrate's court. 'Yes, Adams?'

'I was thinking, sir, that—' I stopped. I'd been dreaming, of course. I had no real interest in art, being hopeless at it. 'It's escaped me, sir.'

'A pity,' said Mr Horton, 'we were all expecting a revelation. However, let me see what progress you've made with your water colour. Would you favour me, Adams, by bringing it to me?'

I took it to him and laid it on his desk. The class of fifteen-year-old boys awaited his comments. Our morning's work was to create a water colour painting of a blue vase standing on a table in front of his desk. He examined my effort, his handsome countenance expressing a willingness to make the best he could of it.

'Sir, I'm not much good at—'

'Adams, what is this?'

'My painting of the vase, sir, as far as I've got.'

'It's something blue, I grant you, definitely blue.'

60

'Well, yes—'

'You've seen nothing of what the light has given to the subject – no browns, no reds, no yellows?'

'Well, it just looks blue to me, sir. That's what I mean, I'm not much good at art, sir.'

'Then you'll have to improve, won't you, or it'll look as if I'm not much good at teaching you. I'll get the sack, Adams.'

'Good lord, sir, I hope not.'

Another titter ran round the class. Mr Horton studied the class with interest, the interest of a man fascinated by the occupants of a monkey house.

'Look at the vase again, Adams. Look at it long and often. It's a glazed blue vase standing in light from the windows. Sunlight, my boy. There are other colours present as well as blue.'

'Yes, sir. I just hope I'm not going colour blind.'

'Oh, I don't think it's that,' said Mr Horton in a friendly way. 'I think you're letting a lack of interest rear its blank head. You have some career in mind, I suppose?'

'I hope to excel in banking, sir.'

'Really?' Mr Horton looked gloomy for me. 'You'd rather work in a bank than communicate with the wonders of colour in a Bloomsbury garret?'

'You starve to death in a garret, sir.'

'Yes, but as a free man, Adams, a free man owing nothing to anyone except me. And who knows? The time has already come when people posing as artists produce canvases so hideous they're acclaimed overnight as geniuses. That could well happen to you, my boy. Go back to your desk, study the vase again, and begin afresh.'

'Yes, sir.'

'Good.'

I went back to my desk and studied the blue vase again. It looked the same as before, a blue vase shining in the light. However, Mr Horton had said, more or less, that there were browns, reds and yellows, so I used some. And some greens as well, to make him think I'd had a burst of

61

imaginative brilliance. Towards the end of the morning, when everyone was thinking about what their mums had put in their sandwiches, Mr Horton walked around the class, peering over each boy's shoulder and making comments approving, disappointed, sarcastic and even incoherent. When he peered at my effort, which looked like a vase struck by a disintegrating rainbow, he seemed most impressed.

'Brilliant,' he said.

'Thank you, sir.'

'Yes, consider yourself a modern genius, Adams, acclaimed overnight. That is all your own work?'

'Yes, sir.'

'Blinding,' said Mr Horton, 'blinding.'

It was French in the afternoon, and I wasn't too bad at that. I'd averaged sixty per cent plus a term. But the master, Mr Ainsley, was in his most Gallic mood. His mother was French, and he considered her language exquisite, which made him very Francophilic about it at times. He listened in dark-faced pain that afternoon to our conversational French, the dialogue opening with, 'Would you kindly direct me to the nearest railway station, please?'

He took exception to my pronunciation.

'Stop,' he said, shuddering.

'Sir?'

'You might understand what you're saying, Adams, and I might disentangle some of your strangulated vowels, but a citizen of France, never. Is there such a thing, I wonder, as cockney French?'

'I don't sound cockney, do I, sir?' My English teacher was given to knocking any pupil's cockney twang for six, and had once told me I'd got a good cosmopolitan accent. I'd looked up cosmopolitan, and its meaning had sent me home feeling very smug.

'Your French vowels, Adams,' said Mr Ainsley darkly.

'What about them, sir?'

'They'll be my death,' said Mr Ainsley.

I went home in a depressed state after such a discouraging day. Walking down the Place, I saw Emily dart out of her house. She reached the gate. Railings fronted the houses, and there was a gate to each house. Seeing me, Emily stopped. I heard her amiable but blowsy mother call.

'Em'ly! Come back in 'ere!'

Emily, much to my surprise, darted back in and slammed the door as I passed. A van was delivering paper to the printing factory, its horse with its nosebag on, and there was a dull, drumming murmur from the drug mills. I entered our house. Sammy and Tommy were in the kitchen, eating slices of bread covered with beef dripping. They and Lizzy came home from school at midday to have their dinner. I took sandwiches and had my dinner while they were having tea. Being Monday, it would be cold beef and bubble and squeak. The house smelt of Monday washing. The line in the yard was full. In the scullery, Chinese Lady had a large cauldron of water heating up on the gas stove. She gave me a straight look.

'You'll have to have yours washed too,' she said.

'What's that mean?' I asked.

'Your head,' she said, and seemed careworn.

'I still don't know what you mean.'

'The clinic lady come to the kids' school today, and went all through the children's hair.'

'Oh, blimey,' I said.

'Language won't help.'

The clinic lady visited the elementary schools regularly, bringing with her a fine-toothed steel comb and an enamel basin full of disinfectant. Dipping the comb, she would ferret around in the children's hair, searching their scalps. If she found lice, the child in question took a slip of paper home to its parents.

'Was it Sammy's head?' I asked. Sammy was the untidiest one, the one who avoided soap and water whenever he could, and didn't like having his hair washed. He complained the soap went into his eyes and blinded him.

Chinese Lady compressed her fine lips.

'All of 'em,' she said, and looked as if the shame of it was killing her.

'All? Not Lizzy too?' Not Lizzy, with her hair her crowning beauty even at thirteen, the hair she brushed and kept so immaculate.

'Lizzy too.' Chinese Lady looked in pain. 'Now don't start rampaging about, talkin' language at them, and don't say nothing to Lizzy. She's in our room. Leave her there. We've all got to have our heads scrubbed, and you've got to go to the chemist's and get some oil of sassafras. It's got to be rubbed in all over your scalps after the scrubbin'.'

'Not mine. My head's clean, and yours must be too.'

'Don't talk silly. If they got it, we've all got it. You don't think them pestiferous lice just pick out them three, do you? Other kids have come home with them notes. Em'ly, she's got lice, and Lily Chubb and Jimmy Hodges, and that's not all.'

'Oh, blimey,' I said again, 'the whole street's infested.'

'What d'you mean, infested? It's not the plague.'

'It's just as catching.'

'Humiliatin', more like.' Chinese Lady bit her lip. 'What your dad would of said I can't bear to think. It's not as if I don't give the kids their baths, it's not as if I don't dust and clean—'

'Of course you do. It's not your fault, Mum.'

'Has your head been itchin' lately?'

'No. Yes, a bit, now I come to think.'

'There you are, then.' Chinese Lady spoke in a defeated way, her almond eyes sad. 'I use gallons of carbolic through the year, but this place, there's dirt all round us. We're on top of factories and them drug mills, and all the smokin' chimneys, and it all comes in, even if you don't see it. Come here.' She led me to the furthest corner of the scullery, the darkest corner. The only light came through the narrow glass panels of the door to the yard and the outside lav. 'Put your hand on the wall, go on.'

I wiped the flat of my hand over the whitewashed brick

64

wall, then went into the light and looked at my hand. It was filthy.

'All right, Mum,' I said, 'this weekend we'll wash down the whole house, every wall and ceiling in every room – with water, soap and carbolic. We'll all lend a hand.'

'Boots,' she said, 'who's going to tell Mr Finch?'

'No one.'

'We got to tell him, in case he's caught them from us. We got to tell him.'

'Yes, all right, Mum. I'll tell him.'

'He'll leave,' she said. 'Anyone would, even the most charitable person. Go an' get that oil, then. Take some money from my handbag.'

I took sixpence. Passing the downstairs bedroom on my way out, I stopped. The door was shut. Lizzy was inside, her scalp lice-infested. I hesitated, then went on my way to the chemist's shop in Walworth Road and bought a bottle of sassafras oil.

Tea was postponed until the disinfecting job had been done. Chinese Lady scrubbed Lizzy's head first, over the scullery sink, with the door shut tight. Lizzy bore it silently, as far as I could hear. Sammy and Tommy weren't sure what the fuss was all about. Lousy heads were common in Walworth. But because of Chinese Lady's manner, they were subdued, playing Ludo on the kitchen table while awaiting their turn, and making only murmured grumbles about tea being late. Sammy kept scratching his head.

Lizzy came out of the scullery with a towel around her head. Silently, she marched through the kitchen back to the bedroom. Chinese Lady went after her.

'Lizzy, let Boots do it for you, while I get on with scrubbing Sammy and Tommy.'

'No! I'll do it for myself!'

'It's always better, lovey, to let someone do it for you. They can see better, get their fingers right into your scalp—'

'No!'

65

I went to the open door of the bedroom, joining Chinese Lady there.

'I'll do it, Lizzy,' I said, 'and you can do it for me.'

'Go away.' Lizzy sat at the old mahogany dressing-table, with its swinging oval mirror, and a bowl and pitcher on one side.

'Sure you can manage by yourself?' I said.

'Yes. Go away.'

Chinese Lady closed the door and went to scrub Sammy's head. I sat with Tommy, who was eating what was left of yesterday's cold Yorkshire pudding. Lizzy called after a while.

'Can I have that oil?'

I took it to her. She sat looking at herself in the mirror. Her hair, still damp, was hanging thickly.

'Here, Lizzy,' I said, offering the bottle.

'We're lousy,' she said.

'It's no one's fault.'

'We're dirty,' she said.

'No, we're not. Chinese Lady wouldn't allow that.'

'She can't stop it. Bein' poor don't matter too much, but bein' poor *and* lousy *and* dirty – we'll all end up in one of them institutional homes.'

'No, we won't. I'm going in for banking, and you'll go in for a nice job—'

'Don't feel like Lord Muck any more, though, do yer, now you know you're lousy.'

'D'you want this oil?'

'All right, you do it.'

I parted strands of her hair. Her scalp looked white and healthy. I applied the oil and rubbed it briskly in with my fingertips.

'It might make your scalp smart a bit,' I said.

'Just do it. I don't feel like any chat.'

I didn't feel too sociable myself. I kept thinking about my own scalp and what might be crawling around deep in my hair. Lizzy's head rolled about under my fingers. She muttered something as the oil began to sting.

'All right, Lizzy?'

66

She didn't answer for a while. Then she said, 'Chinese Lady ain't—' She stopped, as if it was a moment when she could have improved on ain't. Then, because the sky had fallen on her, she said flatly, 'Well, she ain't.'

'Ain't what?' I kept parting other strands.

'Very happy.'

'No, I know.'

'It's even worse for her.'

'Worser.'

'You said worser's not a word, you said it last week.'

'Well, this week's not the same as last week.'

'This week's lousy,' said Lizzy, and gave an abrupt laugh. I saw one then, as I parted fresh strands. Grey and disgusting, it sat there at the roots of her hair, on her scalp. I said nothing, I broke its back with my fingernail and disposed of it amid my massaging. I thought of my own scalp again. Lizzy turned then, put her arms around my waist and her face against my shirt. 'Oh, Boots, ain't it shameful?'

'It's not very nice, no, but it's not your fault, Lizzy, nor Chinese Lady's.'

She wasn't crying. She was simply suffering from unbearable self-disgust. After I'd finished, I attacked Sammy's scalp and then Tommy's, while Lizzy did a furious job of work on our mum's head, in their bedroom. Lastly, after I'd washed and scrubbed my own head in hot soapy water, with even a touch of carbolic in it, Chinese Lady applied the oil to my scalp, in the kitchen. Tommy, Sammy and Lizzy sat quietly watching.

Sammy broke the silence.

'Ain't we goin' to get no tea ever?'

'Shut up,' said Lizzy, 'who wants tea at a time like this?'

'I do,' said Sammy, 'I'm starvin'.'

When Chinese Lady had the whole of my scalp burning, she went into the scullery to wash her hands. I followed her.

'Did you find any in my head?' I asked.

'Didn't I say we'd all got the disease?' She was sharp, her face drawn.

'It's not a disease—'

'Good as. Don't argue. Go and comb your hair. Use my fine-tooth comb. Comb it good and hard. Tell Lizzy to do the same. Keep combing it, all the time, now and tomorrer and every day – go on. Otherwise, we'll all—' She broke off.

'Otherwise what?'

'We'll all have to have our heads shaved, that's what, we'll all have our hair taken right off.'

'Oh, bleedin' hell,' I said, at which Chinese Lady boxed my ears. Lizzy came rushing out. She stared. Chinese Lady's face was flushed, her mouth working.

'Mum, don't take on,' said Lizzy.

'I'm goin' to wash my hands and get tea.'

'I'll get tea,' said Lizzy.

'You go an' comb your hair.'

'I have.'

'Comb it again. Hard. Hard, you hear? Even if it makes your scalp bleed.'

'All right,' said Lizzy.

'Everyone in this house has got to be clean – clean – you hear?'

'Mum, you're really takin' on,' said Lizzy.

Chinese Lady looked at her. We all looked at each other.

'Well?' said Chinese Lady.

'Mum,' said Lizzy, 'Tommy said at least we ain't got fleas.'

'What?'

We all looked at each other again and burst into laughter. Chinese Lady gave Lizzy a hug.

'Oh, Lizzy, you love,' she said.

I took Tommy and Sammy up to our bedroom, and we sat on the beds combing our hair, drawing hard teeth firmly over our scalps. Sammy did it for thirty seconds, then gave up. I made him start again. Ten minutes later, I knocked on Mr Finch's door.

'Enter,' he called.

I opened the door and went in. He was preparing his evening meal of spicy sausages and potatoes on the small gas oven. He had his own gas meter.

'Hello, Boots.' He was in shirt, trousers and braces, with slippers on his feet. He looked strong and healthy, like any man of the sea and the river.

'Mr Finch,' I said, closing the door.

'What can I do for you, my boy, apart from offering you a sausage?'

'Very kind of you,' I said, 'but we're having our own meal in five minutes.'

'You haven't eaten yet? You're late with your victuals tonight, aren't you?'

'Well, it's like this,' I said, and told him about the headlice. He listened very quietly, and with a slightly pensive look. At the end, I said, 'We thought you ought to know. Mum says she'll understand if you want to leave.'

'Leave?' His eyebrows went up.

'If you want to find other lodgings.'

'Sit down, Boots,' he said.

His room had a table, two upright chairs, an armchair, a little dresser and other essentials in addition to the gas oven. It also had its own small range, for winter heating. Every room in the house, except the scullery, had a fireplace or a range. Mr Finch's living-room could have looked a crowded and untidy place, but it didn't. It looked very orderly. But he was very orderly himself, and he could do things for himself that other men couldn't or wouldn't, like sewing a coat or shirt button back on and darning his socks. That came from having been a seaman. I sat down at his table, which he had laid for his supper. He examined his frying sausages, turned them over and lowered the gas flame. On the table, propped against his cruet, I saw a letter with a stamp stuck on, ready for posting. It was addressed to 'Mrs Gertrude Livingstone, 19 Meadow Lane, Chatsford, Kent.' That was his old Aunt Trudy, of course.

'Mr Finch,' I said, as he turned to give me his attention. 'I think Mum is worried you might feel we don't keep clean—'

'I hope,' he said, interrupting me firmly but kindly, 'I hope we needn't talk about other lodgings or about our little failings. What has happened, Boots, isn't a tragedy. Lice aren't our most deadly affliction. They arrive and become stubborn about leaving, but we can drive them out in the end. There are worse things, like typhoid, like bugs and fleas. In Russia—'

'You've been to Russia?'

He smiled.

'Oh, to their Baltic ports during my years as a seaman. In Russia, there are bugs and fleas by the million, by hundreds of millions. In one of their operas, there's even the "Song of the Flea". The rich of that country suffer fleas, as well as the poor.' He smiled again, and the twinkling light entered his eyes. 'The Russians, Boots, are miserably lousy. So don't let's worry about a few headlice. Boots, you said all of you. Lizzy too?'

'Yes,' I said.

'Poor Lizzy,' he said. 'Well, she's our only real worry. Lizzy is very sensitive. This is what you must do. Every evening, every evening without fail, you understand, her hair must be washed, thoroughly washed, with hot water and a special medical soap you can get from a chemist. And every other evening, you must use that oil on her scalp. You must use it sparingly, because otherwise it will have such an irritating effect that it may cause sores. And so, apply it lightly every second evening. And – ah – to your mother's scalp too. The ladies' hair is far more important to them than ours is to us, and they are far more sensitive. Do you understand? What are a few lice to you and me? We can comb them out and massacre them. Our hair won't give them as much nourishment as the crowning glories of the ladies, or quite the same amount of warmth. I've seen dockers' families, Boots, and it's always the girls and women who suffer more. Under no circumstances, my boy, must we risk Lizzy or your mother having their hair cut off. That would be unbearable to them. Tomorrow, I'll bring home some of the finest oil of sassafras, the kind my Aunt Trudy used on me.'

'You had headlice even living with your aunt?' I said.

'Several times. They can come, Boots, from mixing with other boys. Aunt Trudy told me once that the only permanent way of curing my lousiness was to cut my head off.' Again he smiled. 'She was so ashamed of me that I thought she'd do it. Don't look so worried. We shall conquer. And kindly inform your mother I'm so comfortable in her house and am treated so well by all her family that I beg her to say no more about my leaving.'

'Yes, Mr Finch, and thank you kindly.' I got to my feet. Wanting to repay his kindness, I said, 'Shall I get Sammy to post your letter for you?'

'Letter?' he said, and looked quite surprised for a moment. Then he saw it, standing against his cruet. 'No, no,' he smiled, 'I'll be happy to take it myself. It will give me an excuse for a little exercise. It's to my Aunt Trudy.' There was just the hint of a question about that piece of information, but I didn't like to tell him I'd read the envelope.

'Well, I'll go down and have my meal,' I said, 'and thank you again for what you've said, Mr Finch.'

I told Chinese Lady what he had said, and she remarked we had the nicest gentleman lodger anyone could wish for.

'We'll do what I mentioned,' I said, 'we'll clean the whole house at the weekend.'

'I ain't 'elping,' said Sammy, 'not unless I'm paid tuppence.'

'You'll all get an extra penny each,' said Chinese Lady.

'No, we won't,' I said, 'we can't afford it.'

'Ain't doin' no work, then,' said Sammy.

'You better muck in,' said Lizzy, 'or you'll get no food.'

'I'll run orf, I will,' said Sammy.

71

'I'll take yer,' said Tommy, 'I'll take yer to where yer won't know the way back.'

'I wish you'd all speak more proper,' said Chinese Lady, looking tired, 'then I'd have a bit less to worry about. Never mind, get on with your tea.'

CHAPTER SEVEN

One thing about the lice, they kept Emily out of the way for long weeks. Only a few days after the notes from the clinic lady had turned Chinese Lady grey with shame, Emily had her great mop of tangled hair shorn to the roots. Mrs Castle told Chinese Lady it had to be done, there wasn't nothing else for it, what with Emily having let her hair get in such a mess that you couldn't separate one strand from the next. Chinese Lady didn't think all the blame was Emily's, she thought Mrs Castle guilty of neglecting to do what she ought to have done by making sure Emily's hair had never got in such a mess. She didn't say so, of course. But we all knew Mrs Castle was a bit too easy-going over things like that. If Emily said she didn't her hair washed, Mrs Castle would say, 'Well, next week, then, love.' And next week never came.

Mrs Castle told Chinese Lady that Emily was crying herself to sleep every night because she was bald, and Chinese Lady said quite frankly that she wasn't surprised, so would any girl.

Emily went to school with her head swathed in a scarf, but she did not appear in the street, she did not go out to play or come into our house. She stayed indoors. We all felt for her. Chinese Lady tempered her compassion with relief, for she had come to the conclusion we'd all caught the disease from Emily. Poor Emily, she said.

If our lice were relatives of Emily's, we still didn't want them in our house and we got rid of them by constant head-washing and applications of the sassafras oil. We all went to the clinic in Browning Street and were pronounced free of the vermin. Lizzy was so grateful for her deliverance that she joined the church confirmation classes.

Approaching her fourteenth birthday, she was joyously playing cricket with boys after school one day. At the chalked wicket on the wall that was at a right angle from the printing factory, and which made the Place L-shaped, she wielded the wooden bat. She hit the old, solid rubber ball all over the street until Ernie Jones, the bowler, tossed the ball to Tommy.

''Ere, you 'ave a go at yer skin and blister,' he said, 'she's my blinkin' death.'

It was twenty minutes to six. I was standing at our door, watching the cricket and keeping an eye open for bobbies. Lizzy began to flog Tommy's deliveries. Free of the lice, she was full of energy and laughter in her old pinafore school frock and her sturdy school boots. She had been on to Chinese Lady for months about wearing shoes for school, not boots. But Chinese Lady said the way she kicked around at school, shoes wouldn't last any time. Lizzy, nearly fourteen, hated wearing boots now, and Chinese Lady might have had a reckless moment and bought shoes for her. Instead, she was adamant that for school Lizzy should continue wearing boots, like all the other Walworth girls.

Emily was watching from her parlour window, her new-grown hair still very short and covered by a woollen hat. She looked as if her teeth were gritted and her temper fierce. A boy on a bicycle turned into the Place from Browning Street, and pedalled slowly along, looking at the house numbers. He saw me at our door.

'Watcher there, Boots,' he called.

Lizzy, hearing him, turned her head and saw him. She stiffened, and stood so still that the ball bowled by Tommy hit the chalked wicket.

'That's gotcher,' said Tommy.

Ned Somers pedalled up to our gate and dismounted.

'Hello,' I said, 'are you popping in?'

'I'm on my way home from work,' he said. 'I thought it was time I called to see how you were.'

74

He had his back to Lizzy, who was across the way, and who had been hidden from him by the L-shaped nature of the street. And Lizzy was a furious rosy red. In her shabby school clothes and her boots, and hot from wielding the bat, I suppose one couldn't say she was at her best. She dropped the bat and darted. She turned the corner of the wall and hared towards Browning Street, running fast.

'You'd better come in and say hello to Mum, now that you've missed Lizzy,' I said.

'Missed her?' Ned looked around. Lizzy had disappeared. 'Did she pass me, then?'

'Not really. Come on in.'

'Well, I've got five minutes,' he said, propping his bike against the railings. 'Can't stay longer. It's me mum.' He gave me a cheerful grin. It made him cheerfully good-looking, and he was wearing a charcoal-grey suit that added tone to his amiability. 'If I'm ever later than I should be, she starts nattering on about the dangers of riding a bike.'

His bike was a Raleigh. The best. It gleamed. It was every boy's ambition to own a Raleigh. One had to wait for the family ship to come home, of course.

I took him in and he renewed his slight acquaintance with our mum, who was getting tea. She seemed very pleased he'd remembered us, very pleased he'd dropped in. She offered him a cup of tea.

'I'd better not stop, thanks all the same,' he said, 'but I'd like a glass of water. I'm parched.'

It was late June, and hot. I got him a glass of water.

'Well, the '08 vintage burgundy has made a name for itself,' he said. He looked brown-faced and grown up, two inches taller than I was, and I was coming on quite well in my sixteenth year. 'That's only what I've heard.' He gave me another grin. 'I'm still humping Spanish sherry around. But they say the prospects are still good. I hope I'm not being a mug.' Casually, he asked, 'How's your sister?'

'The last time I saw her, she was breaking sprint records.

If you're only staying a few minutes, I think you'll miss her.'

'Oh, well,' he said.

'You met our Lizzy, of course,' said Chinese Lady, obviously taken with his handsome and respectable look. 'On the Sunday, when we come to see Boots in Guy's.'

'And we had another meeting of a kind,' smiled Ned.

'A kind?'

'On the Monday, when Boots was still in, his tonsils still out and Eliza was there with Mr Finch, your lodger.'

'Eliza? Oh, Lizzy, you mean.' Chinese Lady smiled. Her careworn look always seemed to slip away when she smiled, and you could imagine what she was like when our dad had first courted her. 'Well, Boots is better for havin' them tonsils of his out.'

'Mum, can I 'ave a slice of bread an' drippin'?' Sammy had appeared.

'No, your tea'll be ready any minute.'

'Hello,' said Ned.

''Ello,' said Sammy. 'That yer bike outside?'

'Yes.'

'Crikey, you must be rich,' said Sammy.

'I had to save up for it,' said Ned.

'I'm goin' to be rich,' said Sammy, 'except our mum don't want me to be sinful as well. You get a fousand years of 'ard labour in 'ell if you're sinful.'

'A thousand years of hard labour in all that fiery heat?' said Ned. 'Sounds a bit much, even for a rich sinner.'

'You sure you wouldn't like to stay for tea?' said Chinese Lady.

Ned surveyed the kitchen table with its laden cloth, the plates of bread and marge, the jars of jam and the cold apple pie. He seemed quite tempted.

'Nice of you, Mrs Adams,' he said, 'but I'm expected at home and I'm going to be late as it is. Glad Boots is better. You look very fit,' he said, and gave me a friendly pat on the shoulder. 'I'll drop by again, perhaps.'

'I'd make it a Sunday, if I were you,' I said. 'Lizzy never

76

goes sprinting in her Sunday clothes. It's her birthday, by the way, on the 15th July, next month. She doesn't go sprinting on her birthdays, either.'

'I think you're trying to tell me something,' said Ned, smiling. He said goodbye to Chinese Lady and Sammy, and off he went. I watched him ride up the Place and saw the flutter of an old pinafore dress on the street corner. It whisked madly out of sight as he pedalled up and turned the other corner on his way to Walworth Road. A few moments later, Lizzy reappeared, walking haughtily homewards.

'What happened to you?' I asked.

'Nothing,' said Lizzy.

'Ned Somers popped in.'

'Who?' Lizzy was very haughty.

'You remember Ned – you met him at Guy's—'

'Who?' she said.

'Come off it, sis. He asked after you.'

'What for?' Lizzy had her nose in the air. 'What for?'

'Gone on you, I suppose,' I said, and to my astonishment, Lizzy went crimson, her rush of blood instant. Emily opened her parlour window.

'Who was that lanky lemon?' she asked aggressively.

'Just a bloke,' I said. 'How you feeling, Em?'

'None of yer business,' said Emily, 'so shut yer cake'ole. I get enough sarky muck at school – I don't want none of yourn.' She closed the window and disappeared.

'I suppose we ought to encourage Emily back into the land of the living again,' I said, as Lizzy and I went in, 'I suppose she could come to Sunday tea.'

'What, and chance havin' her pull the house down?' said Lizzy. 'She doesn't like anyone at the moment, not even me very much. What did he want?' she asked, as we entered the kitchen.

'Ned? Just to say hello. He was riding home from the City.'

'How posh. In his horse an' carriage?'

'No, on his bike, as you saw.'

'Pity he didn't keep goin', then, wasn't it?'

'Why was it?'

'We don't want him here,' said Lizzy, 'he'll catch something.'

'You two at it again?' said Chinese Lady, coming in from the scullery with my hot meal. 'Just sit down and have your tea and try to be nice to each other for a change. I don't know why I deserve the kind of fam'ly I've got. I was goin' to buy some nice kippers for tea—'

'We can't afford kippers,' I said, 'not while half our belongings are in pawn. We've got to try saving something each week.'

'That's right, boss everyone about,' said Lizzy, 'give yer orders—'

'Now look here, you Lizzy,' said Chinese Lady, seating herself in front of the teapot, 'Boots has got his faults, but it's no help you keepin' on at him all the time – Sammy, sit up straight, don't slummock at the table.'

'Oh, crikey,' muttered Sammy.

'We'll say grace for once,' said Chinese Lady.

'Eh?' said Tommy.

'We'll say grace,' said our mum firmly. 'It's time this fam'ly sat up straight at the table and was a bit more reverent and thankful, then we might get more deservin'.' She clasped her hands, closed her eyes and said, 'Lord, for what we're about to receive, please make us truly thankful. Amen.' She opened her eyes. 'No one said it.'

'Oh, Mum,' said Lizzy.

'Say grace, all of you.' We all said grace. 'That's better. Now you can start your tea.'

'Yes, Mum,' said Lizzy.

'That's a love,' said Chinese Lady, to whom our Lizzy was dear.

Tommy ate with healthy relish, Sammy gobbled and Lizzy chewed a little absently. She eyed a jar of jam thoughtfully and drew it forward.

'He's not comin' again, I hope,' she said.

'Who – Ned?' I said. 'He said he might. I think he will.'

'Other people would wait till they're invited.'

'Lizzy, he's a nice boy,' said Chinese Lady.

'Ugh,' said Lizzy, spooning jam onto her plate.

'He called you Eliza,' said Chinese Lady.

'He's got a sauce,' said Lizzy. 'And catchin' people out like that, comin' here without sayin'.'

'Ah,' I said in the worldly way of Mr Finch. 'Ah,' I said again, and nodded my head sagely.

'What's that mean?' said Lizzy.

'Just something to do with being caught out. I think he wants to take you out.'

Lizzy went rosy red.

'Lizzy's blushin',' said Tommy to Sammy.

'It ain't my fault,' said Sammy, 'I ain't done nothink.'

'It'll be nice, Lizzy, havin' someone take you out walkin',' said Chinese Lady approvingly.

Lizzy took refuge in a large bite of bread and jam.

'I told him a Sunday would be best,' I said.

'Yes, you always look so pretty on Sundays, Lizzy,' said Chinese Lady.

'She can't be caught out on Sundays,' I said.

'Mum, 'it him,' cried Lizzy through bread and jam.

'But a Sunday would be very nice,' said Chinese Lady.

'I'm goin' to scream in a minute,' said Lizzy.

'She's gone all funny,' said Tommy to Sammy.

'Can't we change 'er?' asked Sammy of our mum.

'Sammy, you wouldn't want someone like Em'ly instead of our Lizzy, would you?' said Chinese Lady.

'Oh, gawd 'elp us,' said Sammy, 'not 'er, not Em'ly.'

Chinese Lady gave him a severe look.

'I tell you what, Lizzy,' I said, 'I think Ned would like to see you in that new dress of yours, the sky-blue one.'

'Oh, yes,' said Chinese Lady, regarding Lizzy fondly, 'the one Aunt Victoria give you last time. Now I've shortened it, it looks lovely.'

Lizzy lifted her head, her expression haughty.

Taking off the upper class, she said, 'This is all tewwibly borwing.'

Tommy hooted. Chinese Lady glanced at me, a slight smile on her face. She knew what I knew. Lizzy, almost fourteen, had an admirer. Chinese Lady, naturally, was very pleased for her. The admirer was so respectable.

On Lizzy's fourteenth birthday, there were cards on the mat, and a letter for Mr Finch, postmarked Chatsford, Kent. From his fond old Aunt Trudy, of course. I took it up to him. Sometimes he'd left the house before I went to school. Sometimes he was on a later shift. He was later today. He thanked me for his letter.

'Don't forget Lizzy's party tonight,' I said.

'I'll be home in time for that, have no fear,' he said genially. 'I treasure the invitation. Ah – will you give this to her?' He handed me a parcel wrapped in crisply-new brown paper.

'With pleasure, Mr Finch.'

'The pleasure, Boots, is all mine.'

I took it down to Lizzy, together with the birthday cards. Chinese Lady was out at her charring work, and Lizzy was cooking the breakfast porridge. Porridge was our staple breakfast diet. It made a cheap and nourishing meal.

'Happy birthday, sis,' I said, and kissed her cheek. 'There's some cards.'

'Oh, let me see,' she said excitedly. I gave her the cards and took over the stirring of the porridge. Sammy was washing at the sink. He gave himself a lick and a promise, and a quick wipe with the towel. Tommy took his turn and gurgled and splashed like a happy walrus. Lizzy looked at the cards, with their halfpenny stamps. There was one from us, her family, one from Aunt Victoria and her family, one from a group of school friends, one from Emily, one from Mr Finch and one from – she hid the card behind her back without mentioning the sender.

'Yes, well, who's that last one from?' I asked.

'Nobody,' she said.

'Is that a fact? Not many people get a card from nobody. Porridge ready.' I took the saucepan to the kitchen table and ladled it out into the bowls. Sammy scattered sugar profligately over his. We all began spooning, with Lizzy going through her cards again.

'How'd he know it was my birthday, Boots?' she asked pinkly.

'I mentioned it,' I said. 'What's he written on it?'

'Nothing,' she said.

'Imagine nobody sending a card with nothing on it,' I said.

'You make me die laughin',' said Lizzy.

'Aren't you going to open Mr Finch's present?' I asked.

'When I come 'ome, with me other things,' she said. We had all given her something. Not much, but something. And it was a ritual with Lizzy, not to open her birthday presents until she came home from school and could enjoy doing so at delicious leisure.

I had a good day at school with mathematics, history and English literature, all of which subjects I enjoyed. During the last hour of the day, when the teachers were in monthly conference with the headmaster, the prefects took charge of the classes. I took over a class of third-year pupils, all feeling their feet. My responsibility was to keep them in order. No prefect could do that merely by being older than they were. All prefects on these occasions were Aunt Sallies. So I said I'd write a word on the blackboard, the first boy would pipe up with a related word and so on, all through the class. I wrote 'Circle'.

'Square,' said the first boy.

'Triangle,' said the second.

'Oblong.'

'Oranges,' said Johnson.

'Explain how you associate oranges with oblong, Johnson,' I said.

'Do whatter?' said Johnson.

'How d'you relate oranges with oblong?'

'They're round, and we're being geometric.'

'All right, oranges, then. Now you, Pike.'

'Elephants,' said Pike.

'You sure?'

'Well, oranges are fruit, so are bananas, and elephants like bananas,' said Pike.

'Why didn't you say bananas, then?'

'All right, bananas, then,' said Pike.

'Elephants,' said the next boy.

'Huge,' said the next.

'Tiny.'

'Wee.'

'Widdle.'

A titter ran round the class, followed by a malicious hush. I knew they expected me to make a fool of myself, so I just said, 'Well?' to the next boy.

'Water,' he said.

'Prefects,' said the next.

'Prefects?' I said. 'Prefects, Walker?'

'Well, I s'pose I could have said wet,' said Walker.

'Fifty lines, Walker,' I said.

'You'll be lucky.' said Walker.

'Write them out before you leave. The line will be, "I must not try to be a clever Dick, I'm not smart enough." All right, next boy – proceed from water.'

'I'm not doing any lines,' said Walker.

'Who asked you to pipe up?' I said. 'You're not the next boy. You've had your turn and come a sickening cropper. Now lash yourself to the mast or you'll be chucked overboard. Your turn, Russell. The word is water.'

'Wet,' said Russell.

'Walker,' said the next boy.

An hysterical titter ran round the class.

I went home in a self-satisfied frame of mind. When I arrived, Lizzy was in the bedroom, getting ready for her birthday tea party, and Chinese Lady was preparing it. Seeing some of the food, I said, 'What's gone into pawn?'

'Never you mind.'

The birthday cards were on the kitchen mantelpiece,

and another one had come by the afternoon post – from
Ernie Jones, who was rather keen on Lizzy. All to no
avail, however. Lizzy treated all boys under sixteen as
infants.

I went through the cards. I read the greeting Ned Somers
had written on his offering.

'*Eliza is a girl I met*
On a day in spring,
As I haven't seen her since
Shall I give her a ring?'
He'd added, '*Many happy returns, Eliza – Ned.*'

'You got a cheek!' Lizzy was there, snatching the card
from my hand.

'We always read each other's birthday cards,' I said. 'I
like Ned's poem.'

'Well, you would, wouldn't you? You're two of a kind.'
But Lizzy looked tickled, a blush and a smile lurking. She
was prettier day by day.

'Have you opened your presents?' I asked.

'Yes. Thanks for the hair ribbon and hankie, Boots.' She
kissed me. 'And I had another hankie from Sammy and
Tommy between them, and Chinese Lady give me a new
petti – look.' She tweaked her sky-blue dress, the one that
was lovely, and the lacy hem of a white petticoat peeped.
'Ain't it – isn't it pretty?'

It looked so pretty it must have been expensive. I
wondered what had gone into pawn.

'What did Mr Finch give you?'

'A big box of chocolates,' said Lizzy. 'Ain't he kind? And
Aunt Victoria sent me a new blouse from her family. I'm
havin' my best birthday ever.'

Her guests were four school friends, plus Emily, Ernie
Jones and Mr Finch. She'd invited Miss Chivers, who had
said how sorry she was she couldn't accept. The Witch, of
course, never let her go to birthday parties. There was
always someone in trousers at birthday parties. While
Lizzy was making all the guests comfortable in the
parlour – the parlour was allowed to be thrown open on

83

birthdays – I had a word with Chinese Lady in the scullery, where she was boiling a full kettle of water for tea.

'It don't matter what's been spent,' she said, 'it's Lizzy's fourteenth, and we had to make up for her gettin' them awful lice. I never seen her so upset, nor so sufferin'. Lizzy's sensitive, you know she is, so we had to make her birthday special.'

'I suppose so,' I said.

'Boots, we got to look out for them comin' again.'

'The lice?'

Chinese Lady, watching the kettle, nodded.

'They're breedin' all round us,' she said, 'because some people don't do nothing about them. So you keep a watch on your head. I'm watchin' Lizzy's, and the kids.'

I heard laughter from the parlour, the excited, strident laughter of Emily.

'About what's been spent,' I said, 'we'll have to cut down for the next few weeks and save a few shillings.'

'Yes, course we will,' said Chinese Lady, whose priorities didn't include worrying too much about things she didn't understand, like where the money went to. 'Did you see the nice card Ned Somers sent Lizzy? Fancy him writing a poem about givin' her a ring.'

'I think he meant a telephone call, Mum.'

'Telephone?' Our mum looked as if I'd brought the Shah of Persia into the conversation. 'Only rich people have telephones.'

'Not now. Other people have them, and business firms and shops and stores. Ned's dad has a grocer's shop and might well have one.'

'Well, we haven't, nor likely to, nor need to. It was nice that Ned sent a card, but he hasn't called, like he said he might.'

'I think he'll pop over one day.'

'He better,' said Chinese Lady, 'otherwise Lizzy might start broodin'.'

'Brooding? Mum, she's only fourteen.'

'And you're still only fifteen, which means you don't know as much as you think you do.'

Twelve sat down to tea around the parlour table, and the kids' eyes popped at the spread. Hungry mouths gaped pinkly. I worried again about the cost of everything, but discovered afterwards that Mr Finch had begged our mum to allow him to contribute, and he had brought home with him the iced birthday cake, two dozen jam tarts and two dozen rich pastries.

Lizzy had had the privilege of seating everybody, and with feminine sensibility had co-opted the worldly help of Mr Finch, who had pointed out that as there were six ladies and six gentlemen, Lizzy should seat them alternately, so that each lady could enjoy the courtesy she was entitled to, a gentleman on either side of her. Emily was given a place between Sammy and me. The four school friends, two girls and two boys, sat next to each other, with Tommy completing the sandwich for the girls, and Lizzy gave herself a place between Mr Finch and Ernie Jones, which probably gave earnest Ernie false hopes. Chinese Lady had Mr Finch on her left and Sammy on her right. She presided in upright graciousness over the teapot, and the family handed the food round.

For the first time since her head had been shaved, Emily had it uncovered. Her hair was growing quickly now, as if eager to establish itself again as a great tangled mop. It was, at the moment, a crown of curling auburn tufts, and made her thin face look peakier and enlarged her darting green eyes. It was Lizzy's party, but Emily dominated the tea table with her unquiet voice and her shrieks of laughter. And each time she laughed she gave me a dig that threatened to cave my ribs in. Lizzy was queen, all the same, her chestnut hair burnished by savage comb and stiff brush, and I caught Emily looking at her once with her sighing soul in her eyes.

Mr Finch was in warm relish of everything, including the high spirits of the young and Chinese Lady's huge pot of hot, golden tea. He complimented her on its perfection.

'Well, it's Lizzy's fourteenth,' she said, 'and the family wanted to do her proud.'

'Very right and proper,' said Mr Finch. 'When I was young, my Aunt Trudy also spared no effort on such occasions. But it's not one of my own birthdays that comes most often to my mind. Shall I recount a sea story?'

'Yes, yes!' cried the kids.

'I could tell yer some stories, I could,' said Emily, her voice juicy with jam tart.

'No, yer couldn't,' said Tommy, 'except fer fairy stories an' we've 'eard all them. Come on, Mr Finch.'

'Many years ago, in the South Pacific,' said Mr Finch in resonant and reminiscent fashion, 'when I was first mate on the good ship *Sea Adventurer*, we were running before a high wind. The glass was falling, and Captain Longbags—'

'Capting Whatter?' said Tommy.

'Well,' said Mr Finch, 'perhaps that wasn't his correct name. It was probably Smith or Crusoe—'

'Oh, crikey,' said one of Lizzy's lady school friends, 'not Robinson Crusoe, not 'im, was it, sir?'

'It might have been, little lady, it might have been,' said Mr Finch, 'although I never caught sight of his Man Friday.'

Emily shrieked and scattered pastry crumbs. Her sharp elbow dealt my ribs a fiendish blow.

'Kindly stop trying to make holes in me,' I said. 'Carry on, Mr Finch.'

'Oh, don't he talk plummy, yer bruvver,' whispered the little lady to Sammy.

''E caught it at 'is school,' said Sammy, and Chinese Lady rapped his knuckles with her teaspoon as he stretched for a rich pastry instead of asking for someone to kindly pass the dish.

'The glass was falling,' said Mr Finch, 'and we were under full sail, running for Rarotonga. That's a lonely island in the heart of the South Pacific. Astern was the black doom of a fast-approaching hurricane. Captain Jollybags was on the bridge—'

''E said Longbags before,' said Tommy to Sammy.

'All the same, my boy,' said Mr Finch. 'There he was, on the bridge, roaring and crashing his teeth, exhorting the crew to tighten sail. What a grand if desperate sight we must have been, every sail hoisted in our endeavour to outrun the hurricane. The waves were enormous, breaking over us fore and aft. The sky darkened and turned black, the wind shrieked and howled, the gallant *Sea Adventurer* riding bravely but in perilous plight. At our backs, the hurricane was a great whistling and roaring menace. Captain Shortbags turned about.'

'What, with the 'urricane about to murder yer?' said Tommy, letting a further change of name pass.

'My young friends,' said Mr Finch with due gravity, 'to attempt to run before a hurricane is suicide. You must run into it, if caught by it. If you run before it, it will lift your ship from the sea, whirl it about in the wind like a cork and smash it down and destroy it. With sail reefed, we turned about and ran into the teeth of the shrieking black demon, Captain Jollybags roped to the wheel, the crew roped to the masts. "Avast there, ye sea lubbers!" roared our Captain.'

'That's what pirate captains roar,' said Chinese Lady, while Lizzy's brown eyes danced in delight as she saw Sammy breathless, gaping and agog.

'Oh, I believe Captain Jollybags had a chequered career,' said Mr Finch, 'and probably engaged in a little piracy before he became gallant and respectable. Where was I?'

'In the teeth of the howling black demon of the oceans,' I said, 'with Captain Somebags roaring.'

'Crumbs,' whispered the little lady, 'ain't he posh, your bruvver, Sammy?'

'It ain't my fault,' said Sammy.

'I won't deny it,' said Mr Finch sonorously, 'we feared for our lives as the hurricane smote us and the gallant *Sea Adventurer* was battered by its fury. Mrs Adams, may I have a slice of your own delicious fruit cake?'

'With pleasure, Mr Finch,' said Chinese Lady, and the

kids were left with mouths agape and eyes popping while she cut him a generous slice.

'Mr Finch, you're teasin' us,' said Lizzy, 'you ain't—' She corrected herself, a habit that had begun to grow lately. 'You haven't finished your story.'

Mr Finch took a bite of cake and pronounced it fruitily luscious. The kids' mouths woke up and resumed pastry-munching work as Mr Finch went on.

'The dreadful day threatened to be our last,' he said. 'All was lost, or seemed to be, the shrieking blackness enveloping us, the wind smiting us, and our battered ship running into waves as mountainous as Everest. Masts splintered and cracked. Captain Longbags roared his defiance, and I and the crew sang a hymn.'

'Wasn't you seasick?' asked Ernie Jones.

'Sailors don't get seasick,' said Lizzy, looking sorry for any boy who could ask such an ignorant question.

'What 'ymn did yer sing?' asked Tommy.

'"To Those in Peril on the Sea,"' said Mr Finch. 'What else could we sing, my boy? We were battered, broken and swamped, the sea and the sky as black as darkest night. But just as we thought ourselves doomed beyond salvation, our hymn of prayer was answered and the brave *Sea Adventurer* ran clear. The hurricane, howling in frustration, passed on. With our masts smashed, we lay becalmed in a gentle blue sea beneath the hot sun. Our repairs took us four days. This really is delicious cake, Mrs Adams.'

'I'm pleasured, Mr Finch, to know you like it,' said Chinese Lady.

'Oh, Mr Finch, come on,' said Lizzy.

'On the morning of the fifth day, we took up our course again. There was a cry from our lookout high in the crow's-nest. "Ahoy, below! Boat to starboard! Ahoy!"'

'Cor,' said Sammy.

'I betcher a parrot was in the boat!' yelled Emily, having allowed Mr Finch all the attention for long enough. 'I betcher—'

'Quiet, Emily,' said Chinese Lady.

'Yes, Mrs Adams,' said Emily. Chinese Lady could quell Emily as no one else could.

'No, there was no parrot,' said Mr Finch, 'though I agree, Emily, there could have been. In the boat was a shipwrecked mariner, whose vessel had gone down in the hurricane. He was the only survivor, and as I helped him aboard, sun-scorched and haggard, what d'you think he said to me?'

'Praise be?' suggested Lizzy.

'Is Captain Jollybags at home?' I suggested.

'Is whatter?' said Tommy.

'As if anyone 'ud say that when 'e was all scorched nearly to 'is dyin' breaff,' said Sammy.

'I'll tell you what he actually said,' smiled Mr Finch. 'He said, "Thanks, Mister Mate, it's my birthday today and I thought I was going to have my tea party all on my own."'

The parlour erupted. Lizzy's laughter was rich, Emily's a hurricane screech, and Sammy's so hysterical that he turned red and gasped, 'Oh, I gotter run, Mum.' He jumped from his seat and left the room at a frantic pace.

It was a happy party, with games afterwards. Emily took a leading part in all, creating havoc with her darting, elbowing rushes and knocking Sammy over once when he was careless enough to loiter in her path.

'That Em'ly,' said Tommy, 'she tramples people flat and don't even bother to stop an' see if they're dead or not.'

'Well, you know, Tommy,' said Mr Finch, 'you'll discover when you're older what all we men discover, that we owe so much to the ladies we can forgive them their curious little ways when they're girls.'

'Yes, Mr Finch,' said Tommy, 'but 'ow many of us round 'ere is goin' to live to be men with Em'ly trampling most of us to death?'

'That's a point,' said Mr Finch.

CHAPTER EIGHT

Chinese Lady hadn't said how much Lizzy's birthday had set her back, but it came to light on Wednesday, when the rent man called at a quarter past five. That was a good time to find the women in, when they were having to see to their kids' tea and not dodging him by being down the market.

I heard Chinese Lady say to him, 'I don't have it all, I'll make it up next week.'

'No, you won't, Mrs Adams, you've done it on me too much before an' kept me waitin' too much as well. Besides, you did it on me last week. Four shilling short last week, you were. So this week I want sixteen shilling. Mr Small, the landlord, says there's too many owing as it is, and it's me who gets it in the eye, not you.'

'Seven an' six, that's all I can manage this week. Sammy's had to have new boots – well, good seconds up the Lane, but they cost—'

'Now, Mrs Adams, I got me own kids and me own troubles, I can't afford to be lumbered with yourn as well. Sixteen shilling I want. Sixteen shilling I'll have, if you don't mind.'

'I don't have sixteen shillings, I told you, I only got seven an' six.'

'Well, I'm going to tell you something, Mrs Adams. Have another look to see what you've got. Look good and you'll come up with the rest. Look under a vase or under your pillow.'

'I could look under everything in the house, and still only come up with what I got in my purse – seven an' six. An' tenpence that's got to keep us till Friday. I got to buy something for dinner tomorrer.'

'Sixteen shillling I want, Mrs Adams.'

'Well, come again Friday, and I'll give you the other four an' six.'

'Not four and six. Eight and six. I let you owe me four shilling on last week's rent. I want that four shilling now, Mrs Adams, and the twelve for this week.'

'I can't give you the owings till Friday, I told you.'

In the kitchen, Lizzy looked worriedly at me.

'Mum's done it in this week,' she said.

'Where's the money go to, that's the problem,' I said.

'If you was at work like other boys,' said Lizzy, 'instead of just learnin' to speak posh – '

'I'm not just learning that,' I said. The rent collector was still arguing, so I went to lend assistance to Chinese Lady. 'It'll have to be Friday before we can pay you everything,' I said.

'Don't give me no lip, sonny,' said the rent man. 'Is your lodger in?'

'Not yet. About six o'clock.'

'I'll come back quarter past six. Borrow it from him. You do that, sonny, you borrow it from him. You don't want Mr Small sendin' the bailiffs round to strip your dear old mum of all her belongings, do you?'

'No, I don't,' I said, 'and I don't want Mr Small sending you round to call her old, either.'

The rent man's grin was a little sour.

'You got a real lippy offspring there, Mrs Adams,' he said.

'We can't,' said Lizzy, 'we can't borrer from Mr Finch.'

'That we can't, and we won't,' said Chinese Lady, stiff with anxiety. 'I've never borrered, never. Except from the pawn, which is different, anyway. It's like doing business when you go to the pawn, it's not like common borrering.'

'It'll have to be Friday,' I said, 'they're not going to do a bailiff job on us between now and Friday.'

'I'll loan yer,' said Sammy.

'You'll what?' I said.

91

'As long as I get me fair int'rest,' said Sammy.

'What you talkin' about?' asked Chinese Lady.

'Loanin',' said Sammy. He went upstairs to our bedroom. He came down again with an old bulging sock. He emptied it of coppers. A heap of pennies, halfpennies and farthings sat like a dull small goldmine on the table. 'It's me savings,' he said.

'Oh, crikey,' gasped Lizzy, 'look at all that.'

'Me savings,' said Sammy. 'Nine an' fourpence. I'll count it and show yer.' He counted it. Nine and fourpence. For any young boy it was a small fortune.

'Oh, bless you, Sammy love,' said Chinese Lady, who had typically overlooked asking what he considered was a fair interest rate.

'I loans yer eight an' six – nine bob, if yer like – and you pays me back a bob a week plus me fair interest.'

'Bless you, Sammy,' said our trusting mum again.

'What interest do you have in mind?' I asked.

'He can't charge interest,' said Lizzy indignantly, 'not the fam'ly.'

'I ain't chargin' much,' said Sammy. 'Thruppence a week, that's all.'

'That's all?' I said. 'Per annum, that'll be about a thousand per cent.'

'Wassat mean?' asked Sammy, both hands guarding the coins.

'It means you're a crook.'

'I better not loan, then,' said Sammy, and took up the old sock. I placed my hand over the copper pile.

'Penny a week,' I said.

'Tuppence,' said Sammy, 'there y'ar, tuppence, that's fair, ain't it?'

'You rotten little miser,' said Lizzy.

'Now don't call him names, Lizzy,' said Chinese Lady, 'I don't mind a bit of interest, and it is his savings.'

'A penny on every bob is enough,' I said.

'I ain't loanin' you,' said Sammy, 'I'm loanin' our mum.'

'More shame on you that it is our mum,' said Lizzy, 'that

you're makin' her pay interest. Boots ought to give you a good walloping.'

'Sammy, you're a moneylending shark,' I said.

'Well, as long as it ain't sinful,' said Sammy. 'All right, Mum can give me back a bob a week an' just a penny interest then. I 'ope it don't ruin me.'

There was a knock on our front door. I answered it. Ned Somers stood there, his bike propped against the railings.

'Hello, Boots,' he said cheerfully, 'it's me again.'

Nice and easy, that was his manner, with self-assurance.

Distinctly, I heard a gasp from the kitchen, then the sound of flying feet and the opening and closing of the bedroom door at the turn in the passage. Lizzy had made herself scarce again, caught in her old pinafore school frock again.

'Come in, Ned.'

'Thanks. Can't stop long, and don't want to get in your way, anyway.'

'If you've got time for a cup of tea, Mum'll make you one.'

'Well, I did say I might be fifteen minutes late home, so I'll have a cup of tea with pleasure.'

I liked his way of making himself at home with people. He had no side. But he was a cut above all the boys Lizzy knew, and it seemed to throw her into a panic. I took him into the kitchen, where Chinese Lady, her immediate financial worries solved, gave him a very glad smile of welcome. He said hello to her and the kids.

'He'll have a cup of tea, Mum,' I said.

'I'll make some,' she said, 'the kettle's simmering. I'll turn the gas up.' She hurried into the scullery, and Ned chatted with Sammy and Tommy. It didn't take Sammy long to confess with pride that he was a moneylending shark.

'Oh, does high finance run in the Adams family?' said Ned.

'What's 'igh finance?' asked Sammy.

'The money touch,' said Ned.

'It ain't touched me,' said Tommy. 'Lizzy got a birthday card from you.'

'That's good,' said Ned. 'Where is she?'

'Lizzy?' bawled Tommy.

No answer.

'I'll get her,' I said. I closed the kitchen door behind me as I went to the bedroom.

'Lizzy?' I turned the handle. The door was locked. Lizzy was in full retreat.

'I'm washin' me hair,' she called.

'In cold water?'

'Yes.'

'You don't want to say hello to Ned?'

'Oh, is he here, then?'

'Yes. Come on, Lizzy.' But I knew she wasn't going to show herself, not without changing into something pretty, and if she did that the kids would make pointed remarks. 'You ought to thank him for his birthday card.'

'Oh, blow.' Lizzy sounded beset. She had an admirer, but didn't quite know how to cope with what it meant. Why should she, at only fourteen? 'Tell 'im – tell him I'll thank him when he goes. Tell him I'm washing me hair.'

I explained to Ned she couldn't show herself because she was washing her hair. Chinese Lady, pouring tea, gave me a faint smile.

'She'll speak to you on your way out,' I said to Ned.

'Look,' said Ned, stirring his tea, 'if she doesn't like me, you can say so. I don't want to become a nuisance.'

'Of course she likes you,' said Chinese Lady, 'she was touched you sent her a birthday card. We give her a lovely party.'

'Well, she's a lovely girl,' said Ned without reservation, and Chinese Lady gave him an approving look. We talked some more until he said he'd better be off. He followed that by asking Chinese Lady if he could call after dinner on Sunday and take Lizzy to Ruskin Park.

'Oh, that'll be nice,' she said, 'but you'll ask Lizzy herself?'

'I thought I'd mention it to you first, Mrs Adams.'

'I'm pleasured,' said Chinese Lady.

On his way out, Ned, at my nod, knocked on Lizzy's door.

'I'm washing me hair,' she called.

'Eliza? It's me, Ned.'

'Oh, help.' It was almost an SOS.

'No, it's me, I said, not Jack the Ripper. Glad you had a lovely birthday party.'

'Yes. Oh, crikey. Yes.' Lizzy sounded all nerves. 'Oh, thank you for your birthday card, I'm sure.'

'Pleasure, Eliza. I'll be here at two-thirty next Sunday afternoon, by the way.'

'What for?'

'We could go to Ruskin Park.'

'Who's we?'

'You and me,' said Ned, a smile on his face. 'Shall us do that, Eliza?'

'I might be ill on Sunday.'

'So might I. There's measles about. All the same, I'll stagger here at half-past two. So long, Eliza, be good.'

Lizzy reappeared when he'd gone. She was quite pink.

'All right, Lizzy?' I said.

'He's not really comin' on Sunday, is he?' she said.

'Like to bet?'

'Not for me, though, is he?' said Lizzy.

'Well, it won't be for me,' I said, 'I'm not a lovely girl.'

'Yes, that's what he said, Lizzy,' smiled Chinese Lady fondly. 'What a lovely girl, he said.'

Lizzy's pink flush turned rosy.

I thought I'd like to talk to Mr Finch about girls. They were strange beings.

The rent collector made his return visit, Chinese Lady settled in full and we sat down then to our tea.

Mr Finch, ensconced in his armchair, briar pipe in his mouth, carpet slippers on his feet, watched the blue smoke thoughtfully.

'Girls?' he said.

'Well, I thought you'd know something about them.'

'You've met a pretty young thing, Boots?'

'Me? No. Well, I know a few girls, of course, but I haven't met any particular one.'

'But you might, of course. As an old bachelor, my knowledge of the fair sex is very limited. Your late father, rest his soul, would have been the best man to ask. He was, after all, a soldier and a husband, as well as a father. However, it's my opinion, Boots, that no two girls are alike. It's also my opinion that it's a mistake to expect any girl to act as you would like her to, or as you think she ought. Your sister Lizzy now, our dear Lizzy. Lizzy is a sweet girl determined to become a lady. Nothing will stop her leaving the grey fields of Walworth and entering the green fields of paradise.'

'Paradise?'

'To Lizzy, green grass, green hedges and fresh air represent paradise. Lizzy feels, I'm sure, that one can't be a lady in Walworth. One can be a good and hardworking woman, but not a lady. Lizzy loves fresh, clean clothes. Undarned stockings are bliss to her. To someone who can help her become a lady in her little paradise, Lizzy will give all of herself without question, although she will also ask to be loved.'

'You're saying she'd marry someone for his money?'

'Boots, I didn't say that at all. If you were to take Lizzy to somewhere not very far from here, to Dulwich, say, and show her the great playing fields of the colleges there, and the avenues with their little houses and green gardens, you would be showing her paradise. Lizzy won't ask for mansions, servants and parklands. She'll ask for a house with a garden, a house with a bathroom, and that is very modest compared with what many lovely girls would demand.'

'That's a middle-class dream.'

'Paradise. Then there's Emily, her close friend, and the terror of the neighbourhood. Do you have any idea of what Emily would ask for?'

'Someone she could knock about?'

'Oh, I don't think so, Boots. I think Emily would only ask to be cuddled.'

'Cuddled? Emily?'

Mr Finch smiled.

'I may be wrong, of course,' he said. 'I did say that as a confirmed bachelor I've a limited knowledge of the ladies. I've not been able to look at them with the wiser eyes of a married man.'

'Mr Finch, would you say Miss Chivers is a confirmed spinster?'

Mr Finch watched the rise of a puff of smoke.

'You're thinking you'd like to propose to her when you're older?' he said.

'I'd need to be older now to think that,' I said evasively. I did, secretly, feel romantically disposed towards Miss Chivers.

'Miss Chivers is a spinster because of circumstances,' he said quite sombrely. 'A man wishing to change her state would first have to cut her free from the spider's web.' He frowned. 'I shouldn't have said that. Forget that I did, Boots.'

'Yes. But I think she's lovely, don't you?'

His smile came back.

'My boy, will you drink a glass of ale with me?'

'Thank you kindly, sir, but—'

'You're nearly sixteen. I think a small glass of ale is permissible.' He produced a pint bottle of Watney's and two glasses. He twisted the bottle-top free and poured the ale. Froth swirled and climbed, and the golden ale sparkled. I drank it cautiously. Its tang hit my palate. Mr Finch downed half his glass with good-living relish.

'It's not bad stuff,' I said in a manly way.

'Stuff? Ale, my boy, is God's homely nectar. I've drunk the wine of many countries, and long may wine remain to grace the tables of those who prefer it. It's ale, Boots, that is the drink of the warrior. Empires have been won on hops and malt, and lost on the grape. Shall we drink a toast? To our Empire? To peace? Yes, to peace. No, not even peace. Let's drink to a lady, to your fine mother.'

We drank to Chinese Lady.

'Mr Finch,' I said, 'how do you get on with the people at the docks where you bring the cargo ships in?'

'The London dockers, you mean?' he said, his eyes full of the twinkling light.

'Well, you're very worldly,' I said, 'and they're pretty rough, aren't they?'

'I know the sea and the ships, Boots, and they know I know. If they're rough, they're still fine and hardy men. They know most of my education comes from experience on the seven seas, not from books. My Aunt Trudy once said that whatever kind of a nuisance I turned out to be, I'd get on with people. You are people, Boots, you and your family, and I hope I get on very well with all of you.'

'We wouldn't want anyone else as our lodger.'

'I regard that as a great compliment, Boots.'

Ruskin Park in the sunshine of a July afternoon was a place of green grass and colourful flower beds. The people of Walworth liked to stroll through it on Sundays. It offered peaceful escape from grey streets. You couldn't walk on the grass, of course, or drop litter. The brown-clad park-keepers saw to that. If they caught you on the grass, they had you off it quick, and if they caught you dropping a toffee-paper, they made you pick it up just as quick. If you were middle-class and accordingly received as much as a shilling in the way of pocket money each week, you could play tennis on the courts recently erected. The charge for use of a court was a shilling an hour, so if four of you played it cost you threepence each, which was in line with middle-class spending.

Sammy, Tommy, Lizzy and I liked to stop sometimes and watch the middle-class boys and girls at play on the courts. Some of them – well, most of them – wore white, and that always made Lizzy say, 'Don't they look grand, don't they look posh?' She didn't really mind some people being posh, even if she did occasionally get shirty about me talking like Lord Muck. She often wished we were posh, so that Chinese Lady wouldn't have to worry so much about where the money went to.

On the tennis courts, the boys wore cricket shirts and white flannels, or grey flannels in a few cases. The girls wore frilly white frocks and white hats. The ball plopped gently from girls' racquets, and the boys would yell, 'Don't kiss it, Caroline, hit it!' Middle-class girls had names like Caroline or Charlotte. Our kind of girls had names like Ethel or Vi or Liza.

The paths wound their various ways through the park, around the stretches of green grass and the flower beds, and there were clean-looking public lavs, called conveniences. The tiles inside always seemed as if they'd just been polished. At least, they did in the Gentlemen's. It was probably the same in the Ladies', but neither Chinese Lady nor Lizzy could have confirmed it, for I'd never known either of them to make use of the place. It actually cost a full penny for a wee in the Ladies', which was wicked extravagance to Chinese Lady, and a quite unnecessary expense to Lizzy, who never seemed in need outside of our home, except at Aunt Victoria's.

In the park, the girls of Walworth and Camberwell promenaded in their Sunday frocks, cheap but colourful. If a girl didn't have a Sunday frock, or if it was in pawn, she didn't come to the park, because the park was made for one's best clothes. The girls walked in their twos and threes, the boys likewise, and passed and repassed during their promenading until the first gauche communication was established.

'Hello, we seen you girls before.'

'We seen you boys too. And you was here last Sunday.'

'We seen you lots o' Sundays.'

'Lucky you.'

'I'm Joe. Me mates are Bert an' Stan.'

'I'm Doris. She's Maisie. She's Connie.'

'We'll walk yer 'ome, if yer like.'

'We ain't going home yet.'

'Walk yer round the park, then.'

'Shall we, girls?'

That was the way it was mostly done, and it was a thrill to all.

'Isn't it nice here today?' said Chinese Lady. Sammy, Tommy and I had brought her out for the afternoon. She had her Sunday hat on, the superior black one, and her only Sunday dress, a dark brown one with a brocaded bodice, which Aunt Victoria had given her three years ago. There should have been a cameo brooch pinned at the high neck, but it was in pawn. For ninepence.

Chinese Lady walked at a strolling pace, carrying herself upright, as always, and with her bosom looking proud. A man in a suit and cap, holding the hand of his little girl, gave her a very friendly glance. Chinese Lady stiffened.

'Cheek,' she said, sounding like Lizzy. Lizzy had left the house half an hour before us. Ned had called as promised to collect her. He looked very sporty and casual in grey trousers, striped belt and white open-necked cricket shirt. And Lizzy looked lovely in the sky-blue frock and her best boater. Chinese Lady had given the boater loving attention to bring it looking almost new. Cornered at last by Ned, Lizzy had again been surprisingly shy. Ned had said, 'Well, if you don't look a Sunday treat, I'll eat my hat.' And Lizzy had gone off with him in a state of nerves, lowered lashes and girlish rosinesss.

We reached the tennis courts and stopped to watch the play inside the high wire netting. The players ran about, pursuing the ball with their racquets. The girls ran sportingly, the boys ran determinedly. Watching Walworth kids began to make loud comments.

'Git yer braces on, Claud, or yer trousers'll fall down.'

'"Op lively there, Gladys, yer petticoat's showin'.'

'Oops, mind yer elbow, Dennis.'

'Watch yer bloomers, Maggie.'

One of the middle-class girls approached the wire netting and said very sweetly to the kids, 'Push off, you little buggers.'

'Well,' gasped Chinese Lady, who had heard every word, 'well! Come away, Sammy. You too, Tommy.'

'I like watchin',' said Tommy.

'I don't want any of you watchin' girls like that,' said Chinese Lady, 'that means you too, Boots.'

'Boots likes girls showin' their legs, don't yer, Boots?' said Tommy.

'It's my Sunday treat,' I said.

'I'll box your ears, big as you are,' said Chinese Lady, 'I won't have any of you talkin' about girls' legs.'

The tennis girls' legs were in white stockings. The girl who had stunned the catcalling boys came to the netting to collect a ball. She looked up at me. She was fair under her white hat, and her mouth was sweet and pink. She winked at me.

'Don't go away,' she said. She collected the ball and served, an underarm stroke that dollied the ball over the net. The boy who received it biffed it out. She laughed, turned and gave me another wink.

'Well,' gasped our mum again, 'well! The saucy minx. I don't know what the country's comin' to. We're not stopping here. Boots, you come on now, or you might get into the kind of company your dad would of been sorry about.'

We went on, strolling idly over the paths and enjoying the sunny Sunday look of the park. It was a good outing for our mum. If she'd stayed home she'd have found some work to do, and still been at it when it was time to prepare tea. I never minded preparing Sunday tea myself. She disapproved strongly. She had rigid ideas about what was men's work and what was women's, and was totally against either interfering with the other. But I did get the tea sometimes, with Lizzy helping, and by the time it was ready, Chinese Lady would sit down at the teapot, look at the table and say, 'Well, there's compensations in havin' obstinate children.'

'Mum,' said Tommy, as we strolled, 'that girl what spoke to Boots an' give 'im a wink – was she a tart, Mum?'

'Course she was, wasn't she, Mum?' said Sammy, now ten.

'Oh, you kids,' said our mum.

'Luvaduck,' said Tommy, 'there's our Lizzy.'

Lizzy came into view, side by side with Ned. They were walking slowly. Ned was talking and Lizzy was laughing. She had come to at last. She was alive and flowering. She was fourteen, and she had an admirer who was grown up. She looked at her Sunday best, and Ned looked handsome.

Chinese Lady murmured, 'Oh, don't they look nice together, don't our Lizzy do us proud in her new frock?'

'Don't stop, Mum,' I said, 'and you kids, don't yell at her or I'll clout the pair of you. Just walk by.'

Lizzy saw us coming towards her and Ned. The brim of her boater cast a soft warm shadow over her face, and the shadow deepened because of her sudden rise of colour.

'Can't stop, Lizzy,' I said, 'we're going to the bandstand. See you later, Ned.'

We passed by, leaving them to each other.

'Anyone 'ud think we got measles,' said Tommy.

'Ernie Jones is gettin' pimples,' said Sammy, whose cherubic face was smooth and healthy. ''E's not arf gettin' bovvered about it.'

In a while we passed again the man taking his little girl for a walk. He gave Chinese Lady another glance, and even a smile. It made her quite livid.

'What's he think I am?' she breathed.

'Pretty, I suppose,' I said.

'Don't be silly,' she said.

'We're proud of our Chinese Lady, aren't we, kids?' I said.

'Whaffor?' asked Sammy.

'She makes spiffin' bread pudden, that's what for,' said Tommy.

Chinese Lady looked comforted by that.

We got back home at five-thirty. Tommy and I offered to get tea ready, and Sammy said he'd fill the kettle, put it on and watch it come to the boil for a penny. Chinese Lady said it was very kind of us, but as Ned would be joining us at the tea table she'd rather see to everything herself. She put up with domestic interference sometimes, she said, and although it was a kind interference she could do without it when there was a guest and it was Sunday. However, she allowed Tommy and me to lay the parlour table.

Lizzy and Ned returned then, Lizzy carrying a bunch of flowers, bought by Ned from the seller outside the gates of King's College Hospital, next to the park. He'd bought them for our mum, she said, and she was as sunny as the day. She presented the bouquet to our mum.

'They're from Ned,' she said.

'Oh,' Chinese Lady looked astonished.

'It's a kind of thank you for the loan of your daughter's company, Mrs Adams,' said Ned. 'She's actually managed to talk to me, and I've managed to convince her I'm not someone who bites old ladies.'

'Oh, I never said you did that,' protested Lizzy. 'Now when did I say that? I never did.'

'No, but you thought it,' said Ned solemnly. 'I could see it in your eyes the first time I saw you. I could see your eyes thinking oh, I bet he bites old ladies.'

'No, you couldn't,' said Lizzy indignantly. 'How could anyone see that in anyone's eyes, anyway? Now how could anyone see me thinkin' – oh, you're havin' me on.'

'Anyway, we had a lovely afternoon, Mrs Adams,' said Ned. 'At least, I did.'

'The flowers are – well, I can't remember when I last had such a nice bunch,' said Chinese Lady. 'Thank you, I'm sure. You're stayin' to tea?'

'No, send him home,' said Lizzy, 'he's makin' fun of me.'

'Is there cake?' asked Ned.

'I baked a nice coconut cake this mornin',' said our mum.

'I hope I'm not going to miss that,' said Ned, 'but am I going or staying?' He smiled at Lizzy.

'Oh,' she said impulsively, 'you'll stay, won't yer?' Then

she went pink at being so impulsive, took her boater off and looked intently at it. Ned saw the glossy crown of her chestnut hair.

'Can I put the kettle on?' he said.

It was Lizzy's first time, her first time of having a boy to Sunday tea, and she was alternately laughing and shy. She was laughing when he was teasing her, she was shy when she caught his glance. She was quick with excitement one moment, dreamy with wonderment the next, as if she couldn't understand what interest a handsome young man could possibly have in a girl of fourteen.

It was an intriguing Sunday tea for the family.

When Ned left at nine that evening, he said he'd come again soon, if no one objected.

'We'll be pleasured any time,' said Chinese Lady.

CHAPTER NINE

We all broke up for school holidays. Sammy and Tommy spent most days wandering far and wide, trying to earn pennies. They frequently got as far as Brixton, where the people who lived in the big houses on the hill had servants to answer the door to callers. If Tommy was a bit reserved about knocking, Sammy wasn't.

'D'yer want any jobs done, like walkin' yer dog or cleanin' 'is kennel or diggin' yer garden or clearin' yer rubbish?' Sammy would ask, his cherubic face angelic. Surprisingly, they were given such jobs, and they came home with pennies. Sammy saved most of his. Tommy spent most of his.

Lizzy had a stroke of luck the day after she broke up, getting a temporary summer holiday job at Hurlocks the drapers, near the Elephant and Castle. In their stock rooms. She told them she was sixteen, so they paid her four shillings a week, including all day Saturdays. Four shillings represented riches to Lizzy. She gave Chinese Lady two and six, and kept one and six for herself, and still felt rich. She saved a shilling a week – for a rainy day, she said. Hurlocks let her buy a pair of imitation silk stockings at cost price. They made her pretty legs look lustrous. Chinese Lady wasn't sure they weren't a bit improper on her fourteen-year-old daughter. Lizzy said they were only for Sundays, and that they couldn't be improper on Sundays, could they?

She became a bit down at times, however. I suspected it was because she hadn't heard from Ned since he'd taken her for a walk in the park and stayed for Sunday tea. I casually mentioned he hadn't been round.

'Oh, I expect he's got lots of girls,' she said, just as casually. 'Older ones.'

'But not prettier,' I said, to buck her up.

'I expect he 'as got lots, though, don't you?' said Lizzy.

'No, not really. He doesn't strike me as that kind of bloke.'

'Oh, well,' said Lizzy.

On August Bank Holiday we all went to Peckham Rye, where they always had a funfair every Bank Holiday. Mr Finch had proposed the outing and had insisted on being the host. He provided the picnic we took with us in the shopping bag. There were hard-boiled eggs, corned beef sandwiches made from crusty loaves, tomatoes, rock cakes, Granny Smith apples, and bottles of lemonade and kola water. Mr Finch also paid for the tram ride. Emily had been included in the party, because her mum and dad rarely went anywhere, except to the bottle and jug counter of the pub, from which they brought back beer to drink at home. Emily could get restless on Bank Holidays, and lonely. She behaved herself very well on the tram, but the moment we found a picnic spot on the Rye, she reverted to type, cavorting, pushing, tormenting and generally mucking about.

Even Lizzy told her to shut up. Sitting on the grass in her pretty white blouse, blue skirt and boater, Lizzy was watching the girls who were hand in hand with boys. I felt she wanted a boy of her own, a regular boy. Only yesterday, our mum had said to me what a pity that nice young man Ned had turned out to be a bit casual. Lizzy was growing up, she said. One could see that. Chinese Lady had had to do some keen shopping around to provide her only daughter with two pairs of stays.

'Come along, children,' said Mr Finch, who had been smoking his pipe and talking to Chinese Lady, 'it's my treat for the roundabouts and the Big Wheel.'

Emily rushed off in advance. Sammy and Tommy followed in a more sedate way with Mr Finch. Emily rushed back and tugged at my arm.

'Oh, come on, Boots, you're comin', ain't yer?'

'Thank you kindly, Em, but no,' I said, 'I've got some homework reading to do.'

'Spoilsport,' said Emily. 'Lizzy, come on.'

'All right,' said Lizzy, who understood Emily better than any of us, and the two girls went off.

Mr Finch returned with the kids forty minutes later. He'd treated them to rides on the swings, roundabouts, helter-skelter and Big Wheel.

'Where's the girls?' asked Chinese Lady.

'I thought they came back after their ride on the Big Wheel,' said Mr Finch, looking a very upstanding man in his shirt, tie, trousers and braces. Chinese Lady had minded his jacket and waistcoat for him.

'Boots,' said Chinese Lady firmly, 'go and look for them.'

Peckham Rye on August Bank Holiday was crowded with all kinds of people, including all kinds of young bloods on the lookout for girls. I went in search of Lizzy and Emily. It took me some while to locate them. Lizzy was struggling with two tall skinny grinners from the back streets of Peckham, and Emily was actually rolling about on the grass with another grinner, he attempting to pin her and to pull her hair. Emily was giving as good as she was getting. I went up to the tall skinnies and booted the nearest one up the backside. He yelled, and they both let go of Lizzy and whipped round.

'Hoppit,' I said. I was taller than both of them and not so skinny. I was also bad-tempered. I didn't like anyone laying hands on our Lizzy.

'Ain't yer business,' said the booted one, 'so sod off.'

'See that?' I showed him my balled fist. 'You'll get it smack in your cakehole, and it'll hurt. Lizzy, hop off to Mr Finch and tell him I've got trouble.'

Lizzy ran. The two skinnies eyed me nastily. A crowd was going to collect if fists started to fly or boots started to swing. I ran to the grounded Emily, a screeching fury as the third boy yanked at her hair, now grown thick and tangled. I pulled him off her. People began to gather. The boy leapt to his feet and rushed me. I tripped him up. He

107

fell flat on his face. People cheered. I helped Emily to her feet. She kicked the sprawled boy.

'Buzz off, Em,' I said.

'Oh, yer saved me, yer stopped 'im pullin' me 'ead off,' she gasped.

'Come on, we'll both buzz off,' I said, seeing the skinnies were now undecided, and that a bit of commonsense cowardice might be wiser than another rush of blood. I retreated with Emily, and we met Mr Finch and Lizzy hurrying towards us.

'Is all well?' asked Mr Finch, a reassuring stalwart. 'Alarm set in when Lizzy ran up crying "To the rescue!"'

'Oh, Boots went an' done for 'em good an' proper,' gasped Emily triumphantly. 'Laid 'em all flat, 'e did.'

'All of them?' said Mr Finch. 'How many?'

'Dozens,' said Emily, her hair a mess, her Sunday frock dishevelled. 'They went for Lizzy an' me, didn't they, Lizzy?'

'Only after you cheeked them and stuck your tongue out,' said Lizzy.

'Oh, I never did,' said Emily.

'Or if you did, it was all a misunderstanding,' said Mr Finch.

'Mum's havin' hysterics about you, Boots,' said Lizzy, 'she thinks you're brawlin'.'

'Oh, I'll run an' tell her Boots 'as been 'eroic,' said Emily, and dashed to convey this epic news to Chinese Lady. It cut no ice with our mum. She gave the girls a lecture and me an earful.

'Mum, it wasn't Boots's fault,' said Lizzy.

'Never mind whose fault it was, he's been fightin',' said Chinese Lady severely, 'and he knows I don't hold with that. He should of fetched a policeman.'

'But, Mum,' said Lizzy, 'if he hadn't—'

'Never mind ifs and buts,' said Chinese Lady. 'Your dad would never forgive me if he thought I'd raised a hooligan. When I think, on a Bank Holiday and all, when I think of my only oldest son kickin' boys with people lookin' on, I wonder what my fam'ly's comin' to. And I don't know what Mr Finch thinks, I'm sure.'

'Ah, well,' said Mr Finch tactfully.

'Where's Sammy?' I asked.

'He's not brawlin', I can tell you that,' said Chinese Lady, 'he's wheeling a lady's pram up and down for a penny.'

'Is the lady in it?' I asked.

Emily shrieked, Lizzy giggled, Mr Finch coughed and Chinese Lady gave me a look.

'Your school's turnin' you into a comedian,' she said. 'Well, you watch out, my lad. Banks don't employ comedians, nor hooligans. As for you, Lizzy, sittin' there laughin' your head off, don't you ever get mixed up again with boys like them. There's plenty of nice boys about, like – well, never mind, let's have our picnic.'

When we got back home at four, faces warm from hours in the sun, Emily spoke to me before going indoors.

'Oh, I'll never forget 'ow yer saved me from gettin' all me hair pulled out,' she said, 'you was so brave, Boots.'

'Well, you've got nice hair, Emily, only you ought to brush and comb it now it's grown so thick again.'

'It's my hair, not yourn,' said Emily, and kicked her gate resentfully.

'All right, don't bite my head off.'

'Oh, I wouldn't, honest.' Emily looked at her feet. 'Boots, I ain't goin' to be a wretched girl no more, truly I ain't.'

'Who says you're wretched?'

'Me teachers, all of 'em.'

'Well, you show 'em you're not, Em,' I said, and gave her a pat.

'Oh, I do like yer, Boots, and I won't kick yer no more, honest.'

'Good on yer, then,' I said.

'You're me 'ero,' said Emily, and dashed indoors.

Miss Chivers came to Bank Holiday tea, receiving special dispensation from the Witch, who had recently

109

been screeching at kids playing in the street during the school holidays. Because of her dark face, with great black eyebrows, a bony beak of a nose and glittering eyes, the younger kids were terrified of her. Miss Chivers, her daughter, maintained a quiet and calm front that never crumpled, not to our knowledge, even though the immediate neighbours said her mother was on at her day in, day out. The only apparent effect on Miss Chivers was that her soft look became softer and shyer.

Mr Finch's kind attentiveness was always unobtrusive every time they were at tea with us. After this Bank Holiday tea, she played the piano, as usual. But we didn't sing because Mr Finch had suggested beforehand that certain ears were more alert these days. We knew it would never do to give the Witch the impression that her daughter was enjoying herself more than was good for her. So we sat and listened to her, Mr Finch smoking his pipe, Chinese Lady letting the music bring dreams to her, and Lizzy with almost a wistful look on her face.

At the end of the day, with our guests gone and the tired kids in their bed, Chinese Lady, Lizzy and I sat at the kitchen table drinking our last cup of Bank Holiday tea. Chinese Lady patted my hand.

'Never mind, Boots,' she said.

'Never mind what?'

'Maybe I was a bit hard on you about your fightin'. Still, don't do it again. Call a policeman. I'm off to bed now. Don't stay up late, you two.'

She went to bed.

'Of course, what she really minded was you gettin' hurt,' said Lizzy. 'You're her first-born, you are.'

'And you're her only girl.'

Lizzy gazed at the empty grate of the kitchen range.

'He ain't goin' to come again, is he?' she said.

'Who?'

'He's middle-class, that's what.'

'Ned?'

110

'Oh, never mind,' said Lizzy.

'You're only fourteen, Lizzy. By the time you're sixteen, you'll be able to pick and choose.'

'No, I won't. I ain't educated enough.'

'Speak proper,' I said.

'I ain't goin' to be no Lady Muck,' said Lizzy.

Lizzy was very down.

There were two letters on the mat in the morning. One for Chinese Lady, from Aunt Victoria, and one for Lizzy. Lizzy was dashing about, getting ready to walk to work. She had to be at Hurlocks at eight-thirty.

'Letter for you, Lizzy.'

She came out of the bedroom. Chinese Lady was already at work at the town hall. Tommy and Sammy were still in bed.

'What letter?' asked Lizzy.

'Here it is. And your porridge is ready.'

Lizzy took the letter into the kitchen and sat down to her porridge. She opened the letter. She read it. Her expression became very odd.

'Oh,' she said. 'Boots, he's broke his leg. A horse and cart knocked him off his bike. He's been laid up.'

'The middle-class bloke? Good.'

'Oh, don't be rotten.'

'It's good, because that's why he hasn't been round, isn't it?'

'He's been off work as well.' Lizzy went on reading. A blush swept her, and she folded the letter up and thrust it hastily back into its envelope.

'Sent you his love, sis?'

'Eat your porridge,' said Lizzy, but her eyes were bright. She spoke to Chinese Lady in the evening.

'Mum, d'you think – d'you think I ought to go an' see him?'

Chinese Lady gave the shy question careful thought.

'No, lovey, I don't think so,' she said, 'not unless he's asked you. It's not like you're fam'ly. I don't think

111

you could turn up without his parents or him askin'. Hasn't he said nothing about comin' here when his leg's better?'

'He's hobblin' about on crutches,' said Lizzy. 'He couldn't come on crutches, could he? He said he'd come when he could. Mum, how long does someone have to be on crutches?'

'I don't know, lovey. A few months, I expect.'

'A few months?' Lizzy got to her feet. 'I think I'll go an' brush my hair,' she said, and retired to the bedroom.

'You wouldn't think she was only fourteen,' I said.

'It's not how old a girl is, it's how she feels,' said Chinese Lady. 'Girls is different from boys. You ought to know that by now.'

'Well, I know girls wear stays and boys don't,' I said, 'and that's about all I do know.'

She gave me one of her old-fashioned looks.

'Boys of ten know that,' she said. 'Still, you should be proud our Lizzy's gone into stays when she's only just fourteen.'

Perhaps that was what had caught Ned's eye, the fact that our distinctly pretty Lizzy already had a figure as shapely as that of a young lady. And since he'd only ever seen her in her Sunday clothes, she would have looked much more a young lady to him than a fourteen-year-old schoolgirl. At any rate, something about her must have impressed him, for he turned up the following Sunday. He made the journey from Herne Hill by tram and on his crutches. Sammy answered the door to him just as we'd finished washing up the dinner things. Lizzy heard him saying hello to Sammy and rushed out – to the bedroom, to comb and brush her hair. Ned worked his way through to the kitchen well before she returned, and Chinese Lady made him sit down at once, his crutches resting against the table, his left leg in plaster.

'Oh, we was so sorry to hear about your accident,' she said.

'It could have been worse,' said Ned, who looked his usual well-dressed self in a grey suit and tie. 'I could have lost it.'

'Oh, surely not,' said Chinese Lady.

'You don't mean it could have got mislaid, do you?' I said.

Ned laughed.

'Good old Boots,' he said.

Lizzy reappeared then. Ned gave her a warm smile, and Lizzy just couldn't control her colour. It flooded her. Her hair shone. Most girls wore their hair hanging down their backs, some using ribbon to let it hang tidily, others letting it hang loose. Lizzy's hair, long and thick, was wound around her head, in the same way she dressed our mum's hair sometimes. She used hairpins to keep it in place. She had hairpins in now, but they were all invisible. In her white Sunday frock, she was completely the young lady, even if she was blushing like any unsophisticated schoolgirl.

'Hello,' she said, and she was so shy it almost hurt me. 'I – we – oh, is your leg a bit better?'

'It's a lot better for seeing you, Eliza, you look good enough to eat.' Ned did not suffer from being reserved. 'Don't you think she looks good enough to eat, Boots?'

'I've never heard of anyone wanting to eat their sister,' I said, 'I've heard of fellers wanting to eat someone else's sister.'

'Cor,' said Sammy, 'fancy eatin' Effel Jones – I'd be sick.'

'Not if you ate her with custard,' I said.

'Oh, don't be horrid,' said Lizzy.

'Lizzy,' said Chinese Lady, 'Ned says he could have lost his leg. Isn't it a mercy he didn't?'

'Crikey,' said Tommy, 'the doctors was goin' to saw it off?'

'Not quite,' said Ned gravely. 'It was the mad runaway horse and cart. I was bowled off my bike and the horse came at me with its teeth showing. I suppose that having

113

broken my leg, it thought it might as well have it for supper.'

'Oh, you!' Lizzy laughed and flowered.

Ned stayed to tea.

Lizzy had a boy, very definitely, and when the family realised it, the family said, 'Fancy, that's our Lizzy, would yer believe.'

CHAPTER TEN

I opened the door to an early-morning knock. Miss Chivers stood there, wearing a navy blue dress and hat, a familiar outfit on her working days. With her spectacles on, her eyes through the lenses didn't look shortsighted. They looked very clear. She smiled gently.

'Boots, would Tommy like to clean the outside of our windows? I haven't been able to manage it these last few days, not the outside. I'll give him sixpence.'

'How much?'

'Sixpence.'

Tommy and Sammy could work all day doing odd jobs and not earn that much between them.

'Tommy will do it for tuppence, if it's only outside. No, wait a moment, I don't think Mum would let him climb any ladders.' Chinese Lady wouldn't, for certain she wouldn't. Not with spiked iron railings down below.

'Oh.' Miss Chivers looked softly abashed. 'Well, never mind, I'll do them when I come home this evening.' She would sit on the upstairs sills, with the windows open, and manage them that way, as everyone did.

'I'll do them for you, Miss Chivers.'

'Boots, I couldn't ask you.'

'I'm offering.'

'But you're nearly a young man, and you're studying,' she said. I was studying a book on banking lent to me by Mr Finch, who had got hold of it from somewhere. It wasn't an easy exercise in learning, but I was persevering.

'I'll do them for you, Miss Chivers.'

'If you're sure?' She was shyly diffident. 'Well, the ladder's lying along the passage, and the doorkey's under

115

the step mat. The doctor's due for his weekly call on my mother today.' The doctor attended the old Witch regularly. 'My mother – she's in bed and a little poorly, Boots.'

'The same as usual? I'm sorry.' I was sorry for her, not the harridan. And what she meant was that I wasn't to go into the house and disturb her mother. I wasn't likely to, anyway.

'Leave it to me,' I said.

'Here's the money, then. I insist, and thank you, Boots.' She pressed a sixpence into my hand, which was something I could usefully put away for Christmas. She went off at a graceful, gliding walk.

A voice called fretfully after her.

'You wearing your glasses, Elsie?'

'Yes, Mother.'

The Witch, poorly though she might be, had been watching from her bedroom window.

I did the windows after breakfast, when Sammy and Tommy had gone off down the Lane to offer their services to stallholders. They might come back with a penny, they might come back with a few pounds of specked apples.

Miss Chivers's doorkey was under the step mat. I opened the door and carried the ladder out from the passage. I set to work on the bay windows of the parlour, the net curtains hiding the room. I had a pail of warm water with soda crystals in it, and two cloths. Kids playing in the street watched agog. The water was black after I'd done the parlour windows and one upstairs window, so I got some fresh water for the last window, that of the Witch's room. I climbed the ladder, hung the pail on a hook and dipped the cloth into the water. I nearly fell off the ladder then, for the curtains parted and a face appeared. I saw a white nightcap and lankly hanging black hair threaded with silver. Two glinting black eyes, set in dark hollows, and a great beaky nose, confronted me through the dusty glass. The mouth was a thin gash, bitter and malicious. It opened and crooked, ancient teeth showed. The face didn't say anything, it just glared at me, a screech in its eyes.

'Good morning, Mrs Chivers,' I said from my perch, and the face took on a new dimension of glaring spite, and a hand went up to an ear. 'Good morning, Mrs Chivers,' I called, 'I'm cleaning your windows.'

The lower window shot up.

'I know you,' hissed the Witch, 'you're Mrs Adams's dreadful boy – be off with you – be off!'

'I'm supposed to do these windows first—'

'Disgusting boy!' And the window slammed shut. I cleaned it, and the upper one, all with a feeling she was watching me through the net curtain. The lower window shot up again, smoothly but viciously, and the pane rattled. The sunken eyes glittered and the thin lips writhed. 'I know you – you're the one that's nearly grown up – Elsie didn't say it would be you – get off that ladder – been looking in Elsie's bedroom, that's what you've been doing – I'll give you cleaning windows when all you want is to see her bedroom – you're disgusting – you're like all of them round here, you're all trying to get your dirty hands on her – get off that ladder—' It all shot at me, the staccato hisses of hate and the spittle. A veined, clawlike hand darted and the fingernails scored the wrist of my clinging left hand. I let go and my feet slipped from the rung. I flung both arms around the ladder and slithered downwards, feet flailing to find purchase. Fortunately, I'd placed the ladder outside the iron railings. I missed being spiked as I tumbled to the pavement. Someone ran up and shook a skinny fist at the glaring Witch.

'You old cow – you old ragbag – I'll kill yer – I saw what yer done – yer tried to make Boots break 'is neck! I'll tell 'is mum, I'll tell my mum, I'll tell the coppers! Boots, get up, you ain't dyin', are yer? Oh, if she's killed yer, I'll get the law to 'ang 'er – Boots?'

Emily knelt beside me. The window slammed shut. Emily smothered my head in her bosom. I was surprised to

117

feel two soft bumps there. It hadn't occurred to me that Emily would be anything but skinny all over. There was a faintly sour smell about her, like damp washing that had been left neglected for a few days.

'I'm all right,' I said, and got up, a bit bruised. I dusted myself down. Emily rose to her feet. Her auburn hair had become a thick, tangled mess during the months it had been growing. Her green frock was shabby and marked, and her face looked as if she hadn't washed it yet.

'Boots, she nearly done yer in.'

'No, she didn't, and don't tell Miss Chivers. It'll upset her. The old girl's barmy, mad as a hatter. But I don't think Miss Chivers wants her committed to Bedlam.'

'Oh, Boots, yer do talk nice, even when yer just nearly been done for – it's no wonder some of the girls round 'ere ain't arf gone on yer.'

'They've never told me. Now look, wait till I put this ladder back, then come indoors with me. I'm going to do something about your hair, and I'm also going to heat a saucepan of water. Well, no, forget the water.' I could do something about her hair, but to get her to take a bath would incense her mum. It wasn't my business, either her hair or her personal cleanliness. But it wouldn't hurt to do her hair a bit of good.

'Me 'air?' she said.

'Yes.'

'Me mum does me 'air.'

'When?'

'Ev'ry Christmas, if she's got time.' Emily retreated a little while I stowed the ladder back along the Chivers's passage. I replaced the doorkey under the outside step mat. 'Boots, I ain't goin' to let yer muck me 'air about.'

'I'm not going to muck it about. Come on, there's no one in. Our mum's gone to our Aunt Victoria's for the morning. But I still don't want any screaming.'

'I ain't goin' in your 'ouse by meself with only you there,' she said, but coming with me all the same. 'You'll – you'll—'

118

'I'll what?' I said, opening our door.

'Boots, you ain't goin' to lark about, you ain't goin' to pull me clothes up, are yer?' Emily seemed very unhappy.

'Be your age, Em,' I said.

Entering the passage with me, she muttered, 'Only – well, I ain't got – well, I ain't got nothing pretty on.'

She was talking about her petticoat and drawers. Poor Emily. Mrs Castle was a fond mum, but a careless one. Mr Castle looked at Emily, saw only what he wanted to see, a daughter with green honey in her eyes, and said proudly what a caution she was. Both parents seemed unaware that they neglected Emily in many ways. Mrs Castle never seemed to mind dirt. She was the kind of woman who, if she dropped a slice of bread and marge on the floor, would pick it up and put it back on the plate, saying a bit of clean dirt never hurt anyone. In respect of Emily's clothes, Mrs Castle would let her wear the same things over and over until they were ready to drop off, then go out and buy her new things and let the process repeat itself. None of Emily's clothes ever looked properly laundered.

'Stop being soppy, Emily,' I said. 'Go and sit at the scullery sink.'

I went upstairs and got a large, fine-toothed steel comb and a stiff hairbrush. When I came down, Emily was prowling jerkily around the scullery. I pulled a chair in from the kitchen and told her to sit on it, facing the sink.

'Won't,' said Emily, but she sat down and bent her head over the sink. I began to use the comb. She yelled. It was like trying to rake barbed wire. But I kept at it, doing little tufts at a time. The dirt that was movable began to come out. And other things. Emily's headlice were back and thriving. I didn't say anything, and Emily had her eyes shut tight with pain, and her teeth clenched. I turned the tap on and let the swirling water carry the lice away. 'Oh, crikey,' she gasped, 'that comb ain't arf 'urtin'.'

'If you used a comb every day,' I said, 'it wouldn't hurt at all. But you don't, so you've got to put up with it now.'

'What you doin' it for?'

119

'Because you've got nice hair, and because you live next door.'

'Oh.'

The comb tugged and Emily winced.

'Stick it, Em,' I said.

'All right,' she said, and she did, bravely. It took me an hour to get all the nits out, all the tufts untangled, and I made her keep her head over the sink the whole time. What lice came out were drowned or smothered, I hoped, in the sewers of Southwark. I'd put on a large kettle of water and it was now steaming. Emily, head up, ran a hand through her hair.

'Don't move,' I said.

'I ain't goin' to move, Boots. I know what you're doin'.' Her expression was sad. 'I'm lousy again, ain't I? It serves me right, don't it, for not lookin' after me 'air. But don't let 'em cut it all off again, I ain't got nothing good except me 'air.'

'Why don't you keep it washed and combed, then?'

'Oh, I dunno. Boots, you goin' to wash it for me?'

'You might prefer to wash it yourself. If I go and do a bit of reading for half an hour, will you give it a really good scrub and wash?'

'I promise,' said Emily.

'You Em'ly, you there?' It was Mrs Castle's voice, shouting fatly through the letterbox. You could tell it was a fat voice because the echoes seemed to billow through the passage.

'She ain't goin' to like this,' said Emily.

'Well, we won't answer, then, that's the best thing.'

'She'll use yer latchcord and come in.'

'No, she won't, it's on this side of the door.'

'Em'ly, you there? You there with Boots?' The voice was enquiring, but not concerned. We didn't answer and she went away.

'She only wanted me to run an errand, I bet,' said Emily.

I went upstairs and did some studious reading. I came down after thirty minutes and found Emily still scrubbing her head, the large enamel bowl in the sink full of soapy water, with a faint smell of disinfectant to it. Emily's head was a mass of lather, her face red and wet. Her green eyes blinked amid dripping foam.

'That's very good, Emily.'

'I done it twice already, this is the third time. Boots—?'

'Well?'

'It feels nice.'

'Clean and untangled?'

'Yes.' Her hands scrubbed vigorously. 'I'll get to rinse it in a minute, shall I?'

'Good idea. Plenty of rinsing to get the soap out. There's a towel. When you've dried it, I'll put some oil on.'

'Yes, all right,' said Emily.

'You wouldn't like a nice hot bath, I suppose?' It was back again, the interfering impulse.

Emily turned her lathered head, her eyes blinking again.

'Oh, you ain't goin' to be wicked, are yer, you ain't goin' to chuck me all naked into yer bath, are yer?' Her face looked wetly hot.

'You're being soppy again.'

'But I got to undress to 'ave a bath.'

'I know that, Em. But you don't think I'm going to hang around, do you?'

'You ain't goin' to look at me nakedness?'

'Leave off, Em.'

'Oh, could I 'ave a bath, then, could I? Me dad filled our tub for me last Easter, but it's a bit of a trouble for me mum, carryin' 'ot saucepans – could I use your tub, then? I got some pennies, I could put some in yer gas so's yer mum wouldn't 'ave to pay – and yer won't look, will yer?'

'I'll put the cauldron on,' I said, 'and leave the rest to you. You'll look good when it's all over. What'll you tell your mum, though?'

'Nothink,' said Emily, 'she won't notice. Oh, yer so good to me, Boots.'

Sammy brought a little packet to me in the evening.

'Em'ly said to give yer this.'

Inside a folded brown paper bag was a bar of Nestle's chocolate, with a slip of paper containing a pencilled message.

'*With fond grattitude from Emily next door.*'

Lizzy laughed.

'Oh, Boots, ain't that sweet?' she said. 'What's she give it to you for?'

'Christmas, I suppose.'

'Christmas? It's not Christmas, it's still summer holidays.'

'Well, don't tell Emily, she might come and take it back.'

'Cor, you oughter see that Em'ly,' said Sammy. 'All done up clean and shinin', she is, 'air as well.'

But three months later, Emily was a mess again. And Sammy was scratching his head again. Lizzy stared at him in horror over tea one evening. Sammy was eating bread and jam out of one hand, and scratching his head with the other.

'Oh, no,' cried Lizzy, and wouldn't even finish her tea.

Chinese Lady regarded Sammy unhappily, and the grey entered her face. The kitchen was warm, the range fire alight. Everywhere else, except in Mr Finch's sitting-room, the house was full of damp November cold. The kitchen still held the aroma of freshly-baked bread pudding, fruity and spicy.

'Wassup?' asked Sammy.

'Finish your tea,' said Chinese Lady, 'then it's into the bath for you and Tommy, and a good hot head-scrubbing.'

'Barf? It ain't Friday,' said Sammy.

'What we done?' asked Tommy.

'Sammy's scratching his head,' I said.

Tommy thought.

'Mine's been itching a bit, Mum,' he said.

Chinese Lady looked sad. Lizzy looked stricken. Little shudders shook her.

'I got to write to Ned an' tell him not to come this Sunday,' she said.

122

'No, you haven't,' I said.

'Oh, yes, his fam'ly would like that, wouldn't they, me sharin' my headlice with him. I probably been sharin' them with him already.'

Ned had been seeing Lizzy every Sunday, and had taken her to his home twice. Much to her relief, his home wasn't impossibly grand. He, his parents and his sister lived in the flat above his dad's grocer's shop in Herne Hill, although Lizzy did say the rooms were furnished quite posh. What had pleased her most was the friendly way his parents received her.

'Lizzy,' I said, 'you don't—'

'I could go to his home and share them with his whole fam'ly,' said Lizzy, and her brown eyes looked tragic.

'Well, look,' I said, 'Mr Finch said on the last occasion—'

'Yes, I know,' said Chinese Lady quietly, 'but we don't want a long oratorical offerin' from you, Boots.'

'It's not serious,' I said. 'We keep as clean as we can, we bath every Friday, and we look after our hair. What we've got we've caught from Emily. Emily's always in and out, and she can't keep away from Lizzy or the kids. She and Lizzy go to school together, and put their heads together.'

Lizzy shuddered, but still wasn't disposed to be disloyal to Emily. She said, 'It's not her fault, it's the way her mum and dad live. They just don't bother about the things our mum does. They're fond of Emily, but they don't look after her, and it's made her so that she don't bother, either. I bet they're chronic with lice themselves.'

'It's funny, but they're not,' said Chinese Lady tiredly. 'Last time it happened, I talked to Mrs Castle. Well, at least she never takes offence, and she and Mr Castle managed to stir themselves enough to go to the clinic, and the clinic didn't find a single lice on either of them. Em'ly had them all, poor girl. It did seem unfair, only Em'ly. Now she's probably goin' to have all her hair cut off again. She'll hate it, but she just don't do anything about herself.'

'We're going to have a scrub-up after tea?' I said.

'We got to,' said Chinese Lady, 'all of us.'

'Shall we do Emily as well?' I asked.

'Her mum might not like us interferin',' said Lizzy.

'Her mum won't notice,' I said, 'so I'll go and get Emily in a moment, and I'll talk to her.'

'No, you won't,' said Chinese Lady. 'Your trouble is you're too flippant. What Emily needs is someone to put the fear of God into her.'

I put the fear of God into Emily. I walked up and down the cold, damp and dark street with her and frightened her to death about what the headlice could do to her.

'And what's more,' I said, 'it could be worse than going permanently bald, it could mean you getting sent to a lepers' colony.'

'Oh, gawd, stop it,' said Emily.

'No, you've got to be told. You could get to the stage where the lice get under your scalp and your head breaks out in leprous sores. The sores will eat the top of your head off, then start on things like your ears and nose.'

'Oh, yer lyin' bleeder,' gasped Emily.

'All right, go round to the town hall and ask the sanitary inspector. I can't understand you – anyone would think you didn't like living next door to us.'

The gaslight of the single street lamp peered palely at Emily's shocked face.

'Yer not to say that, I like that best of all – oh, yer wouldn't go away, would yer, Boots, you and yer fam'ly?'

'Well, you seem as if you want to get away from us, you seem as if you can't wait to get sent to a lepers' colony, with no skin to your head and your nose half-eaten—'

'You keep sayin' things like that an' I'll die, I will! That's what yer after, ain't yer? Yer want me to drop dead at yer feet, then yer wouldn't 'ave me around bein' a rotten nuisance to yer.'

'Now did I say that, did I?'

'Boots, I ain't been a nuisance to yer lately, yer know I ain't.'

'I'm not talking about that, I'm talking about you looking after yourself a bit better than you do. Now listen, you're going to get all those nits out of your hair again tonight, you're going to let us scrub your head and oil your scalp. And every night for a fortnight at least, you're going to do it yourself. You're going to wash your hair every night, and you're going to comb and brush it six times a day. Or we will move.'

'Oh, yer wouldn't – Lizzy's me best friend, and I like yer home and comin' in to see yer fam'ly.'

'I know Lizzy's your best friend, but Lizzy doesn't like headlice, Em.'

'Oh.' The penny dropped. 'Oh, she don't catch 'em from me, does she?'

'You'd better think about that. Are you coming in for a scrubbing or not?'

'Yes, I'll come. It's blinkin' cold out 'ere, anyway. Boots, yer don't like me much, do yer?'

'Of course I like you. Would I be out here, walking you up and down in the perishing damp, if I didn't? I'm trying to be a help to you, Emily.'

'Oh, yer so good to me, Boots,' she sighed.

Three weeks later, when Emily was looking cleaner and neater every day, Lizzy said it wasn't me who had cured Mrs Castle's harum-scarum daughter of her slovenliness, it was Chinese Lady. Chinese Lady had talked to her like a fond mother, telling her she could be one of the nicest girls around if she'd only keep herself presentable.

'That cured Emily, just telling her to keep herself presentable?' I said.

'Well,' said Lizzy demurely, 'what really did it was when Chinese Lady mentioned your name. She told Emily you'd always had a soft spot for her, and that you'd said what a pity she never looked anything but ragged and mucky.'

125

'I've got a soft spot for that holy terror?'

'It did the trick,' said Lizzy, prettily smirking. 'You been Emily's hero for months. And she's not been tormentin' you lately, has she?'

'She's not going to start following me about, is she?'

'Only in a protectin' way,' said Lizzy.

'You're barmy.'

'I'm fourteen,' said Lizzy. 'So is Em'ly. You're only sixteen.'

'I can't work that one out.'

'Course you can't, you're not grown up yet. Em'ly and me are.'

'I'll tell Mr Finch that. I'd like to hear what he has to say about it.'

Mr Finch, who had spent his usual week with his Aunt Trudy during the summer and reported her as being livelier than a cricket, spent only a few seconds on thinking about Lizzy and Emily being grown up. Then he said yes, he thought they were both grown up, since Lizzy had already decided what she wanted out of life, which meant she was mentally mature, and that Emily had put aside irresponsible self-neglect, which meant she intended to become a credit to her friends.

'Emily?'

'I think that's what's in her mind. We must both hope she succeeds. I believe her efforts have been inspired by your understanding mother assuring her she has a heart of gold and shouldn't go through life trying to prove she hasn't.'

'And what about Lizzy telling me I'm not grown up myself, even though I'm two years older than she is?'

Mr Finch smiled.

'Clever Lizzy,' he said. 'In implying she's more mature than you are, she's put you in self-doubt about your role as head of the family after your mother. Be prepared, Boots, for her to usurp you.'

'It's all too much for me,' I said.

'The ladies, my boy, are all too much for every man.

126

Our only defence is to look wise and profound, to nod our heads and merely to say yes or no. This can confuse them.'

'Can it?'

'Yes, but not much,' said Mr Finch.

CHAPTER ELEVEN

The winter of 1912 was cold and damp, with sooty smoke rising from the forest of domestic and industrial chimneys. Yellow fog descended on Walworth. Tram headlights peered blindly, and tram bells clanged muffledly. The kerosene lamps hanging in the market stalls shed foggy light over the wares, making blood-red oranges look palely green. Ragged boys and girls used the fog to dart unseen under stalls and grope for what they could snatch from crates.

Chinese Lady suffered spasms of irritation on Mondays, when the washing on the yard line hung limp in the fog. Mrs Castle waddled in one Saturday morning to talk to Chinese Lady about Emily. Fat, heavy and placid-looking, she sat down in the kitchen with a brown shawl over her shoulders and loose hairpins showing.

'That Em'ly,' she said, 'what's come over her ain't 'ardly normal. Taken to doin' 'er own washin' an' ironin' these last Saturdays, she 'as. Won't trust 'er old mum to do it for 'er, she won't – me what's been givin' 'er clothes a good wash nearly once a month at least. I miss sometimes, of course, I ain't got six pair of 'ands. I ain't one to go on at Em, but she's got that fussy lately I don't know that I won't ask 'er dad to give 'er a talkin' to. Know what she just said to me?'

'What?' asked Chinese Lady, who'd been back an hour from her shopping and still had her coat and hat on. The coat might come off, the hat wouldn't.

'"You got to do something about washing-up, about gettin' it done proper, it's always 'anging about in the sink." That's what she said. Me, as if I got time to wash up

128

every cup an' saucer straight away. It's bad enough 'er gettin' so fussy, but when she starts findin' fault with 'er old mum, it's time 'er dad took 'is strap to 'er. But 'e won't, 'e says it ain't right for girls to be walloped, least of all Em'ly. I got so upset about 'er remarks I just 'ad to come in 'ere for a sit-down and a cupper tea. Is Boots goin' to put the kettle on?'

'All right,' I said.

'Yer a real love,' said Mrs Castle, her red, beery face creasing in a kind, fat smile. 'Yer got a nice boy in Boots, Mrs Adams, that yer 'ave. I ain't sayin' I ain't proud of our Em'ly, but what's took 'old of her lately, I don't know. The 'ot water she uses. Always washin' 'er 'air and havin' a bath. She'll wash all 'er 'air off, if she ain't careful, mark my words, an' scrub 'erself in the bath till there's nothing left of 'er.'

'Still, she's looking very nice, Mrs Castle,' I said from the scullery, 'she's looking a credit to you.'

'You sure?' called Mrs Castle. 'I 'adn't noticed about bein' a credit – she don't look 'ealthy to me. Pale as a ghost, she is, sometimes.'

'Clean,' I said to the kettle, sitting on the gas.

'What's that?' called Mrs Castle.

'I said she's a credit to you, Mrs Castle.'

'I dunno about that,' said Mrs Castle, who was puzzled rather than greatly upset. 'Don't you think she's got a bit fussy an' queer, Mrs Adams?'

'She's growing up,' said Chinese Lady.

'So she is, that's right.' I heard Mrs Castle heave with relief. Her chair creaked. 'I never thought of that. All them funny ways she's gettin' – of course, she's growin' up. I'll tell 'er dad that. Where's yer Lizzy?'

'Doin' a little Christmas shopping,' said Chinese Lady.

Lizzy was continuing to blossom and to see Ned every Sunday. And she was carrying herself more and more like our mum, very upright, with her young bosom proudly pouting.

On Christmas Day we had our family party. Aunt

Victoria, graciously head-patting, Uncle Tom, who knew his place – slightly to the rear of Aunt Victoria – and Cousin Vi, who was sweet if rather tepid, called in the morning to drink a little Christmas port with us and to bring presents. They stayed an hour. Aunt Victoria did all the talking so that after they'd gone we weren't sure if Uncle Tom and Cousin Vi had actually been present.

Our party started with Christmas dinner of roast beef and plum pudding, Mr Finch being guest of honour. Chinese Lady had bought several white candles and we had them alight instead of the gas. The parlour fire was blazing. Chinese Lady had had her usual rush of Christmas blood, letting the money run away, and among other things had bought three hundredweight of coal at the mad price of a shilling per hundredweight. Everything that could be pawned had been, except Grandma's tea service. That had to be at home for Christmas Day and Boxing Day.

Mr Finch gave us all presents. There was a new willow-pattern dinner service for Chinese Lady, which made her eyes light up at what the pawnbroker would loan her on it. The old service had suffered breakages over the years, necessitating the use of odd plates. Sammy was given a clockwork train set, Tommy a stamp album of leather, and Lizzy a lovely, warm-looking, plum-coloured winter coat, which fitted her perfectly. A friend, said Mr Finch, had helped him choose it. Lizzy was so overwhelmed her eyes misted up, and she flung her arms around his neck and kissed him. Mr Finch coughed. He gave me a set of Rider Haggard novels, knowing I was an avid reader.

We had all clubbed together with pennies to give him a present, a new briar pipe and two ounces of his favourite tobacco. We had given each other little things from the penny bazaar, and again had clubbed together to buy Chinese Lady a pair of black kid gloves. Lizzy got them from Hurlocks. The gloves retailed at a shilling, a strain on our resources, but Lizzy got them for eightpence, much to

Sammy's relief. Mr Finch's present had cost us almost a shilling.

Mr Finch made a speech of thanks, bringing in Christmases with Aunt Trudy, where he had to sit up straight, and Christmases at sea where the jar of rum was locked away by the skipper after it had been round four times.

There was a lot of food left over from dinner and also from tea, and Chinese Lady said to me in the scullery that it was just as well because it would have to last us the rest of the week. She'd only got a few pennies left in her purse, she said.

I handed her a cup to dry from the sink. We were washing up the tea things. The others were playing young people's games in the parlour.

'What about Wednesday's rent?' I asked.

'We'll have to manage somehow.'

'With a few pennies?'

'Well, your grant might come through early, and so might my pension.'

'Or you could borrow from Sammy again,' I said sarcastically.

'Oh, I never thought of that,' she said. 'Yes, course I could. I only owe him two shillings from the time before.'

'But that was months ago, and you were going to pay him back a shilling a week.'

'I know that, I don't need telling,' she said. 'But there's four of you to feed and clothe, remember, an' the money just runs away, what little we got of it. Anyway, Sammy don't mind waitin' as long as he gets his extra interest.'

'Extra?'

'Well, it was his savings, it's fair he gets an extra penny a week interest when I can't pay him. Now don't start – I can see from the look on your face you're going to say something. Just be thankful Sammy earns all the pennies he does and saves 'em.'

'You'd better get something in writing from Sammy about his interest rates so that when you're put in the poorhouse by your only youngest son you'll know how it happened.'

131

'Well! That's a nice thing to say about your own brother, and on Christmas Day and all.'

'I don't know what comes over me sometimes.'

'Don't give me that kind of lip, my lad, or you'll get a saucepan on your head.'

Boxing Day was bright and crisp, and the Christmas spirit reigned on. Lizzy had a new dress, bought with her small amount of savings. She was in a slight ferment in the afternoon while awaiting the arrival of Ned. She was always like that when Ned was due to call, as if she could never quite believe he was coming on her account, as if it was difficult for her to accept that a handsome young man of eighteen could be seriously interested in a girl of fourteen. Since Ned was obviously very taken with her, I couldn't think why she had these moments of self-doubt.

When I mentioned it to Mr Finch once, he said, 'Boots, my boy, Lizzy has already mapped out her future, but of course it takes two to establish it.'

'Her future? But she's only fourteen.'

'It's no use your harping on that point. Your sister is in love.'

'What, at fourteen?'

'That's still irrelevant.'

'Sorry.'

'Don't be sorry. You're fond of your sister. Lizzy is a lovely girl. Ned's a fortunate young man.'

'But he's not very old himself.'

'Eighteen now, I believe. Four years older than Lizzy. Just right. Lizzy needs to see a man, not a boy. But we mustn't anticipate, Boots. The patterns of life are constantly changing. Our wishes are changed by events, our emotions are changed by time. And even our strictest loyalties can be disturbed, although not so much by events or time as by our relationships with people.'

'Well, yes, that's it. Lizzy can't really know now what she'll want in five years, say.'

'We'll see, Boots, we'll see. Let's hope that all stays

132

right with the world and with Lizzy's enjoyment of life.'

Ned arrived at three on Boxing Day afternoon, his leg perfectly healed now. Lizzy in her new dress was at once told she looked better than Christmas itself. That put warmth into her eyes and calmed her down. Then Ned asked where the mistletoe was, and Emily went into fits of the giggles. Emily had been invited by Chinese Lady to join us for the afternoon and for Boxing Day supper of cold beef, fried potatoes, pickled onions, pickled red cabbage and what was left of the Christmas pudding. Emily was rapturous at being with us.

Ned, an extrovert young man, conducted a theatrical search for mistletoe in the parlour. Emily shrieked with laughter, and Lizzy clapped her hands. There was no mistletoe, however. Nor was there a Christmas tree. Chinese Lady had at least exercised economy there. And the paper chains festooning the parlour and the kitchen had been made by us out of strips of coloured paper.

Ned, giving up his mistletoe search, did not carry the issue further. He was extrovert, but not brash. He treated Chinese Lady with a kind of cheerful respect that did not run to familiarities. Chinese Lady approved of young men being respectful towards family figures like mums and dads. Ned gave Lizzy the respect due to an equal. He teased her, yes, and pulled her leg, but never talked down to her or drew attention to what was fact – that he was a young working man with prospects and Lizzy was still a schoolgirl. That pleased her very much. The street boys called her a schoolkid, which, coming from fourteen-year-old males whom she very much considered kids themselves, might have made her wonder exactly how Ned regarded her. He always gave me the impression that he certainly didn't regard her as just another girl, whether still being educated or not. He talked to her, and in a way that made her blossom and flower. And he never pawed her, not in front of us, and probably not in any case. That was one thing Lizzy wouldn't have stood for. She had our mum's sense of propriety.

Emily was watching them, seeing how he looked at Lizzy, seeing how Lizzy's eyes danced. Emily was amazingly clean and neat. She too had a new frock, bought for her by her fond mum, now reconciled to Emily's strange addiction to hot water and soap. The frock was apple green. It enhanced the dark auburn colour of her hair, now thick and springy. Regularly combed and brushed, it was free of all nits and tangles. It looked rich and healthy, and made her thin face seem all eyes, green eyes.

'Come on, Eliza, let's take a walk,' said Ned, 'I need some exercise after all the groceries we ate at home yesterday. Would you like a walk?'

The day was crisply cold, but Lizzy had a new winter coat.

'Oh, yes,' she said.

'Who else?' said Ned. 'Come on, Boots, you too. And you, Emily.'

'Oh, yer don't want me,' said Emily, 'I can play Snakes an' Ladders with Tommy.'

'I'm not playin' Snakes and Ladders with you,' said Tommy, 'you cheat.'

'Oh, I don't,' said Emily, who did.

'Come on, Emily, stir yourself,' I said, and she jumped up then.

'I'll 'ave to go an' put me coat on,' she said, and rushed out. She still couldn't go anywhere, not even from one chair to the next, without darting or rushing.

Lizzy put her new plum-coloured coat on, and I saw Chinese Lady give her a look of maternal pride. The new coat made Lizzy look like a princess. With it she wore a cream-coloured tam-o'-shanter. Chinese Lady's eye had alighted on it on a market stall. Threepence, it had been, and good as new. Chinese Lady had got it for tuppence. It would last Lizzy ages.

Emily returned with a skip and a jump, wearing a plain navy blue coat and a knitted woollen hat. We went out, walking along Walworth Road to the Elephant and Castle, just for the exercise. Ned and Lizzy walked ahead, hand in hand. Emily kind of pranced beside me. It got on my nerves a bit. She gave me a glance. My expression must have been a bit peevish or sulky, and she must have been a bit telepathic, for her physical jerks melted away and she walked in what Chinese Lady would have said was a more ladylike fashion.

Walworth Road was almost deserted except for the occasional Boxing Day tram and the odd couple of people or so. The bright, crisp day lightened Walworth's greyness. Smoke from chimneys drifted straight up. I thought of Lizzy's paradise. Green grass, open air and a proper bath. Yes, Lizzy would like that, a proper bath, instead of a Friday-night dip in our tin tub. We all took a dip on Friday nights.

Watching Lizzy hand in hand with Ned, I thought her new coat gave her quite an elegance, especially as she had the same kind of upright walk as our mum. Lizzy was a young lady. That was what she wanted to be, a lady. Lice horrified Lizzy. They didn't really horrify Emily.

'You're not sayin' much,' said Emily.

'I was thinking how nice you're looking, Emily. You're doing wonders with your hair.'

'Do yer like it, Boots, now I wash an' brush it?' she said. 'I do it all the time, every day, like you told me to, like your mum said I should. It's not a mess any more, is it?'

'Nice hair like yours shouldn't ever get to be a mess.'

'I didn't know it could feel so good, keepin' it clean and all. And I 'ave a bath very reg'lar, especially Saturday nights when Mum and Dad are at the pub up King and Queen Street. I 'ave it all to meself then. Don't hot water make you feel all dreamy? An' I do all me own launderin', would yer believe, ironin' as well. It feels ever so good, wearin' clean things, especially me drawers and petti. Boots, ain't Lizzy swell in her new coat, don't she look so pretty? And ain't she got the nicest boy? Did yer 'ave a lovely Christmas Day? I wished I could of been with yer. We 'ad Uncle Bert and Auntie Maud come, an' you should of seen the beer bottles. You got such a nice 'ome, Boots.'

135

'It's the same as yours, Emily.'

'Yourn is the best, though. It's—' Emily did some puckered-up thinking, her nose peakily pink with the cold. 'Well, it's more cosy, like. You got a nice fam'ly too. Ain't Lizzy a love?'

I felt quite warm towards Emily.

'Well, you're a love too, Emily.'

'You're 'avin' me on,' said Emily, 'ain't yer?'

I gave her thin shoulders a squeeze.

'No, I ain't, Em,' I said.

'You're givin' me a cuddle, and in the road too,' said Emily, with a giggle.

'It's Christmas.'

'Fancy that,' said Emily.

We sat around the parlour fireside after supper. Chinese Lady said what a pity we hadn't thought of buying some chestnuts to roast. Anything that helped us acquire a well-fed Christmas look had a place in our mum's heart.

Faces glowed in the heat. Coal at a reckless shilling per hundredweight burned and flamed. Lizzy smiled as Ned poked the fire. She liked him making himself at home.

Ned, turning the coals, said, 'By the way, I'm going to learn a lot more about sherry. The firm's sending me to Spain in a week's time, to the place where it's all produced. Jerez de la Frontera, but everyone just calls it Jerez. That's where the name of sherry comes from. The firm says I'm to have an apprenticeship. I'll be there about a year, and I'll learn the language as well as other things. It seems I really do have prospects.'

He was still poking at the coals. I didn't know why he'd chosen to tell the whole family, instead of just Lizzy. I didn't know why he hadn't first broken the news to her. It was obvious he hadn't, for her face was stiff, her eyes on the fire. Chinese Lady looked a little sad.

'Your firm must think a lot of you,' I said.

'Oh, I suppose if they feel you're going to be of real use to them, they've got to see you know all the processes

136

which make the stuff drinkable,' said Ned. 'I've got to get down to things in Jerez – burn the candle at both ends for a year – but everyone at the firm says it'll be worthwhile. Don't think I'll forget you lot while I'm away. I won't. With any luck, I'll walk in on you about this time next year to wish Eliza a merry Christmas in Spanish. What'll you think of that, Eliza?'

'I don't know any Spanish, so I won't know what you're talking about, will I?' said Lizzy, eyes still on the fire. I knew what she was thinking. In going to Spain, Ned was departing from her ordinary world and entering a new and exciting one. Spain. A foreign country that was far beyond her horizons. Different people, different customs, different sights. He would meet Spanish girls with dark eyes. He would grow out of being the young man she knew. He would think Walworth a very drab place, its people much too common.

'My parents said I'd better make the most of it, and I naturally want to,' said Ned, but he didn't seem all that excited about it. He was still fiddling with the poker, a frown on his face. Chinese Lady glanced at me, her expression rueful, and I felt she was thinking what I was thinking, that his parents had probably advised him to concentrate on his prospects and not to be diverted by his feelings for a girl who was only fourteen. I supposed that could be counted as sound parental advice. I wondered if he'd promised them to do that, to forget any diversions that could be rated unimportant in comparison with his career. Such as writing letters to young girls. I wondered exactly what his feelings for Lizzy were.

I'd thought, when talking to Mr Finch, that since she was only fourteen, one couldn't expect Ned to consider that his future was bound up with hers. It was more reasonable to accept she was his girl of the moment. In a month's time, probably, Lizzy would be in the past tense. Lizzy knew it. Her face showed it. And Emily, still with us, was sitting up stiff and straight as if she knew it too.

'Spain,' said Lizzy with a brave little smile, 'imagine

that. It'll be so excitin' for you. You'll come back lookin' like a peccador.'

I could have told her she meant picador, but I didn't. Nor did Ned.

He said, 'D'you fancy me looking like a peccador, Eliza?'

'I don't know, I'm sure,' said Lizzy, staring at her feet, 'I never seen one.'

Chinese Lady was very quiet, and Tommy was puzzled by the change in the atmosphere.

'It ain't dangerous, goin' to Spain, is it?' he asked.

'Well, he won't get eaten,' I said.

'That's all right, then,' said Tommy.

It was worrying, however, when Ned said goodbye a little later, because Lizzy was really not equipped to cope with such a body blow at her age. Her teeth were positively clenched, her eyes unable to meet his. Ned looked quite disturbed.

'Well, Eliza—'

'Yes, it's been nice,' she said muffledly, 'Boots'll see you out. I got to make a sandwich for Mr Finch.'

Mr Finch was out. He sometimes did go out in the evenings, to meet friends, and he was out tonight. He had said he'd be back about nine-thirty, and Chinese Lady had said that as it was Boxing Day she'd like him to have a nice cold beef sandwich when he returned.

'Yes,' said Ned, 'but I'll come and see you the moment—'

'Yes, it's been nice,' said Lizzy again, and left the parlour to go to the kitchen.

I saw Ned to the front door after he had said goodbye to everyone else. Emily had been very stiff and haughty.

'Eliza's upset with me,' he said.

'Well, she's very young.'

'I know that, don't I?' He was suddenly angry. 'I keep being told that by my parents, I don't want you shoving it down my throat as well. I've also been told I've a long way to go before I'm mature. I suppose you can't make too

138

many plans at my age, I suppose things might be different after a year, or even six months. But I can't not go. There aren't all that number of really good jobs about.'

'I'd go like a shot myself,' I said.

'And leave your girl behind, and do nothing for a year except study?'

'I'd have to, I suppose. But how do I know? I'm not going to Spain and I don't have any girl.'

'Fourteen.' Ned muttered the word. 'It beats me.'

'What beats you?'

'Fourteen, you chump. That's what beats me. But I'll be back, Boots.'

'That's what you feel now, that you'll be back?'

'Yes. So keep an eye on Eliza for me.'

Emily came to the front door almost as soon as Ned had gone.

'I'm goin', Boots,' she said, 'it's just fam'ly now.'

'What's just family?'

'What Lizzy's sufferin'.'

'Is everyone daft round here? Lizzy's still a kid.'

'Well, I'm not,' said Emily fiercely, 'an' Lizzy's older than me, so she's not, either. She's got a breakin' 'eart, she 'as. He won't come back again, you know he won't, an' she knows it too. You got to be nice to her, Boots.'

'Goodnight, Emily.'

A few minutes later, with Lizzy back in the parlour, Chinese Lady told Sammy and Tommy to go up to their bed.

Lizzy said, 'No, let 'em stay up a bit longer. It ain't all that late, Mum, and we ain't got to get up for school, it's Christmas holidays. You Sammy an' Tommy, yer mum's lettin' yer stay up a bit. Come on, we'll all play Snakes an' Ladders.' Lizzy wasn't trying any more. She was back to her cockney best.

'I wish you'd speak more proper,' said Chinese Lady sadly.

'What for?' said Lizzy brightly.

'Lizzy, don't take on—'

139

'I ain't,' said Lizzy. 'He's gone, that's all.' She shrugged. 'Oh, well, nice while it lasted. Come on, you kids.'

Lizzy's dream of early paradise had been very brief.

'Never mind,' said Mr Finch the following evening.

'You don't think it matters too much?' I said.

'Oh, it matters a lot to Lizzy, obviously. Would you like a pipe of tobacco, Boots?'

'I haven't taken it up yet, thanks all the same. You don't think it matters as much to Ned?'

'I think he's right to go. I think his firm see him as a very good prospect indeed. They're investing in him. Whether the year in Spain will change his outlook, we don't know, Boots.'

'He won't feel like looking Lizzy up again, you mean?'

'In a year, Boots, perhaps Lizzy won't want him to?'

'I don't know. I don't know anything.'

'Are you sure?' Mr Finch smiled. 'Boys of your age are convinced they know everything.'

'I must be simple, then. I don't know anything. I'd like to be a bit like you. You know such a lot.'

'My guess, Boots, is that the year ahead is a testing time for a young man of eighteen and a girl of fourteen. But guesswork isn't knowledge. What I do know is that our loyalties sometimes conflict with our attachments.'

'Attachments?'

'Our affections,' said Mr Finch.

'In what way?'

'Well, to answer that, I'll refer to my dear old Aunt Trudy, as I often do. She took me in, a miserable orphan, looked after me and brought me up. She's my family, all the family I have. I owe her all my loyalty. But if she and your sister both fell into the Thames, and their only hope was lifebelts, and there was only one lifebelt, could I be sure I'd throw it to Aunt Trudy, perilously aged, and not to Lizzy, heartbreakingly young? Or if it were any of your family? No, I'm not sure I would throw it to Aunt Trudy, I'm not sure who I would save.'

'You'd save both, Mr Finch. You'd throw the lifebelt to one and dive in after the other.'

'Would I? But I can't swim, Boots.'

'You can't swim after having been at sea so many years?'

'A great many seamen can't swim, my boy.'

'Well, I'm jiggered.'

'Quite so, Boots. So, there is Lizzy, very young, and Lizzy seems to have lost her first admirer. We must keep an eye on her.'

'Sammy, how much savings you got?' asked Chinese Lady.

'How much d'yer want?' asked Sammy.

'It's the rent,' said Chinese Lady. 'The rent man's comin' tomorrer. Sammy, have you got eight shillings you could lend me?'

'Eight shillings?' I said. 'But you've got Mr Finch's six, haven't you? That leaves you six short, not eight.'

'I had to use two shillings of Mr Finch's,' said Chinese Lady, 'there wasn't a penny in the house, and there was food and everything. Sammy, can you lend me eight?'

'Well, yer gettin' to owe me a bit, Mum,' said Sammy, and brought a grubby notebook out of his pocket. He thumbed through it. 'Since I loaned yer first time for the rent, yer've 'ad a shilling, then ninepence, then another shilling, and then one an' six.' He examined thickly pencilled figures. 'Yer owe me ten shilling an' sevenpence.'

'How d'you make that out?' I asked. 'She only owes you two shillings from that first grasping loan. The other loans amount to four and thruppence, and she's paid some of that off, hasn't she?'

'Only one and tuppence,' said Sammy.

'That makes she owes you five and a penny,' I said, 'not ten and sevenpence.'

'Oh, yerse?' said Sammy in high dudgeon. 'There's the interest, ain't there? I ain't runnin' no charity, I'd be ruined if I was. Me savings is me business, an' it's between me an' Chinese Lady, ain't it, Mum?'

'Sammy, you sure I owe you that much?' said Chinese Lady.

'I ain't in business to do yer down, Mum,' said Sammy.

'I can't believe I got a Shylock for me brother,' said Lizzy, 'I'm goin' to be sick.'

'Sammy, you got enough savings to loan me for the rent?' asked Chinese Lady, prepared to plunge deeper into Sammy's clutches.

'I got eleven an' fourpence,' said Sammy, 'but yer got to start payin' me back proper, like yer said first time.'

'Where'd you get all that money?' I asked.

'Earned it slavin',' said Sammy.

'You'll end up as a pawnbroker,' I said.

'Yus, I'm thinkin' about it,' said Sammy.

CHAPTER TWELVE

Life went on. Miss Chivers continued to suffer the Witch uncomplainingly, and Mr Finch continued to be a kind and untroublesome lodger. They met every month when Miss Chivers came to Sunday tea, and no two people could have been more circumspect. Not by even a glance could Mr Finch have given the Witch cause to believe he had disgusting male designs on her daughter. Nor by a single word could Miss Chivers have made her chronically possessive mother think she welcomed such designs. She was the most charming of women, shyly virtuous, with a cultured air that really made her totally out of place in Walworth. She would have fitted a little country cottage, but her mother, the old harridan, had been the daughter of a Walworth tailor, and seemed set to live and die in the Place.

Chinese Lady still never knew where the money went to, and there was stuff in pawn that looked like never being redeemed. We made her stop buying Sunday joints and do toad-in-the-hole instead, with corned beef and mashed potatoes on Mondays. She said she'd never be able to hold her head up again, but we told her it need only last until Lizzy and I got jobs. Lizzy never mentioned Ned. But I think she still wanted to be a lady, and pleased our mum by speaking a lot more proper. She decided she wanted to work in a dress shop, if possible. She left school at Easter, when she was on her way to fifteen. Emily also left, and so did I. I was a few months short of seventeen. It was now up to me to repay Chinese Lady for the two extra years I'd spent at school compared with most other Walworth boys. I had passed my exams, and had my matriculation

143

certificate, and I wrote to the head offices of banks. I was given interviews, and forms to fill in, and I then waited for one of the banks to grab me. But it seemed 1913 wasn't a good year for banking, because I only received letters advising me my qualifications had been noted, my application filed and my services, accordingly, would be called on as soon as a suitable position in a branch was vacant. Since Lizzy secured an immediate job with a store called Gamages in Holborn, and in their ladies' wear department – much to her delight – my superior education hardly looked as rewarding to the family as her elementary one.

Chinese Lady and Lizzy were keeping all of us, for my school grant had ceased. Lizzy brought home nine shillings a week and gave our mum six, which induced in Chinese Lady the most reckless rushes of blood.

'Ain't Boots goin' to do no work?' asked Sammy one evening. I'd spent the day looking for jobs in City offices without success.

'Course he is, when some bank comes to its senses,' said Chinese Lady. 'Boots is just waitin' for one of them to wake up.'

'Wake up to what?' asked Tommy.

'His many gifts,' said Lizzy, growing up every day. She was going to be a beauty. And she was acquiring boys, boys from outside the neighbourhood, which was always a sign that the girl in question was going to be more of a winner than others. Lizzy brought strange faces home to Sunday tea. The faces changed quite frequently. She did not appear especially gone on any of them, she only appeared to like having a boy to go about with. Chinese Lady got a little irritated by the way one face succeeded another, and asked Lizzy what she was up to. It wasn't nice, she said, for Miss Chivers and Mr Finch never to know who they were going to meet next.

'They don't mind about me going out with boys,' said Lizzy, 'and it ain't – it's not as if I bring them all home at once to Sunday tea.'

'Good as, in a way,' said Chinese Lady tartly, 'and I

don't want any of our friends or neighbours thinkin' you're turnin' into a flirt.'

Lizzy became fierce at that.

'I'm not a flirt – don't you say I am!'

'Well, all them different boys—'

'Never mind – don't you ever call me a flirt!'

'I'll call you what I think's fittin', my girl.'

'You don't call Boots nasty names, oh, no,' said Lizzy. 'Other boys are slavin' to bring home wages, but you let Boots sit idle day after day.'

'Oh, Lizzy,' said Chinese Lady sighingly, 'Boots is walkin' his feet off lookin' for a job.'

'Well, he still hasn't got one,' said Lizzy. 'All that education and all, all his Lord Muck talk about bankin', and he ends up eatin' us out of house and home.'

'Lizzy, you want me to feed him bread and water till he's earnin'?'

'I'm goin' out in the street,' said Tommy, who didn't like family arguments.

'You finish your tea first,' said our mum.

'I finished,' said Tommy, and made a rapid exit. Sammy sidled out after him. Lizzy, her hot dinner only half-eaten, pushed her plate aside, got up and went to the bedroom. That left just Chinese Lady and me.

'She didn't mean it, Boots. She's just not very happy.'

'I'll go and talk to her.'

'No, leave her be a while.'

I finished my tea, then went to see Lizzy. She let me in, gave me a look and then made a grimace.

'Goin' to dress me down, are you?' she said.

'What for?'

'Oh, I'm sorry, honest – I didn't mean it.' She gave me one of her impulsive hugs. 'It's rotten for you, not havin' a job, but you'll get one soon, you'll see. Only I'm not a flirt.'

'Of course you're not. You've just got a few boys running after you. But you know what Chinese Lady's like. She's always thinking about what the neighbours will say.'

145

'Mr Finch don't think I'm a flirt, does he?' Lizzy was fond of our lodger.

'No, he just thinks you're finding out that there's a lot of fun in life for you youngsters.'

'Youngsters? Listen to you.' Lizzy laughed. She looked very much the ladies' wear assistant in a black dress with white collar and white cuffs. That was her working outfit. She seemed nearer seventeen than just over fifteen. 'Let's go up the West End when I leave work tomorrow,' she said, 'it's early closing. I'll help you look for a job. We just might find one.'

'All right, I'll meet you outside Gamages at about ten past one.'

Emily popped in later. She was still as much in and out of our house as her own. She too had found a job, after a month of nothing. She had tried to follow Lizzy into Gamages, applying for any kind of work they could give her, but with no luck. So she took a job in a bottle-cleaning factory near Waterloo Road. It was a hard slog from eight till six, and a half day Saturdays. They paid her five shillings a week. But her mum only took a shilling from her, and Emily kept the rest. She was still thin and plain, although she did have a wealth of striking auburn hair, and maintained her clean and neat look, without having Lizzy's flair for making the most of the cheapest kind of clothes. She hadn't yet shed the habit of being pushy and noisy, of laughing louder than others, but she was improving, she was calming down in stages. She hung on grimly to her friendship with Lizzy, sharing the company of boys whom Lizzy knew. Whether or not the boys thrilled to that, I didn't know, but it would have made no difference to Lizzy. She was loyal to Emily. They had something in common, though I'd no idea what it was.

I met Lizzy when she came out of Gamages that summer afternoon, and we headed west. Lizzy studied the office buildings along High Holborn, and pushed me into two or three. The answers to my enquiries about a job were very similar.

'Nothing doing, young man.'

'Oh, never mind,' said Lizzy eventually, when we were heading for the Strand, 'let's go into a nice teashop and I'll treat you to tea and a toasted bun. We ain't – we haven't been in a nice teashop since as long as I can remember.'

She made her own choice of teashops, taking me into one in the Strand, almost opposite Charing Cross Station. It was quite select. Lizzy, a giggle in her eyes, framed our word for it with her mouth. Posh. Seated at a table, we awaited the arrival of a waitress. One materialised with a smile. Lizzy looked at me. I'd never given a waitress an order before, and I wasn't sure I ought to now, because it was Lizzy's treat. I couldn't have paid, anyway, I didn't have a bean on me.

'Yes, sir?' said the waitress, a cheerfully plump woman in her forties.

Lizzy, slightly pink because we were being very grand, said to me, with an upper-class take-off, 'You may order me a toasted bun with tea, thank you kindly, Bobby.'

The waitress glanced at her, at the bright brown eyes under Lizzy's everyday working boater, and the waitress smiled.

'A toasted bun for you, madam,' she said, 'and for the young gentleman?'

'I'll have the same,' I said.

'Yes, sir,' said the waitress, and departed.

'You spoke very grand, Lizzy,' I whispered.

'Well, it's so posh in here,' she whispered back, 'I hope they don't charge us for—' She stopped, and her eyes widened. I followed her gaze. We were shyly tucked away in a corner. Lizzy was looking at a couple just leaving the teashop, which was fairly crowded. The couple were Miss Chivers and Mr Finch. In a blue suit, his hat in his hand, Mr Finch was smiling at Miss Chivers as he opened the door for her to precede him into the Strand. Neither of them noticed us. They were looking at each other, and she was smiling too, in her soft, myopic way, her glasses off. They lingered for just a second or two at the door, and then I heard her say, 'Oh, I really must get back.'

Outside, they parted. Through the shop window I saw their hands touch for a moment, and then they went their separate ways.

'Oh, would yer believe,' whispered Lizzy in excitement.

'No, I wouldn't,' I said. 'No, perhaps I would.'

'Ain't it nice, really?' breathed Lizzy, thrilled by the magic of what seemed a secret romance.

'Ain't it just?'

'Speak proper.' Lizzy's eyes were dancing. 'They're courtin', that's what, only they don't want the Witch to know. Boots, supposing they'd seen us, though?'

'I'm glad they didn't,' I said, 'Miss Chivers would've been overcome.'

'We better not say anything.'

'Our lips must be forever sealed.'

Lizzy softly giggled.

'What with Miss Chivers bein' overcome and our lips forever sealed,' she said, 'you sound like a *Peg's Paper* serial. No, but ain't it—' She made a face at herself. 'I'm supposed to speak posh in Gamages ladies' wear. But I don't want to turn into Lady Muck.'

'One Muck's enough in the family, I suppose.'

'No, but isn't it nice, Mr Finch and Miss Chivers goin' courtin' in secret, takin' time off their work to meet?'

'It could give the Witch fifty fatal fits.'

'She's never goin' to let Miss Chivers get married, never,' said Lizzy.

'Not unless lightning strikes and the old hag disappears in fire and smoke.'

Lizzy burst into giggles, then blushed as people looked. The waitress brought our order on a tray.

'Thank you,' said Lizzy.

'A pleasure,' said the motherly waitress. She set the things out and put the bill beside my plate. 'If I may say so, you do make a nice-lookin' young couple.'

She went away with a smile, leaving Lizzy smothering more giggles. The toasted buns, buttered, were luscious, the tea fresh and hot.

'Boots, I met a new boy, the brother of one of the girls at work. He's nice.'

'Well, I suppose we'll get two looks at his face before he sinks without trace,' I said. 'Lizzy, you don't have to be in such a hurry, do you?'

'What d'you mean?' Lizzy was eyeing the teapot, conscious that it was her privilege to pour.

'About finding a boy to get fixed up with when you're only fifteen.'

'Who's talkin' about gettin' fixed up?' whispered Lizzy hotly. 'I'm sure I'm not, so you can mind yer business. Going out with boys don't mean I'm thinkin' of marrying any of them.'

'Sorry.'

'Oh, help, I'd better pour the tea, I suppose.' Lizzy was slightly pink, the teashop looking so posh to us, with the lady customers wearing elegant hats. But she poured the tea bravely and we began to enjoy the toasted buttered buns. 'Anyway,' she went on, 'it's about time you had a nice girl.'

'What, me without a penny in my pockets?'

'A nice girl wouldn't mind about that.'

'I would.'

'You wouldn't if you were common like the rest of us. Boots, isn't the toasted bun scrumptious? Real butter and everything?'

I stole a look at the bill. I nearly fell off my chair. It came to ninepence. Ninepence for just a pot of tea and two currant buns? Lizzy couldn't afford all that, even though she was earning a wage.

'Lizzy, it's ninepence,' I whispered, stricken.

'How much?' breathed Lizzy.

'Ninepence.'

'Oh, crikey,' said Lizzy, and blinked. 'Oh, well,' she said, 'we don't do it every day. I don't mind just for once,

149

Boots, it's like being Lord and Lady Muck. And we can have two cups of tea each. You better pay.'

'Me? I ain't got two farthings to rub together.'

'No, I'll give you the money, silly, and we better include a penny for a tip. You have to in posh places. Oh, wouldn't Chinese Lady like it here, with butter on the toasted buns?'

'As soon as I get a job, we'll treat her,' I said. 'Thanks for my treat, sis.'

'Oh, well, you're not too bad sometimes, you could be worse,' said Lizzy.

Mr Finch called me up to his room on Friday evening.

'Boots,' he said, 'I'm sorry banking's passed you by for the moment. Would you like to apply for a job as a junior clerk with a firm on the wharfside at Blackfriars?'

'I'll apply for anything, Mr Finch,' I said. No one would have thought from the frankness of his look that he had secrets. Lizzy and I hadn't said a word to anyone about him socialising with Miss Chivers in a Strand teashop.

'It's twelve shillings a week,' he said.

'Twelve shillings?' Silver loomed glitteringly before my eyes. 'Twelve shillings?'

'They won't pay more.'

'Oh, I'm not thinking of asking them to. Twelve shillings is a godsend.' It was. It would make me the biggest wage-earner in the family. Chinese Lady would rush about in reckless circles.

'Then present yourself to the manager of the retail distributive department of Weddell's at this address on Monday morning, and providing you're in your usual form I think you'll be asked to start on Monday week.' He handed me a slip of paper. His eyes twinkled at my expression. 'You're good at figures, aren't you?'

'Yes, Mr Finch. Mr Finch, I—'

'Don't embarrass me now. During these last six years, Boots, you and your family have been my friends. Just go and deliver the promising news to your mother.'

'Thank you kindly, Mr Finch.'

Chinese Lady was quite overcome.

'Well,' she said, 'well!'

'Yerse, it's a blessin',' said Sammy.

'Our Mr Finch, he's so kind to us,' said Chinese Lady.

'Yer could treat me to a toffee-apple just fer luck, Mum,' said Sammy. Toffee-apples from the shop in King and Queen Street were two a penny, and the shop stayed open until eight in the evening.

'All right,' said Chinese Lady, almond eyes brightly reflecting her appreciation of God's goodness.

'Get me one too,' said Tommy.

'It'll cost yer,' said Sammy. 'An 'a'penny.'

'Mum's going to give yer the penny,' said Tommy.

'No, I mean you got to pay me an 'a'penny for going,' said Sammy.

Chinese Lady, giving him a penny, said, 'Get two, one each for you and Tommy, but don't let me hear no more about makin' Tommy pay you for going or you'll get your ears boxed, and quick.'

'Crikey,' muttered Sammy, as he went, 'it ain't Christian what they expect yer to do for nothing in this 'ouse.'

'That Sammy needs talkin' to,' said Chinese Lady. 'Oh, Boots, twelve shillings a week – that's nearly what some men earn navvying. We'll be so well off, we won't hardly know how to spend it. You needn't give me more than half.'

'I haven't got the job yet,' I said, 'but if I do, I'd better give you the same proportion as Lizzy.'

'She gives me six, you can give six.'

'No, Lizzy gives you two-thirds of her wages, so I must give you the same. That'll be eight shillings.'

'But you're a boy, you need more than a girl,' said Chinese Lady. 'Boys have to have money in their pockets to pay for things for girls when they take them out.'

'I'm not taking girls out, not yet, so I'll give you eight bob. It's only fair.'

'All right,' said our mum, 'until you get a girl, then.

151

Young men have got to hold their heads up when they're in work, and girls like it when they get treated. Oh, won't Lizzy be glad to hear the news when she comes in?'

Lizzy was out with her new boy, whom we hadn't met yet.

We met him on Sunday, when Miss Chivers took tea with us and Mr Finch made his usual well-rehearsed entrance. Lizzy brought the new face home just before tea was on the table. His name was Martin, and he came from Brixton Hill, where all the big houses were and where some theatre people lived. He was a very good-looking new face, but painfully diffident and mumbling. Lizzy was in full control of him, as with all the boys who had come and gone. There was none of the quite acute nervousness she had shown so often with Ned. She fussed over Martin's requirements at the tea table, positively stuffing him with food. Mr Finch smiled at her perky possessiveness, and Miss Chivers seemed sweetly intrigued, casting her soft, smiling glances at them. She cast not a single glance at Mr Finch, keeping her eyes lowered whenever he and she exchanged their usual kind of polite words. I was far more interested in them than in Lizzy's relationship with Martin, thinking they might just give themselves away by a look or a gesture.

Emily was with us. She was coming in more and more on Sunday afternoons, and Chinese Lady couldn't bring herself not to ask her to stay for tea. Emily viewed Lizzy's new boy with what I thought was frank disparagement, and after tea, when we sat listening to Miss Chivers playing waltzes on the piano, she began to whisper to me.

'Boots, that boy ain't Lizzy's cup of tea, he ain't got one ounce of stuffin' in him. What's she doing, pickin' up such soppy boys like she is?'

'Martin's very nice-looking.'

Martin was sitting on the sofa with Lizzy and looking dreamy, and Lizzy was actually holding his hand. She had never been as gauche as that before in front of the family.

'Look at that,' breathed Emily in disgust. 'Imagine Lizzy being as soppy as he is, when she could have a real manly chap, if she wanted. Look at him, he's just a baby. He ain't no good for our Lizzy. I wouldn't even 'ave him meself, and I ain't ever going to 'ave the pick of what's going.'

'You will when you're really pretty, Em,' I murmured.

'Some hopes,' said Emily, thereby implying she was no longer relying on her facial bone structure to work wonders for her. 'But I'm going to buy meself a nice costume at Gammidges next week. You know, where Lizzy works. She said they got lovely ladies' wear. I got some money saved, I ain't spent hardly anything from me wages.'

'Good for you, Em.' I was watching Miss Chivers at the piano, her glasses on to enable her to read the music, her dark blue Sunday dress flowing over her figure, which I thought very shapely. Mr Finch, standing beside her, was turning the pages of the old music book for her, but without any hint that he desired to do far more for her than that. She did not look up at him, she kept her eyes on the music and nodded each time she wanted a page turned. She gave the impression of being softly committed to the piano and its tinkling sociability.

I heard Emily whisper, 'I hope I can get Lizzy to serve me, I ain't never been in a store.'

'I'd better come with you,' I said.

'Eh?' said Emily.

'To make sure you choose something nice.'

'Boots? Oh, lor luvaduck,' breathed Emily, 'would yer really come with me, would yer?'

Chinese Lady gave our whispering faces a look.

'I'll come,' I said.

'Oh, crikey,' said Emily, 'you're bliss to a girl, you are.'

When Martin said an inarticulate goodbye later, Lizzy gave him a kiss. Chinese Lady looked startled, and also none too pleased. But no one said anything.

I was accepted by Weddell's as a junior clerk, and told to be in the office at eight o'clock next Monday morning. I broke the good news to the family and later to Mr Finch, who gave me a slap on the shoulder and a glass of ale.

'Well done, Boots.' He smiled. 'Well played, my boy.' His twinkle arrived. 'That's what you say, I believe, at the game of cricket.' He shook his head at himself, just for a second. He followed that with a very broad smile. 'Well, let's make life a game. All is at peace with the world, now the silly war in the Balkans is over. Let it remain so, eh? Well played, Boots.'

'You did it for me, Mr Finch, thank you kindly and very much. Mr Finch, excuse my cheek, I'm sure, but it can't really be much fun for you here. I keep wondering why you don't live somewhere just outside London, in a little country cottage, for instance, and perhaps get married. I'm sure with the nice ladies there are around, you could meet your fate quite easily.'

'Meet my fate?' Mr Finch chuckled, his eyes very bright.

'Some lady would love to live in a country cottage with you, I'm sure.'

'Oh, I'm very set in my ways, Boots, and having missed meeting my fate so far, I doubt if it will catch me up. In any case, it's very comfortable here, and very convenient. Perhaps when Aunt Trudy passes on, she'll leave me her little house in the country. She has no children, so who knows? Meanwhile, my home is here, and the Turkish baths, which I enjoy twice a week, aren't very far. That keeps me fit. I'm not yet fat and sagging. And my friends are here, Boots. Friends are important to a confirmed old bachelor.'

But he wasn't old. He was a strong-looking man who couldn't be much over forty. And there was Miss Chivers, of course. Here, he could keep an eye on her. Miss Chivers to me was most desirable. I wondered if she was to Mr Finch as well.

Lizzy looked very much the pretty and competent assistant as she attended to the wants of a customer in the ladies' wear department. And Emily was very much the

154

nervous virgin shopper as she stood as far out of reach as possible, poor girl, while we waited in the hope of getting Lizzy to attend to us. The atmosphere was almost upper-class to us, with the floor actually carpeted and frocks and blouses and coats on palatial display, and dressed dummies looking haughtily elegant.

With Lizzy still engaged, another assistant approached us, a woman of about thirty, with a sweet, gracious and helpful smile.

'Oh, my gawd,' breathed Emily in panic. She had never bought her own clothes before. Her mother had always shopped for her, and in careless fashion, so that Emily had grown up looking as if everything she wore had been made for someone else. Even so, her idea of spending saved-up wages on a jacket and skirt must have come from a sound feeling that a costume would be smart and practical for a young working girl. She would, however, have almost certainly bought the first one offered to her, and probably without trying it on, so agitated were her nerves. She had never been in a place like Gamages, and it seemed, with the approach of the assistant, to be giving her heart failure.

'Buck up, Em,' I whispered.

'Oh, my gawd,' she breathed again.

The assistant, most gracious in her desire to be of service, stopped and addressed Emily.

'Can I help you?' she asked.

Emily cast a look of fright at me. As far as a ladies' wear department was concerned, I was a virgin myself. But Emily needed help.

'This is Miss Emily Castle,' I said, 'and she wishes to look at some costumes.'

The lady assistant seemed enchanted by that. She surveyed Emily. Emily, in a straw hat decorated with a bunch of cherries, and a brown skirt and white blouse, which were clean and neat if nothing else, turned a desperate pink.

'What size does madam wish?' asked the lady assistant.

'Oh, my gawd,' breathed Emily yet again.

155

'Pardon?' said the charming assistant.

'I dunno, I never heard what me size was,' said Emily, who was picking up her aitches better these days. That came from listening to Lizzy's aitches.

'Oh, that needn't be a problem, madam,' said the lady assistant. Emily was nearly falling over at being called madam by so superior a being. The assistant summed her up, and her smile became very kind. 'I think we can make a good guess at size, and if madam has no particular colour in mind—?'

'Brown,' gasped Emily.

'Bottle green,' I said.

'Eh?' Emily looked aghast. 'I'm not going to wear no green. Mum said brown 'ud be nice.'

'You're always wearing brown, Miss Castle,' I said. 'Try bottle green for a change.'

'Are you the young lady's gentleman friend?' smiled the assistant.

'No, I'm Miss Adams's brother,' I said, and nodded at Lizzy, who gave us a little wave.

'Oh, our Miss Eliza. How nice.' The lady assistant's smile was very kind. 'Young madam would like to look at a brown costume, perhaps, and also a green?'

'Well, yes, you can do that, Miss Castle,' I said, and the lady assistant smiled again and led the way.

'What d'yer mean, callin' me Miss Castle?' hissed Emily.

'It's just the thing, in Gamages,' I whispered.

We waited at the counter while the assistant went to a recessed rack on which costumes hung.

'Green don't suit me,' said Emily. 'It's Irish, and them Irish is unlucky with all the trouble they cause.'

'Don't fuss,' I said. 'You've got auburn hair, so green will suit you. Bottle green, that is. I didn't come with you to have you buy something that doesn't suit you. I'll tell you what you look best in.'

'Oh, would yer, Boots? Me nerves are chronic.'

'How much money have you brought?'

'Two pound ten,' she whispered.

156

'That much?' I said, and whistled.

'Oh, ain't it going to be enough? I'll pass out if it ain't and she gives me a look. I wouldn't mind if it was Lizzy.'

Lizzy was still busy.

'You shouldn't need more than thirty bob, if that,' I said.

'Boots, I dunno how I'd manage without yer – yer so nice to me.'

The charming lady assistant seemed to be taking a great deal of trouble in selecting suitable offerings for Emily, although there were several customers requiring attention. Lizzy and two other assistants were doing their best. When she was sixteen, Lizzy would qualify for commission on each sale she made.

Our lady assistant brought the offerings, placing them neatly over the counter. A brown costume lay beside a bottle green one. Emily approached them nervously. Her hand sought mine and gripped it desperately. The assistant began to point out the virtues of the brown costume. It was all right, but it wouldn't make Emily look like the Queen of Sheba.

'Yes, it's nice,' gasped Emily, 'I'll take it.'

'No, you won't,' I said, 'not without considering the green one.'

'They're both very smart, I think,' said the lady assistant. 'Would young madam care to try them on?'

Emily turned crimson.

'Oh, no – I'll just have the one Boots says.'

'Try them on first,' I said.

'If you'll come this way, madam?' smiled the lady assistant, gathering up the costumes.

'No, I ain't going to,' gasped Emily, 'I ain't going to get undressed.' She pulled me aside and whispered, 'Boots, me drawers and everything – a lady like her seeing them.'

'Well, they won't bring the store manager to have a look.'

'Oh, yer cheeky bleeder,' gasped Emily.

'Go and try the costumes on,' I said. I spoke to the lady assistant, who seemed in a quite fascinated state. 'It's just that my friend, Miss Castle, hasn't bought a costume before. How much are these?'

'The chestnut brown is one pound, one shilling and elevenpence, the bottle green is one pound, four shillings and elevenpence. The wool in the green is a finer quality, but the brown isn't inferior. I do recommend you try them on, madam.'

'He says I got to,' said Emily with a resigned blush. She disappeared with the assistant. I might have worried a bit about the state of her petticoat and drawers in the past, but I felt whatever she was wearing now would be clean. Lizzy looked up from trying to please a stout and pernickety lady. She gave me an encouraging smile. The lady assistant reappeared, a little smile on her face.

'Miss Castle has decided she'll need a blouse. She says would you choose one for her.'

'Does it get like this for a married man?' I asked.

'For some married men, Mr Adams,' she said. 'The nicer ones.'

'How much are blouses?'

'Oh, all prices from one and elevenpence to seven and sixpence.'

'Give her a treat. Pick one at about four or five bob.'

'Yes, Mr Adams.' The lady assistant seemed to be enjoying herself. I wondered if Emily was. 'Silk. White? Cream? Ivory?'

'Pale green,' I said.

'I see. You're very determined, aren't you?'

'She's got auburn hair.'

'And green eyes.' She smiled, opened a drawer and delicately ruffled through blouses. She picked one out, a very pale green. She took it to the dressing-room.

Emily emerged a few minutes later. She was pink. The chestnut brown costume looked smart. She was still wearing her white blouse.

'What d'yer think, Boots? It's nice, don't yer think? I'll have it, shall I?'

'Try the green one on first.'

'Oh, yer makin' me suffer, you are,' said Emily, but went, the lady assistant following.

Out she came again, our Emily, and to me the bottle green costume was perfect. Emily looked a picture, and because she was thin and because the lady assistant had taken the trouble to find exactly the right size, she also looked quite elegant. Lizzy, with a moment to spare at last, came across, and Emily stood there, pink and nervous, but very smart indeed. The bottle green was her colour all right. With the long jacket caressing her slim hips, the skirt gracefully draping her thin legs, and the visible V-shaped section of the pale green blouse soft and delicate, Emily was as good to look at as never before. And she had obviously used her handbag comb on her hair. It looked crisp and shining.

'Is it all right, Boots, will it do?' she asked.

'Em'ly, it's lovely,' said Lizzy.

'Grand,' I said.

'Doesn't she look sweet?' said the lady assistant, and Emily stared at her, and a quiver hit her.

'Can I buy it, Boots?' she asked.

'Course you can,' I said. 'Ain't yer grand in it, ain't yer swell?'

Emily laughed in nervous excitement, and the lady assistant took her away to get her changed. More customers appeared, and Lizzy attended to an enquiry about gloves. I wandered around, but retreated in haste when I found myself surrounded by dummies swathed in things like stays and corsets. Emily was paying her bill, the lady assistant having packed the costume and blouse in a white cardboard box and wrapped it in brown paper. Receiving her change, Emily said, 'You been so nice to me.' Emily was always grateful for the smallest kindness these days. Chinese Lady had done the trick with one or two motherly lectures, I thought.

'A pleasure to have served you, Miss Castle,' said the lady assistant.

'I'll come again when I got more savings to spend,' said

Emily, 'it's took me four months to save what I had before I paid for these.'

'We'll still be here in another four months,' said the lady assistant, who seemed to have taken to our awkward, plain-faced Em. 'Bring our Miss Eliza's brother with you again. He has an eye for what suits you.'

Emily gulped.

'Yes, thank you, I'm sure,' she said.

The lady assistant gave me a smile, and we left. Emily scuttled through the store, down the stairs and into Holborn.

'What's the giddy rush?' I asked.

'Oh, I dunno if I'm comin' or going,' said Emily. 'Can we go home now so's I can put me new costume on an' wear it this evening?'

'Lizzy's boy Whatsisname is coming. Shall we all walk up West and see the lights?'

'Oh, crikey, would yer do that with me, Boots, would yer walk up West with me?'

'It'll help you give your new costume an airing.'

'Ain't yer swell?' said Emily. 'You ought to have a nice girl, honest you ought, she wouldn't half appreciate how swell you was.'

We had a nice walk up West that evening, Lizzy with her hand in Martin Whatsisname's. She looked very animated. He looked as if he'd be more comfortable sitting at home with a comic. Emily kept muttering worriedly about Lizzy chucking herself away on a boy who'd lose a fight with a rice pudding.

'Don't get so worked up,' I said, 'Lizzy's only having fun.'

'Crikey, yer call that fun, holdin' hands with a wet leek?' said Emily, who seemed taller and more upright in her proudly-worn new costume. 'Why don't she get a boy more like you now her best one's gone and drowned himself in Spanish sherry?'

'I don't think sisters fancy boys who are like their brothers.'

'Still, ain't she swell, though? Look at her, ain't she swell?'

'So are you now, in your new costume.'

'Oh, would yer come and 'elp me buy more new things when I got more savings?' she asked, as we all stopped to watch upper-class people alighting from carriages to enter a theatre.

'All right, if you're desperate,' I said.

Impulsively, Emily gave me one of her old-fashioned digs. It made me totter. And that made Emily gulp.

'Oh, sorry,' she said.

'I'm starting my job on Monday,' I said, 'so try not to put me in hospital.'

'Oh, yer ain't cross with me, are yer? I didn't mean it. Look, yer can hit me back, if yer like.'

'Not here, Em. Wait till we get back home.'

'Oh, yer so forgivin',' said Emily.

CHAPTER THIRTEEN

The office at Weddell's was out of Dickens. It had a low ceiling, small windows on which Victorian dust still lay, and two long double-sided desks, sloping, with five inkwells on each side. They provided working space for twenty clerks. There were seventeen clerks and three junior clerks, including me. One either sat on a high stool or did one's work standing, if that was more comfortable. There was also an office boy. For the twenty clerks and office boy there was a lav at the rear of the office, with a sink and a gas ring. The latter was used to boil water for morning and afternoon tea, the office boy's job. The hours were from eight until five, with an hour for lunch. That was what they called it, the lunch hour. We had heard of lunch, our family, and even of luncheon. Chinese Lady said the middle classes took lunch and the upper classes took luncheon. I took sandwiches.

The manager's office was adjacent to the general office, and had glass observation panels to enable the manager and under-manager to keep watch on the clerks. No talking was allowed. If anyone broke the rule, the under-manager came out and stared frowningly at the offenders. You had to sign your name in a book on arrival in the morning, and a red line was drawn on the stroke of eight o'clock. The manager's first job, when he arrived at nine o'clock, was to inspect this time-keeping book and to call in, one at a time, any clerks whose names were inscribed below the red line. To be late, even if only by a minute, was to invite a rebuke. To be consistently late was to invite the suggestion that one's talents could be put to better use elsewhere.

Junior clerks called the established clerks Mr Smith or Mr Jones or Mr Whatever. You left the junior echelon after three years service. My job was to summarise, on huge squares of lined and columned paper, the orders for retail shops that were loaded into vans by a night shift. The office was attached to a large cold storage complex for frozen meat and offal. The retail shops in question were butchers' shops, all belonging to a vast organisation called the Union Cold Storage Company, with big interests in South America. The atmosphere of the cold storage complex always managed to seep into the office in winter, when it became freezing and caused the elderly clerks to wear mittens.

The manager was a basically kind chap, about forty-five, but pernickety in his expectation of clerical perfection. Whatever human failings we had outside the office, he disliked us bringing them to work. The first time I was late, after I'd been clerking for a month, he called me in.

'Adams, you were five minutes late this morning,' he said. Whenever one had to sign below the eight o'clock line, one had to write the exact time of arrival.

'I'm sorry, sir, but the trams were all crowded. It took me ages to find room on one.' The trams were crowded every morning between six-thirty and eight, and one had to cope with a terrible pushing and shoving. I explained this to the manager.

'Pushing and shoving?' Mr Barratt looked pained. 'You should form an orderly queue, Adams.'

'I do, sir, but no one else does. Believe me, sir, jungle law prevails at tram stops in the mornings.'

Mr Barratt's pain increased.

'Jungle law?'

'It can get like a charge of elephants, sir.' I was keen to let him see I had a good excuse. I didn't want my twelve shillings a week to be at risk.

'I hope, Adams, you aren't going to bring your feverish imagination to the office. Kindly leave it behind. You must give yourself more time to catch your tram. You must

163

allow for these things. It wouldn't do for you to become a slipshod time-keeper when you've only been with us a short while.'

'No, sir. I'll make sure I don't become that.'

'Very well, Adams. Since you depart punctually at five every evening, kindly see to it that you arrive punctually at eight every morning.'

'Yes, sir.'

'Are you still gettin' on all right at your work, Boots?' asked Chinese Lady, when winter was on us.

'Nothing to it, Mum. It's just figures and additions.'

'Well, it's good practice for bankin', and it's good money too. We're able to have nice meals nearly every day, and nice roasts on Sundays, and Sammy and Tommy both got new boots and clothes – well, nearly new.'

'Have we got anything put aside?'

'We did have a few shillings,' said Chinese Lady, 'but it all went gettin' stuff out of pawn and paying off Sammy what I still owed, though I still got some interest owing to him. Still, we'll manage, and we don't have to go to the pawn like we did. With you and Lizzy both earnin', we never been so well off.'

'If we don't have any savings, we aren't well off.'

'Well, we are, considerin'. Christmas won't be long, and you'll all be able to have nice presents. Boots, I just remembered, a card come for Lizzy. From Spain, would you believe.'

It was November, and Saturday, and I'd just got home from my morning's work. On the mantelpiece, against the tin clock, stood a card. I picked it up. It was a picture postcard of a Spanish bullring. On the back were some pencilled words.

'Hello, Eliza, this is from me still burning Spanish candles at both ends – caramba! It was a scorching summer here – whew. Are you growing up, Eliza? Are you, Eliza? Love, Ned.'

'What's he mean, askin' her if she's growing up?' said Chinese Lady.

'I think he's really asking her if she's forgotten him,' I said.

'I suppose she's over him,' said Chinese Lady.

'Yes, I suppose.'

Lizzy was fancy-free at the moment. Despite having appeared to be well-favoured by Lizzy, Martin Whatsisname had sunk without trace, like all the preceding boys, and she was now going out and about with a girl friend from Gamages. She always took Emily along too. The three of them made a perky and animated trio, and Emily was obviously grateful that Lizzy was still a firm friend, even if my sister's horizons were broadening.

When she arrived home from her long working day that evening, glowing in her warm winter coat that Mr Finch had given her, I pointed out the card that had come from Ned. Lizzy took it down, looked at the picture, read the message, tore the card up and put it on the fire.

'Oh, Lizzy, fancy doin' that,' said Chinese Lady.

'It don't mean anything, that card,' said Lizzy. 'He's probably sent one just like it to every girl he knew. What's for tea? I'm starving, and me and Em are going out with Clara later.'

Clara was the new friend.

'I'm doing fried sausages an' mash,' said Chinese Lady. 'I'll go an' cream the mash with butter and milk.'

'Butter and milk?' I yelled, as she disappeared into the scullery.

'Mash is lovely with butter and milk,' she called back.

'What's wrong with marge, pepper and salt?'

'Oh, leave her be,' said Lizzy.

'Look,' I said, 'if we could only save something she could have a holiday. D'you realise she's never had a holiday? Aunt Victoria and her family have a week at Southend every year.'

'I never thought of that,' said Lizzy more quietly. 'But she wouldn't go by herself, she wouldn't leave Sammy and Tommy.'

'If we saved a decent bit, they could go with her.'

'It's a nice thought.' Lizzy smiled. Working in Gamages ladies' wear was giving her quite an air. On her way to sixteen, she was very much the young lady. 'Still, you ought to get a girl, Boots. You don't want to end up always being mum's boy, do you?'

'Well, I like that, I don't think. Just because—'

'Don't start one of them speeches,' said Lizzy, taking off her hat and coat. Preparing to carry them to the bedroom, she was obstructed by the entrance of Sammy, a vegetable sack in his arms. He bumped Lizzy with it. 'Oh, don't mind me,' she said, 'I like havin' dirty old sacks up against me frock.'

Sammy dumped the sack on a chair. His face was grimy, his jersey dirty.

'What's in the sack?' I asked.

'Apples,' said Sammy. I lifted the sack from the chair and put it on the floor. Sammy looked as if his family was a puzzle to him. Chinese Lady came out of the scullery. Sammy dived into the sack and brought out apples. He placed twelve on the table, laid for Saturday high tea. 'There y'ar, Mum,' he said.

'Oh, they're cookers,' said Chinese Lady, 'I'll make a lovely apple pie for tomorrer's dinner. Where'd you get them from?'

'Down the Lane, under a stall,' said Sammy. 'They said I could 'elp meself from a box wiv specked ones in it, but there's 'ardly no bad specks – yer can see there ain't. Well, only 'ere an' there. Yer can 'ave that lot, Mum.'

'Bless you,' said Chinese Lady.

'It's about four pounds, that lot,' said Sammy, 'but I'll only charge yer thruppence. I sold Mrs Jones some, an' Mrs 'Iggins, an' Miss Chivers. I charged 'em tuppence.'

'And you're charging Mum thruppence?' said Lizzy.

'Well, I'm sellin' 'er more, ain't I? Tommy'll be back soon, Mum. 'E's been tryin' for oranges. I told 'im which stalls was the best to duck under. We're goin' out this evenin' to sell 'em to neighbours.'

'You can't sell rotten oranges,' I said.

'Yer can if they ain't too rotten,' said Sammy, 'I done it before. What's fer tea, Mum?'

'Fried sausages an' mash,' said Chinese Lady. 'You can sit down when you've washed your face and hands. I'm only charging you fourpence.'

'Fourpence? Whaffor?' said Sammy.

'Your sausages an' mash.'

'I ain't payin' no fourpence,' said Sammy.

'Then you can go hungry,' said Chinese Lady.

'Crikey,' said Sammy, 'what a bleedin' sell.'

At which, Chinese Lady boxed his ears so resoundingly he fell over his sack of apples.

He still went out later to sell bruised oranges with Tommy. Lizzy went out with Emily and Clara, and I went out with Charlie and Frank, two ex-school friends of mine. But I spent most of the time wondering why Lizzy had torn up Ned's card so positively. It seemed to me the card had told her he had not forgotten her. Lizzy must simply have gone off him. Well, I'd told Mr Finch that at fourteen she was too young to think about permanent relationships.

Wonder of wonders, Miss Chivers was to have Christmas dinner with us. Wonder of wonders, the Witch had been carted off to hospital the day before Christmas Eve with pleurisy. It was touch and go, Mrs Castle said. Miss Chivers said it wasn't as bad as that. Her mother had a remarkable constitution and was expected to recover.

Miss Chivers dutifully went to see her on Christmas morning. Mid-morning, I answered a knock on the front door. It was Emily. Emily used the latchcord most times and simply walked in.

'Hello – merry Christmas, Em.'

'Oh, yes – merry Christmas – an' this is for you, Boots.' She pushed a little solid packet into my hand and fled. I opened it. I stared. It was a pocket watch and must have cost her all of six bob. Its case shone like gold, its black figures clear on its white face, its time correct and its tick steady. I went and knocked on her door. Mrs Castle opened it, looking red-faced and blowsy, but kind-hearted.

'Well, look who's 'ere,' she said, giving me a plumply fond smile because it was Christmas.

'Merry Christmas, Mrs Castle. Is—'

'Aincher growin' tall and all?' she said. 'I seen yer all of a puny babe, now look at yer, all of a young man.'

'Can I speak to Emily?' I said. Somehow, I didn't think I'd let on that Emily had spent a lot of her hard-earned money on me.

She turned.

'Em'ly! Boots is 'ere to see yer, to give yer a Christmas kiss – Em'ly!'

Emily came out of the kitchen.

'You don't have to wake the dead, Mum,' she said.

'Wait, I'll get the mistletoe, I know we got some somewhere, only I ain't 'ung it yet.' Mrs Castle hefted her heavy way to the kitchen, rummaged around and reappeared, a sprig of mistletoe in her hand. In the passage, which her fulsome bulk seemed to make a small and crowded place, she held the sprig over Emily's head. 'There y'ar, Boots,' she beamed, ''elp yerself.'

Emily, far from thrilled, said, 'I wish you'd act yer age, Mum.'

'Oh, yer shy,' said Mrs Castle fondly, 'it's 'cos I'm 'ere. Well, I'll leave yer to be cosy an' private.' She went back to the kitchen and said loudly to Mr Castle, 'Boots is givin' Em'ly a mistletoe kiss.'

'No 'arm in that,' said the fruity voice of Mr Castle, 'but just leave 'em be, old girl.'

'Come in 'ere,' said Emily, looking uncomfortable, and took me into the parlour. There were a few paper chains hanging, and some bottles of beer stood on a table. And the room looked as if a good tidying-up was long overdue. 'I'm doin' it over this mornin',' said Emily. 'It ain't much at the moment, is it? But Mum don't seem to have a lot of time.'

'It's nice enough,' I said. 'Emily, this watch—'

'Oh, it's all right, isn't it?' She seemed anxious.

168

'Emily, you can't give me something as expensive as this.'

'Yes, I can.' Her eyes darted and flickered. 'You been so nice to me, and I ain't always been very nice to you, I been a little Turk sometimes – oh, not lately, not since I been grown up. Is it a nice watch?'

'It's too nice for me. The money you must have spent on it.'

'Oh, I got me savings. You'll keep it, won't yer, Boots, as long as it's all right for you?'

'Emily, it's grand.'

Her flickering eyes travelled over the furniture. She pushed back a curling strand of thick, clean hair.

'I don't want nothing from yer, Boots, honest. You been nice to me in a special way, you made me be a help to meself and keep me clothes all clean. And me 'air – hair. Just as long as you like the watch—?'

'I like it very much, Em.'

'Well, happy Christmas, then,' she said, and picked up a duster and ran it along the top of the sofa.

'Have you got friends and relatives coming today?' I asked.

'Just Uncle an' Auntie, same as usual. They'll have a nice booze-up with Mum an' Dad.'

'Well, you don't want a booze-up, do you? If your mum and dad don't mind, why not come and join us after your Christmas dinner? We'll be having a cup of tea and Christmas cake at half-past four and Christmas supper later. Want to come in, Em?'

Emily turned, her face flushed.

'Oh, could I, Boots, could I? Will yer mum mind if I do? My mum won't. She an' Dad'll be havin' a knees-up with Uncle and Auntie.'

'Come in after dinner, then.'

'Oh, Christmas Day with all of yer, ain't that lovely?' Emily's green eyes shone. 'I won't be no trouble, honest.'

'Trouble? You're past all that – or you'd better be. The watch is grand, Em. Thank you.'

I told Chinese Lady I'd invited Emily.

'You sure you want Em'ly here Christmas Day?' said Chinese Lady.

'Well, she's in and out the rest of the year, so she might as well be in and out Christmas Day. And she's not like she was. Lizzy's growing up fast, so Emily is determined she's not going to be left behind. Look what she's given me for a Christmas present, by the way.'

Chinese Lady gaped at the watch.

Lizzy said, 'Did you give her a kiss for it?'

'I gave her an invitation to join our party.'

'You could have give her a kiss as well.'

'She wasn't keen on that.'

Lizzy laughed.

Miss Chivers came in a little while before dinner was put on the table, and we all wished her a merry Christmas, and she said oh, how lovely and warm our kitchen was. Chinese Lady, flushed from the heat of ovens, asked how she had found her mother, and Miss Chivers smiled gently and said she was much the same.

'Her pleurisy's much the same?' asked Chinese Lady.

'Oh, no, that's improved,' said Miss Chivers, 'it's her mania that's much the same.'

'Her anaemia?' said Chinese Lady.

'Mania,' I said. It was the first time Miss Chivers had ever made any reference to the Witch's chronic tendency to make her life a misery.

'Oh, I meant anaemia,' said Miss Chivers confusedly. 'Do forgive me. And do let me give you these.'

There was a Christmas present for each of us. There were gloves for Lizzy and me, a toy each for Sammy and Tommy, and handkerchiefs for Chinese Lady. Mr Finch had already handed us gifts. We had been prepared for that, and the family had bought him carpet slippers, Lizzy having got them at a discounted price from Gamages. Chinese Lady had thought we ought to be prepared for Miss Chivers too, and Lizzy had rushed out late on

170

Christmas Eve to the chemist's shop and bought her some Yardley's lavender soap and scent. We had all contributed, Tommy with relief at finding a penny to spare, and Sammy with disgust at the unexpected strain on his hoard. Handing over two halfpennies, he had said, 'I 'ope this ain't goin' to be reg'lar.' Chinese Lady had said what a good job we were richer now, or she'd have had to go to the pawn, and on Christmas Eve too.

Miss Chivers seemed enchanted with her gift. I thought she looked lovely, her hair softly shining, her deep blue dress softly caressing her, her eyes framed by long thick lashes. Mr Finch came down and wished her a very happy Christmas, and Miss Chivers gave him the gentlest of smiles and said how very nice it was to be with all of us.

We were seven at Christmas dinner, and Chinese Lady begged Mr Finch to do her the honour of carving the huge rib of roast beef. He felt the honour so much that he made a speech while carving, which I thought very sophisticated of him. We all had enormous platefuls of food, and Miss Chivers smilingly declared that if she managed to finish hers she would end up as big as a balloon.

'Oh, we'll tie yer down, Miss Chivers, so's yer don't sail orf,' said Tommy.

Miss Chivers laughed.

'This is a banquet, Mrs Adams, a banquet,' said Mr Finch. 'Miss Chivers, may I pass you the gravy boat?'

'Thank you,' said Miss Chivers, 'how kind everyone is.'

Lizzy's eyes met mine across the kitchen table, and a little smile danced.

The range fire glowed, the kitchen was warm, knives and forks became busy and Mr Finch entertained us with sea stories. At the end, when Christmas pudding with hot custard had been consumed, Sammy groaned.

'I'm bustin', I am,' he said, 'I ain't never felt more bustin'.'

'Do speak proper,' said Chinese Lady.

'Yes, Mum,' said Sammy, 'but you done us real swell.'

'I second that,' said Mr Finch.

'I third it,' said Lizzy.

'I fourth it,' I said.

'May I fifth it?' smiled Miss Chivers.

'What'll I do?' asked Tommy.

'You say passed unanimously,' I said.

'I'm not sayin' that,' said Tommy, 'it don't sound nice. I'll second it, like Mr Finch done – no, can't I first it?'

'Sammy firsted it,' said Mr Finch gravely.

'Well, all I can say is Mum did do us swell,' said Tommy.

'Passed unanimously,' said Miss Chivers gently. 'Mrs Adams, thank you so much for a perfectly lovely dinner.'

'Oh, I'm real pleasured,' said Chinese Lady.

'I now suggest,' I said, 'that me and the kids clear away and wash up.'

'Me?' said Sammy.

'Yes. You're one of the kids.'

'All right,' said Sammy, 'I'll 'elp for tuppence.'

'It's Christmas,' said Lizzy.

'All right,' said Sammy, 'just a penny, then.'

'All right,' I said, 'as it's Christmas.'

Emily joined us at four o'clock, when we had transferred to the parlour. She arrived wearing her bottle green costume with the pale green blouse, her hair as burnished as Lizzy's. She really did look elegant, and I thought what a pity that despite her big green eyes, her thin face, pointed chin and peaky nose made her such a plain girl. Miss Chivers told her she looked lovely, and Mr Finch told her she reminded him of his romantic youth, when he mooned mournfully about in unrequited love for a young lady who lived near his Aunt Trudy.

'Oh, yer kiddin' me, Mr Finch,' said Emily.

'No, no, on my honour, Emily,' smiled Mr Finch.

'Such a lovely costume, Emily,' said Miss Chivers.

'Boots chose it for me,' said Emily, 'at Gammidges, where Lizzy works.'

'Then Boots is a young man we ladies must favour,' smiled Miss Chivers. 'The colour is perfect for you, Emily.'

172

'Oh, you going to take him shoppin' with you next time you buy new clothes, Miss Chivers?' said Emily ingenuously.

'I accept,' I said, at which everyone laughed, except Emily, who had asked the question quite seriously, and Sammy, who thought it all sounded barmy.

We had afternoon cups of tea, with Christmas cake, and then played games. Lizzy, with a teasing smile, eventually suggested Postman's Knock.

'Oh, crikey, not that soppy game,' said Tommy, 'you 'ave to do kissin'.'

'Don't think you'll have to do it with me,' said Lizzy.

'But, Lizzy, you only got Mr Finch,' blurted Emily, 'you—' She blushed and stopped.

'Well, you've got Boots and Tommy and Sammy *and* Mr Finch,' said Lizzy.

'It'll cost 'er sixpence if she gets me,' said Sammy.

'Lizzy, you need more people for playin' Postman's Knock,' said Chinese Lady.

'There's eight of us,' said Lizzy, 'that's enough.'

'I'm not playing,' said Chinese Lady.

'Yes, you are,' said Lizzy, 'and it won't matter if you get one of the boys, you deserve a kiss from all of them, especially at Christmas.'

'I second that,' said Mr Finch.

'You go out first, Em'ly,' said Lizzy.

Emily said, 'Oh, no, let someone else be first.'

'All right, eeny meeny miny mo,' began Lizzy, and ended up pointing at Chinese Lady. 'Out you go, Mum.'

'Can't Tommy go?' said Chinese Lady, comfortably ensconced beside the fire.

'It's you, Mum, you, Mum!' shouted Tommy and Sammy.

'I don't know, I'm sure,' said Chinese Lady, 'if I've got to play this kind of game at my age, it's as well Christmas comes but once a year.'

But she went out very gamely and waited in the passage. Lizzy numbered the males off. One, two, three, four. Mr

Finch was numbered three. Chinese Lady's favourite number was three.

'What number, Mum?' she called.

'Three,' called Chinese Lady, of course.

'Mr Finch, Mr Finch!' cried Emily, Tommy and Sammy, and Miss Chivers, looking very shy and retiring, smoothed her dress over her knees and studied the effect shortsightedly.

Smiling, Mr Finch said, 'One must play the game in the right spirit, eh, boys?' Lizzy opened the door for him and he went out to our waiting mum.

'I 'ope Mum don't box 'is ears,' said Sammy.

The door opened and our mum returned, looking quite herself.

'Spirit all right, was it, Mum?' I asked.

'I'll have a little drop of port,' said our mum.

I poured her some while Lizzy numbered the ladies off, one two three four. Miss Chivers was number three.

'What number, Mr Finch?' sang Lizzy, pretty as a picture.

'One,' called the deep voice of Mr Finch.

'Lizzy, Lizzy, you, Lizzy!' cried Tommy.

'Goodness me,' said Lizzy demurely, and tripped out. Miss Chivers gave me a smile.

'Isn't Lizzy growing lovely?' she said.

'Oh, she's grand,' said Emily, answering for me.

Mr Finch came back, and I took over the job of numbering the males for Lizzy.

'What number, Lizzy?' I called.

'Four,' said Lizzy.

'You're the lucky one,' I said, 'you've got Sammy.'

'I don't want him.'

'Shall I sell yer my go for tuppence, Mr Finch?' asked Sammy.

'Done,' said Mr Finch, 'tuppence is the bargain of the year.'

'Sorry, not allowed,' I said.

'All right,' said Sammy, 'but I ain't goin' to kiss 'er. I'll

174

give 'er a tickle, that's what I'll do. Can I give 'er a tickle, Mum?'

Chinese Lady, fortified by a little port, said, 'Well, it is Christmas and Christmas is supposed to be fun for the young.'

Out Sammy went. Two seconds later, the passage resounded to Lizzy's shrieks. Emily nearly cried with laughter, and Miss Chivers seemed to have eyes full of soft delight. Chinese Lady twinkled.

Lizzy came flying in.

'Oh, that Sammy,' she gasped, 'can't you sell 'im, Mum?'

'When Christmas is over,' said our mum.

The game continued. Lizzy numbered the ladies, Sammy called number four, and number four was Miss Chivers.

'Oh, my goodness,' said Miss Chivers.

'Come on, Miss Chivers,' said Lizzy, 'and give him a wallop for me.'

'Oh, heavens,' said Miss Chivers, 'I really don't know, I've never played Postman's Knock – oh, dear.'

'With Sammy, you'll only have to stand up to a good tickling,' I said.

'Oh, Boots.' Miss Chivers looked confused.

'Well, ain't yer comin', whoever yer are?' bawled Sammy from the passage.

'When faced with the unknown, Miss Chivers, one must be brave,' said Mr Finch.

Miss Chivers suddenly smiled.

'Very well, out into the unknown,' she said, and out she went. Sammy came back in a few moments later, a grin on his face.

'Did yer get a kiss, Sammy?' asked Emily.

'Ain't telling,' said Sammy, and Lizzy numbered all the males off again.

'What number, Miss Chivers?' she called.

'Two,' said Miss Chivers.

'Boots, it's you, Boots!' yelled Tommy.

'Oh, my goodness,' I said, and Mr Finch roared with laughter, and Emily giggled her head off.

I went out. Lizzy closed the door on us. In the gaslit passage, Miss Chivers smiled at me.

'It's all right, we'll just pretend,' I said.

She laughed very softly.

'But it's Christmas, Boots, and all such fun,' she said, 'and you're all so sweet.'

And she kissed me. She put a soft mouth to mine, she put her soft bosom to my chest, and her mouth pressed. It was a warm and generous kiss, a loving kiss as far as I was concerned, and it lingered.

'Well, I never,' I said.

'Now you have to kiss me, don't you?' she said. She looked lovely.

'Good idea,' I said, and took my turn. Her mouth was so good, so warm, so lingering. Her bosom was like velvet cushions.

'Oh, you sweet boy,' she murmured. 'Now you stay, don't you, and I go back.' She returned to the parlour, and I heard her say, 'One can survive the unknown.'

'Oh, ain't it a lovely giggle?' said Emily, who had been left out so far. The old Emily would have created about that.

Lizzy closed the door, then called to me, asking what number I wanted.

'I'll try Emily,' I called back.

There were yells at this.

'No, you got to call a number,' said Lizzy.

'Two, then.'

'Em'ly, Em'ly!' yelled Tommy, and Emily came out and the door closed.

'Oh, lawks,' said Emily, and dropped her head.

'Well, come on, Em.'

'You don't want to kiss me,' she said.

'If you mean you don't want me to, I'll give you a tickle instead.' I put my fingers to her ribs. Emily stiffened, her thin body going rigid.

176

'Oh, I'll scream,' she gasped.

'Kiss or tickle?'

She lifted her head. She was rosy red. I kissed her on her mouth. Emily had a very nice mouth. She gurgled, quivered, jerked and floundered.

'Oh, crikey,' she gasped.

'It wasn't too painful, was it?'

She drew a breath and looked up at me. Her eyes were a lustrous, shining green.

'Oh, Boots, ain't Christmas grand in your house?' she said.

The game went on for a little longer and ended when Mr Finch was out in the passage and called Miss Chivers's number.

'Dear Lizzy, I think not,' she said gently.

We all knew there was the Witch to consider. It might reach her ear, it just might, that her daughter had been kissed by Mr Finch during Postman's Knock.

We enjoyed a hearty supper and then some rousing music hall numbers on the piano, with all of us singing. Not until midnight did Miss Chivers and Emily depart.

Emily said, 'Oh, you give me such a lovely Christmas, Mrs Adams, thank you ever so much – you got a family that's blessed with overflowin' goodness.'

It was quite a speech from Emily.

And Mr Finch, just before he retired upstairs, simply said, 'Mrs Adams, Emily was right.'

I had something on my mind on Boxing Day. I remembered what it was. Ned had said a year. He had said last Boxing Day that he might walk in this Boxing Day. But it passed without any sign of him. I mentioned him to Lizzy.

'I thought he might have come,' I said.

'Who did you say?' asked Lizzy, straight-faced.

'Ned.'

'Don't be daft,' said Lizzy.

'But he did say—'

177

'Oh, sometimes you ain't got as much sense as Sammy, even if you are the eldest,' said Lizzy, near to angry irritation. 'D'you think anyone who's spent a whole year in Spain is ever going to be seen in Walworth again? He won't even think much of his home in Herne Hill. So leave off about him.'

'All right, sis.'

'That game of Postman's Knock was much more interestin' than someone who's gone for good.'

'Why was it?' I asked, remembering Miss Chivers kissing me and me kissing her, and the warm pressure of soft, lingering lips.

'Well, didn't you realise I suggested it to see what would happen if Mr Finch an' Miss Chivers had to kiss?'

'We wouldn't have seen anything, not with them out in the passage.'

'No, but it would've been interestin' to see how long they stayed out there, only they avoided it, didn't they? She wouldn't go.'

'That was because she didn't want the old Witch to hear about it.'

'I bet she didn't dare let Mr Finch kiss her in case she was overcome,' said Lizzy with a smile.

'Overcome?'

'With passion,' said Lizzy, and laughed.

'Now who's being daft?'

'Not me,' said Lizzy. 'Mr Finch kisses lovely.'

'So does—' I stopped. 'So does Emily, would you believe.'

At the office, New Year was the time when clerks were notified of wage rises. They were called yearly increments. But one didn't qualify if one was a new clerk who hadn't been there a full year. The manager, Mr Barratt, explained to me that providing my work continued to be satisfactory, my reward would come next New Year. He was kind enough, in his well-fed portliness, to buck me up by saying 1914 was expected to be a better year for business than 1913.

'But times are still hard, Adams. By the way, I'm told you

talk a lot when you arrive in the mornings. You're not paid for that, you know, so don't let it become a habit.'

'I only talk up to eight o'clock, sir. I usually arrive about ten to.'

He seemed a little shocked that I was disputing the matter.

'My information, Adams, disagrees with that.' He got all such information from the under-manager, of course. The under-manager's starting time was the same as the clerks', eight o'clock. The under-manager was also out of Dickens. Uriah Heep. 'Return to your work.'

I went back to my desk to get on with earning my much-wanted twelve bob a week. The office boy was taking orders for hot toast. He was allowed to slip out and get it from a nearby cafe. The clerks ate it with their morning tea, and it cost a penny a round. I saved my pennies by eating Chinese Lady's rock cakes, and she also provided me with sandwiches for my midday meal. I always went out and ate them in a churchyard or somewhere else where there was a seat. For company, I usually had Sid Nicholls, another junior clerk.

'You got a girl, Adams?' he said one day.

'I know girls, I haven't got any of them.'

'You better come an' meet my sister, then. I think she might fancy you.'

'What makes you think that?'

'She likes lah-di-dah blokes.'

'I'm not lah-di-dah, faceache. I can't afford to be. We're bleedin' poor at home, I can tell you. We're in and out of pawn like—'

'Like a sailor with a tart?'

'How do I know? I don't know any sailors, or any tarts.'

CHAPTER FOURTEEN

Four days into the New Year, a Christmas card from Spain arrived for Lizzy. In it, Ned wished her a happy Christmas, with love. It upset Lizzy.

'I wish he wouldn't, he knows it don't mean anything and so do I,' she said, and put it on the fire. Chinese Lady sighed.

'You haven't been to Sunday church lately, Lizzy,' she said. 'Nor have you, Boots.'

'Sundays are my only full free days,' said Lizzy, 'I don't have time for church.'

'You should make time, so should Boots. It's not right to think that now you both got jobs you don't owe nothing to God.'

'All right, we'll go next Sunday,' I said.

'I'm not,' said Lizzy, 'I got my laundry to do.'

Chinese Lady's lips compressed. Lizzy laundered her underwear herself now, like Emily had been doing for months. Emily did hers because of her mum's indolence. Lizzy did hers for a different reason. She washed it on Sunday mornings and ironed it Sunday nights. It was because she was a private and fastidious person. But as far as Chinese Lady was concerned, it was because her own laundering efforts weren't good enough for her only daughter. A little acrimony was creeping in.

'I can do your laundering,' she said.

'No, I'd rather do it myself,' said Lizzy.

'I don't do it good enough, I suppose,' said Chinese Lady.

'Mum, I just like doin' it myself,' said Lizzy.

'Your dad never complained when he was home, and he

180

was that fussy he could even find fault with a Chinese laundry. He never found fault with me.'

'Mum, I'm not finding fault. As if I would.' Lizzy squeezed our mum's shoulders, but Chinese Lady still looked put out.

'What's going on in the scullery?' I asked. Grating metallic noises had been going on for a while.

'It's Sammy,' said Chinese Lady, 'he's making holes in cocoa tins.'

Sammy came in then, placed a cardboard box full of pierced cocoa tins on the table, and lifted a businesslike face to our mum.

'Can I 'ave some of the rags, Mum?' he asked.

'You know where they are,' she said. An old wooden box in the scullery was always full of rags. Chinese Lady never threw even the tattiest clothes away. She cut them all up into rags for cleaning and polishing, and for dishcloths.

'What's your new fiddle, Sammy?' I asked.

'It ain't a fiddle,' said Sammy, 'it's business. I'm makin' winter-warmers what'll be fog-lighters as well.'

'All right, let's hear the worst. What for?'

'Whaffor? People who need 'em, of course. I stuff 'em wiv rags dipped in meffs—'

'Meths?' said Chinese Lady sharply. 'Now don't you go playin' about with meths, my lad, you'll set fire to the house and us as well.'

'Course I won't,' said Sammy, 'I got more sense than that. When I light the rags, they burn just right in the tins. I make 'andles out of long bits of wire, and the tins keep yer warm, an' they glow too, so's other people can see yer comin' in the fog.' Outside, Walworth was shrouded in thick yellow fog. 'Tommy and me's goin' out to sell 'em at tuppence each. I'm givin' Tommy a farving for ev'ry one 'e sells.'

'Couldn't you give him something lower than a farthing?' I asked.

Sammy considered it.

'There ain't no arf farvings,' he said, 'I better give 'im an 'ole one.'

181

'You're not going out selling them tonight,' said Chinese Lady, 'you'll get lost in the fog.'

'No, he won't,' I said, 'he can light one of his lamps.'

'Don't put ideas into his head,' said our mum, 'he's got too many there already.'

'All right, I'll stuff 'em wiv rags and sell 'em tomorrer,' said Sammy.

And he did. He and Tommy knocked on people's doors and out of a score of dads and mums found eight mugs. Tommy made tuppence on the deal, and Sammy made one and tuppence, less tuppence for the meths. Tommy was also a mug.

Lizzy was blossoming into a very ladylike ladies' wear assistant, and was given a rise to bring her wages up to ten bob. It wouldn't be long before she was sixteen and earning commission on her sales. She acquired a new boy at the end of February, the brother of her colleague Clara. His name was William Something-or-other. He was a bright-looking young blood, and as lively as a cricket compared with the vanished Martin Whatsisname. Unfortunately, his liveliness didn't abate when he was drinking a cup of tea, and it got on Chinese Lady's nerves the very first Sunday that Lizzy brought him home. One of the several things our mum was rigidly unyielding about was the correction of noisy eating and drinking, and when Sammy was younger he had been consistently banished from the table for slurping and slopping. William slurped like a rhinoceros at a muddy pool. Lizzy didn't seem to notice, or at least to let it worry her, which was strange, because of her fastidiousness. Perhaps the fact that William was tall, extrovert and manly-looking was more important to her than his noisy relish at the tea table.

In March, on the second occasion when Lizzy brought William home for tea, Miss Chivers was due for her monthly visit. The Witch had come out of hospital in January and was more the screeching old hag than ever, giving the street kids earfuls of complaining abuse from her window. And back it came, according to those who heard it at about half-past eight in the mornings, when Miss Chivers left for her work.

'You got your glasses on, Elsie?'

Lizzy showed William into the parlour, then came into the kitchen, where Chinese Lady was slicing bread and trying to stop me buttering some slices and putting marge on others. Interference, she called it.

'William's here,' said Lizzy, ravishing in a new Sunday hat, acquired at a privileged price from Gamages. 'Is there fruit cake? He likes fruit cake.'

'You didn't say you was bringing him to tea,' said Chinese Lady, obviously upset at the thought of him slurping away in front of Miss Chivers and Mr Finch, especially as our lodger had been working long hours on the river of late and needed a bit of civilised behaviour at a tea table.

'I brought him before,' said Lizzy, 'so I can bring him again, can't I?'

'Miss Chivers is comin',' said Chinese Lady.

'I know that,' said Lizzy, and looked about to take sensitive offence. 'You're not trying to say William's got measles, are you?'

'Of course not,' I said, 'Mum's just pointing out Miss Chivers and Mr Finch already make seven.'

'Oh, really?' Lizzy was stiff. 'Isn't William stuck-up enough for you? You're gettin' worse, you are. All the girls round here laugh themselves silly at you – you're Lord Muck in person now you're a clerk—'

''Ere, Lizzy,' said Sammy, barging in.

'What do you want?' asked Lizzy fretfully.

'There's a bloke come,' said Sammy with a grin, ''e says 'e's a Spanish peccador, an' can 'e come in?'

'What?' Lizzy looked stunned.

'It's 'im, your nice feller,' said Sammy. ''E's come back and 'e don't arf look swell.'

A silence descended. Lizzy's colour drained. She paled, she really paled. And Ned came in then.

'Hello, family – hello, Eliza,' he said, and Lizzy stared at him. Her colour rushed back, flooding her, and I saw her teeth bite on her bottom lip. Ned was nineteen, coming up for twenty. He was tall and brown and smiling, his hat off, his grey overcoat unbuttoned. He looked lithe and fit and, compared with all her other boys, very mature. His eyes seemed fascinated by the way Lizzy had advanced in shape and stature. He had left a girl. He had come back to a young lady. 'You really have grown up,' he said.

They were looking at each other. Lizzy was silent and trembling, her colour going and coming. Not far off sixteen, she was a very promising ladies' wear assistant, but she was gulping like a schoolgirl and still no words came. And I felt I knew then what had made her think a year's absence in Spain meant the end of her relationship with Ned. She had never been able to believe he could be seriously interested in a schoolgirl.

Chinese Lady interceded.

Quite calmly, she said, 'After all this time, Ned, you'll stay to tea, won't you?'

'If I'm not to be chucked out, yes,' said Ned. 'Are you chucking me out, Eliza?'

Lizzy managed to speak then.

'It's nice of you to come and see us again,' she said with an effort, 'but my young man William is here.'

Ned sighed, then smiled resignedly.

'Well, that had to happen, I suppose,' he said. 'Kind of you, Mrs Adams, but I'd better not stay.' He gave Lizzy a wry little grin. 'I might tread on William's face. My word, you do look good, Eliza. Mrs Adams? And Boots – so long. Lots of luck.'

He left without any fuss. Lizzy stood quite still, her lips trembling, her eyes blinking.

'Have you done the right thing, Lizzy?' asked Chinese Lady sadly.

Lizzy looked at me.

'Well,' I said, 'who's William, anyway? He's only the latest in your stamp collection.'

Lizzy came alive. She laughed. She turned and ran, out of the house, flying in pursuit of Ned. I told Sammy to ask William to come out here, as I wanted a word with him.

I had a word with him. Privately, in the scullery.

'So you see,' I ended, 'it'll only be embarrassing, especially as they'll probably get engaged later this year.'

'Well, I tell you,' said William, 'I don't like being a bleedin' gooseberry, but don't I get any tea, neither?'

'That wouldn't be fair,' I said. 'Have tea with me in the kitchen. Our mum won't mind.'

'All right, you're on,' he said, 'I hope there's fruit cake.'

'And Sunday-fresh rock-cakes.'

'That's all right, then. I can get other girls, anyway.'

'How'd you get them? I can't.'

'Easy. You just—'

'Tell me over tea,' I said.

He told me over tea. You just needed to have a sister. Your sister always knew other girls. Your sister would always sort you out one who hadn't got a feller and was in need of one. It sounded very plain sailing. I'd have to talk to Lizzy sometime. Lizzy might know a very nice girl who was in need of me.

After finishing up all the cake Chinese Lady had apportioned, William left and I went into the parlour, where Miss Chivers was playing romantic tunes on the piano. Lizzy was sitting on the sofa with Ned, he already looking very much at home, very much as if he belonged, but Lizzy looking as uncertain as a gazelle who had scented a lion. Or perhaps it was a look of disbelief. However, as I sat down she glanced at me, and her eyes were shining. She might have been finding it difficult to believe Ned had come back, but she was very happy.

Over tea, Ned had talked about his time in Spain, about Jerez and its sherry, about how he had had to study everything from the spring treatment of the vines, the growth of the grape, its harvesting and its progress from ripe fruit until it became fine golden sherry. He could distinguish the difference between a very good sherry and

185

an excellent one, and he could speak Spanish. He was qualified to participate in buying and selling, and to know exactly the tastes and requirements of every important customer.

Miss Chivers was impressed with him. So was Mr Finch. Mr Finch liked his lack of conceit, his natural friendliness, and his ability to get on with everyone. Mr Finch liked more than anything his devotion to Lizzy, which had survived his fourteen months in Spain and the natural doubts of his parents. That, Mr Finch told me, made him far more admirable than his knowledge of sherry ever would.

It seemed that Ned's return even affected the carefully conducted relationship between Miss Chivers and Mr Finch, for as he turned the music for her she smiled up at him, and he responded with the kind of smile that put the twinkling light into his grey eyes. It was quite a mellow Sunday evening.

Ned left at the same time as Miss Chivers. I think he knew he had overwhelmed Lizzy. What she had said to him when she flew from the house to bring him back, I didn't know, but all the time he was there she seemed as shyly sensitive as she had been when she first knew him. Ned avoided any anti-climax by departing fairly early. And Mr Finch went up to his room not long after to leave Lizzy with us.

She sat in an armchair, looking into the fire.

'I've got to grow up,' she said suddenly.

'You're growing up very nicely,' said Chinese Lady, softly happy for her only daughter. Chinese Lady was very fond of Ned.

'No, I haven't grown up at all,' said Lizzy. 'I don't have any sense.'

'Well, you're still a bit young,' said Chinese Lady.

'He kissed me,' said Lizzy, half to herself.

'That's nice,' said Chinese Lady placidly.

'Hadn't he ever kissed you before?' I asked.

'Of course not,' said Lizzy, 'that's only for when—' She

coloured. 'Well, it's only for when you're properly walking out with a young man, otherwise boys don't have any respect for you. You wouldn't have any respect for a girl who let every boy kiss her, would you, Boots?'

'I suppose not,' I said. I had a lot of respect for Miss Chivers, who'd let me kiss her. I was even in love with her.

'Your dad never kissed me till our engagement,' said Chinese Lady.

'Kissing's soppy,' said Tommy.

'Anyway, I've got to get some sense in my head,' said Lizzy. 'I was so silly, sulkin' like a child because Ned went to Spain and me not believing I was really his girl. I didn't even know what to say to him when I run after him and caught him up.'

'You must of said something,' smiled Chinese Lady.

'I didn't. I couldn't think of anything. Except how silly I'd been, and I wasn't going to say that.'

'Not saying you'd been silly was very sensible of you, lovey,' said Chinese Lady. 'It don't do to admit that sort of thing to men, it makes them think the only sense comes from them. You only have to listen to Boots sometimes, and he's not even a man yet. But didn't you say anything to Ned at all?'

'He stopped when I caught him up,' said Lizzy, 'an' waited for me to say something. When I didn't, he kissed me. Right there in the street, with Ernie Jones lookin'.'

'If your dad had done that to me in the street – well, I don't know what I'd have done meself,' said Chinese Lady.

Lizzy laughed, blissfully.

The following evening, Mr Finch, at ease in front of his fire, said, 'I'm delighted, Boots. Well done, Lizzy. Brave girl. She cast aside all pride and ran to bring Ned back. So there we are. All is now in the dark laps of the gods, as Wagner might say.'

'Who?'

'Oh, the composer. Not quite our cup of tea, my boy.'

'If I get a girl, I hope I don't have problems like Lizzy's had. I mean, not being sure if a girl's keen on me or not.'

'Oh, there'll be problems, Boots.'

'I'd better keep off girls, then,' I said, thinking I might be content to love Miss Chivers from afar.

'There's no chance of that,' said Mr Finch. 'Life won't let you. And some particular girl also won't let you. Await her arrival with rapture and resignation.'

'Life has let you escape,' I said, and watched him covertly then. He took his pipe out of his mouth, and the always alert light in his eyes seemed to darken, as if his thoughts were casting shadows. Stretched comfortably in his armchair, he regarded his carpet slippers, the ones we had given him for Christmas.

'You call it escape, Boots, because you're a little shy with girls.'

'Shy? Me? I'm not shy. It surprised me to find Lizzy is. Have you noticed that, Mr Finch?'

'That's not shyness, Boots. That's a girl in love. Perhaps we should say you're a little wary, then, in case a relationship gets too much for you.'

'Oh, I think I'm old enough now not to let anything get too much for me.'

Mr Finch pointed his pipe at me.

'Be warned, Boots. There's a saying that he who stalks the tiger with a smile on his face is blind to the fact that the beast is behind him.'

'I've only heard that it's the tiger which has a smile on its face.'

'Yes, that's when it's got behind you.'

CHAPTER FIFTEEN

Lizzy's sixteenth birthday party was such a feast of food that I felt sure Chinese Lady had left herself penniless. Ned was there, of course. So were Mr Finch and Emily. And so was Miss Chivers. Lizzy had pressed her to come, and for once Miss Chivers defied the Witch. She said, when she arrived, that her mother disapproved, but that she simply could not miss Lizzy's sixteenth.

Lizzy looked a dream in dark red velvet. Chinese Lady had said velvet, would you believe, when Lizzy brought it home. But the hem was badly stitched, and Gamages had let her have it at a throwaway price. Chinese Lady restitched the hem and made a perfect job of it.

I could see Ned thought Lizzy a dream. She was. And she no longer seemed uncertain. She matched Ned in her self-assurance. And her lashes fluttered teasingly, and her eyes danced. Was our Lizzy really in love? Mr Finch drew me aside after we had been eliminated from Musical Chairs and whispered, 'Don't look so mystified, Boots. Lizzy only has her mind on the lifting of her veil.'

'What veil?'

'Her bridal veil.'

'She hasn't said – Ned hasn't said – no one's said anything about a wedding, or even an engagement.'

Miss Chivers let her hands rest, the piano music stopped, and Sammy gave a yell of frustration as he was robbed of one of the remaining chairs. Emily, a quick, darting figure in bottle green, beat him to it. Sammy hit the floor.

'Oh, gawd, that Em'ly,' he said.

Emily laughed, Lizzy laughed and Ned roared.

'Lizzy has made up her mind,' murmured Mr Finch, as Sammy removed a chair and the music began again. 'She's finally realised what was obvious, that in coming back to her Ned showed that his interest in her had never been casual. She knows now that she matters to him, and she's intent on completely captivating him. She's thinking not about when he'll propose to her, but when the wedding will be. She's thinking will your mother consent to her being married at seventeen or advise her to wait until she's eighteen.'

'All your years at sea and on the river have given you wonderful insight,' I said, and Mr Finch smiled and shook his head modestly.

Lizzy was scampering around the remaining chairs, Ned behind her and Emily following in darting rushes. Chinese Lady was still in, moving decorously. Miss Chivers stopped playing. Emily shrieked, leapt and sprang. She gave Ned a flying shove, grabbing the chair he thought he'd won, and Ned fell over. Chinese Lady seated herself calmly, and Lizzy plunged down onto the last chair amid a flurry of red dress and white petticoat. She looked at the grounded Ned, and laughed and laughed.

Emily won the game. She was like quicksilver.

Later, she said to me, 'Boots, ain't Lizzy happy? Ain't she lovely? Ain't you glad for her?'

'Well, I ain't crying, Em, and that's a fact.'

'No, but ain't he nice, her young man? Ain't he flash? With all them prospects he's got, I bet he'll keep Lizzy in silks an' satins, an' make her look grand every day.'

'Would you like to look grand every day, Em?'

'Oh, I ain't got the looks for lookin' grand,' said Emily, 'I'll be lucky if I'm kept in flannel. Boots, yer family won't move away when Lizzy marries, will it? You won't leave, now you're workin' at a respectable job, will yer?'

'It's not that much of a job. When Lizzy goes, our mum will have less to bless herself with.'

'Oh, but you're not really poor, not now. Look at Lizzy's lovely party and all, and all the food your mum give us. It must've cost near to a fortune.'

'Oh, I don't suppose it's made us poor, Emily. Just penniless.'

'Oh, yer do say funny things, Boots, and yer talk lovely.'

'Have you got the rent money?' I asked Chinese Lady on Tuesday evening. The rent was due tomorrow.

'Course I have,' she said.

'Show me.'

'Well, I haven't got it all, not at the moment. Sammy's going to make it up for me.'

'Oh, Mum, you shouldn't keep borrowing from Sammy,' said Lizzy, 'it's getting shameful.'

'It ain't shameful to me an' Mum,' said Sammy, 'it's business, ain't it, Mum?'

'Sammy,' I said, 'are you getting rich at the expense of Chinese Lady?'

'Some 'opes,' said Sammy.

'How much you short, Mum?' asked Lizzy.

'Only about four shillings,' said Chinese Lady, getting up to bustle divertingly around. 'Well, say four an' six.'

'Boots and me will make it up,' said Lizzy.

''Ere, me an' Mum 'ave got an arrangement,' protested Sammy.

'You mean you're squeezing her dry,' I said.

'He's drivin' her to drink, that's what,' said Tommy.

'Now Sammy's been very obligin',' said Chinese Lady, 'so don't go on at him.'

'How much interest does Mum owe you, Sammy, that's what I'd like to know,' said Lizzy.

Sammy licked through his grubby notebook.

'Only a pound and ninepence,' he said.

'A pound and ninepence?' said Lizzy. 'Interest?'

'Well, she don't pay me back reg'lar, like,' said Sammy, 'an' I ain't the kind to be 'ard on 'er, seeing she's our mum. She don't mind the interest mountin' up a little bit, do yer, Mum?'

'Boots,' said Lizzy, 'take him upstairs and give him a hiding. Take his trousers down. Use our dad's old belt.'

191

'I ain't goin' upstairs,' said Sammy, 'nor takin' me trousers down.'

'Boots, leave him be,' said Chinese Lady.

'I don't mind us being penniless,' I said, 'I do mind Sammy ruining us.'

'I'll wallop 'im for yer, if yer like,' said Tommy the willing one.

Sammy got up.

'All right, I'm goin' upstairs,' he said, 'but only to get some of me things. I'm leavin' 'ome.'

'All right,' I said, 'see him out, Tommy.'

'Stop this talk,' said Chinese Lady, 'it's not nice. As for you, Sammy, it's not the first time you've talked about leaving home. Once more, my lad, and you'll get your ears boxed so hard they'll ring for a week.'

'I ain't leavin' right away,' said Sammy, 'I'm makin' me will first in case I get run over. I ain't leavin' nothing to anyone except you, Mum. Like me train set, what yer could sell for ninepence, if yer wanted.'

'What about your hoard of money?' I asked.

'I ain't leavin' that,' said Sammy, 'I'm takin' it wiv me. I ain't barmy.'

Chinese Lady didn't box his ears. She persuaded him to give the family one more chance. The family didn't want him to go off and get run over, she said.

'Yes, we do,' said Tommy.

Lizzy and I made up the rent. We knew Chinese Lady had blown most of the required six shillings on the birthday party.

The summer arrived hot and sunny.

Emily darted out of her house one evening to arrive at our open front door in a flash of white cotton. I was just about to go and lean against our gate and try some open air, even if it was full of Walworth dust. Emily looked as if she had just washed her hair and had a bath. Her hair was damply fiery in the sun, and her cotton dress hung limply on her thin frame, except for where it clung around her budding breasts. It seemed to me she hadn't got a thing on under the dress. There were two protuberances. She was growing nipples. Nipples? Emily?

'Is your house on fire?' I asked.

'Course it isn't.'

'You left it in a hurry.'

'Oh, I just thought I'd come an' see you quick – just for a sec – I ain't properly – ' Emily blushed. She'd obviously been sparked by a sudden idea, and typically had made an unthinking dash to communicate it. Her eyes flashed about everywhere, except at me. 'Well, yer see – I got lots more money saved, I don't hardly spend nothing of me four bob a week.'

'You're still only getting five bob?' I said. Emily worked hard at the bottle-washing factory. Her hands showed it. They were beginning to redden.

'Oh, I'm grateful to 'ave a job,' she said, 'an' Mum only stops me a bob. Boots, seeing it's summer, I thought – well, would you come with me like you did before an' help me buy new frocks an' things?'

'Frocks, yes. Things, no.'

'Oh, I don't mean drawers an' suchlike,' said Emily, who was no more coy than other Walworth girls about 'things'. 'I mean gloves, like, an' stockings. I thought imitation silk stockings – they'd be nice, wouldn't they?'

Above her auburn head, across the street, the factory wall looked grimy. Emily looked very clean and eager.

'Not stockings,' I said, 'stockings is things. Where'd you want to go?'

'Oh, where we went before – Gammidges. Lizzy's ladies' wear place, where that nice lady served us.'

'You sure you need me? Lizzy and the lady could see to you, couldn't they?'

'Oh, but would yer come with me an' help me choose, would yer, please?'

'All right, Em.'

'I got to tell you, Boots, that you're blessed with goodness,' said Emily.

'If you get a nice frock and look grand in it, I'll walk you up the park on Sunday.'

'Up the park?' Emily's green eyes ran all over our feet. 'Oh, I never been walked up the park before.'

'Well, you're getting to behave yourself nicely. Now go and put some clothes on.'

'Oh, crikey.' Emily blushed and fled.

Mr Finch came down.

'I'm sorry to say I heard all that from the top of the stairs, Boots,' he said. 'Well done, my boy. Emily needs you and your family. You're her ready-made brothers and sister. An only child can get very lonely. Incidentally, you were quite right. Frocks, yes. Things, no, even if she does look at herself as unexciting.' He smiled, passed me, put on a trilby hat and strolled up the Place to go for a walk. He sometimes liked a walk.

I stood at the gate, watching the street kids. The girls were playing hopscotch, the boys kicking a rag ball about. Mrs Blake and Mrs Higgins stood gossiping. Miss Chivers appeared, a letter in her hand. She glided along, halting as she reached me.

'Good evening, Boots,' she smiled.

I rather expected a window to go up, a head to poke out and a complaining voice to make itself heard. But nothing happened.

'Going to post a letter, Miss Chivers?'

'Yes.' Her glasses were on, her eyes clear behind the lenses. 'I must catch the eight o'clock collection at the post office. Isn't it hot, Boots?'

'Yes, but nice and peaceful,' I said. 'Summers always seem more peaceful than winters, don't they? I suppose that's because we don't feel so energetic when it's hot.'

'Less aggressive?' she ventured with her soft smile. She lingered for a moment, and that put me in mind of Postman's Knock and her lingering lips, which had felt very warm and loving. 'Peacefulness has much to commend it, Boots,' she said, and smiled again and gently walked on.

I couldn't help thinking Walworth was a bit unlovely for a woman like her, just as it seemed very unexciting for a man like Mr Finch, who had sailed the seven seas. But I remembered that one Sunday evening they'd both agreed Walworth had a heart charged with the vitality of people grown strong in the struggle to survive.

As for peacefulness, Miss Chivers probably got less of that than anyone when she was home. Her closest neighbour, Mrs Blake, often said that when she was in her back yard she could hear the Witch carrying on as if her daughter was a constant trial to her.

Lizzy came out and stood at the gate with me.

'Whew, it's hot indoors,' she said. She had changed out of her working frock into a very light dress. Very light.

'Emily was here a few minutes ago,' I said, 'and she wasn't wearing anything under her dress, either.'

'What big eyes you've got,' said Lizzy.

'If Ned came round the corner—'

'What?' Lizzy essayed a quick, instinctive glance in the direction of Browning Street.

'If he saw you in nothing but that frock—'

'Yes, what would he do, then?' asked Lizzy with interest.

'I don't know. What would a bloke who's been to a hot country like Spain do if he caught his girl in almost nothing?'

'Don't you really know?' asked Lizzy.

'Not for sure, no.'

'Oh, help, neither do I,' said Lizzy. 'Ain't it—'

'Ain't? Ain't?' I said, knowing that she now wanted to be a lady because of Ned and was very careful indeed when he was around.

'Oh, all right. It just don't come easy to me to be Lady Muck like Lord Muck comes easy to you.'

'Oh, I don't know. I think you're going to finish up as a natural Lady Muck. You already won't eat fish and chips except with a knife and fork.'

'Chinese Lady says behavin' nice at the table isn't

195

anything to do with being stuck-up, and I just agree with her, that's all. Anyway, I was going to say isn't it a mystery, Boots, all the things we don't know about even now we're grown up?'

'Like exactly what Ned would do—'

'Yes, that.'

'We can make guesses – I mean, what we're talking about is what goes on when you find yourself on honeymoon—'

'Who said I was talking about that?' said Lizzy, pinking.

'I did. I think you ought to ask Chinese Lady.'

'She'd faint,' said Lizzy.

'Well, I'll ask her. I don't want to end up not knowing exactly what to do when I get married.'

'You'll ask her?' Lizzy giggled. 'You wouldn't dare. She'd faint twice over. Anyway, you know a bit about what happens, don't you? I bet you do.'

'Yes, but I've got a feeling it's like a sacred ritual and there's a lot more to it than we know about.'

'That's what I feel,' said Lizzy. 'I ain't – I don't have the face to ask Chinese Lady. Go on, then, you ask her. Then you can tell me.'

'It might be too mysterious for a feller to tell his sister.'

'Go on, ask her.'

'What d'you mean?' Chinese Lady quivered.

'You know, when there's just me and my bride, is there something special you have to do besides – besides—'

'Besides?' Chinese Lady gave me a severe look.

'Come on, Mum, you and Dad went on honeymoon, didn't you?'

'Mind your business, you saucy devil. Well, I never heard such a thing come from someone who's still a boy and wanting his own mother to tell him what he's got no right to hear. You wait until you got a bride, then you can talk to the vicar. If your dad hadn't been careless enough to get his head blown off, you could of talked to him.'

'Well, you're our mum and our dad, and don't think

196

we're not grateful. I don't mind you telling me if there's something special to remember.'

'Well,' said Chinese Lady in shock, 'well! I never thought my only oldest son would turn out an impudence. Almost being a hooligan is bad enough. I wonder this kitchen floor don't open up and swaller you. When your time comes, you go an' ask the vicar.'

'If I do ever have a bride, I don't want—'

'Just be nice to her,' said Chinese Lady.

'Nice?'

'And loving,' said Chinese Lady.

I told Lizzy it all seemed to add up to the bridegroom being nice and loving.

'Oh, how sweet,' said Lizzy, 'that'll suit me.'

There had been news in our paper about an Austrian archduke being assassinated, and about Austria being very angry. It seemed to worry Mr Finch.

'A pity, Boots,' he said, sitting with his jacket and tie off, and his braces loose. 'A great pity, when the summer is so beautiful.'

'Well, it's not going to bring the rain, is it?'

'Never mind the rain, my boy, as long as we don't all get caught in a storm,' he said, and looked quite sombre.

CHAPTER SIXTEEN

Emily and I arrived in Gamages ladies' wear department just after noon on Saturday afternoon. Emily was wearing a quite decent boater, together with her pale green blouse and the skirt of her bottle green costume. She had decided she ought to present herself as a nicely-attired customer. She almost looked attractive, because nervous excitement gave her a warm flush that took the peakiness out of her thin features and made her green eyes come alive. And she did have a very nice mouth. She was sixteen now, and no longer an adolescent, but all the same she began to hang behind me. Several customers were present, and all four assistants, including Lizzy and the kind, gracious lady, were busy.

'Come on,' I said, 'while we're waiting why don't we look at some of the frocks on display?'

'It's even posher 'ere than I remembered,' muttered Emily, 'I should've gone to the shop in the Walworth Road.'

'They'd have sold you something that didn't fit and didn't suit, and I'd have made you take it back.'

'Oh, yer so bossy I can't think why I likes yer.'

'Now don't behave like you did before, as if you're having an operation. Stand up straight. Go on, now. Straight. That's it, shoulders back – good for you, Em – no, wait, ease off a bit.'

Emily, having come to nervous attention with her shoulders well back, had had a sensational effect on her delicate silk green blouse and the thin vest she wore beneath it. Her firm young breasts positively pouted and pushed. Amazing. As thin as a flat kipper, yet there she was, sprouting girlish abundance. She needed to wear a corset, like Lizzy did now.

'Ain't I standin' right?' she whispered.

'You're standing like a soldier, Em. I bet my dad would have been proud of you. But relax a bit. That's it. Just right. Now you look as good as any customer here.'

I ordered her to make an inspection of garments on display. One had to give Emily orders in a place like this. She made her inspection. The colours were expressive of bright summer. Better not think of green again. Primrose or white. No, Emily's mass of dark, fiery hair would kill the primrose. Why not white? She was virginal, and it was summer. She regarded everything shyly, but excitement was there, her eyes alight with it. Such moments were eventful for her, after so many years of having her mum buy everything for her.

The gracious lady assistant had seen Emily. She detached herself from a customer who was making a prolonged survey of blouses, and came over.

'Good afternoon, Miss Castle,' she said with a smile.

Emily jumped.

'Oh, hello,' she croaked.

'Good afternoon, Mr Adams,' said the lady assistant. 'How smart Miss Castle looks. That was a very good choice you helped her to make a few months ago, wasn't it?'

'You remember?' said Emily.

'Of course.' The lady assistant gave her blouse customer a glance. 'What can we do for you this time – with the help of Mr Adams again, I'm sure?'

'Can I 'ave a nice frock, perhaps two?' said Emily in a nervous rush. 'An' some nice gloves an' stockings an' things.'

'Things?'

'Undergarments,' whispered Emily hoarsely. She looked beseechingly at me. 'I saved lots of money, Boots, I got three pounds fifteen shillings.'

She had been saving very religiously. She walked to and

from her work in all weathers. She took sandwiches to eat, like I did. She had a job that paid five shillings a week and didn't want to lose it. The bottle-washing factory had girls waiting for every vacancy. Emily didn't seem to worry that the work was making her hands very red. I'd better get her to do something about it. She had nice hands, with slender fingers. It didn't seem right, letting them turn red.

'Ladies' undergarments are on the other side of this floor,' smiled the lady assistant. 'Excuse me a moment – oh, I'll send our excellent Miss Eliza to you.'

Lizzy's customer had departed. The lady assistant sent her over and returned to her own customer.

Lizzy, approaching with style, addressed Emily in an upper-class voice.

'Madam wishes to see some frocks and gloves?'

'What yer talkin' like that for?' whispered Emily.

'If madam will come this way?' said Lizzy. 'Oh, we don't need you, Boots, so hoppit.'

'No, he's got to stay,' said Emily, 'he knows what suits me.'

'Once was all right, last time,' said Lizzy, 'twice is makin' you look daft, Em'ly.'

'But if 'e don't like what I get,' said Emily, ''e'll make me bring it back. And I did ask 'im special to come.'

'I know you did,' said Lizzy, tastefully attired in her white-collared working dress, 'and I never heard nothing more barmy. What's more, he'll boss you about.'

'I'll go and sit down somewhere,' I said.

'But yer got to 'elp me choose,' said Emily, 'yer promised.'

'Oh, come on, Em'ly, you daft ha'porth,' said Lizzy, 'he can come and look when you're trying frocks on.'

'Buy a white frock, Em,' I said, 'while it's still summer.'

'Buzz off,' said Lizzy.

I went to the far side of the department where two chairs were available for tired customers who wished to take the weight off their feet for a while. I sat down. There was reading matter available on a small table. I picked up a manufacturer's catalogue. It was full of illustrations of ladies' things, including photographs of ladies actually wearing them. I wasn't sure Chinese Lady wouldn't have boxed my ears if she'd caught me studying the form of the models coyly displaying corsets of varying styles.

After a while, Emily floated into distant view in a cloud of summer white. Floated? Emily? I went across to inspect her. The white frock had a lace-adorned bodice, a skirt that hung in delicate folds, a red sash and a rich shimmer.

'That's nice,' I said.

'Oh, do yer like it, Boots?' she burst out. 'Can I 'ave it? Oh, and what d'yer think? It's silk.'

'And only eight and elevenpence,' said Lizzy encouragingly. She'd get commission, of course.

'Eight and elevenpence?' I said. 'For a frock? You can get decent frocks for half a crown anywhere.'

'Anywhere's not here,' said Lizzy haughtily. 'And that's a creation, that is, not a frock. Em'ly's saved up for something special, so mind your business.'

'Oh, can I have it, Boots?' begged Emily.

'Course you can,' said Lizzy, 'you don't have to ask him. It's lovely. Come on.' She took Emily away. Emily bought the white frock and a cheaper yellow one. She also bought a pair of white gloves. Then, under the pressure of new customers, Lizzy directed her to the underwear department. At which point, I retreated.

Emily disappeared. After a few minutes, she reappeared, frail with nerves again.

'Oh, could yer come, Boots? I don't know no one in ladies' undergarments, and I'm not meself by meself. Boots, yer don't mind really, do yer? You can tell me what petticoats is the prettiest, like, and 'elp me choose some nice drawers—'

'Are you off your chump? Your mum would have a fit, so would my mum and so would I.'

'But it's not like you don't have a sister,' said Emily, who seemed desperate for help. 'I mean, you seen Lizzy's drawers, ain't yer? When she's been ironin' them and all?'

'I'm not going into ladies' undergarments, Emily, and that's flat.'

'Just this once, won't yer, Boots?' she said. 'I ain't got the courage by meself. Look, they got some on dressmakers' models – we can look at them – I seen some only half a crown.'

'Half a crown? For a pair of drawers?'

Emily blushed.

'They're silk,' she said, 'an' just for Sundays, like. Honest, I won't wear 'em for work. I can buy others for work, cheaper ones. I still got lots of money left. I ain't never worn silk—'

'Nor has my mum all her life, I bet. You're going to end up penny wise, pound foolish, you are.'

'Oh, just this once, come and help me, won't yer?' she begged.

'You'll be my death, Em, you will.'

I had a terrible time, the lady assistants following my progress with popping eyes and audible giggles. Emily, fluttery and bashful, yet strangely determined, kept me beside her while she inspected things on display. We finally arrived at the counter, where two assistants could hardly contain themselves when Emily inarticulately gabbled her wishes and desires, and I had to translate. Things were produced and laid on the counter. Petticoats, drawers and stockings.

'Oh, it's them I want,' said Emily, pointing to a pair of snowy white drawers with flirting lace threaded by pink ribbon, 'them silk ones. Can I have 'em?'

'With pleasure, madam,' said one assistant.

'Yes, thank you,' said Emily, 'but it's me friend I'm askin'.'

The assistant put a hand to her mouth and coughed. The other assistant looked as if the whole thing couldn't be true.

'Kindly wrap them up,' I said, desperate to be gone.

'I want two pairs,' said Emily.

'Two?' I said.

'An' two pairs of them, for weekdays,' said Emily, pointing again. 'An' that petticoat, the one what's got pink ribbon too.' She thought. Her eyes darted about. She swallowed. 'I better 'ave a corset,' she said strangledly.

'That's it, don't mind me,' I said, and the assistants breathed deeply.

'I don't want no stays,' said Emily hoarsely, 'I want a proper corset, a nice one.'

'If you'd come this way—?' said one assistant drunkenly.

'I'll go and sit down,' I said, but Emily gripped my sleeve and we followed the assistant to a dummy wearing a white corset with trimmings.

'Oh, Boots, ain't that fancy?' breathed Emily.

'It's just a dream to me,' I said, 'I'm hoping I'm not really here.'

'Oh, yer being grand,' she whispered, 'yer give me lots of courage.'

When we eventually emerged into the hot afternoon sunshine, I was laden with boxes and parcels.

'I'm going to take a long time to recover from this,' I said.

'Boots, I only spent a bit over thirty-three bob,' said Emily breathlessly, 'and see what I bought, two frocks, gloves, stockings, all them pretty drawers and a petticoat and that fancy corset. I still got lots left.'

'I suppose you know that what you spent would take a corporation dustman nearly three weeks to earn?'

'But that's what I saved it for,' said Emily, 'and it took me months. Boots, Lizzy said – she said you went to a teashop with her in the Strand once, so can I treat yer? Would yer take me there?'

'Well, I suppose we've got time,' I said, and remembered her Christmas gift of a pocket watch. 'But it's my treat.'

'Oh, ain't yer lovely?' she said. 'I'll carry some of them things.' She relieved me of some, and we began to walk to the Kingsway. With offices closed, the traffic in Holborn wasn't as thick as usual. Emily eyed a passing hansom cab.

'Boots – oh, crikey, let's 'ave a cab to the teashop. I'll pay. You'll let me, won't yer? I never been in a cab.'

'Nor have I.'

'Well, go on, call one like you was a proper swell, an' ask 'ow much to the teashop. It won't be more'n a tanner, will it?'

'It better not be. We could buy our own cab for a bob.'

Emily, on a note of high excitement, impulsively called to an approaching hansom.

'Hi! Mister!'

The cab pulled up at the kerbside, and the cabbie gave us a grin.

'Where yer want, me lord?' he asked from on high.

'Charing Cross Station,' I said. I couldn't remember the name of the teashop, but it was almost opposite the station.

''Op in, me lady. 'Op in, me lord.'

'Here, wait a tick,' said Emily. ''Ow much you chargin'?'

The cabbie surveyed her upturned face from his perch. His grin widened at her look of peaky-nosed suspicion. All the same, peaky-nosed or not, Emily in her boater, delicate blouse and lushly green skirt, had a certain astonishing elegance, and the cabbie's grin became fatherly.

'Well, me lady,' he said, 'I ain't askin' no more'n what I'd ask any young toffs. Would yer say a quid's fair?'

'A quid?' gasped Emily.

'All right, fourpence,' said the cabbie, 'and I leaves it to yer worshipful graces to pay me what yer cares to in the way of a tip.'

'We'll give yer a penny tip,' said Emily.

'Will yer now? Temptin' me with riches, are yer? All right, 'op in.'

We got in and the cabbie took us on our way at a smart trot, which put Emily in transports of rapture.

'Ain't it something, Boots, us in a cab? Don't yer think it's the grandest? People'll think we're real swell. It's the best day I ever 'ad except for Christmas.' An excited smile

204

darted. 'You kissed me at Christmas, cheeky. Boots, I better let you 'ave the money for the fare, you better pay. We don't want the cabbie to think you ain't a proper toff.' She opened her handbag and took out her purse, heavy with silver and coppers. 'Here y'ar, Boots.'

'No, I'll pay,' I said.

Her face fell.

'Boots, ain't yer goin' to let me treat yer at all?'

'All right, Emily, you pay the cab fare and I'll pay for the tea.'

'Oh, yer so good to me,' said Emily, and handed me fivepence.

We alighted at Charing Cross Station, boxes and all. I paid the cabbie.

'Thank yer kindly, me lord,' he said.

'That's all right,' I said, and he drove off grinning. We waited for a break in the traffic, busier here, then crossed the road to the teashop. Emily took one look through the window and began to hang back again.

'Oh, I can't,' she said.

'Can't what?'

'Go in there. It's too posh.'

'You look posh yourself.'

'Me?' Emily quivered. 'Oh, you're bliss to a girl, you are.'

'Go on, in you go.'

She went in, flushed and twitching. Customers looked at her. That so unnerved her that she advanced blindly. To prevent her walking into an occupied table, I nudged her towards a vacant one. She sat down with a soft bump, and darted scared looks at tables, patrons and waitresses.

'Oh, 'elp,' she gulped, 'it's all fancy.'

I loaded a chair with boxes and parcels. I sat down. The aroma of currant buns toasting was mouth-watering. A young waitress arrived. I ordered a pot of tea and two toasted buns each.

'Thank you, sir,' said the waitress and tripped away. Cups chimed and teaspoons tinkled. Outside, motor taxis chugged by, business beginning to build up for Saturday evening.

'Oh, you give the waitress the order like you was up from yer castle,' whispered Emily. 'I'm fair shakin' all over meself. It's like Buckingham Palace, ain't it?'

'Well, I really can't say, Em, I've never been invited.'

'Boots, when you get a girl, I bet you'll pick a real princess, I bet she won't 'alf like you. You deserve the best, honest you do. Did yer see the way Lizzy served her customers in Gammidges? Didn't she look as if life was treatin' her grand? She's 'ead over 'eels, ain't she?' Emily chattered on, her face animated beneath her boater. Her pale green blouse moved gently over her budding breasts. They pouted at me. How did thin girls grow ones like that?

The tea and buns arrived, and Emily sighed with bliss at the melting butter. She watched me cut mine with a knife, then followed suit. I saw her hands and the scourge of redness.

'You've got very nice hands, Em,' I said. I didn't mind not minding my own business. As I'd told Chinese Lady once, you have to interfere when it's for the good of friends or neighbours. Chinese Lady had said that anyone who poked his nose in as freely as I did would get it badly damaged one day. For the good of friends and neighbours, it was a risk I willingly took, especially as there were times when minding one's own business was simply a way of refusing one's help. 'Have you thought about what nice hands you've got, Em?'

'Me?' said Emily, swallowing a crisp bit of bun in a startled fashion.

'Yes, you. You don't want them to look permanently chapped, not nice hands like yours. Pour the tea, Em.'

'Oh, no – you,' said Emily in fright.

'Put the milk in first.'

'Boots, I can't – not in 'ere – everyone wearin' posh 'ats—'

'Look, if you can drag me into ladies' corsets, you can pour tea. Go on.'

'Oh, blow yer,' she muttered, but did it, and in praiseworthy fashion once she realised no one was looking. 'Whadjer mean about me 'ands?' she asked.

'You ought to smother them with some Vaseline cream just before you start work each day, then the water wouldn't get at them.'

Emily took a look at her hands.

'Ain't they pretty, either?' she said.

'Well, of course they are. That's why you should look after them.'

Emily put a piece of bun in her mouth and chewed it angrily.

'Bleedin' cheek,' she said.

'I'm only trying—'

'Mind yer own business.' Emily's rag was out.

'Suit yourself. It just seems a pity, that's all, when you've got such nice hands.'

Emily ate another piece of bun.

'Oh, all right,' she muttered.

'You can get some kind of protective hand cream, can't you?'

'How do I know? I ain't never seen none in our house.'

'From the chemist's shop.'

'Oh, all right,' she said again.

'I'd better mind my own business.'

'No, you're being kind, really,' she said.

'I can only think of Vaseline myself. Well, never mind.' I consulted the Christmas gift. The watch always felt snug in my waistcoat pocket. It was taking it out and consulting it that turned ownership into self-importance. Emily visibly perked up. 'Time's getting on,' I said, 'it's ten to three.' And Emily looked proud of my close relationship with her gift.

'Oh, it do suit yer, Boots, 'aving a watch,' she said.

We enjoyed our tea and toasted buns. I paid the bill and left the waitress tuppence for a tip. Emily looked proud again. We walked to the Embankment to catch a tram home. The placard of an evening paper caught our eyes.

'AUSTRIAN ULTIMATUM TO SERBIA – GERMANY SPEAKS.'

'What's an ultimatum?' asked Emily.

'Well, it's like a final demand for the rent.'

'Serbia don't owe rent to Austria,' said Emily.

'I didn't say she did.'

'Them Austrians is after Serbia,' she said.

'What's that?' I said, and she blushed a little.

'It's me school hist'ry,' she said, 'I didn't do bad at hist'ry. I bet there'll be a war with Austria an' Serbia. That's silly, going to war.'

When we got home, I said, 'I hope your mum and dad'll like what you've bought.'

'Oh, can I come in an' show your mum first?'

'Only the dresses,' I said, 'not the things. You show her the things and I'll get a flea in my ear for going into ladies' underwear with you.'

'I'll just show her the corset—'

'No, you won't.'

Emily's eyes flickered, darted and landed on the top button of my waistcoat. A smile, positively impish, peeped. I hadn't known she had it in her to be like that.

'Only me frocks?' she said.

'Yes.'

'All right.'

Lizzy had just got home and had told Chinese Lady about Emily's frocks. Emily displayed them. Chinese Lady said things like my goodness, Emily Castle, and well I never, they're fit for a lady. And Lizzy looked at me with laughter in her eyes, and I guessed the assistants in ladies' undergarments had told her what a terrible time Emily had given me.

'Oh, Lizzy an' Boots been a great help, Mrs Adams,' said Emily, holding the white frock up against her body, 'they been really swell. I 'ad to 'ave Lizzy pick them out for me, I didn't want Boots to make me take them back.'

'I should hope he wouldn't interfere with what don't concern him,' said Chinese Lady. 'Make you take them back? The very idea. That's not being a great help, that's stickin' his nose in.'

'Oh, I don't mind, Mrs Adams, it's nice 'aving someone who—' Emily stopped, gathered up the frock and placed it carefully back in its box. 'Oh, would yer believe it, Mrs Adams, there's probably going to be a war.'

'A war?' Chinese Lady looked as if Emily needed to see a doctor. 'What d'you mean, a war?'

'Oh, not our war,' said Emily knowledgeably, 'just the Austrians an' Serbians.'

'Serbians?' Chinese Lady was mystified. 'Who's the Serbians?'

'They're in the Balkans, Mrs Adams, next to Austria,' said Emily, 'an' they all wear black moustaches an' long daggers for doing people in with.'

'All of them?' I said. 'The Serbian ladies as well?'

Lizzy shrieked with laughter.

'Em'ly, have you caught a fever or something?' asked Chinese Lady.

'No, I just learned about hist'ry an' geography at school, with Lizzy,' said Emily.

'I remember about the battle of Hastings and King Charles having his head chopped off,' said Lizzy, 'but I don't remember nothing about the Serbians.'

'Oh, they was in the hist'ry books, an' I read all the books all the way through,' said Emily earnestly. 'I like books, like Boots does. Them Austrians is after Serbia. Oh, what d'yer think, Mrs Adams,' she said, going off on a new tack, 'me an' Boots went an' had toasted buns in a teashop in the Strand. Talk about swanky, but Boots give the waitress our order like a real toff.'

'Yes, but stop talking about a war,' said Chinese Lady, who had been widowed by a minor one.

'Yes, Mrs Adams,' said Emily, 'only the Austrians think it was them Serbians that done their archduke in. The archduke was going to be Austria's next ruler, so they're all worked up about 'im being all stiff an' dead now, and I bet they'll go for Serbia.'

'Em'ly Castle, you stop this,' said Chinese Lady. 'Anyone would think you've been having a private talk with them.'

'No, it's been in the papers, Mrs Adams, honest. Ain't yer read about it in yourn? And now the Kaiser's beatin' his chest as well.'

'The Kaiser?' Chinese Lady was floundering.

'The Emp'ror of Germany,' said Emily, eager to impart all she knew. 'Oh, crikey, if there's a real bust-up, I expect we'll 'ave to get cross an' send our Navy to quieten them down, don't you?'

'That'll be something, sending our Navy to Serbia,' I said.

'Well, foreigners can get very excitable,' said Emily. 'I expect Miss Chivers is worried.'

'Miss Chivers?' said Lizzy. 'Em'ly, are you having 'ysterics? Boots has had some today, are you having some now?'

'But, Lizzy, Miss Chivers works at the Admiralty, don't she?' said Emily, who had a lot more inside her head than I'd ever suspected. 'I mean, she might be one of the people that'll 'ave to work out where our battleships are an' how many we got.'

'Em'ly Castle, I never heard such nonsense in all my born days,' said Chinese Lady. 'You go on like that, my girl, and you'll talk us into war, that's what you'll do.'

'Oh, I wouldn't want to do that, Mrs Adams, really I wouldn't,' said Emily. 'Me dad 'ud say perish the thought. Anyway, our Navy could put the fear of God into them Austrians an' Serbians, couldn't it? Well, I'll go an' show me mum an' dad me new things now.' She had left the more delicate things in the passage. 'I've had a swell day, really swell. Boots 'as been a godsend, honest. Ain't yer proud he's your only oldest one, Mrs Adams?'

Collapse of Chinese Lady.

CHAPTER SEVENTEEN

Lizzy and I went to church the next morning to please our mum. Our mum didn't go to church too often herself. Having a family didn't give her time. But she said she'd gone very regularly as a girl, she said it gave young people a belief in goodness. She said the miracles of Jesus were all acts of simple goodness, except when He walked on water. What was that, then? The tide was probably going out, she said.

Emily came to church with us. One didn't need to avoid her, for she was no longer the hoyden dreadful. She wore her new dress of white silk and looked so much the demure virgin that boys gaped. She sat with Lizzy and me, and when she sang the hymns her voice rang clear and sweet, her articulation very correct. It's always been curious to me, the fact that we London cockneys, when singing, don't sing with a cockney accent but a cosmopolitan one. We don't sing 'All fings bright an' beautiful'. We sing 'All things bright and beautiful'. Very curious.

Emily was so demure that no one would have thought she'd waltzed me around ladies' corsets yesterday. I think she was wearing hers, because she looked shaped by her clothes, her young bosom proud. Lizzy was lovely in primrose, her hat with its cluster of flowers a concoction she'd picked up for a song in Gamages' millinery. She dreamed her way through the service, her lips a little parted, her eyes far away. Emily was almost reverent in her attentiveness, and guilty of not a single twitch or jerk. Her new white gloves covered her hands.

Mr Finch, walking with us after the service, was at his kindest in his conversation with Emily, expressing himself enchanted by the prettiness of her new frock.

211

'Boots done it,' said Emily.

'Ah?' said Mr Finch gravely. 'Done it?'

'He said buy a white one or he'd make me take it back. 'E – he don't mess about, Mr Finch. That don't suit you, he says. Throw it away. You know, just like that, yer see.'

'Bossy Boots, that's what Sammy calls him,' said Lizzy, upright and graceful.

'Boots has a future,' observed Mr Finch.

'Yes, but what sort of a future?' said Lizzy.

'A captain of commerce?' said Mr Finch.

'With a peaked cap an' uniform?' said Emily. 'Oh, won't yer look grand in that, Boots?'

'It'll probably have to be a bowler hat and a grey suit,' I said, 'but I won't mind that if the money's good.'

'Oh, 'e'll make his fortune, won't he, Mr Finch?' said Emily. 'An' I bet he'll marry a lady duchess, don't you? I mean, don't he talk as grand as any lady duchess would want?'

'Boots has made good use of his schooling,' said Mr Finch, sauntering along with us in the warm morning sunshine. Walworth looked almost colourful this summer.

'Mr Finch, d'yer reckon – ' Emily paused for reflection. Grown-ups like Mr Finch and Chinese Lady often made her look at herself. And there was the fact that Lizzy, her best friend, was speaking much more proper these days. 'Mr Finch, do you think Miss Chivers is feeling worried about what we might 'ave to do about stopping Austria makin' war on Serbia, like gettin' our Navy ready to fire its guns if they go on being silly? I mean, we got a big Navy, ain't – haven't we?'

There was Emily again, Emily with her elementary education and her surprising theories and questions. She was a bit weak on her geography, of course, but she was strong on earnestness.

Mr Finch was quite startled.

'Good heavens, Emily,' he said, and I thought his surprise was followed by a sad look.

'Dad's Sunday paper said swords are rattling, Mr Finch.'

'Let us pray they won't be drawn,' said Mr Finch.

'Oh, I prayed in church that there wouldn't be no war,' said Emily. 'I just wondered if Miss Chivers was 'avin' to get busy at the Admiralty, where she works. I mean, our Navy's got to rule the waves, hasn't it, when foreign countries is rattling their swords, like. I expect Miss Chivers in her work 'as to be able to tell the admirals where all our battleships are, don't you?'

'I really don't know,' said Mr Finch.

'Miss Chivers is only an Admiralty clerk, isn't she?' I said.

'I really can't say,' said Mr Finch.

Lizzy glanced at me. A little smile peeped. I gave her a wink. Mr Finch excused himself and crossed the street to go to the pub for his usual Sunday half-pint.

'Em'ly, you're getting barmier,' said Lizzy.

'But if you read the papers,' said Emily, 'you—'

'Shut up,' said Lizzy, 'we don't want any more silly talk about wars.'

Lizzy had invested all her dreams in peace.

Miss Chivers passed by as I opened our front door at twenty-five to eight on Monday morning. Sometimes she worked an earlier turn at the Admiralty, about one week in four, and sometimes her departure for work coincided with mine. But I never walked up the Place with her, especially now that I was taller. The Witch, her head invariably out of her bedroom window, would have had it in for Miss Chivers if she'd seen a lengthy pair of trousers moving along beside her daughter's skirts. So I usually let Miss Chivers reach Browning Street before I left our doorstep.

Standing there, I heard the old bag.

'Elsie, where's your glasses?'

'I'm wearing them, Mother,' called Miss Chivers.

I stayed where I was for a minute or two, then went on my way. I sensed the eyes at my back, bloodshot and glinting, and the feeling was almost eerie. I caught up with

Miss Chivers at the top of Browning Street, where she was waiting to cross Walworth Road to the Manor Place tram stop.

'Hello, Boots,' she said, with a softly wry smile. It was wry because of her mother. She knew I'd heard the old harridan. She'd seen me at our front door.

'Good morning, Miss Chivers.'

We crossed the road. The road sweepers were already at work. The large amount of horse-drawn traffic kept them busy most of the day. One thing you could say about Walworth, and that was what a good job its road sweepers did. They were worth twice what they were paid, the sweepers, the dustmen, the council navvies and the men who looked after the council's many horses. They were characters of friendly cheer.

'Take a bit round for me old lady's winder-box, will yer, Claude?' was a question often aimed at a road sweeper.

'Like it in a brown paper bag, would yer, Cecil?'

'Nah, a choc'lit box'll do.'

There was a queue for trams, as usual. You got cheap tickets if you travelled before eight o'clock. For a penny, a tram would carry you to Blackfriars Bridge and bring you back in the evening.

Two trams came along, and the queue turned into a scrambling rush. Miss Chivers and I scooted for the second tram, a number 18, that went to the Victoria Embankment. I only went as far as Stamford Street, off Blackfriars Road. Miss Chivers always went on to the Embankment and walked to the Admiralty from there.

Workers shoved about at the boarding step of the tram. The conductor took them to task.

'Mind the ladies there – mind your manners – plenty of room upstairs.'

That was a change. Someone who wasn't minding his manners elbowed Miss Chivers. I gave him a shove with my hip, took Miss Chivers by the elbow and drew her aboard. She mounted the stairs to the top deck. I followed. Her light summer skirt swayed, the lacy hem of a white petticoat frothily peeped and imitation silk stockings shone. I experienced a sensation strangely pleasurable. It made me think of a bedroom, a bed, with Miss Chivers in soft, frothy underwear beneath the sheets and me with her. It was only a momentary madness, but it was immensely pleasurable. We sat on the back seat, and once we had paid our fares we talked.

'Did you have a nice weekend, Boots?' Her soft voice, gently warm, was very musical to my ears, her eyes clear behind her glasses.

'I had a terrible Saturday afternoon. That Emily is a caution, like her dad says.' In a whisper, I told Miss Chivers how I'd gone with Emily to help her spend her savings not only on clothes, but things as well.

'Things, Boots?'

'Yes, you know. Ladies' undergarments.'

'Oh, things,' she said, and softly laughed. The tram clanged.

'Would you believe it, Emily dragging me into that kind of department?' I whispered. 'The assistants had fits. I mean, corsets as well.'

'Oh, my word,' said Miss Chivers with gentle gravity.

'My own fault, I suppose. Well, I always feel Emily needs a leg-up, but I never thought she'd land me in ladies' undergarments. She didn't seem to have any idea of what was proper, she just said she couldn't face up to the assistants by herself.'

'Boots, what fun.' Miss Chivers wasn't blushing. She actually seemed tickled. 'And was it educating too?'

'No, an ordeal. I'm still feeling ill.'

'How sweet,' she smiled. 'Dear young Emily, so in need of someone to share life's modest excitements with.'

'Modest? Crikey, it wasn't modest. How's your mother, Miss Chivers?'

Miss Chivers sighed.

'She's never very well, you know.'

'I expect Walworth doesn't suit her. She probably needs clean, fresh air.'

'Oh, she wouldn't move, Boots.' Miss Chivers gave me a soft smile. 'You're not trying to get rid of me, are you?'

'Oh, bless you, Miss Chivers, never.'

'Boots, what a sweet young man you are,' she murmured, and put her left hand on my knee and lightly pressed. Her touch brought back the pleasurable sensations, and the pleasurable thoughts. How thrilling the lacy hem of her petticoat had looked, delicately dancing around her stockinged legs. The tram clattered and rattled over the tangle of steel lines at the Elephant and Castle. Horse-drawn carts plodded placidly. Everything else hurried, but horse-drawn carts never did. The neatly-gloved hand on my knee rested there.

'When we left Gamages,' I said, 'I took Emily to a teashop opposite Charing Cross Station, where we had tea and toasted buns.'

I waited for a reaction. Miss Chivers only smiled.

'Emily must have liked that,' she said. 'I know that teashop. I go there myself sometimes, when I can snatch a few minutes away from my office. It's very pleasant.'

'Emily thinks Austria's going to war with Serbia, and that the British Navy will have to steam up the Danube and fire off its guns to make them behave.'

'Emily thinks that?' Miss Chivers's hand tightened on my knee, then dropped away. Her eyes clouded. 'Emily?'

'Emily reads history books and newspapers. Emily's a surprise.'

The tram entered Blackfriars Road.

'Imagine that from Emily,' said Miss Chivers in a very low voice.

'Why, is the Navy going to sail, Miss Chivers?'

'Oh, my goodness, Boots, what an alarming question. And it's not one I could answer.'

'No, of course not. I just like talking to you.'

'I like it too,' she murmured, 'and I treasure the hours I've spent with you and your family. I've so enjoyed watching Lizzy grow into a lovely girl. Boots, don't you have a girl yet?'

'I don't feel in any hurry,' I said. 'Actually, if I were older, I think I'd run off with you.'

Miss Chivers seemed to quiver, and faint pink touched her cheeks. I thought her beautiful.

'Oh, Boots,' she whispered with a tender smile, 'this is so sudden.'

'I think I'm in love with you.'

Through her glasses, the light in her eyes looked almost teasing.

'Oh, Boots, that it should come to this, when you're so young and I'm so old, and we're riding to work on a tram. Alas.'

'And alack. Oh, well, my stop's coming up.' The tram was slowing on its approach to Stamford Street. 'Farewell, Miss Chivers.'

'For ever?' said Miss Chivers.

'Well, until tomorrow morning, perhaps.'

I left the tram and walked to my work. I felt quite dreamy. The lacy hem of a white petticoat danced before my eyes in the morning sunshine, and I thought again of how exciting it would be to hold Miss Chivers in my arms, she clad in soft, snowy froth. That was what came from going into ladies' undergarments with Emily.

On Saturday, Miss Chivers knocked at our front door on her way home from her morning's work. She looked quiet and sober.

'Boots, will you please tell your mother I'm unable to come to tea tomorrow?'

'Something's happened?' I said.

'No, it's not that. Unfortunately, my mother—' She stopped and seemed to wince at an unhappy memory.

'She's found out that Mr Finch is often with us?'

'It's very difficult. She only has me. I'm so sorry.'

'Does this mean you won't be able to come at all?'

'I'm so sorry. Please apologise to your mother. I shall miss you all.'

She hurried away to her house. Undoubtedly, the old

Witch had found out. I told Chinese Lady, and Chinese Lady was upset. She felt responsible for having brought the hag's wrath down on the head of gentle Miss Chivers.

Emily appeared. She popped in and out of our house as if it were her own. She was wearing her other new frock, a rich yellow colour.

'I been tryin' it on since I come home from work,' she said to Chinese Lady.

'It looks very pretty,' said Chinese Lady.

'Is it nice, Boots?' asked Emily.

'If it wasn't, I'd make you take it back,' I said.

'Me dad says you got lovely taste, he says he ain't – he hasn't seen me lookin' nicer. Well, as long as you an' your mum like it too, I better go back an' wash me hair.'

I went to the front door with her.

'You're making a marvellous job of your hair, Em,' I said. Emily, I thought, always needed a bit of a boost.

'Oh, you're nice to a girl, you are,' she said. 'If I wear this frock tomorrer, can I come to church again with you an' Lizzy? I won't mess about, honest.'

She hadn't messed about for ages, anyway.

'We'll walk you there,' I said.

She cast her quick eyes at my feet.

'Could I – can I come to tea too?' she asked jerkily. 'I mean, me hands are better now. I got some cream from the chemist – he said it was his 'ighest recommendable. See, look, they ain't so red now.'

Her hands showed a distinct improvement in only a week. But I felt I ought to have left her alone, I felt I ought to have said nothing.

'Bless you, Em, you can kick me next time I don't mind my own business.'

Her head came up, and she looked shocked then.

'Oh, no – I want yer to mind my business – I didn't mean to say bleedin' cheek – specially not in that nice teashop. Oh, yer won't stop being a help to me, will yer, Boots? I'll do me hands reg'lar, like I do me hair, honest.'

'Come to Sunday tea, Em.'

218

'I'll bring a cake,' she said. 'I been doing cookin'. Mum don't mind me using the oven. I'm bakin' a fruit cake this afternoon.' Her green eyes fastened on my tie. 'I like bakin'. You don't mind me tryin' a fruit cake an' bringing it? I got to be good at something else besides washing bottles. If it don't turn out nice, I'll go an' buy one from Hall's. If yer mum won't mind.'

'Well, I'll tell you, Em, it'll probably save her going to the pawn to raise a bob to buy a marzipan cake.'

'Oh, ain't yer got no money, Boots?' Emily looked shocked again.

'Lizzy and I have got a little. Our mum never has any. What she has got she spends on us, to make sure our bones don't stick out and our boots don't let water.'

Impulsively, Emily said, 'Oh, I'll always loan yer fam'ly anything out of me savings. It don't seem right, your lovely mum having to go to uncle's. You needn't pay me back till yer all well-britched, honest.'

'You're a sport, Em, but it's not as bad as that. Lizzy and I can always find a bob or two.'

'It's just that yer got a lovely fam'ly, Boots.'

Ned came over on Sunday afternoon. He arrived like one of the family, letting himself in by the latchcord and walking into the kitchen to ruffle Sammy's hair and to present Chinese Lady with a bunch of roses. Chinese Lady was touched. Lizzy, expecting him, was prettying herself in the bedroom. Tommy was in the parlour, reading a comic. Ned cheerfully pointed Sammy doorwards, with the suggestion he might like to join Tommy.

'I ain't dyin' to,' said Sammy, 'but I will for a penny.'

Receiving a penny, he went. Ned closed the kitchen door.

'It's like this, Mrs Adams,' he said, 'it's like this, Boots. Will you mind if I talk seriously to Eliza?'

'Oh, my goodness,' said Chinese Lady, catching on at once.

'Yes, I know she's very young,' said Ned, 'that's been the

219

problem all along. But I know my own mind. I thought I'd mention it to you first. There's not going to be anyone else for me except Eliza. I need to pop the question, and that's a fact. I've got next year in mind. Say August or September. She may turn me down. If she doesn't, what d'you think about it? You're not turning pale, are you, Mrs Adams?'

'Ned, you and our Lizzy?' breathed Chinese Lady, and I saw gladness in her, a gladness for Lizzy. She could never have wished a better choice for Lizzy. 'You're going to propose to her?'

'My mind is like iron,' said Ned.

'You'd better talk to her in the parlour,' I said. 'I think she'd prefer the parlour. I'll turf the kids out.'

I turfed them out. Ned came in and began walking around the furniture. I asked him if he was worried.

'All right, clever Dick,' he said, 'but wait till you get struck by lightning.'

'I'll call the lightning,' I said, and went and knocked on the bedroom door. 'Lizzy? Ned wants to talk to you, in the parlour.'

Lizzy came out, colourful in her primrose frock. Excitement enlarged her eyes. Ned's arrival at any time always seemed to make her blood run.

'What're you lookin' so pleased about?' she asked.

'I don't know, do I? It hasn't come to pass yet.'

'You're as potty as a banana.'

'I like bananas. I didn't know they were potty.'

Lizzy entered the parlour with no idea of what was in store for her, and I popped upstairs to speak to Mr Finch. He was sitting at his table, writing a letter.

'Sorry we shan't be seeing Miss Chivers for tea,' I said.

'Yes, a pity, Boots. Such a pleasant lady.' Mr Finch blotted his letter and put the pen back in the inkwell. 'Sunday tea with your family was something she enjoyed. Possessive maternalism is an unhappy thing, my boy. You might say my Aunt Trudy was a little afflicted. That might tell you why I went to sea. All the same,

220

Boots, all the same, don't let it be said I've no affection for her.'

'I came up to tell you Ned and Lizzy are in the parlour, and that he's proposing to her. I thought you'd like to know.'

Mr Finch smiled warmly.

'I'm delighted,' he said. 'It was inevitable, of course. It was only a question of when. Who could resist Lizzy? She and Ned—' He drew his brows together then, and a little sigh escaped him. It made me think of Miss Chivers's sad look when I told her Emily had talked about a war. Today's papers were screaming about what was going to happen if Austria did go to war with Serbia, because Germany was promising to support Austria, and Russia was threatening to support Serbia. 'No, no,' said Mr Finch, almost to himself, 'life couldn't be so unkind to Lizzy.'

I heard her voice.

'Mum! Boots!' It was high with excitement.

I ran downstairs. In the passage, Lizzy was holding Ned's hand, her eyes moistly glittering.

'Who's on fire?' I asked.

'Never mind that,' said Lizzy, drawing a breath to calm herself. Chinese Lady arrived. 'Mum, don't reach for your smelling salts – but would you believe, Ned's been and asked me to marry him. It's all right, isn't it? I mean, next year? I'll be old enough then, won't I?'

'Course you will, lovey,' said Chinese Lady, and actually pressed Lizzy to her bosom. Briefly, of course, but definitely. 'There, I'm that pleasured for you.'

Lizzy smiled.

'You don't mind you're not losing a daughter, but gaining another son, Mum?'

'He's an improvement on the present lot,' said Chinese Lady.

'Good on yer, Lizzy,' I said, 'good on yer, Ned.'

We had a celebratory Sunday tea, and Emily's fruit cake, which arrived in style on a stand, two inches in advance of her budding bosom, was a luscious success. Emily, given the glad news of the engagement, was so happy for Lizzy that she cried. It made Tommy ask if there was any difference between an engagement and a funeral.

CHAPTER EIGHTEEN

War arrived like a thunderclap. The people went mad. The shops sold paper Union Jacks at a halfpenny each and people went about waving them at other people, and at passing tramcars. Chinese Lady grimly refrained from having anything to do with such behaviour. Wars didn't do anything except turn women into widows, she said, and she should know, she said. Soldiers were all right, she said, they were good men and brave, and there was nothing wrong with what they stood for, which was keeping the peace. The trouble was, she said, that Governments went out of their minds every so often and claimed that what soldiers really stood for was to fight each other. Our dad had been a good man and brave, she said, and had joined the Army to keep the peace of the Empire, and it must have saddened him, she said, when that shell come and blew his head off.

When Sammy came home one day with an armful of Union Jacks, she looked at him in stern sorrow.

'It's silly enough going out and wavin' one flag,' she said, 'but to go out and wave them by the dozen is something I won't stand for.'

'I ain't going to wave 'em,' said Sammy, 'I bought twenty-five for a bob, an' I'm going up Dulwich, where it's posh, and sell 'em for a penny each. I'll ask tuppence each first, then tell 'em all right, a penny, and they'll think they're gettin' a bargain.'

Sammy was already alive to the prospects of becoming a war profiteer. Tommy, almost fourteen, talked about joining up as soon as the Army would let him. Our mum didn't like the sound of that at all, and fires burned in her almond eyes.

223

'Don't you talk like that,' she said, 'you're not in long trousers yet, and you're not joinin' no Army, in any case, not while there's a war on and I'm still living and breathing. Soldiers is for keepin' the peace, like I've told you, not for killing each other.'

'But, Mum, suppose the Germans come an' invade us?' said Tommy.

'Then I'll go to Dover with lots of other women and tell them to go home sharp,' said Chinese Lady. 'I don't know where all this talk about young men going to war is coming from. We've got a proper army, with proper soldiers, and they'll do what's asked of them, even if they don't like doing it. The country don't need anyone from this family. They've already had your dad. They're not having you, nor Sammy, and nor you, Boots, either.'

'They still got to 'ave drummer boys,' said Tommy.

'You keep on like that, my lad, and I'll box your ears so hard your silly head'll fall off.'

Lizzy went about her life as if the war was something the newspapers had thought up. What the newspapers thought up could always be ignored. She went about with her engagement ring on her finger, and smiled very brightly at all little jokes. Whenever Ned was present, she was as resolute as Chinese Lady in discouraging all war talk. Single-mindedly, she discussed with him plans for their future. She knew, as all Walworth people did, that marriage was no bed of roses. But she knew our mum had had good years with our dad, that our mum held our dad's memory in respect, even if not his carelessness, and that, I think, gave her confidence in her coming marriage to Ned. That event was to take place in August next year, and it had received the blessing of Ned's parents.

Miss Chivers began to go early to work every day after the British Expeditionary Force had taken a hiding and our ships started to be sunk all too regularly by German U-boats. And the country woke up one day to find impressive posters pasted on hoardings. They showed the stern, commanding face of Lord Kitchener, our war chief, with his finger pointing. And they bore the words, 'YOUR COUNTRY NEEDS YOU'.

There were rumblings at the office. The free flow of imported meat into the country was being affected by the war at sea, and the manager, Mr Barratt, began to look like a man whose department was doomed.

I met Miss Chivers quite often at the tram stop in the mornings. I still avoided any temptation to walk with her up the Place. With a war on, her mother was more horribly watchful than ever, probably because some newspapers reported that German soldiers were prone to outrage hapless French and Belgian ladies. There were no German soldiers in Walworth, certainly, but the occasional British Tommy appeared on the streets, and the Witch wasn't a woman to have charitable thoughts about any soldier, foreign or otherwise. She had typical thoughts about me. She called after me one morning, when I began my walk in the footsteps of her daughter, already out of sight.

'I'm watching you, I know what's in your mind, you disgusting boy – you ought to be locked up.'

'So ought you, Mrs Chivers, and for good.'

She nearly fell out of her window in her rage.

A German zeppelin came over one night, and the maroons went off to warn people that bombs might drop on them. The sound woke me up. Sammy and Tommy, however, sound asleep in their bed, did not even twitch. I got up, put on a coat, and went downstairs. The front door was open and someone was standing there. It was Mr Finch, in an old woollen dressing-gown. Our lodger was very sad about the war.

'Can you hear anything?' I asked.

'Yes,' he said, and we went outside to stand in the middle of the street and to listen. I heard a low droning high in the black sky.

'It's up there, right above us,' I said.

'Yes,' he said sombrely.

'Imagine, Germans up there in that sausage.'

'They're probably more nervous than we are,' Mr Finch spoke quietly and without hostility. 'If things go badly wrong at sea, Boots, there's still a chance for the crew. If things go wrong in the sky, there's no chance at all. Dirigibles are frail ships of the air.'

'I feel frail myself, with bombs hanging over my head,' I whispered.

The dark street seemed to murmur, as if the drone of the zeppelin was awakening families. A shadowy figure flitted.

'Boots?' It was a murmur from Miss Chivers. She was wrapped in a coat, her hair softly loose. In the darkness, her face glimmered.

'There's a German zep up there,' I said.

'Yes, I heard the maroons,' she said. 'Mr Finch?' She whispered his name. Mr Finch gave her a silent nod, and she seemed to be drawn to him, she seemed to edge up to him without giving any distinct impression of movement. A bomb dropped. She quivered at the sound of a faint, muffled explosion. The bomb hit a house in Camberwell, killing a man and his wife, as we discovered later.

'Oh,' breathed Miss Chivers, 'was that a bomb?'

'I'm afraid so,' said Mr Finch.

'How terrible it all is,' she whispered. A window opened, and she stiffened.

'Elsie? Elsie?' The voice was a whine. 'You there? You're out of your bed – you're out there, I know you are. You've left me here all alone. Who's that with you, who's out there in the dark with you? You come in at once, you hear?'

Without saying a word, Miss Chivers went back into her house. The night was silent, the droning zeppelin far off, and Mr Finch and I returned to our beds.

At work three weeks later, there was an announcement on the notice board. It said that because of unavoidable circumstances brought about by the war, the clerical staff was to be reduced by half. Senior men received two weeks' notice. Junior clerks received a week's notice. I was among

226

them. I took the bad news home with me. Chinese Lady took it bravely, saying there would soon be plenty of jobs for boys of my age. Boys my age, she said, would replace men who were volunteering to go off to the war. Prior to Kitchener's posters, Chinese Lady had been calling me young man. Now she referred to me as a boy my age. I knew what she was getting at, but didn't say anything.

When Ned brought Lizzy home later that day, after an evening out with her, she didn't bring him in. She said goodnight to him at the front door, and when she entered the kitchen, she was pale-faced and stricken. Ned, she said, had decided to volunteer for the Army, to help get the war over quickly. He had said it needed to be got over quickly, so that we could all go back to a peaceful existence. Lord Kitchener wanted a million men, and Ned intended to be one of them. Lizzy's mouth was compressed, her eyes glittering.

'Oh, Lizzy love,' said Chinese Lady, and her careworn look surfaced.

Lizzy said tragically, 'I didn't think I'd take second place to Lord Kitchener.' And that was all she said. Her dreams lay shattered and she was numb amid the wreckage. I'd have liked to talk to Mr Finch about her and Ned, but he wasn't home. Because of the war, he was working all hours on the river. But he was in earlier the following evening, and when I told him about the effect Ned's decision had had on Lizzy, his fine and expressive eyes grew quite dark.

'The war, Boots, makes one lose faith in the men who command us.'

'I feel Lizzy has lost faith in Ned.'

'Never,' said Mr Finch, sombre but positive.

I had to work out my week's notice. I wouldn't get paid if I didn't.

Miss Chivers passed by as I emerged one morning, giving me a fleeting smile. She was carrying a shopping bag, as well as her handbag. Like Mr Finch, she was very sober these days, as if saddened by the war. And working as she did at the Admiralty, she was probably far closer to the perils of the war at sea than most people. But she never talked about her work.

As usual, I waited a while before showing myself in the street. But for once, the Witch didn't call after her to ask if she had her glasses on. For once, there was no dark, inimical face to be seen. For once, there was no eerie feeling of ugly eyes boring into my back.

I caught Miss Chivers up at the tram stop. She gave me a faint smile. The morning was wet, chilly and gloomy, and she had on a grey raincoat and felt hat.

'Glad to see you're wearing your glasses,' I said jokingly, and she smiled again.

Not for the first time we rode together on the upper deck of a number 18 tram. I told her about Ned's decision to join up. I said I supposed next year's wedding might depend on whether the war was still on or not.

'Boots, I'm so sorry. Poor dear Lizzy must be feeling terribly low. It's going to be a horrid war.' Miss Chivers was sadly but warmly sympathetic. 'It shouldn't have happened, it's affecting so many lives. Do give Lizzy my love. She's been so happy.' Miss Chivers sighed for Lizzy, her gloved hands on her handbag, her handbag on her shopping bag, resting on her lap.

'D'you know what she said? That she didn't think she'd have to take second place to Lord Kitchener.'

'Oh, dear.' Miss Chivers shook her head and smiled. Then she said gently, 'Kitchener – our warlord.'

'Well, we're in the war and someone's got to run it, I suppose. But Lizzy surprised me, saying that. Emily was a surprise too. Of all people, she was the one who said there was going to be a war when nobody else was even thinking about it. Now she's wearing a little Union Jack in her buttonhole. And she's quite optimistic. We'll beat 'em, she says.'

'We all surprise ourselves sometimes at what we say and do,' said Miss Chivers with another smile, a soft and faraway one.

'I'm losing my job, you know. I'm finishing on Saturday. They said it's the war.'

'Oh, Boots.' Miss Chivers came to, and was newly sympathetic. 'That's such a blow to you and your family.'

'It's a blow to Mum all right. It means her going back to pinching and scraping. She's really had enough of that. I suppose I'll have to think about joining up myself.'

'Let Lord Kitchener go first,' said Miss Chivers in a low whisper.

'What?'

'You have your family to think of,' she said.

'Yes. But – oh, well. How's your mother?'

'She'll never be any better,' said Miss Chivers, which was the first time, to my knowledge, that she'd departed from saying something like oh, just the same.

It was paralysing, the news I walked into when I got home that day. For a start, all the neighbours were at their street doors, gossiping or gawping, eyes watching me as I walked down the Place. For another thing, there was a uniformed constable guarding the door of Miss Chivers's house. Our front door was open. In the kitchen, Chinese Lady was sitting at the table, her hat on. She looked stiff-faced and pale.

'Something's up,' I said, 'there's a copper outside Miss Chivers's house.'

'Sit down, Bobby,' she said. Something had to be up for her to call me Bobby. 'I've sent Sammy and Tommy upstairs to the bedroom for a while.' She drew a painful breath. 'The police have been. They're still in Miss Chivers's house. The doctor found her mother dead when he called two hours ago.'

'Dead?'

'Yes, Bobby, dead.'

'I'm sorry,' I said, although I wasn't. I simply thought how free Miss Chivers was now, and how she could burst into life. She must have had a premonition. She had said on the tram that her mother would never get any better.

'It's worse than you think,' said Chinese Lady palely. 'Her throat was cut.'

'Oh, bloody Moses,' I said, and it was then that I felt paralysed.

Chinese Lady winced.

'An ambulance came,' she said. 'They took the body away only a little while ago, after the police sent someone to fetch Miss Chivers home. She's here now, lying down in my bedroom, and in a terrible state, all collapsed. The police are going all over her house. Someone must of broke in, someone must of—' Chinese Lady winced again.

'Someone could have found the key and just walked in. Miss Chivers always left it under the step mat on the days when the doctor was due to call.'

'Whichever way, it don't bear thinkin' about,' said Chinese Lady. 'Poor Miss Chivers, so dreadfully white and shocked. What it'll do to her, I can't think. And I suppose the police'll knock on all the doors and ask questions like did anyone see anything or hear anything.'

'Did you?' I asked, thinking of Miss Chivers and her mother with her throat cut.

'Course I didn't,' said Chinese Lady, 'I'd of told the police if I had.'

'She didn't scream murder, then, the old woman?'

'If she did, I didn't hear her. But she must of had the horrors when she saw the knife comin' at her throat. Who could of done it, Bobby? Who could of cut an old lady's throat and left her dead?'

'Let the police worry about that, Mum. You've got enough on your plate. I'll make a pot of tea. Should I offer Miss Chivers a cup?'

'No, leave her be,' said Chinese Lady quietly, 'she's got grief and nightmares to fight. I don't know how you can be so calm.'

'I'm not. I'm shaking, Mum, I can tell you. I'll make the tea.'

'I'll do it.' That was Emily's voice.

Chinese Lady jumped. Emily had come in very quietly.

She was in the hat and coat she wore to her work. Her thin face was pale.

'Em'ly, I didn't hear you,' said Chinese Lady.

'Your front door's open.' Emily spoke through stiff lips. 'Anyone could've walked in. Anyone could've—' She strove for self-control. 'I closed it. Mum's just told me about Mrs Chivers. She's havin' to brace herself with dad's special medicine.' Mr Castle's special medicine was whisky. He was a beer-drinker who kept whisky for a crisis. 'But it's worse for you. You was all Miss Chivers's best friends. I'll make the tea for you. I won't get in the way.'

Emily picked up the kettle from the range hob. It was always kept on the hob in the winter, when the range was alight. It saved on the gas, for the water was usually hot when the kettle was transferred to the scullery gas stove for boiling. Emily disappeared into the scullery.

'She's gettin' to be a good girl,' said Chinese Lady mechanically. 'Well, it's just as well Lizzy won't be home yet. Ned's meeting her at her work to take her out this evening. I hope she won't quarrel with him about him joining up, only she's in the mood to. If she has a row with him, she'll come home all upset and then have this to face. I still can't believe it. It's – it's—'

'Murder,' I said, and Chinese Lady winced yet again.

'And almost next door to us,' she said. 'I won't get no sleep tonight.'

'I don't think the murderer's going to come back, Mum.'

'I don't mean that, and even if I did, I got you here an' the kids. I mean I'll be thinkin' of poor Miss Chivers and what's going through her mind. The doctor's give her something to help her sleep tonight, but she'll still have nightmares. We ought to offer to put her up somehow – she can't go home, she can't sleep in a room next to where her mother's been murdered in her bed.'

I heard Emily moving about in the scullery. I got up and put out cups and saucers from the dresser. Emily came in and put the milk can on the table. We always kept the milk in the scullery, the coolest place. Emily got a jug and poured some of the milk into it. She was very subdued.

'I'm not in the way, am I?' she said. 'Only I want to do something. Oh, Mrs Adams, I'm awf'lly hurt for you, an' just terribly sick for Miss Chivers – there, the kettle's boiling.' She returned to the scullery, taking the milk can with her. She made the tea and brought the pot in, with its cosy.

'Sit down, Em'ly,' said Chinese Lady, 'Bobby's put out a cup an' saucer for you.'

Emily sat down, milked the cups and poured the tea. She was surprisingly competent and self-controlled, her hand quite steady as she handed tea to us. But her lashes flickered as she loooked at me, her green eyes dark with worry.

'It's awful,' she said.

'Yes,' I said.

Someone knocked on the front door.

'I'll go,' said Emily, and did. She called, 'It's the police, Mrs Adams.'

'Bring them in,' I called back.

She brought them in, two men in plain clothes. One was tubby and round-faced, the other tall and thin.

'Sorry to disturb you,' said the thin one. 'I'm Detective-Sergeant James, and my colleague is Detective-Constable Brown.'

'It's all right,' said Chinese Lady. 'Would you like a cup of tea?'

'Well, that's very nice of you, Mrs—?'

'Mrs Adams,' I said.

'And you're—?'

'I'm Robert Adams, her son. And this is Miss Emily Castle, from next door.'

'Oh, yes, we've seen Mrs Castle,' said Detective-Sergeant James. 'The tea would be very welcome, Mrs Adams.'

Emily looked as if it was a relief to know police liked tea as much as ordinary people, and she quickly put out two more cups and saucers. She poured the tea.

'Sit down, if you like,' said Chinese Lady, and the two men took their hats off and sat down.

'Just a few questions,' said Detective-Sergeant James, and the other man produced a notebook and a pencil. 'You understand?'

'Of course,' said Chinese Lady, but her face was stiff. Emily's pointed chin jutted bravely.

'First, which of you were here during the day?'

'Only me,' said Chinese Lady. 'I got home from me work at the town hall at ten this mornin'. Bobby's only just got home from his.' She didn't mention Sammy or Tommy, and I knew she wasn't going to have them brought down from the bedroom if she could help it.

'I only just got home too,' said Emily. 'Boots an' me – Bobby an' me's been at our work all day.'

Detective-Sergeant James smiled at the little challenge in Emily's voice.

'Please don't worry, Miss Castle,' he said. 'Mrs Adams, during any time of the day, did anything come to your notice, anything out of the ordinary?'

'No, nothing,' said Chinese Lady, sipping her tea. The policemen took thirsty gulps of theirs.

'You heard nothing?'

'You mean screams?' said Chinese Lady painfully.

'I fancy you didn't hear screams.'

'I'd of run out in the street if I had,' said Chinese Lady. 'I didn't hear a thing that was suspicious. Mrs Blake, she lives closest to Miss Chivers – their back yards face each other. Didn't she hear nothing?'

'It seems not,' said Detective-Sergeant James in a perfectly friendly way. Detective-Constable Brown was taking notes. 'You didn't, I suppose, see any strangers about?'

'I don't know any strangers,' said Chinese Lady with nice logic. 'People come an' go in the Place, to the print fact'ry and drug mills. They're customers, I suppose. I don't think of them as strangers. Anyway, I've spent all day indoors, doing mendin' and ironin' and suchlike, and getting food ready.'

'I don't know who did it,' blurted Emily, 'but it don't seem

233

right, askin' Mrs Adams questions like you thought it was her.'

The policemen eyed her brightly. Emily crimsoned and bent her head.

'We're only asking questions,' said Detective-Constable Brown paternally. 'It's a way of picking up clues. Clues, y'know? People can be a great help in a nasty business like this. They notice more than they realise. Asking them questions makes them think. We don't like upsetting anyone, but we have to ask, y'see?'

'Sorry,' said Emily, blushing redder.

'Take Miss Chivers now,' said the constable, 'the poor lady's daughter. We're going to have to ask her lots of questions that'll be very upsetting to her, as soon as she's feeling well enough to answer them. But it's something that's got to be done, don't y'see?'

'Oh, it's awful for her,' said Emily.

'Mrs Adams,' said Detective-Sergeant James, 'we understand you and your family were close friends of Miss Chivers.'

'She come to Sunday tea once a month,' said Chinese Lady.

'What would you say was her relationship with her mother?'

Chinese Lady frowned in dislike of the question.

'Her mother was a bit retiring,' she said, 'and an invalid, and Miss Chivers looked after her and give her care and attention. Some mothers get a lot less from some daughters.'

'The relationship was affectionate?'

'Seeing how Miss Chivers took such good care of her mother, you couldn't ask for more lovin' kindness than that,' said Chinese Lady with a certain asperity. She knew as well as anybody that the Witch had made her daughter's life a misery, but she had never been one to gossip about it, and she obviously had no intention of doing so now. It had nothing to do with the person who had murdered Mrs Chivers, anyway. Her asperity was a reminder to the policemen of that.

Detective-Sergeant James tried a different question.

'Does Miss Chivers have other friends, Mrs Adams?'

'She might, at her work,' said Chinese Lady, 'I don't know of any others otherwise.'

'Do you mean men friends?' I asked.

'Well, I'll tell you,' said Detective-Sergeant James in friendly confidence, 'we've found no sign of breaking and entering, no sign of any disturbance, although Miss Chivers has told us that what little jewellery her mother had is missing. Now, if someone who knew Mrs Chivers – a friend of her daughter's, say – also knew the doorkey was sometimes left under the step mat – well, the point is, were there any men friends?'

'If Miss Chivers told you about the jewellery, didn't she answer that question herself?' I said, and Emily gave a little nervous hiss.

'Miss Chivers, when she was brought home from her office, gave us some information, but because of her state of distress, we asked her very few questions. We'll be talking to her later. Meanwhile, we're asking around, as the saying is.'

'I honestly don't think you'll find anyone who can tell you if Miss Chivers had any men friends,' I said. 'She devoted herself to her mother. But even if there were men friends – at her office, say – why would one of them want to cut her mother's throat? Someone might have wanted to pinch Mrs Chivers's jewellery, but cutting her throat into the bargain – well, I can tell you, people round here will want to know what the world's coming to.'

Emily bent her head. Whether they'd meant it or not, there were more than a few people round here who had said the Witch ought to be done in. Emily knew that, and so did I. So, probably, did Chinese Lady.

'No gentlemen ever called on Miss Chivers?' The question was put to Chinese Lady.

'Not that I know of,' I said.

'Nor me,' said Emily.

'Nor me,' said Chinese Lady.

'Miss Chivers will tell you, anyway,' I said, 'when you ask her.'

'All in a day's work, sir,' said the constable.

'You know she's here, lying down, do you?' said Chinese Lady.

'Yes, we know, Mrs Adams,' said Detective-Sergeant James. 'Later on, if we might talk to her here—?'

'Yes, you got to talk to her, I suppose.'

'We'll leave a constable outside your door.'

'I don't want no constables doing that,' said Chinese Lady.

'He'll keep newspaper reporters from disturbing your privacy. It won't take any reporter long to find out Miss Chivers is here. So if you'd let us post a constable—?'

I had an odd feeling this was as much to do with keeping an eye on the movements of Miss Chivers as with guarding our privacy, and the feeling disturbed me.

Chinese Lady, looking distinctly upset, said, 'Newspaper reporters? I'm not answering the door to anyone from a newspaper. Newspapers? We're not going to be in them, are we?'

'It'll all be in the morning papers,' I said.

'Well, we shan't,' said Chinese Lady.

'We'll post a constable,' said Detective-Sergeant James.

'That's kind of you, I'm sure.'

'I'm sorry for all the trouble.' Detective-Sergeant James and his colleague rose from their chairs and picked up their hats. 'Thank you for the tea, Mrs Adams. If we need to call on you again, you won't mind?'

'You got your job to do,' said Chinese Lady.

The policemen left.

'Oh, crikey, I'm all shakes,' said Emily. 'I never thought – well, a murder in our street and listenin' to police askin' questions, it don't seem real, it seems like some awful dream. Well, I better go back to Mum now in case me dad's not home yet. He ought to be.' Emily, on her feet, seemed uncertain about what to do. 'Still, I better go.'

'You're a good girl, Em'ly,' said Chinese Lady.

'I do feel for you, Mrs Adams, really I do,' said Emily. 'Goodbye, Boots,'

'So long, lovey,' I said.

Later that evening, the police came back. This time, Detective-Sergeant James was accompanied by a Detective-Inspector. They talked to Miss Chivers in the downstairs bedroom. They were with her for ages. Lizzy arrived home while they were still there, and Lizzy was shocked and horrified by the news of the murder, which Chinese Lady imparted to her as gently as she could. I had told Mr Finch about it when he entered the house a little after nine. He looked quite weary from his long day on the river, having left for his work well before seven-thirty in the morning.

He said, when I met him in the gaslit passage, 'There's a police constable outside. He asked me who I was before he allowed me in. What's the trouble, Boots?'

I told him, and he seemed to become lined and haggard before my eyes.

'We're living a nightmare,' I said.

'God in heaven,' he breathed, and put a hand on the banisters, as if he needed support. 'It can't be true. Murdered in her bed?'

'We heard that that was what her doctor said. Miss Chivers is here, by the way. In Mum's room. There are two policemen with her, asking her questions.'

'My God, you're a cool one, Boots.'

'Don't you believe it, Mr Finch. I'm paralysed.'

Mr Finch took his hat off and wiped a film of sweat from his brow.

'Murdered, Boots, murdered in her bed?' he said in haggard disbelief.

'Yes.'

'Who would do such a thing?' he said, and turned and climbed the stairs like a man whose vigour had drained from him.

He too was interviewed by the police after they'd

finished with Miss Chivers, but they were only with him for five minutes. They left then, and we made a pot of tea. Chinese Lady took a cup to Miss Chivers, and I took one up to Mr Finch. Sammy and Tommy, uncomfortable and uneasy, had gone early to bed.

'Mr Finch? We thought you'd like a cup of tea.'

'I would, Boots. Thank you.' He was sitting at his table. His face seemed to have taken on Chinese Lady's drawn and careworn look. His eyes, which, in their alert brightness, always seemed to reflect his mental robustness, were unreadable in their darkness. 'A terrible business,' he said, and drank the hot tea gratefully.

'Horrifying for Miss Chivers,' I said.

'Thank God she has you and your family to turn to.'

'And you too,' I said. 'You're just as much her friend as any of us are, and she needs someone now, don't you think so? Someone very strong as well as very kind? What did the police say to you?'

'They simply asked me how well I knew Miss Chivers, and how well I knew her mother. I said I knew Miss Chivers very well, but that I'd never met her mother and never spoken to her.' Mr Finch filled his pipe and put a match to it. He drew in smoke and exhaled it. It drifted upwards. 'I told them my friendship with Miss Chivers was that of a neighbour, that we met about once a month at Sunday tea in your parlour. They asked me what I thought of her. I told them I considered her a charming but retiring lady. They asked me what I thought of her mother. I told them that since I knew so little of her mother, I had no opinion to offer. They thanked me and left.'

'Did they tell you that the person who did it made off with some jewellery belonging to Miss Chivers?'

'No, Boots, they didn't tell me that,' said Mr Finch, deep in sombre thought. 'Jewellery? In Walworth? Does anyone in Walworth own jewellery?'

'Mrs Chivers owned a little, apparently. Miss Chivers reported its loss to the police.'

'Good God,' breathed Mr Finch, 'murdered for a little

238

jewellery? Boots, tell Miss Chivers that if I can be of any help at all, I will. There are some things even worse than war. I don't wish to be out of order, by the way, not at a moment like this, but you'll be out of a job next week, because of the war. So I've been looking around to see if I can get you a new job, on the river. Would you work on a barge?'

Because of the terrible thing that had happened, I felt he was being a little out of order, that my own problems counted for absolutely nothing, but I also felt he found continued discussion of the murder unbearable. His face was so drawn. He loved Miss Chivers, I was sure, and his thoughts about her at a time like this were his own.

'Mr Finch, that's kind of you, but I'm thinking of joining up,' I said.

He looked as if I had wounded him.

'Don't do that, Boots, you're still very young.'

'I'm eighteen.'

'Too young,' he said, and shook his head. 'Don't do it. There'll be jobs for everyone soon, in the new industries of war, in all kinds of departments, and you'll earn good wages. Your family needs you as an earner, Boots, not as a soldier. There are millions of men the Army can take before they need the younger ones.'

'Mum, as a widow, will get an allowance from the Army if I join up. I've checked.'

'A few paltry shillings, Boots. Have you spoken to her?'

'Not yet.'

He sighed. He seemed very weary.

'She won't like you putting her second to Lord Kitchener any more than Lizzy liked Ned doing it to her. The country shouldn't make demands on the young in wartime when it does so little for them in peacetime.'

This was a new Mr Finch, a troubled and unhappy Mr Finch, and almost a little bitter. I knew it was because of Miss Chivers and her murdered mother. But at least the Witch was not in his way now. He could comfort Miss Chivers quite openly.

Lizzy was in the passage when I went downstairs. She drew me silently into the parlour. She was as surprisingly self-controlled as Emily had been.

'Mum's with Miss Chivers,' she said. 'Boots, about what the police asked you and Mum, about Miss Chivers havin' men friends. I think that's what they're going to be on about, don't you? They're going to look at any close man friend she had. I bet they're thinking about the key under the step mat, and someone knowing it was put there for the doctor. I mean, if the old – if Mrs Chivers was murdered in her bed, someone must have walked quietly in and up the stairs and – oh, don't it make yer shudder?' In her horror, Lizzy lost her ladylike desire to speak more proper. 'Don't it make yer blood run cold?'

'I suppose she must have been in her bed. But she was always up when Miss Chivers went to work, and she was always at one window or another, peering and making ugly faces at the street kids.'

'Yes, but what I mean is I don't think we should tell anyone we saw Miss Chivers and Mr Finch together that day. We know Mr Finch couldn't have done it, and wouldn't, but the police'll get after him if they hear he and Miss Chivers were seen out together. So if they come and ask more questions, we won't say anthing. That's best, not saying anything. It would only make things more upsetting for Miss Chivers.'

'I know what you mean, sis, but I'd think Miss Chivers would have told the police everything about any men friends. I shouldn't think there'd be any point in her keeping quiet about them now, as she doesn't have to worry about what her mother would say. If the police feel the poor old lady was done in by someone who knew Miss Chivers fairly well, someone who knew about the key, I'm sure Miss Chivers would give them all the information she could. I think she'd have probably already told them if she'd been meeting Mr Finch – and I've just thought, perhaps they met accidentally in that teashop? When I mentioned to her I'd taken Emily there, she said she went

240

there herself sometimes, so she might have bumped accidentally into Mr Finch. Well, that makes me think you're right – it's best we don't say anything about it. Anyone could've done the deed. Some crook might have known or might have guessed Mrs Chivers had a bit of jewellery. And some crooks might do an old lady in to keep her quiet.'

'We don't have crooks like that round here,' said Lizzy.

There were a few old lags in Walworth, and a few up-and-coming ones too, the kind who picked pockets or went and did a house in Dulwich, but there were no thugs.

'Well, the police'll find whoever it was,' I said, and we went into the kitchen to warm ourselves at the fire. A moment later, Chinese Lady came in with Miss Chivers, who was terribly pale and dark-eyed. But she spoke quite gently.

'It's dreadful, isn't it? I'm so sorry for the distress it's causing everyone,'

'Oh, what can we say?' said Lizzy. 'You're the one who's got such a burden of suffering.' She sounded just like our mum. 'We'll do anything we can to help.'

'Dear Lizzy,' said Miss Chivers emotionally. 'What should I have done without you all, without the comfort of your kindness? It's all so—' She visibly shuddered. 'I'm not quite sure whether I've really taken it in yet. I feel very numb. But I must go back home now.'

'I've told her she shouldn't, that she ought to sleep here, but she won't,' said Chinese Lady.

'I'm not afraid,' said Miss Chivers. 'I'm very shaken, but I'm not afraid.'

'I'll come with you, if you like,' I said, 'and sleep in an armchair in your front room. Just so that you won't be alone, that you'll have someone in the house with you.'

'How kind of you, Boots, how very kind,' she whispered, and her suffering eyes misted. She was not wearing her glasses.

'Yes, let him do that, Miss Chivers,' said Lizzy, 'we couldn't bear you being on your own, and neighbours wouldn't think much of us as your friends if one of us didn't do that much for you.'

'Boots is a tall and strong boy now,' said Chinese Lady, 'especially for his age.'

'Boots is a fine young man,' said Miss Chivers.

'Boys his age might look – well, never mind,' said Chinese Lady. 'He'll come and sleep in an armchair, Miss Chivers, and keep you safe. It's no more than he should do.'

'I'm so grateful,' said Miss Chivers. 'Thank you, Boots.'

There was still a police constable outside our front door when Miss Chivers and I emerged. The street was dark and quiet. Everyone had at last quit the scene except this policeman.

'I'm taking Miss Chivers to her house,' I said.

'Ah,' said the constable, and fingered the chinstrap of his helmet. 'I'll come along with you, sir.'

'There's no need. Miss Chivers is going to try to get some sleep, and I'm going to sit in an armchair in her front room.'

'That's very neighbourly of you, sir. I'll be going off duty at eleven. I'll keep a watch until then. You never know what sort of people might come knocking on the door. You'd be surprised the kind that hang around when there's been – well, when there's been something out of the ordinary happen.'

'Yes, goodnight, officer,' said Miss Chivers. I walked with her to her house. The constable followed, deliberate and ponderous in his tread. Miss Chivers let herself in with her key and turned the gas up in the passage. I closed the door. In the light, she looked at me. The house was uneasily quiet, and I thought her very courageous in her willingness to face up to it. 'Are you sure you don't mind, Boots?' she said in a low voice.

'About something out of the ordinary? Well, yes, I mind about that because of what it must have done to you. But I don't mind about being here.'

'You think I might get silly and frightened?'

242

'I don't think you'll get silly.'

'I'll light the gas in the parlour for you.'

She lit the gas mantle above the mantelpiece. The room looked tidy and clean, the linoleum softly shining. There were armchairs and a sofa, all leather-covered, and a cabinet filled with books. Miss Chivers drew the curtains to.

'I'll manage now,' I said, 'you go up.'

'Do you want anything, Boots? A cup of cocoa and a biscuit, perhaps?'

'No, nothing, thanks. I'll leave about seven in the morning without disturbing you. I'll need to get a wash and shave before—'

'A shave, Boots?' Almost there was a smile in her voice.

'I've been shaving for over a year, I'll have you know.'

'Yes, you have grown manly. I'll go up, then – oh, I'll bring you some blankets down or you'll freeze.'

'Thanks.'

She went upstairs. I took off my jacket, waistcoat and tie. I inspected the books in the cabinet. I was certain I wasn't going to find it easy to sleep. A read would be the thing for a while. I waited for the blankets to arrive. I heard Miss Chivers moving about upstairs for several minutes, and then there was only silence. The parlour began to feel wintry, and in just my shirt and trousers I began to feel uncomfortably cold. I continued to wait, borrowing a book and sitting down to read it. Time went by and there was still no sign of Miss Chivers and the blankets. Then, suddenly, there was the sound of movement from above, followed by a kind of whispering rush down the stairs, and Miss Chivers appeared at the open door of the parlour.

'Boots – oh, I'm terribly sorry, I actually forgot about the blankets – I actually went to bed without giving them a thought – do forgive me.' Her voice was a whispering rush too. 'But here they are.'

I went and took the blankets from her. She stood with the passage gaslight behind her, and I was aware of her hair flowing and loose. The blankets, folded, came thick and warm into my hands. The light above the mantelpiece bathed her. I stared. She was clad in a black silk nightdress. Black silk. It hung around her, delicately draping her figure. Semi-transparent and softly translucent, it gave her white body an allure that was breathtaking to me. Firm, fulsome breasts glimmered. My mouth went dry and I was unable to speak. Her eyes looked so dark, so shadowed.

'Miss Chivers—' That was all I managed to say.

'You must have been so cold – I'm so sorry – I might even have gone to sleep and forgotten the blankets completely – my mind was on other things – then I remembered and rushed down – I brought two – will they be enough to keep you warm?' Every word was a soft murmur.

'Yes. Thank you.' I stopped looking at the misty whiteness of breasts and made a vague inspection of blankets. 'It's all right – don't worry.'

'Dear Boots, how sweet you are,' she whispered.

'I borrowed a book.'

'Yes, of course. Thank you so much for being here.' She put her hands lightly on my shoulders, reached up with her mouth and kissed me on the cheek. A compulsive reaction made me turn my head, and I kissed her lips. Her silken-draped breasts pressed against the buffer of the blankets. Her lips were soft and warm and sweet. She did not retreat in modesty and alarm. She kissed me without reserve, and lingeringly. 'Goodnight, Boots.'

She was gone, closing the door behind her.

I slept in fits and starts on the sofa.

CHAPTER NINETEEN

It was in the papers the following morning, of course. The headlines and the story made me feel sick. I couldn't concentrate on my work. That hardly mattered, anyway, for I only had a couple of days to go. My mind was full of imaginative pictures of the murdered Witch one moment, and of dreams of Miss Chivers in a black silk nightdress the next.

No one in the office realised the murder had taken place in the street in which I lived, which was a great relief. The manager called me into his office during the afternoon. He had one of my worksheets in front of him.

'You're making some unaccustomed mistakes, Adams,' he said.

'It's probably because it's on my mind that I'll be out of a job next week,' I said.

Mr Barratt frowned.

'Yes,' he said, 'I understand. I'm sorry, Adams. But your work has always been very good, and I'd have liked you to have maintained that standard to the end. Your accuracy has been a pleasure to me, and I shall be happy to give you your written reference. Without any mention of your indifferent performances this week. Or the fact that you were three minutes late this morning.'

'Kind of you, sir.'

'I'm sorry to lose you. Good luck. Be on time tomorrow.'

When I got home, Chinese Lady had a bread pudding in the oven, and its fruity, spicy smell invested the kitchen with a mouth-watering aroma.

'Good old Mum,' I said, 'any news?'

'Worries, that's all,' she said, and told me that people from newspapers had been nosing around. Some had knocked on our door, pushed their noses in and asked her nosy questions. She'd answered a few, then shut the door on them, and one or two noses had narrowly escaped injury. Mrs Castle, of course, had invited them in, so had other neighbours. And the police had been in Miss Chivers's house again.

Emily came in later, her attitude restrained. She and Lizzy went and sat in the bedroom to talk.

Tommy made a comment.

'Us kids ain't 'alf popular at school. Everyone wants to know about the murder. Anyone 'ud think me an' Sammy an' the other kids seen it done.'

'I been thinkin',' said Sammy, 'I been thinkin' I might go to the *South London Press* tomorrer.' The *South London Press* was our local newspaper. 'I could tell 'em lots about the old – well, Mrs Chivers, like. Newspapers pay yer good money if yer tell 'em lots about people who been murdered.'

'If you do that,' I said, 'don't bother to come back. Just keep going until you reach a rundown orphanage.'

'Here, you ain't our dad,' said Sammy, 'you can't send me orf to an orphanage, can he, Mum?'

'But I can, you nasty boy,' said Chinese Lady, 'and I will. Don't you talk to anyone about Mrs Chivers, you hear?'

Sammy, conceding that for once money wasn't everything, said, 'All right, Mum, I won't say nothink to no one.'

When he and Tommy had gone up to bed, after putting away a mug of cocoa and a slice of bread pudding, Mr Finch came down to sit with us for a while. Last night, he had been a man shocked. Tonight, he was calmer.

'I thought of calling on Miss Chivers, to offer whatever I could in the way of help and to give her my sympathy. But I think she would rather be left alone for a few days. In similar circumstances, I know I would. It troubles me, Mrs

Adams, that you're so close to the unpleasantness of it all, you and your family.'

'You're as close as we are,' I said.

'Yes, I am, Boots.' He lit his pipe. He found pleasure in his pipe. 'I admit a feeling of unhappiness. I'm sure we're all unhappier about this than about the war at the moment. But time will help us, and Miss Chivers. I don't want to talk too much about it. Endless talk is exhausting.'

'Yes, I know what you mean, Mr Finch,' said Lizzy.

'What I really came down for was to say that as the war has brought a rise in the cost of things, including food, I think it only fair, Mrs Adams, to pay you an extra two shillings a week on my rent. Please allow me to do that. Here is the rent that's due for next week, the new amount. Eight shillings.'

'Mr Finch,' said Chinese Lady, 'I really – '

'I insist,' said Mr Finch. 'I don't know any man who's lodged more comfortably and kindly than I am.'

'Thank you, I'm sure,' said Chinese Lady, 'I'm pleasured to have you, Mr Finch.'

'Ned joined up today,' said Lizzy.

'The war,' said Mr Finch, shaking his head. 'Lizzy, I'm sorry.'

'I think we all ought to have a nice cup of tea,' said Chinese Lady, rising.

'Yes, a nice cup of tea works wonders,' said Mr Finch. 'That's the saying, isn't it?'

'Name?' said the recruiting sergeant, hardly looking up from his desk.

'Robert Adams.'

'Age?'

'Eighteen.'

'Address?'

'Number two, Caulfield Place, Walworth.'

'Next of kin?'

'My mother, Mrs Maisie Adams, same address. She's a widow.'

'A widow – right.'

'A war widow.'

He looked up.

'Your father was a soldier?'

'He was.'

'You're welcome, son. What regiment?'

'West Kents.'

'West Kents. Right.' He made a note on the form. He completed his entries. 'Sign there, then take the oath.'

I signed. An officer stepped forward, and along with a number of other recruits, I took the oath to serve my King and Country.

'Company! Company – on pa-raaade!' The huge voice of a warrant officer rang out over the square of the training camp deep in the heart of Kent. Some four hundred recruits waltzed untidily about in all directions before miraculously resolving into eight separate drill squads, each squad under the command of a sergeant assisted by a corporal.

Sergeant Harris, in charge of C Squad, watched silently as forty-eight men, including me, arranged ourselves in four ranks of twelve. Corporal Purvis ordered us to dress from the right, and we shuffled and sidled, right arms extended sideways to ensure we finished up at the correct distance from each other. We had been at the camp a week, and had been told that after three or four months we might, if we looked like soldiers by then, receive our first seven days leave before being posted to a new battalion. As yet, we had no rifles. The camp was awaiting a consignment from an overworked ordnance factory.

'Squad – squad – shun!' bawled Corporal Purvis. Corporal Purvis almost always bawled. Sergeant Harris almost always spoke quietly but clearly. 'All present and correct, Sergeant,' said Purvis.

Sergeant Harris eyed us bleakly. He was long, lean and rock-hard, and coming up to forty. He had fought in the Boer War, and at Mons and Le Cateau, where he'd been badly wounded in the leg. His hero, Lord Roberts, who had finally put paid to the Boers, had just died, leaving him dourly pessimistic about the Army's present leadership. In France and Belgium, the battles were desperate. The Allies were holding the Germans, but only just. Sergeant Harris, a fighting man, did not seem to think much of his current job as a drill NCO.

'Stand easy,' he said. We stood easy. The other squads were already being marched about on the enormous square. Sergeant Harris ignored that. 'You've been here a week,' he said, 'and I want to tell you, my lads, that some people might say you're shaping up and some might not. In my opinion, you're still falling over your feet. I suppose you know you've all got two feet. One's your left, the other's your right. This is the left.' He pointed to his polished left boot. 'This is the right.' He pointed to his right boot. 'It might be confusing to some of you, but you'll learn. Well, you'd better, because by the end of your training here, you'll either be soldiers or you'll get your legs broken. C Squad's leg-breaking machine is Corporal Purvis. Your time on the square fits you for knowing your left from your right, for obeying commands, for coming smartly to attention and for making you capable of all marching in the same direction at once. I've already told you this, but half of you seem to have cloth ears. Corporal Purvis, who's that man scratching himself?'

'Private Anderson,' bawled Corporal Purvis.

'Well, inform him sometime that his King and Country don't allow him to do it on parade.'

'It's me flannel vest,' said Private Anderson. Such vests had been issued to all.

Sergeant Harris fixed him with a cold eye. Private Anderson visibly shrank.

'On parade,' said Sergeant Harris, 'you speak only when you're asked to. Right, then. Squad – squad – atten-shun!'

We came to attention and the morning's square drill began.

It was the following morning, at breakfast in the great draughty dining hall, that the man next to me, having finished his porridge and his bread and sausages, pulled out a newspaper and began reading it.

'Blimey,' he said.

'Blimey why?' I asked.

'They nicked someone for that Walworth murder – the daughter, would yer believe.'

Ice ran down my spine.

'Mind if I look?' I asked, and he passed me the paper. There it was, brief but horrifying. It stated that Miss Elsie Chivers, thirty-one, had been arrested and charged with the murder of her mother, Mrs Daisy Chivers.

I received a letter from Chinese Lady next day.

'*Dear Bobby, something awful's happened, did you read it in the papers, they've been and arrested Miss Chivers, no one can believe it and even Mr Finch looks struck down. Lizzy cried her eyes out and I feel ill. I don't know what you're doing of in the Army when you ought to be home at a terrible time like this. There's talk about people here being called as witness, you'd better come home and be one, you can talk a lot more convincing than some of us, you can stand up for Miss Chivers. Emily says no one could do it better than you, Emily's got a good head on her shoulders and knows what she's talking about, she says do you want her to knit you some socks. She's never done any knitting but she's started to learn, although with this awful thing about Miss Chivers hanging over our heads we can't settle to anything much. Ask the Army if you can come home for a while. Lizzy says what with Ned in the Army as well as you, and now Miss Chivers in peril of her life through injustice, it's hardly the best time we've ever known, and she's right. She and the kids send their love though what you went and joined up for we'll never know, your affec. Mother.*'

I managed to have a word with Sergeant Harris before we were called on parade. I told him my troubles. His granite-like face became very bleak.

'Where d'you think you are?' he asked.

250

'In the Army, Sergeant.'

'Well, that's something. I thought you thought it was Sunday school.'

'My mother's a widow.'

'So's mine.'

'My father fought in the Boer War.'

'Mine fell off a bridge.'

'Mine was killed later on the Northwest Frontier.'

'Hard luck.' Sergeant Harris was unmoved. 'What regiment?'

'West Kents.'

'And you're taking his place, are you? Well, listen, Private Adams, it's the West Kents you're in all right, and it's my job to make you deserve the West Kents. I can't do that if you come and ask me to ask the Adjutant if you can go home every time your mother drops a saucepan on her foot.'

'She hasn't dropped a saucepan on her foot.'

'I know, I know. I'm sure she's a good mother. Everyone's mother is good, but we can't go and bring them into the Army with us. In their nice way, they'd muck things up. No, you can't go home. You couldn't help, even if you went with the blessing of Lord Kitchener himself. It's not your mother who's been arrested, it's just a neighbour. Everyone's got neighbours, some good, some bad and some lousy. But there's a war on, lad. Worry about that, not your neighbour. She'll get a fair trial before they hang her.'

'I wish you hadn't said that, Sergeant.'

'Don't rile me, son.'

'She's not going to like this,' I said.

'Who's not?'

'My mother,' I said, as a bugle sounded.

'Kindly go away,' said Sergeant Harris, 'or we'll fall out. Get yourself on parade.'

I wrote to Chinese Lady, explaining my difficulties, and back came another letter from her a few days later, full of tart comments about the Army and my lack of sense in joining it. She went on to say that Miss Chivers's solicitor had been to see her and other neighbours, and that he wanted her as a witness for the defence. She was quaking at the thought of that, she said, but she was going to do it for the sake of Miss Chivers. The solicitor also wanted Mr Finch to appear, and Mr Finch had agreed to do all he could as a witness. Mr Finch was very upset about the arrest, he said the law was out of its mind. She had asked the solicitor to call me as a witness too, but the solicitor said that wasn't necessary, especially as I was busy preparing to do my bit for the country.

It was two months before the new rifles arrived. Sergeant Harris began the morning parade with a homily.

'Stand at ease,' he said. We stood at ease. He eyed Private Parks stonily. Private Freddy Parks was a mate of mine. 'I said stand easy, I didn't say flop about like a dying penguin.' Private Parks pulled himself together. 'My lads, today's your lucky day. This morning, you'll all draw rifles. Drill fits you for marching, rifles fit you for soldiering. You can't soldier without them. Each man will make a note of his rifle number and memorise it. You hear that?' We all stood in silent assent. 'Losing your rifle or mislaying it is a crime against the King's Regulations, and any offender will be stood up against a wall and shot by men who haven't been as careless as he has.' Sergeant Harris was dry and straight-faced. If he had a sense of humour, it never showed. 'You'll receive your rifles with gratitude. They're going to be your best friends. Some of you think your mothers are your best friends. You can forget that. From now on it'll be your rifles. You'll cuddle 'em, clean 'em, love 'em and cherish 'em. You'll need 'em when you come face to face with the enemy. What enemy, you may ask. Yes, my lads, what enemy?'

Unable to resist supplying the answer, I said, 'Sergeant, it's the Germans, Austrians, Hungarians and Turks.'

'Did I hear someone, Corporal Purvis?' asked Sergeant Harris.

'Private Adams,' bawled Corporal Purvis.

'It was him, was it?' said Sergeant Harris. 'Well, inform Private Adams he'll be first tomorrow to fix his bayonet and charge the Germans, Austrians and all the other fanackapans.'

He was as good as his word. I led the charge against the stuffed dummies of the enemy, and not a smile disturbed his granite features as one swung violently back and knocked me off my feet.

'Dear Boots, I hope you don't mind me writing, your mum give me your camp address so I thought I'd write, but only if you don't mind. It's heroic you're a soldier now, though your mum don't think much of it. She give me an earful last week when I said you were going to help us win the war, she said you'd get your head blown off more like, but she didn't mean it. She's that upset about Miss Chivers, like we all are, what with going to court and the magistrate saying Miss Chivers had got to go for trial at the Old Bailey. Who would have thought it, the Old Bailey? She couldn't have done it, not when she's so nice and Dad says she hasn't even got it in her to harm the hair of a dog.

'It's put everyone in a state, but at least I've got a new job now, in a war factory making haversacks and things for the Army, I like it much better than the bottle-washing factory, which was ruining my hands. I can wear nicer things at my new work. I still keep my hair nice and still save lots of my wages, which are more than I got for washing bottles. I went and bought some very nice lonjery at a ladies' shop, it's what Lizzy told me to call it, lonjery, she said it's a French word that ladies use, and I've got a nice boy too. His name's Arthur and he works in the factory office and I've been out with him twice, would you believe. Fancy me having a boy. He took me up West, where we saw lots of soldiers and sailors strolling about and having a fling flirting with girls.

'Are you getting on well in the Army? We all hope you'll soon come home on leave, your family misses you, but

you're a soldier now and it can't be helped. My mum and dad send you all the best and my dad says don't forget to duck when you get to France. Everyone's sad about Miss Chivers, but we're all hoping for the best, they say the trial starts in a fortnight and your mum's going to stand up for her in court and so is Mr Finch, isn't he a kind man? I hope this reaches you as it leaves me in good health, yours faithfully Emily Castle.'

I replied to Emily, thanking her for thinking of me and wishing her good luck with Arthur. I told her the word Lizzy had mentioned was lingerie, which I agreed was more ladylike than drawers and things. I said I was due for leave fairly soon, and that I was sure Miss Chivers would never be found guilty. I told Emily to cheer up Mum and Lizzy, and to tell her dad I'd not forget to duck as I didn't fancy getting shot through being careless. That wouldn't help anybody, I said, and wouldn't do me much good myself.

I tried not to think about Miss Chivers. I tried to tell myself that Chinese Lady and Mr Finch would convince the jury she was simply too gentle a person to do the slightest harm to anybody. Mr Finch was bound to be particularly convincing. His Aunt Trudy had brought him up to be a kind and forthright man.

Thinking of his Aunt Trudy made me remember she lived in Chatsford, which wasn't all that far from the camp. I asked Sergeant Harris if he could help me get a pass to go to Chatsford.

'Where?' he said, looking not quite so impassive for once.

'Chatsford. It's not very far. A relative of our lodger lives there. I thought I'd call on her and have a chat. I'm keen to meet her.'

'Who is she, your lodger's young and innocent sister?'

'No, his aunt. I need a pass if I want to go there, don't I, Sarge?' We were allowed out in Maidstone on Saturday afternoons, but a pass was usually required if you wanted to go somewhere else. You could get a pass if you had a relative next door to death, but it was difficult otherwise.

'Apply to the duty officer,' said Sergeant Harris.

'I thought you might put a word in for me.'

'Sometimes, Private Adams, I get a feeling that you think I'm fond of you.'

'No, I'd just like to get a pass—'

'Shove off,' said Sergeant Harris.

But despite his apparent lack of comradeship, he must have put in a kind word on my behalf, because on Saturday morning an orderly room clerk handed me the necessary pass. I thanked Sergeant Harris.

'I think I should tell you, Private Adams, that that pass and the King's uniform don't entitle you to muck the place up.'

'Pardon?' I said.

'If I hear anything about raping and pillaging, I'll have you shot in the places where it most hurts.'

'I don't go in for that sort of thing,' I said.

'That's what they all say.'

I took a train to Canterbury and changed there for Chatsford. Arriving at the station, I asked the ticket collector where Meadow Lane was. He gave me directions and I walked. It was a fine March day, crisp and bright. Chatsford was a large village of cottages, houses and gardens, with a wide and attractive high street. A farm cart stood outside the farrier's shop. The horse was inside, and I stopped to watch in fascination the shoeing of the placid beast. Going on, I got the eye from two girls because of my uniform, and I saluted them. They burst into country giggles and fled. I was feeling these days that I needed a girl to go out with. Most of the other recruits talked about their girls at home. I could have talked about Miss Chivers, who aroused such pleasurable sensations in me, but I didn't, of course. I kept very quiet about her.

I turned left off the high street, walked fifty yards and turned right into Meadow Lane, which looked very countrified with its hedgerows and cottages. Reaching number 19, I opened a wrought-iron gate, walked up the path and knocked on the front door. It was a pretty

255

cottage, with latticed windows and creeper on the walls. The door was opened by a studious-looking man, near to middle age, with a pipe in his mouth and a copy of *The Times* in his hand. He took the pipe from his mouth and smiled.

'A visit from the Army?' he said.

'Excuse me,' I said, 'but I'm looking for Mrs Gertrude Livingstone.'

His eyebrows went up, giving him a startled look. Then he said, 'Good lord, who are you?'

'My name's Adams, Robert Adams. Mrs Livingstone is the aunt of a friend of mine – well, he's the lodger in our house in Walworth, south-east London. Mr Finch. He's talked to us a lot about her, and as I'm at the West Kents' training camp, I thought I'd come and call.'

'Oh, I see.' He smiled again. 'Unfortunately, Mrs Livingstone is away. Did Mr Finch know you were coming?'

'No. I only made up my mind yesterday. We get Saturday afternoons off, and I thought it would make a nice change to come and meet Mrs Livingstone instead of traipsing around Maidstone.'

'A pity,' said the studious-looking gentleman. 'Had Mr Finch known, he could have told you his aunt was away.'

I heard a woman call, 'Who's that, dear, the curate?'

'No, just someone enquiring after Mrs Livingstone,' he called back. 'I've told him she's away.'

'When's she expected back?' I asked.

'Not for some time. I'm renting this place from her while she's away. I've some writing to do.' His smile was kind. 'I needed somewhere restful and quiet. We live in London normally, my wife and I. Sorry your journey's been for nothing.'

'That's all right.'

'I'd ask you to come in for some tea, but we're going out in a few minutes.'

'That's all right,' I said again. 'Goodbye.'

'Goodbye,' he said. He stood at the door and gave me a friendly wave when I reached the gate. A woman appeared. She smiled at me over his shoulder.

I walked back to the high street. There were quite a few shops, and three pubs. There were several people about. I saw a teashop. I thought of Emily, quivering with awe because the teashop in the Strand was so grand. This was a homely teashop, and I went in to treat myself to a cup of tea and a slice of cake or something. There were a number of tables neatly laid. At one sat a healthy-looking country couple, enjoying a large pot of tea and buttered scones. Behind a counter was a handsome woman with a full figure. I sat down. She came up and gave me a smile. She had rich red lips and white teeth.

'Good afternoon, Captain,' she said. Her voice sounded lush and fruity.

'I'm not a captain yet,' I said, 'I'm just a recruit. Could I have a pot of tea and some scones? Wait a sec, though, I'd better see if I can afford it first. How much will it be?'

'Thruppence for the pot of tea, soldier, and thruppence for four buttered scones. Only it's not butter now there's a war on. Still, nearly as good as butter. I make it myself, with a margarine base.'

'Sixpence altogether?'

'Just sixpence. We don't take tips from soldiers.' Her full lips seemed to dance around her white teeth. 'I'll get Rosie to serve you while I go and look at the scones. Rosie?' Through the open door at the back of the shop, a girl appeared. She wore a black dress with a white front, signifying her status as a waitress. 'Rosie love, serve the captain here with a pot of tea and four scones. I need to look at the oven.'

Rosie was about seventeen, with hair as black as Chinese Lady's kitchen range, a healthy complexion and bright, lively eyes. She was almost as pretty as Lizzy. Behind the counter, she made a pot of tea with boiling water spouting and steaming from an urn, and she buttered the scones. She brought everything on a tray.

'Here we are, Captain,' she said in a warm country voice. 'That's your teapot, and them's your scones.'

'I'm glad you told me,' I said, 'or I might have drunk the scones and eaten the teapot.'

Rosie laughed exuberantly. The country couple laughed heartily.

'Cheeky, aren't you?' said Rosie.

'So are you,' I said. 'Where's the milk?'

'Here,' she said, lifting the attached lid of a pewter jug.

'Thank you kindly.'

'Oh, my, you're a one,' said Rosie, and lingered. 'What's your name?'

'Robert.'

'I'm Rosie.'

'Yes, I think I've just met your mother.'

'Mum's a corker,' she murmured.

'What's a corker?' I asked, filling my cup.

'Oh, go on, I bet you thought her peachy.'

'No, I just thought her scones looked nice. You're the peachy one.'

'Golly,' murmured Rosie, 'you're lively, you are. No wonder soldiers have got girls in every port.'

'I thought that was sailors,' I said, eating a freshly-baked scone.

'Same thing,' said Rosie, still lingering.

'Don't tell the sailors that.'

'I like you,' said Rosie.

'You're nice yourself,' I said.

'Rosie,' called her voluputous-looking mother, 'come and take these scones.'

'I won't be a tick,' said Rosie, and danced away with her tray, and her rounded bottom received a light smack from her mum.

'You're flirting again,' said her mum, and the country couple smiled at each other, then at me.

'I'm just talking,' said Rosie, and brought out a dish of hot scones, which she placed on the counter. Two stout ladies came in and filled a table.

'Pot of tea, Rosie,' said one.

'And some scones,' said the other.

'Got your soldier boy in today, Rosie?' said the first.

Rosie smiled.

Emily would have liked this kind of cosy teashop. I finished the scones. They were delicious.

'Penny for them,' said Rosie, appearing beside me again.

'I liked the scones.'

'D'you want another one? We won't charge, seeing you're a soldier.'

'No, no more, thanks.' I poured a second cup of tea. Rosie eyed me smilingly. She picked up my cap and looked at the brass badge.

'You're West Kents,' she said. 'I go into Maidstone some Saturdays.'

'We could meet,' I said, 'if your mum won't mind.'

'Honest?' she said.

'If you are.'

'I'll have to be back home by eight,' she said.

'Next Saturday, then, outside the town hall?'

'Three o'clock?' said Rosie.

'I'll be there. You sure your mum won't mind?'

'Not unless she fancies you herself,' murmured Rosie.

'I'm a bit young for someone's mother.'

'I still like you,' said Rosie.

CHAPTER TWENTY

Ned wrote.

'Dear Boots. I got your address from Eliza. How are things with you in the West Kents? The East Surreys have sent me to this place. I'm an officer cadet. If I get my commission, I shan't take any more lip from Eliza. I'm not too popular with her at the moment, as you no doubt know, but you and I both, we can't help the way things are. It's stiff and grim here. The discipline's a swine, but that's how good officers are made, I'm told. I only hope I come out of this place alive.

'It's pretty bloody terrible, this business of Elsie Chivers coming up for an Old Bailey murder trial. Could a woman like that have actually murdered her own mother? Like you and your family, I find it unbelievable, I find it impossible to think of a guilty verdict – God, you know what that would mean, don't you? I'd like to get some leave and cheer Eliza up a little, but there's no chance at the moment. It's concentrated training and swotting day after day. It's making me feel second lieutenants are highly-prized cannon fodder, that they're shaped to fit the barrel of a field gun and fired at the Germans. If you land on one and knock him cold, you're promoted to first lieutenant. If you miss the target, you pick yourself up, and go back to get fired again.

'Well, there are all ways of fighting a war, I suppose. Eliza's not very happy about the shortcomings of men. She's convinced they not only like to get themselves into a war, they like getting themselves blown up into the bargain. Perhaps she's right. Let's hear from you sometime, Boots, and let's hope we bump into each other

when we get to France. All the very best, Ned.'
I sent a reply in very much the same vein.

Rosie was already waiting when I got to the town hall on Saturday at five to three. Her smile was vivacious.

'You're nearly late,' she said.

'Then you're nearly early. Still, nice to see you, Rosie. I wasn't sure you'd turn up.'

'And I wasn't sure you would, seeing how larky you were about it,' said Rosie. In a dark blue coat and hat, she looked tingling and healthy in the cold air. Traps and buggies trotted by, and some motor vehicles, including omnibuses, belched about, giving Maidstone a taste of things sure to come. 'I told Mum you were just a laugh.'

'A joke?'

'No, a laugh. That's not the same as a joke.'

'What does that mean, that your mum trusts you with a laugh, but not a joke?'

'Gracious me,' said Rosie, 'you're tying me in knots, you are. Where you going to take me?'

'Would you like to go to a teashop?'

'I've just left one. Well, good as just left.'

'So you have. That wasn't very bright of me, was it?'

'I wasn't actually complaining,' said Rosie, 'and I'd like some tea.'

'So would I. I was brought up on a teapot. We drink gallons at home.'

'My dad says the whole country swims in it and that it'll drown itself one day. He says no one'll cry for help, only for more sugar. Come on, then.' Rosie put her arm through mine and we began our stroll amid the wartime shoppers. Khaki uniforms were plentiful, and the girls of the town were out and about, boaters bobbing as they perkily sized up the soldiers they most fancied. Rosie was hardly shy. Her arm hugged mine, bringing it close to her warm breast. She tripped along beside me as if her body enjoyed movement, and she gave me the impression she considered we were already old friends. I stopped at a teashop. 'No,

261

not that one,' she said, 'everyone goes in there. I know a much nicer one, where you get treated decent.'

The nicer one, in the main shopping thoroughfare, was what Emily would have called posh. It had lace curtains and a little bell that tinkled when the door opened. There were alcove tables, Madeira lace tablecloths and the glint of silver cutlery. Among the customers were delicate-looking old ladies and two officers with young ladies. There was an elegant manageress, and there were two prettily-uniformed waitresses, one of whom gave Rosie a quick, knowing smile. Rosie sailed through like a blue-clad swan on a smooth-flowing river, and the officers glanced at my private's greatcoat. I thought about saluting them, then remembered one didn't have to in places like teashops or restaurants. It was assumed, in any case, that privates wouldn't patronise the same establishment as officers. Rosie sat down at an alcove table. I removed my peaked cap and my greatcoat, hung them on a peg, and sat down with her. The waitress who had given Rosie a smile with a wink to it arrived to take our order. She gave Rosie another smile.

'Nice,' she said.

'Oh, hello, Lily,' said Rosie.

'What would you like, Rosie?' I asked.

'Tea and toast and a slice of fruit cake,' said Rosie.

I ordered the same for both of us. Lily, the waitress, gave me a wink all to myself before departing.

'She's very friendly,' I said.

'Well, she's looking for one of her own,' said Rosie.

'One what?'

'Soldier, silly,' laughed Rosie. 'D'you like it here?'

'Your teashop's homelier.'

'It's my grandma's place, really. Mum does the home-made cakes and I help at the tables and Grandma counts the takings. Grandma likes takings and counting them, and Mum likes baking and meeting people.'

'I can't make head or tail of that, Rosie, unless you mean your mum really does pop people into her oven before saying hello to them.'

'Oh, you cuckoo,' said Rosie, and her eyes filled with giggles. 'You're a real laugh, you are. I like meeting people myself, don't you?'

'I liked meeting you.'

'I expect you say that to all the girls.'

'All what girls?'

'Don't you have a girl at home?' she asked.

'None I can think of.'

'Never mind, I still like talking to you. But no girl, really, and you so thrilling?'

'I'm steady, not thrilling.'

Our tea arrived in a silver pot, followed by hot buttered toast – or it might have been margarine – and slices of rich, dark fruit cake.

'Service with a smile,' said Lily, the waitress.

'Buzz off,' said Rosie. She poured the tea and we ate the hot toast. 'I'll be your girl, if you like,' she said.

'Pardon?'

'Well, if you like,' she said.

'That's very kind of you, Rosie.'

'It's only if you fancy me,' she said.

'I do fancy you. You're a lovely girl.'

'Have some cake,' said Rosie, pushing the dish my way. I took a slice. 'Well, shall I, then?'

'Shall you what?'

'Be your girl.'

'Rosie, you don't even know me.'

'Well, gracious me,' said Rosie, 'what's that matter? I'm only going to be your girl, not your keeper. Anyway, of course I know you. And Mum said you were an improvement on some she could mention.'

'I don't see how your mum—'

'D'you want some more tea? Pass your cup.'

I passed it and she refilled it. She might have been only seventeen, but she had as much bounce as Nellie Wallace. She was good for me, she took my mind off Miss Chivers. One of the reasons why I'd joined the Army was to take my mind off Miss Chivers, but it didn't work all the time.

Rosie was a great help.

'Your mum only saw me for about thirty seconds,' I said.

Rosie's smile was sweet.

'Oh, it only takes Mum a tick to make up her mind about soldiers,' she said.

'Was she a sergeant-major, then, before she started baking cakes for your grandma's teashop?'

'The things you say – aren't you a lad?' said Rosie, and her lips looked red and her teeth white, just like her mum's. She exuded rich vitality. 'You don't mind that I fancy you, do you?'

'Well, if we fancy each other, that's a nice coincidence.'

'You said your name's Robert.'

'Robert Adams. Robert's a bit stiff.'

'I'll call you Bert,' said Rosie, cutting up her slice of fruit cake with a knife. She popped a neat square of it into her mouth and made a luscious little meal of it. 'Bert's a nice name for a soldier. My surname's Harris – that's in case you want to write love letters to me.'

'Love letters?' I'd had no idea I was in as deep as this already.

'Well, if you like.'

'We've got a drill sergeant called Harris.'

'That's probably my dad,' said Rosie, eating more fruit cake.

'Pardon?' I said.

'He was wounded in the retreat from Mons,' said Rosie, 'and he's been doing a drill sergeant's job for a while. Is he the one you mean?'

'Sergeant Frank Harris, that's his name.'

'That's my dad,' said Rosie, 'it's nice you know him.'

'Nice? He'll murder me.' I wished at once that I hadn't used that word.

'Only if you've got two left feet.'

'He's not going to like one of his awkward recruits getting off with his daughter.'

'Oh, you needn't take any notice of that,' said Rosie

blithely. 'He was made acting company sergeant-major at Mons, then he got wounded and lost the promotion to another sergeant, so he's been a bit cursed about things. But he's just been told he'll be made up when the new battalion's formed, so he'll be kind to you from now on. Would you like to take me round the shops before you put me on my train back home?'

'As long as I don't have to go into ladies' shops and look at things.'

Rosie's eyes filled with new giggles.

'Aren't you comical?' she said. 'Shall we go?'

'I'd better pay the bill first,' I said. I picked it up. The pot of tea was fivepence, the toast for two was threepence and the fruit cake was fourpence. A shilling in all, and I left Lily tuppence for a tip. I had to learn to live.

Rosie took me on a prolonged tour of the shopping areas. Like all girls, she found shops irresistible, even if there was no purchase in mind. She was a vivacious and bubbly window-gazer, and an enthusiast in her inspection of interior wares. Her exuberance was infectious. She took me into clothes shops, china shops, stationery shops, furniture stores and even a hardware shop. In the latter, she surveyed a range of wallpapers.

'Grandma wants new wallpaper for our teashop,' she said. 'D'you like that one?'

That one was a cream-coloured wallpaper with a pattern of richly red roses climbing around bamboo.

'Very jolly,' I said.

'Jolly?'

'Bright and cheerful. Like you.'

'I'm jolly, bright and cheerful?' said Rosie.

'And pretty too, of course.'

'You're beginning to be a favourite of mine,' said Rosie, then spoke to an assistant. 'I'd like some rolls of that one, the one my soldier friend likes.'

'Certainly, miss.'

'Wait a minute,' I said, 'hadn't you better take a sample home to your grandma first? If you buy it and she doesn't

265

like it, I'll get the blame.'

'Better you than me,' said Rosie. 'No, Grandma told me to please myself, and this'll do. You've got good taste.' She took a slip of paper out of her handbag with figures on it. She studied them and worked out her requirements with the assistant. Her requirements came to five rolls, which were parcelled up and paid for. She went through the transaction enjoyably, and we left the shop, the long solid parcel under my arm. With time running out, she asked me if I'd like to walk her to the station.

'Of course.'

So she put her arm through mine again, and we walked to the station.

'You can help me do it Sunday week,' she said.

'It?'

'The wallpapering. We can't do it except on a Sunday. Grandma wouldn't close on a weekday because of her regulars. You can do wallpapering, Bert, can't you?'

'I once did our bedrooms at home when the landlord sent round some remnants.'

'That's all right, then.' Rosie bobbed along. 'We'll do it together Sunday week.'

'Sorry, Rosie, but we're not allowed out on Sundays. Just Saturdays. It's church parade Sunday mornings and hush on Sunday afternoons.'

'Don't worry, I'll speak to Dad. He'll be home for the day tomorrow. He'll see you get a pass.'

'Don't you believe it.'

'But you'll come, won't you, if you do get one?' she said, the cold night air making her lashes glimmer as if the frost was settling on them.

'All right, I'll come, Rosie,' I said, as we turned into the station.

'Come early, then you can have Sunday dinner with us. Gracious me, that's my train coming in.'

'Goodbye, Rosie, it's been really nice.'

'Well, come on, then, give us a kiss,' said Rosie, lifting her face and pursing her dewy lips. I kissed her. Her

266

mouth, touched by the frost, was cold and tingling-fresh before melting into warm softness. Her young bosom pushed at me. I kissed her twice. She kissed me back. 'Mmm, I like you,' she said, and ran for the platform.

'The wallpaper?' I shouted, and ran after her. She turned and I gave her the parcel. She laughed and ran on.

Outside the dining hall on Monday morning, Sergeant Harris stood in silent observation of recruits filing out after breakfast. His bleak eyes took note of my emergence.

'That man – yes, you – come here.'

I approached.

'Yes, Sergeant?'

His grey eyes glinted.

'Private Adams, I presume?' he said, and it was all there, in his eyes, the knowledge that I'd had the gall to get off with his daughter.

'I had no idea, Sergeant, honest, that—'

'Don't come the old sweat with me,' he said, 'I've eaten six like you for afters, you pillaging delinquent.'

'Pillaging?'

'I thought you went to Chatsford to see your lodger's aunt, not to rut about in search of virgins.'

'I did, Sergeant, but she was away.'

'What's her name?'

'Mrs Livingstone.'

'Never heard of her.'

'Well, Chatsford's a big village—'

'Where's she live?'

'Meadow Lane. The postman would know her, he delivers our lodger's letters to her.'

'I don't think I'm going to like you, Private Adams.'

'I just went in for a cup of tea, Sergeant, I had no idea your family—'

'Shut up. Stand to attention.' His face was expressionless. 'Anyone would think that men who join up to fight in this kind of war would represent the backbone of the country, not its leavings. What's all this lead-swinging

267

business about wallpapering the teashop next Sunday?'

'Well, it was like this—'

'Don't tell me, I'll die laughing.' Sergeant Harris became a study in dark marble. 'For your information, there's a war on, and you're in it. Furthermore, you ponce, you've got yourself out of your class, and if you didn't notice it that means you're all flat feet and no savvy. D'you know what savvy is, Private Adams? It means recognising what's in front of your eyes. Now, are you still keen on wallpapering?'

'Well, I did promise, Sergeant – but only if I can get a pass, of course.'

A kind of wintry pity pained his face.

'You're a mug, Private Adams. Right, about turn. Right, double march and keep going until you fall off the cliffs of Dover.'

I had another letter from Chinese Lady. It was all about the worries of the coming murder trial. The trial was to begin next Tuesday, and she said I mustn't think she wanted to spoil my first leave. I was due home on Monday. I was to have a nice seven days, she said. The solicitor had told her it wouldn't be a long trial, as there weren't many witnesses. Mr Finch had said that if it was to be a short trial, the prosecution must be inflicted. She didn't say inflicted by what or whom. She did say she had the shakes, but that that wasn't going to prevent her speaking up for Miss Chivers, and she also said the war must be sending the country mad. It could only be that, she said, which made the country put poor Miss Chivers on trial for her life.

I replied to say that all being well, I'd be home on Monday, that I'd like to go to the court and perhaps the solicitor could make sure I got a seat. I told her to keep her pecker up, that Miss Chivers couldn't possibly be guilty, that she was going to be tried simply because the police had failed to lay their hands on the real murderer. I said to tell Mr Finch I'd called at his Aunt Trudy's house, only to find she'd gone away for a while.

I tried to have faith in my belief that Miss Chivers would be set free, and I tried not to think about her in her black silk nightdress. Thoughts of Rosie helped, so did thoughts of her dad, Sergeant Harris, who professed himself indescribably blissful at finding I was on target with my rifle at the butts.

On Saturday, I was called to the orderly room and given an all-day pass for Sunday.

The teashop in Chatsford high street was closed. I peered through a window. I saw tables and chairs piled in the centre. I saw two stepladders and a plank. The counter was covered by an old sheet, and the old wallpaper had been stripped off. I knocked. Rosie came through the shop and opened the door.

Her smile got into her eyes.

'You've come,' she said. 'That's nice. Still, I told you not to worry.'

'Well, I'll tell you something, Rosie. Your dad's not as keen about this as you are.'

'Oh, I can always manage Dad,' she said, letting me in and closing the door. 'I can't always manage Mum, but she's a woman, of course.'

'My mum's a woman too,' I said. 'I like your Sunday outfit, by the way.'

Rosie's shapely figure was covered by a blouse and skirt, over which she wore a huge apron. A scarf was wound around her hair.

'You don't mind I look awful?' she said with a smile, and I thought the smile implied she knew she was so pretty that she could never look awful, not even in a sack. She had more self-confidence than Lizzy. Lizzy would have died sooner than let Ned see her in an old apron and a headscarf. 'We've got some overalls for you. You'd better come through and meet Grandma. You've already met Mum.'

I went through the shop and Rosie took me into a living-room where a grey-headed lady sat reading a

Sunday newspaper. She pushed her steel-rimmed glasses down her nose and gave me a sharp, enquiring look.

'Who's he?' she asked Rosie.

'I told you he was coming, he's my soldier friend,' said Rosie. 'He's at Dad's camp and he and Dad are pals. His name's Robert. You can call him Bert.'

'I like to know what's going on,' said the elderly lady.

'Now don't fuss, Gran,' said Rosie, 'just say hello.'

'None of your cheek, missy.'

'Good morning, madam,' I said.

'What's he call me?' asked Grandma Harris.

'He's being polite,' said Rosie.

'Well, now you're here,' said the old lady to me, 'don't knock things about or break any windows. Just put the wallpaper up nice and tidy. Rosie, is he staying to dinner?'

'I told you, Gran, yes,' said Rosie.

'You and your soldiers,' said Grandma Harris, and returned to her paper.

'We're only young once, Gran,' said Rosie. 'Come on, Bert, the overalls are in the shop. You go and put them on, and I'll bring the bucket of paste. I've mixed it. Mum's doing the dinner. She'll come and have a look at you in a minute, to see you're behaving yourself, or if I am.'

I went and put the overalls on, taking my khaki jacket off first. Rosie, a live wire, danced in with the bucket of paste.

'Well, here goes,' I said, 'but I can't guarantee perfect results.'

'Never mind being gloomy,' said Rosie, 'let's have fun. Roll out the paper – on the counter. I've got all the measurements.'

'You're a girl wonder, you are.'

'Well, give us a kiss, then,' said Rosie, and came close, put her apron up against my overalls, and lifted her mouth.

'Won't your dad mind?' I said.

'He would, if you kissed him instead of me,' said Rosie, eyes bright. I gave her a thrilling kiss. She gave me one, even more thrilling. We coincided with the next. 'Help, don't make me faint,' she said.

'To work,' I said, 'but say a prayer first.'

'A prayer? What for?'

'That your grandma won't make us do it all again.'

Rosie pealed into laughter. From the depths, from the kitchen, I supposed, her mother called.

'What's going on out there?'

'Just the wallpaper, Mum,' called Rosie.

Her mum came in. She was wearing something knitted, and it clung warmly around her bosom, making her breasts look boldly pushing. Sergeant Harris had got a wife whom Emily's dad would have called a cuddlesome armful. One would have thought he ought to look happier than he did.

'Hello,' said Mrs Harris, 'blessed if you aren't the young captain.'

'I'm just a private,' I said.

'You don't look just a private, you've got the looks of a chirpy young captain.' Mrs Harris smiled and her lips looked lush. 'Well, some girls get all the luck, only they don't always have the sense to realise it. All right, get on with things, then.'

She returned to her kitchen.

'Gracious me,' said Rosie demurely, 'Mum fancies you too.'

'God help me with your dad, then. Come on, don't talk drippy stuff about your mum, let's cut the wallpaper.'

We started the work. What a struggle it was at first. With the old paper having been stripped off – by Sergeant Harris himself, last Sunday, Rosie said – we only had to paste and hang the new paper. Rosie was in constant fits, because for the amateur a strip of pasted wallpaper is a thing malicious and perverse. Prolonged wrestling bouts took place, most of which I lost during the first hour. Mrs Harris came in once to see why Rosie was hysterical.

'Are you being tickled?' she asked.

'Oh, Mum, not while I'm down here and Bert's up the ladder,' said Rosie.

'Grandma wants to know who's larking about.'

271

'I'm having one or two problems, Mrs Harris,' I said, 'but I'm ironing them out.'

'You'd better,' said Sergeant Harris's voluputous wife, 'or you'll catch it from Grandma Harris.'

'We'll win, Mum,' said Rosie. 'We're not fighting the Germans because we're losers.'

We did win in the end, although not until after five o'clock. In between, I had Sunday dinner with Sergeant Harris's family. It was luscious, thick-gravied, dumpling-packed mutton stew. Meat was short, and the mutton Mrs Harris had bought was only fit for stewing, she said. The result was as good as any of Chinese Lady's winter stews. Grandma Harris tucked in with relish, even if she did keep asking Mrs Harris where Rosie had found me. Rosie had giggles in her eyes.

When the final strip of wallpaper was in place, I came down from the ladder weary but triumphant. Rosie hugged me, pressed close and kissed me. Her lips smacked into mine.

'Oh, good on you,' she said, 'I'll tell Dad to make you a colonel. Give us another.'

She was nice to kiss. She was warm, cosy and clinging. We both smelled of paste, but it was the aroma of victory.

Mrs Harris said we'd done a very good job, and put on tea, with lots of home-made cake. Grandma Harris asked what I was still doing here.

'He's having tea, Gran,' said Rosie, 'he's earned it.'

'Made enough noise putting on a bit of wallpaper,' said the old lady, 'it's not the kind of Sunday I'm used to. I don't know, all these soldiers, coming in and going out. Be the fire brigade next, I shouldn't wonder.'

Rosie laughed. She walked to the station with me afterwards.

'I'll tell Dad what a good job you did,' she said.

'I shouldn't, if I were you. He'll only saw my legs off. Tell him I didn't turn up. He'll like me better for that.'

'Grandma was pleased, anyway,' said Rosie.

'That's news to me.'

'Oh, she wouldn't have said so in case it made you think of charging her. Wasn't it fun?' Rosie's arm hugged mine. 'I'll meet you in town next Saturday, shall I? Town hall, three o'clock?'

'Not next Saturday, Rosie. I'm starting a week's leave tomorrow.'

'What?' Rosie sounded disgusted.

'We could make it next Saturday week.'

'You didn't say anything about any leave.'

'I didn't know I had to. I'm just mentioning it now. Saturday week, though, is that all right?'

'Oh, thrilling,' said Rosie.

CHAPTER TWENTY-ONE

I arrived home at a moment when Sammy and Tommy were eating their midday dinner of mashed potatoes and fried fish rissoles. Chinese Lady had a magical way of turning cheap fish or leftover meat into very savoury rissoles. Although it was only the end of March, 1915, the Sunday joint was disappearing and with it the customary washday dinner of cold beef and bubble-and-squeak. Bubble-and-squeak, fried until it had a crisp coating, had to have been created by some kitchen genius. Probably an unlauded and forgotten country housewife.

Chinese Lady was eating a sandwich herself, and having a cup of tea with it. My arrival brought hoots from the kids and a critical look from our mum. It was my uniform that made her frown. She couldn't dissociate it from our blown-to-bits dad, bless her.

'Well, here I am, Lord Kitchener's mightiest warrior, and how's life, Mum?' I said, and kissed her on the cheek. She had her black hat on.

'We're bearing up,' she said. She gave me another look. 'I'm glad you're still in one piece, but I'm sorry we got so many worries this week.'

She meant the trial. It was to open tomorrow. The kids looked uncomfortable. Chinese Lady sighed. She and other neighbours were to appear as witnesses, and she wasn't looking forward to taking the stand.

'Miss Chivers will get off,' I said, pouring myself a cup of tea.

'Of course she will,' said Chinese Lady, 'but it's not my idea of happiness, standin' up at the Old Bailey and having them lawyers askin' me questions I'm not expecting. Mr Lawrence, the solicitor, told me to be calm and just speak the truth. It's all right for him, but the Old Bailey's not the sort of place I'm used to.' She sighed again, her careworn look in evidence. 'I've got some rissoles for you, they only need frying.'

'I'll do them,' I said, 'you take it easy.' I hung up my greatcoat and cap.

'Where's yer rifle?' asked Tommy, due to leave school at Easter.

'Deposited in the quartermaster's stores.'

'You ain't much of a soldier if you don't have no rifle,' said Tommy. 'Suppose the Germans come?'

'Well, I'll have to hide in the coalshed,' I said, 'and when they ask you where I am, you can tell them you'd rather be tortured to death than give me away.'

'I don't fancy that,' said Tommy with sturdy candour.

'Nor me,' said Sammy, 'I'll give 'im away.'

Chinese Lady managed a faint smile, and I fried my rissoles. Tommy and Sammy went back to school, and I talked to Chinese Lady about the trial in an effort to convince her it wouldn't be too unbearable.

In the afternoon, I went to the public baths in Manor Place and treated myself to a wallowing time in gallons of hot water, while using a huge chunk of yellow soap. I'd done that once a week when I was working. Chinese Lady had asked if our zinc bath was no longer good enough, and I'd said good enough, yes, but big enough, no. At the camp, bath parade was weekly and communal, the facilities primitive.

In the evening, I looked forward to seeing Lizzy again, but Emily appeared first. Sammy and Tommy were sitting beside the fire eating dripping toast as a run-up to tea, and Chinese Lady was laying the table.

'Oh,' said Emily, seeing me. She was wearing a warm-looking woollen dress of light brown, and was still growing. She was slender now rather than skinny, with a nicely rounded bosom. But her face was still thin, her chin still pointed, her eyes still large and green. Her hair was a mass of dark rich auburn, healthy and clean.

'Hello, Emily,' I said.

'Oh, you're home,' she said, and plucked at the skirt of her dress. 'I just got in from work myself and wondered if you was here yet.'

'I think this is me,' I said.

'He still says things that don't make sense,' said Chinese Lady.

Emily looked my uniform over, then glanced at Chinese Lady.

'He don't look too bad, not really,' she said, but it was more of a tentative suggestion than a definite opinion. She knew Chinese Lady thoroughly disapproved of my enlistment.

'It's not how he looks, it's what he's let himself in for,' said Chinese Lady.

'Oh, he'll take care, Mrs Adams,' said Emily, 'won't you, Boots?'

'The time it's taking to train me, it could be all over before I get to France,' I said.

'He ain't brought 'is rifle,' said Sammy.

'Just as well,' said Chinese Lady, 'we don't want him showing you how to fire it.'

'Boots is going to hide under the bed if the Germans come,' said Tommy.

'So am I,' said Emily, playing with a brooch at the neck of her dress.

'Which bed, yours or mine?' I asked, trying to bring a little cheer to the troubled atmosphere.

'Oh, crikey,' said Emily, and Chinese Lady gave me a look.

'Don't bring loose talk home with you,' she said. 'I don't care how big you are, I won't have it, especially in front of Tommy and Sammy.'

'I'll try a joke, then,' I said. 'A soldier stopped a wandering sailor in the street and asked him if he'd lost his ship. "No," said the sailor, "it's on the end of this piece of string." And the soldier said, "I don't see no piece of string." "Well," said the sailor, "if you can't see me ship, how d'you expect to see a piece of string?"'

276

Tommy and Sammy looked mystified, Chinese Lady looked blank and Emily burst into laughter.

'We won't have no more jokes,' said Chinese Lady, 'not with poor Miss Chivers in her kind of trouble.'

Emily stopped laughing, and Lizzy came in. Her plum-coloured winter coat was still her favourite. Carefully preserved, it helped to make her a warm, glowing picture. She was almost seventeen. She looked almost eighteen. She had the same kind of vivacity as Rosie, but the similarity ended there. Lizzy had the air of a young woman. Rosie was brightly girlish.

'How's Ned?' I asked, after the greetings were over.

'I don't know, do I?' said Lizzy. 'I haven't seen him lately, have I?'

'Hasn't he written?'

'Of course he has. Twice a week.'

'Then hasn't he said how he is?'

'He says he's fine.' Lizzy poked the range fire, and glowing ash dropped sparking into the grate. 'I don't know how he can say that. What's fine about training to go to war? It's like saying you're enjoying something that could lead you to your own funeral.'

'Lizzy love, don't go and get worked up,' said Chinese Lady.

'That Lord Kitchener, taking young men from their girls, and older men from their wives, he ought to be put on trial, not Miss Chivers,' said Lizzy. Gloom settled again. Lizzy, aware she was responsible, straightened up, and gave Emily a bright smile. 'What d'you think, Em'ly, d'you think Boots is looking good?'

Impulsively, Emily said, 'Oh, he looks just—' Then she stopped, for of all things she never liked to go against Chinese Lady, and Chinese Lady didn't want anyone to say life in the Army suited me. 'Oh, not so bad, really.'

'It's rotten round here,' said Lizzy forthrightly, 'with everyone thinking more about the trial than the war, and the war's bad enough.'

'I got to go,' said Emily unhappily, 'Mum'll have dinner ready for me now.'

I went to the front door with her.

'I'm pleased about your new job,' I said.

'Oh, I'm all right,' she said, 'but your mum doesn't half miss yer, y'know, and it's all so upsettin', Miss Chivers going on trial and all. It's awful. Still, it's nice for your family that you're home again, and I bet you'll get a girl now. All the best ones'll come running now you're a soldier, you wait. Your mum's upset and everything, but I think she's proud of you really. You look grand, honest you do. Boots, I – I like you for joining up, for going off to fight the Germans, even if your mum don't feel too pleased. I like Ned for doing his bit too, though Lizzy hates it. You an' Ned, you're both real men. We got to beat those Germans, and we won't, will we, unless we got enough real men for it. Dad says you're doing the country proud.'

'That's very nice of your dad. Anyway, do you like your new job?'

'I like the wages,' said Emily, 'I get twelve bob a week, would yer believe. I'm saving most of it.'

'What for?'

'Oh, you never know.'

'And how's Arthur?' I asked, keeping Rosie in the background.

'He's nice,' said Emily. 'Imagine, me having a boy.'

'Well, why shouldn't you? You're nice too, Em.'

'You didn't use to say that.'

'Well, you were a bit of a brat.'

'I wasn't grown up like I am now,' said Emily, darting a smile. 'Arthur was going to take me up West again next Saturday, but he's doing weekend overtime.'

'All right, I'll take you, if Arthur doesn't mind.'

'Oh, crikey,' said Emily, 'd'you mean that?'

'Of course.' At the back of my mind was a desperate hope we'd have something to celebrate, the release of Miss Chivers. 'We could do a music hall, and take Mum and Lizzy with us. I've got a few bob saved from my pay.'

'Oh, ain't you a lovely soldier?' said Emily.

'Don't tell that to my drill sergeant,' I said, 'or he'd call me a fairy.'

'What's a fairy?'

'It's what soldiers call a cissy.'

'Well, you're not a cissy,' said Emily, 'your mum wouldn't stand for it.'

I invited myself upstairs during the evening to sit with Mr Finch. He welcomed me warmly. The light in his eyes was still healthy and alert, but I thought him a little thinner and not quite so exuberant. Miss Chivers, of course. He produced a bottle of beer. I produced a packet of cigarettes. He shook his head and pointed to his pipe. He poured the beer and handed me a foaming glass.

'That's the stuff that makes men of the Britons, Boots,' he said. 'They know how to brew their beer and their rich stout. All those fine English hops, eh? Get that down you, young soldier. So, you're wearing your uniform now as if you were born in it. What's the expression, Boots, chips off the old block? Cheerio.'

We drank the beer in front of his fire.

'How's work on the river?' I asked.

'Oh, they're still arriving at London's docks, the merchant ships – those that haven't been sunk by U-boats,' he said, lighting his pipe. 'It's a stern business at sea, Boots. The U-boats are dangerous hunters, and know where to find many of our ships.'

'German spies, I suppose.'

Mr Finch took his pipe from his mouth and pointed it at me.

'You've hit the nail right on its head,' he said. 'Spies, undoubtedly. By the way, your mother told me she had a letter from you in which you mentioned you'd called on my old Aunt Trudy. That was a very friendly gesture. You knew where she lived?'

'Yes, I saw her address on a letter you had ready for posting once, and I remembered it. I hope you don't mind that I called.'

'Not a bit, Boots, not a bit.' Mr Finch smiled. 'It was a pity you found her away.'

'I was quite disappointed, I thought meeting her was going to make the day for me. She's let her cottage to some friends from London.'

'Yes, she'll be away some time,' said Mr Finch. 'It didn't occur to me to let you know.'

'No, of course not. Mr Finch, I suppose I'm trying to avoid talking about Miss Chivers. Perhaps we both are. I thought the police must have made a silly mistake when they arrested her, but I've realised since that they must think they've got a good case.'

Mr Finch's eyes darkened.

'Did you read an account of the hearing before a magistrate?' he said.

'Well, no, I didn't. I don't get hold of too many newspapers at the barracks. In any case, I don't think I wanted to read it, I think I knew it would depress me.'

'The prosecution produced only one witness and some medical evidence. The witness was Mrs Blake.'

'Mrs Blake?' She was the neighbour who lived next door to Miss Chivers. Their back yards adjoined. 'Mrs Blake was a witness for the prosecution?'

Mr Finch stared into the fire.

'She made a statement to the police, like most people here did,' he said, 'and the poor woman found it was to be used for the benefit of the prosecution. As I think you know, Boots, the unfortunate Mrs Chivers was extremely critical of her daughter, and her complaints were constant and sometimes loud. The prosecution used Mrs Blake as a means of establishing that mother and daughter were always quarrelling.'

'I never heard any quarrelling,' I said, 'I never heard Miss Chivers speak a single angry word to her mother. What I did hear was Miss Chivers being nagged. I never once heard her answer back.'

'Mrs Blake was asked questions at the hearing about what she heard from her yard. The questions were

280

designed to draw from her a picture of mother and daughter hating each other. Mrs Blake, a single soul, fell into the trap. But it was the medical evidence the prosecution liked best. Boots, the doctor established that death took place between six-thirty and seven-thirty in the morning, before Miss Chivers left for her work and when only she could have been in the house with her mother. It was that fact, obviously, that led to the arrest of Miss Chivers, and it's that fact, Boots, which makes it all so serious.'

'Oh, bloody O'Reilly,' I said, and thought of how Miss Chivers had passed our house that morning, at twenty-five to eight, how silent the street had been, with the Witch not sounding off, for once. 'I don't like that, Mr Finch.'

'I wonder,' said Mr Finch quietly, 'will the defence ask Miss Chivers to take the stand herself to testify about what time she got up, what time she left the house and to explain all she did in between?'

'The defence lawyers sometimes don't ask a client to take the stand, do they?'

'The defence sometimes don't want a client to,' said Mr Finch.

'You're a defence witness, Mr Finch?'

'I am,' he said stoutly.

'You'll do your best for her?'

'I will. So will your mother. We were asked to appear after the hearing, and agreed, of course.'

'I'm going to be there,' I said.

'I thought you'd want to.'

CHAPTER TWENTY-TWO

What about the missing jewellery, I thought, who had taken that?

I had other thoughts as I travelled up to the Old Bailey with Chinese Lady and Mr Finch. Chinese Lady wore a new black hat, which Lizzy had got very cheaply for her, and a black coat. I knew she wanted the court to see she had respect for her widowhood. At the Old Bailey, she and Mr Finch passed into the care of Mr Lawrence, the solicitor, who was pleasant of face, calm of manner and soothing of voice, and who helped me find a seat at the back of the court. I was surprised to discover how small the wood-panelled court was. In my imagination, it had been large, magnificent and awesome.

It was soon full. People had queued all night to get seats. It wasn't often that a murder trial featured a woman accused of cutting her own mother's throat. There came the moment when Miss Chivers appeared in the dock from below, a policewoman with her. I had a glimpse of her profile before she sat down with her back to me. I thought her face pale, but her composure wonderful. She was wearing her glasses. Her hat was a dark brown velour, her coat light brown. A moment after she had seated herself amid a buzz, she took her glasses off and placed them in their case. Why had she done that? She was very shortsighted. She would not be able to clearly see the judge, jury, the counsel and the people. It was because of her gentleness, her reticence and her shyness, perhaps. She perhaps preferred not to observe the faces of those in judgement of her.

The counsel in their white wigs and black gowns

consulted papers. People whispered and murmured. Miss Chivers sat quite still.

Everyone was asked to be upstanding for the entrance of the judge. In his wig and his colourful robes of office, it was his arrival on the scene that brought to the court the awesome atmosphere I'd expected. He seated himself and everyone followed. With the court packed, the judge in elevated majesty, the barristers and the jury in repose, the trial began.

Amid a hush, the prisoner came to her feet and the clerk read the charge. It sounded terrifying – that she did on such and such a day, at such and such a place, do that which brought about the felonious death of her mother, one Mrs Daisy Chivers.

'Do you plead guilty or not guilty to the charge?'

In a low but firm voice, Miss Chivers replied, 'Not guilty.'

She fascinated me. She was so calm. The brim of her hat shaded her face, and her coat caressed her slenderness. Her back was quite straight. She sat down again, and counsel for the prosecution came to his feet. He was a large man, with a square jaw, and exuded a bruising confidence in his brief. He looked capable of reaching the verdict himself, without any help from the judge or jury. In a clear and resonant voice, he began to outline the case for the Crown.

He would, he said, deal only with the facts and the factual conclusions. There was the fact that Mrs Chivers had been found dead in her bed. There was the further fact that there was no trace of blood anywhere outside the bed. These two facts led to the conclusion that she had been murdered in her bed, perhaps while still asleep. No one had heard any cries or screams for help. It would be shown from medical evidence that death took place between six-thirty and seven-thirty that morning. The police had found no signs of a break-in, no signs that an intruder had been in the house, which meant, unless defence could prove otherwise, only the accused and her mother were

283

present at the time. The weapon, either a very sharp knife or an open razor, had not been found. The conclusion was that the murderer had removed it from the house and got rid of it. What was the nature of the accused's relationship with her mother? An acrimonious and bitterly quarrelsome one, as evidence would show. Indeed, prosecution would prove it an unnaturally hostile relationship.

It did not take long, the presentation of the Crown's case.

Defence counsel took his turn. I knew his name. I'd picked it up from the morning newspaper. Sir Humphrey Dunbar. He was distinguished in his looks, and his voice was bland and untroubled. He merely said prosecution's case was based on what was anathema to a British jury – circumstantial evidence. It was quite wrong to conclude that because no traces of blood had been found anywhere outside the bed, the murder had taken place there. It was quite wrong to conclude that because the police had found no signs of an intruder, only the accused could have committed the act. Because such a conclusion was agreeable to the Crown, that did not make it the right one. The defence would show, irrefutably, that the accused was incapable of killing a fly, let alone her own mother.

Prosecution's first witness was Dr Michael Edwards. He explained that Mrs Chivers was a patient of his, that he called once a week at her request, although he did not consider this necessary. She insisted, however, that she was a semi-bedridden invalid. Her condition was one of anaemia and acidity. He let himself into the house by the key left under the step mat. Sometimes Mrs Chivers was up, sometimes in bed. She did not, however, like answering the door to anyone, not unnatural in elderly women when they were alone. On the day in question, he called just before four in the afternoon. It was his opinion that the house was in its usual tidy state. Mrs Chivers not being downstairs, he went up to her bedroom, as was usual. He found her in bed with her throat cut. He confirmed that the subsequent examination established she had died sometime between six-thirty and seven-thirty that morning.

Defence counsel asked only three questions of the doctor.

'Was Mrs Chivers's bedroom door open when you went up?'

Dr Edwards thought.

'Yes,' he said.

'Was that normal?'

Dr Edwards thought again.

'No,' he said. 'Usually it was closed.'

'Whenever you called and had to go up to her bedroom, her door was closed, whatever time of day it was?'

'Yes.'

'Thank you, Dr Edwards,' said Sir Humphrey Dunbar.

Detective-Sergeant James gave his evidence, beginning from the time when he arrived at the Chivers's house at twenty-five past four. He quoted from his notebook. Mr Braithwaite, prosecuting counsel, was interested in the police investigation of the house. Detective-Sergeant James detailed the exhaustive search that had been made then and on the following day. Nothing was found that might have had any bearing on the murder.

'Is it your opinion there had been no intruder?'

'Objection,' said Sir Humphrey languidly. 'My learned friend has said he'll deal only with facts. An opinion is not a fact, m'lud. An opinion is an irrelevance, the more so when related to Crown's stated intentions.'

'Would you rephrase your question, Mr Braithwaite?' asked the judge kindly.

'Pleasure, m'Lord. Sergeant James, were there no signs at all of a possible intruder, no signs at all that anything had been disturbed?'

'Objection,' said Sir Humphrey. 'How could witness know what might have been disturbed unless he had prior knowledge of the house, its contents and its arrangements? How could he know, for instance, if a cushion had been turned over, a pillow moved or a door opened?'

'Mr Braithwaite?' said the judge just as kindly. One felt he already sensed that Sir Humphrey was going to be blandly pedantic.

'Sergeant James,' said Mr Braithwaite, 'did you detect any signs at all of a possible intruder?'

'None.'

'Your witness,' said Mr Braithwaite, not at all put out.

Sir Humphrey rose.

'The murder weapon has not been found?'

'No, sir,' said Detective-Sergeant James.

'Is it suggested, then, that the accused carried it all the way to her office that morning? Or left it on a tram? Is it suggested she carried with her a carving-knife?'

'What the weapon was hasn't been established.'

'My learned friend suggested it was either a carving-knife or an open razor. Since neither the accused nor the deceased had need of a razor, a carving-knife seems to be reasonable.'

Detective-Sergeant James referred to his notebook.

'In answer to a question of mine,' he said, 'the accused informed me her late father used an open razor.'

'But it was not in the house?'

'No, sir.'

'Did you find a shaving brush, a shaving mug, a shaving soap and a sharpening strap?'

'No, sir.'

'Did you ask the accused what had happened to these items?'

'No, sir. I did ask her what had happened to the razor. She replied that she supposed her mother had got rid of it years ago.'

'With the rest of the shaving equipment, do you think? And why not? So we're left with the carving-knife, Sergeant, one that can't be found. One that you might suggest the accused carried to work with her?'

Detective-Sergeant James said, 'I can only say that although we found no carving-knife, we established with Mr Brady, a butcher in Walworth Road, that joints of meat were bought by the accused from time to time. I asked the accused how the joints were dealt with when roasted, since there seemed to be no carving-knife in the kitchen or elsewhere. She replied that it should be somewhere in the kitchen, but that if it wasn't, then someone had taken it.'

Mr Braithwaite, lounging like a well-fed lion, showed the ghost of a smile.

'Sergeant James,' said Sir Humphrey, 'for some reason, my learned friend asked you no questions about jewellery that was reported missing. I am correct, I think, in saying you received such a report?'

'From Miss Chivers, sir.'

'She itemised the missing pieces?'

'Yes, sir.' Detective-Sergeant James again referred to his notebook. 'Three silver brooches, a silver ring – '

'Yes, several items, I believe, all belonging to the deceased.'

'So the accused said, sir.'

'Why should she not say so? It was her duty as a citizen, surely, to give you all the information she could. It's the duty of every citizen to do that when a crime has been committed. Indeed, Sergeant, isn't it a felony to withhold any information that may be of help to the police?'

'As much, sir, as it is to give false information,' said Detective-Sergeant James.

'Really?' Sir Humphrey seemed pleasantly intrigued. 'Now why do you say that?'

'I thought it helped to answer your question.'

'Come, Sergeant, it was an implication, was it not, that the accused may have lied to you about the jewellery, that either there were no such valuables or, if there were, she removed them herself. I suggest that that is what you meant, didn't you?'

'I meant, sir, that accused persons have been frequently known to give false information. The accused in this case, having made a search of her mother's room at our request, stated that the jewellery in question was missing from a drawer in the dressing-table. She later presented us with a list of seven items.'

'You drew the conclusion that the deceased had been robbed as well as murdered?' said Sir Humphrey pleasantly.

'I drew the conclusion that it seemed so,' said Detective-Sergeant James, as collected as Sir Humphrey was bland.

'By an intruder?'

'After an investigation, by the accused, sir. If the jewellery was ever there. There were no fingerprints other than those of the accused and the deceased, and none of the detailed items of jewellery were insured, according to the accused.'

'Very interesting, Sergeant James. The jewellery was not insured, so you concluded it did not exist. Are you married?'

'Yes, sir.'

'Does your wife own any jewellery?'

'Two rings, including her wedding ring, and a silver crucifix.'

'Are they insured?' enquired Sir Humphrey.

'No, sir.'

'It would upset you if I declared they did not exist? How much was the jewellery detailed by the accused worth?'

'She put its total worth at twenty pounds.'

'I suggest a great many people have jewellery worth that modest sum, and that most of them haven't insured it. In drawing the conclusion you did about the jewellery in question, I suggest you did a grave injustice to the accused.'

'I fail to see that,' said Detective-Sergeant James.

'It made you decide, did it not, not to pursue the possibility of an intruder. The jury, I hope, will not fail to see that. No further questions.'

Mr Braithwaite rose to repair the damage.

'Sergeant James, it's been established the deceased died between six-thirty and seven-thirty. What time, according to the statement the accused made to you, did she leave the house to go to her work?'

Without consulting his notebook, Detective-Sergeant James said, 'Twenty-five minutes to eight.'

'Thank you,' said Mr Braithwaite.

'You may stand down, Sergeant James,' said the learned judge.

The court then adjourned for lunch. I watched as Miss Chivers was led down to the cells. She really did look very calm, very composed. I wondered how Chinese Lady was feeling, and whether or not she'd be called this afternoon. Mr Finch at this moment was escorting her to a nearby public house to buy her a glass of fortifying port and a cold beef sandwich. I wandered out and about, and found a seat by St Bart's Hospital. There I ate the cheese sandwiches I'd brought with me. Office girls, perky in skirts and white blouses, for it was a nice day, gave me all kinds of looks. I supposed they didn't see a sitting soldier eating cheese sandwiches every day. The food had little flavour. I was in worried travail.

The court returned to awesome majesty after lunch. The prosecution called for Mildred Mary Blake to take the stand. Mrs Blake was the immediate neighbour of Miss Chivers. She and her husband were a homely couple, their children married and off their hands, and Mrs Blake often gave Sammy a penny to run errands for her. Chinese Lady would be having the horrors at knowing such a nice woman was actually a witness for the prosecution. Mrs Blake, of course, was the victim of statements she had made truthfully and innocently to the police. I was sure she bore Miss Chivers no ill-will.

After taking the oath and going through the formal preliminaries, which quickly reduced Mrs Blake to nervous apprehension, Mr Braithwaite opened his questioning.

'Mrs Blake, am I right in saying the back yard of your house adjoins the back yard of the accused?'

'Yes, me Lord.'

'Only His Lordship, the judge, is addressed as my Lord, Mrs Blake. I am merely Mr Braithwaite.' He gave Mrs

Blake a large and encouraging smile. Mrs Blake twitched. 'Because of the proximity of these back yards, were you able to overhear the accused and her mother sometimes?'

'Yes, sir.'

'What was your impression of their relationship?'

'Oh, I – well, I didn't think – well, it didn't seem very happy.'

'Why did it seem like that to you?'

'Well, you could hear them – you could hear Mrs Chivers raisin' her voice, specially in the summer when their kitchen winder was open. Mr Blake – my 'usband – used to say the old – he used to say she's off again.'

'Do you mean you often heard them quarrelling?'

'Well, it was never very friendly, like.' Mrs Blake looked at the judge, as if silently appealing for help. He gave her a kind nod. 'Mrs Chivers, poor woman, always seemed cross about something or other.'

'How long, to your knowledge, had this unhappy relationship existed?'

'I don't know, sir. It was going on when me and Mr Blake moved in seven years ago.'

'You've been aware of it all these seven years, Mrs Blake?'

'Well, on and off, like.'

'Obviously, you wouldn't have overheard them every day, but you did hear them frequently enough to give you the impression their relationship was a permanently disagreeable one?'

'I never – nor did my 'usband – we never heard them being nice together, sir. I don't want to speak ill of the dead, but Mrs Chivers, she was very disagreeable – '

'Quite so, Mrs Blake.' Mr Braithwaite's restrained resonance gentled the nervous witness. 'Would you say neither liked the other?'

'I don't know about that, sir, but it often sounded as if Mrs Chivers didn't like what Miss Chivers got up to – I mean, what she thought she got up to – I mean, I couldn't believe Miss Chivers—'

290

'Got up to? Could you explain that?'

Mrs Blake cast a worried and embarrassed look at the prisoner in the dock. Miss Chivers, with her glasses off, seemed detached. I couldn't see her face. I wanted to, for I was sure her expression was gentle and her eyes softly myopic.

'I sometimes heard Mrs Chivers telling Miss Chivers she was – well, disgustin' – that she only thought about – about lust and men, that she didn't have any decent feelings, nor any consideration for her own mother – all she wanted was for her to be in her grave so's she could bring men home and do disgusting things with them there – she often said that sort of thing.'

I could imagine that. I could imagine the Witch saying it every day. And in the summer, with a window open, I could imagine the Blakes listening to that spiteful voice with mouths agape and ears numbed. The Witch never whispered her obscenities.

'Mrs Blake, can you remember the kind of thing the accused said on these occasions?'

'Well, you couldn't hear much of what Miss Chivers ever said, she being a very quiet-speakin' lady. There was just one time when I was in the yard and I heard Miss Chivers fairly clear. I remember she said, "Mother, you are sick."'

'"Mother, you are sick"?' repeated counsel.

'Yes, sir. Mr Blake was there as well, and he said it was too true.'

'That was the extent of the accused's sympathy for her mother, to tell her she was sick?'

'Objection,' said Sir Humphrey. 'Witness can't know—'

'Objection sustained,' said the judge pre-emptively.

'Mrs Blake,' said Mr Braithwaite, 'we can at least assume, from what you overheard, that the accused considered her mother sick.'

'Well, she was, sir,' said Mrs Blake, 'she was always havin' the doctor.'

'I don't think the accused meant physically sick, and I don't think your husband meant that, either. We shall ask him when he takes the stand. I'd like the jury to be absolutely clear about one particular fact – the fact that to your knowledge, the accused and her mother suffered this unpleasant relationship during the whole of the seven years you lived next door to them?'

'Well, yes, sir.'

'Thank you. Mrs Blake, were you ever aware of the accused having men friends?'

'No, sir.'

'No men ever called on her or entered the house?'

'No, sir, not to my knowledge. Of course, I don't stand at the door, watching, like.'

'Thank you, Mrs Blake. Your witness, Sir Humphrey.'

Sir Humphrey stood up.

'Just a few questions, Mrs Blake,' he said affably. 'You said you heard the accused clearly only once, when she said, "Mother, you are sick." Was it your impression that she was speaking angrily?'

'I don't know if she was angry, sir, she just spoke very clear, like.'

'But not loudly?'

'Oh, she was never loud, sir.'

'You never heard her in an angry or hostile mood?'

'Not as I could tell, sir, and she wasn't like that, anyway.'

'You never heard her threaten her mother?'

'Oh, goodness, no, sir.'

'Would you say she cared for her mother?'

'She must of – she 'ardly ever left her, except to go to work or do some shopping.'

'Thank you, Mrs Blake,' said Sir Humphrey tenderly.

Mrs Blake stepped down with relief. Her husband was called next. He drove a horse-drawn coal cart, and coal dust had left its blue mark on his lined face. Mr Braithwaite questioned him resolutely, and he confirmed much of what Mrs Blake had said. He confirmed he too had been in the yard when Miss Chivers called her mother sick.

Mr Braithwaite, imposing in his bigness, said, 'Was it your impression that the accused had rounded on her mother in a fit of temper?'

'Rahnded on 'er?' said the coalman.

'That she'd lost any patience she had? To tell one's mother that she is mentally sick is a cruel thing, Mr Blake – you agree?'

'The old – beg yer pardon, yer honour – but she was sick.'

'And the accused told her so in no uncertain fashion?'

'She told 'er all right, she come out with it very clear, an' with their kitchen winder open, the missus an' me 'eard it very clear. It was Sunday afternoon an' I was 'elping the missus to fix a new washing line fer Monday, an' Mrs Chivers, she'd been goin' on as usual – '

'Yes. Could you say if you ever felt the accused was on the verge of striking back? We accept that the deceased was highly critical of her daughter. Did you ever feel there were times when the accused was close to losing control of herself?'

'Now 'ow do I know?' Our homely coalman, far less nervous than his wife, snorted. ''Ow would anyone know if they wasn't there lookin' Miss Chivers in the face?'

'Not one of your better questions, Mr Braithwaite,' said the judge mildly.

'M'Lord,' said Mr Braithwaite, 'Mr Blake in his statement to the police said he wouldn't ever have been surprised if the accused fetched her mother a wallop.'

The court buzzed with murmurous laughter. The judge was quite unamused.

''Ere,' said Mr Blake, 'I'd 'ave fetched anyone a wallop meself if they nagged me day in, day out, but that don't mean I'd 'ave kicked 'em to death.'

'Nevertheless,' said Mr Braithwaite, 'we've established you and your wife overheard the accused in a moment of cruelty—'

'Objection,' said Sir Humphrey. 'Really,' he added.

'Mr Braithwaite,' said the judge, 'it's not my view that

you've established there was cruelty in the mind of the accused at the moment in question.'

'M'Lord, I made a suggestion.'

'You made a statement,' said the judge. 'Jury will disregard it.'

'Mr Blake,' said Mr Braithwaite, losing none of his resolution, 'your wife's impression of the relationship between the accused and her mother was that it was an unhappy one. What was your impression?'

'That they'd been better orf livin' separate – it might've give Miss Chivers a bit o' peace.'

'Thank you,' said Mr Braithwaite, at which the coalman looked a little worried. 'Mr Blake, would you say the accused was an attractive woman?'

'Yes, I would,' said Mr Blake, as if that put right anything that had been wrong with his previous answer.

'Attractive to men?'

'Eh?' said Mr Blake, obviously thinking the question daft.

'Do you think her attractive to men?'

'If a lady ain't attractive to men, she ain't attractive, is she?'

I saw members of the jury smile.

'Did her mother discourage her from associating with men?'

'Yus, she did,' said the coalman.

'How do you know?'

''Ow do I know? Well, we 'eard the old – beg yer pardon – we 'eard Mrs Chivers tell 'er daughter more'n once to keep away from men, that men would—' Mr Blake's blue-lined face took on an expression of honest distaste. 'She said men 'ud make 'er daughter as lustful as they was. I reckon no wonder Mr Chivers went early to 'is grave—'

'No, thank you, Mr Blake,' said Mr Braithwaite gravely, 'no comments, please. Would you say the accused was a repressed woman?'

'Objection,' said the languid Sir Humphrey. 'Leading the witness, m'lud.'

'Don't do it, Mr Braithwaite,' said the judge patiently. 'Objection sustained.'

'Dear me,' said Mr Braithwaite. 'Do you know what a repressed woman is, Mr Blake?'

'Yus, I do,' said the coalman. 'She's one what ought to 'ave a 'usband but can't git one, and if you ask me—'

'I'll ask you, Mr Blake, what your opinion of the accused is.'

'She's a nice lady what's been frustrated,' said the coalman determinedly.

'Yes, so you said in your statement to the police. Thank you, Mr Blake.' Mr Braithwaite turned the witness over to the defence.

'Just one question, Mr Blake,' said Sir Humphrey placidly. 'Was it your impression that the accused cared for her mother?'

'Course she cared, she wouldn't 'ave put up with what she did if she 'adn't,' said Mr Blake. As a witness for the prosecution he had done what he could for the defence.

It was worrying. The prosecution had a very clear-cut case because of the estimated time of death. They were using the trial in an attempt to establish the motive. Mr Braithwaite meant to convince the jury that Miss Chivers had reached the end of her tether. The suggestion was that she had not only had to put up with every kind of spiteful whining, but with the denial of her natural desire for a husband. At thirty-one, the suggestion was that she turned murderous in her sense of frustration.

The last of the neighbours as witnesses for the prosecution was Mrs Higgins, who lived opposite Miss Chivers. The same kind of questions were put to her regarding what she felt of the relationship between mother and daughter. Mrs Higgins, as plump and motherly as Emily's mum, but never slatternly, plainly wished herself anywhere but where she was. Her eyes turned constantly to the prisoner in the dock. Miss Chivers probably only saw her as a blur. I felt Miss Chivers could exist peacefully when everything was a blur. In sharp focus, the court and its significance would have added sharply to her suffering.

Mr Braithwaite changed tack.

'Did the accused and her mother ever entertain, Mrs Higgins?'

'Not as I know of.'

'Were you ever entertained?'

'Well, yes, I did go in once. I was coming home from the shops when Mrs Chivers actually opened the door, which she hardly ever did, and asked me to have a cup of tea with her.'

'The accused never invited you in? Only her mother?'

'Well, yes.' Mrs Higgins cast another glance at the dock.

'Mrs Chivers was prepared to be hospitable – at least, on this occasion?'

'I wasn't partial to her, but I didn't want to be unneighbourly.'

'What was her attitude? Friendly?'

'Complainin',' said Mrs Higgins uneasily.

'Complaining? About her neighbours?'

'No. About her daughter, as usual.'

'As usual? You mean she often complained to you and other neighbours?'

'Well, out of her window sometimes. She'd call a body and say things like she wished she could be sure her Elsie was doing an honest day's work like other people and not going out from her job and meeting men. She said that to me too many times, and it made me uncomfortable. When she give me this cup of tea, she said her daughter was mad about men.' Mrs Higgins was staccato in her agitation. 'I said I'd never noticed. She said that was because her daughter was too sly and crafty. She said no woman had a more crafty daughter than she did. I said—'

'Thank you, Mrs Higgins, that's all.'

Defence counsel rose to address Mrs Higgins courteously.

'What was it you said, madam, that my learned friend had no desire to hear?'

Mrs Higgins blurted, 'I told Mrs Chivers she was lucky to have a daughter like her Elsie, I said her daughter was a lady who was nice to everyone.'

'Thank you, Mrs Higgins,' said Sir Humphrey, and sat down.

'One moment, Mrs Higgins,' said Mr Braithwaite, rising again with the suspicion of a pleased smile. 'What did Mrs Chivers say to that?'

Mrs Higgins glanced yet again at the dock.

'She – she said I didn't know the half of it, she said her daughter would be happy to see her dead. I got up and left, I couldn't stand any more talk like that.'

'Thank you, Mrs Higgins,' said Mr Braithwaite in a large booming way.

A cold lump hit my stomach and stayed there. Miss Chivers showed no reaction. Her demeanour, as far as I could tell, was still calm. The judge had a word with respective counsel and adjourned until tomorrow morning, when the defence would begin calling its witnesses. The court was upstanding for the exit of His Lordship, and then Miss Chivers was again taken down to the cells.

I met Chinese Lady and Mr Finch in the hall, together with Mrs Pullen, who lived at number 6. Mrs Pullen was also a defence witness. The solicitor, Mr Lawrence, was talking to them, assuring them that all had gone as well as could be expected. That remark made Mr Finch frown. Mr Lawrence said they would take the stand tomorrow, and that they would be required only to speak the truth. Chinese Lady said no one would get her to speak anything but the truth.

We went home. On the way, I thought Mr Finch looked more sombre than ever. I wondered just how close he and Miss Chivers had become, and whether or not the Witch had come to suspect an attachment. She had suddenly stopped Miss Chivers coming to Sunday tea with us. If she had suspected, she might have spent weeks tongue-lashing her daughter until Miss Chivers had—

I blanked it out of my mind. Other thoughts took over. According to medical evidence, the Witch had been dead when Miss Chivers passed me by on her way to the tram stop. Caulfield Place had been silent, the factory and drug mills, which opened to their workers at eight o'clock, still closed. Miss Chivers and I had talked on the tram, and she had been her usual sweet and gentle self. I had asked her how her mother was, and her eyes had clouded. And she had said her mother would never be any better. Knowing or unknowing, how right she had been.

We made a pot of tea when we got home, and Mr Finch sat in the kitchen to share the beverage with us. I told him and Chinese Lady what the prosecution witnesses had been asked and what they had replied.

'I'd never have believed they'd speak up for the prosecution,' said Chinese Lady.

'I think they just made honest statements to the police and then found themselves trapped,' I said.

'I still don't think much of them,' said Chinese Lady, 'and are you sure it's legal you telling us all this?'

'Mr Lawrence didn't say I shouldn't, and after all, you and Mr Finch aren't on the jury. I think it's only the jury that can't discuss the case with people.'

'From what you say, Boots,' observed Mr Finch, deep in thought, 'it seems the prosecution tried to present Miss Chivers as a woman who might have been considered inoffensive by her neighbours, but was considered immoral by her mother. They used Mrs Higgins to bring out the reason why Mrs Chivers was so critical of her daughter. Did you feel the jury might have believed this?'

'What they believed, I don't know, but it made me feel sick.'

'There was also, was there, an attempt to show that Miss Chivers was driven by her mother to an extreme act of retaliation? We shall have to be careful, Mrs Adams.'

'Careful?' said Chinese Lady, almond eyes alarmed under the brim of her hat.

'We'll be asked questions that will invite us to paint our own picture of Miss Chivers, a picture of a good woman incapable of murder. I hope we're not asked to emphasise her mother's vindictiveness. The more we say about that, the more the prosecution will try to show that in the end Miss Chivers could bear no more. To make the most of the time factor, they only need to establish a motive. I think

298

you said, Boots, that Mr Blake was asked if he ever felt Miss Chivers was close to losing control of herself. Yes, we must be careful, and we mustn't allow ourselves to be provoked.'

'Provoked?' said Chinese Lady.

'Rattled,' I said.

'That's it, Boots, that's the word,' said Mr Finch, with just a little of his old cheer.

CHAPTER TWENTY-THREE

Chinese Lady was the first defence witness to be called the following day. She entered the court in her black coat and hat, and I was pleased to see she carried herself in her usual upright way. She took the stand and the oath, repeating the words in a voice throaty with nervousness. But she did not look nervous, she looked bravely defiant. She went through the preliminaries without stumbling, Sir Humphrey forsaking his blandness in favour of friendly encouragement. He touched on the fact that she was a soldier's widow and that our dad had died an heroic death, although Chinese Lady had always said it was a careless happening.

'The Army sent me his medals, of course.' For all the awesome atmosphere, Chinese Lady sounded caustic, and her almond eyes sought out the judge, as if he had something to do with that higher majesty responsible for bestowing a minute pension with the medals. Miss Chivers turned her head and glanced at her. I saw her face. Without her glasses again, I doubted if Chinese Lady was clear to her, but her expression was soft with compassion. She knew it was an ordeal for Chinese Lady.

'You have the court's sympathy, I'm sure, Mrs Adams,' said Sir Humphrey. 'Now, will you tell us how long you've known the accused?'

'Ten years. When we moved out of Peabody's Buildings to Caulfield Place in 1905, Miss Chivers and her mother was already living there.'

'Ten years must have enabled you to form a firm opinion of the accused?'

'One year would have been enough.' Chinese Lady was speaking up. 'Miss Chivers is a lady.'

'What kind of a lady?'

'She's a lady.'

Sir Humphrey smiled.

'I think my learned friend might insist there are all kinds of ladies.'

'A lady's a lady.'

'Would you say the accused was a good lady? Or insensitive? Or impatient?'

'Miss Chivers is the nicest and kindest person I know. That's why she's a lady.'

'Have you entertained her in your home?' asked Sir Humphrey.

'Many times she's come to Sunday tea with us.'

'Is she a friend of yours and your family?'

Chinese Lady looked slightly affronted.

'We don't invite people to Sunday tea who isn't our friends,' she said.

'Did you ever discuss her mother with her?'

'We only ever asked her how her mother was.'

'Why did you ask that?'

'Her mother was always under the doctor.'

Having mixed with all kinds of boys at school, and all kinds of men during my few months in the Army, I half expected a titter or two. But the court was silent and engrossed.

'What did she say in answer to your enquiries, Mrs Adams?'

'She always said her mother was just the same.'

'That was all? She never complained about her mother, or criticised her, or said she was difficult?'

'Never.'

'Might I suggest there had to be some occasions when she was critical of her?' said Sir Humphrey in an obvious attempt to have Miss Chivers's tolerance emphasised.

Chinese Lady, misreading Sir Humphrey's purpose, said tartly, 'You can suggest what you like, but you'd still get the same answer.'

'Mrs Adams, I'm more than happy with your own

answer. You and your family seem to have been the accused's closest friends.'

'We still are.' Over her nerves, Chinese Lady was still tart.

'I believe you. I merely want to suggest that if the accused disliked her mother or lacked sympathy for her, you and your family, as her closest friends, would have come to know this.'

'Miss Chivers never complained about her mother to us, never, if that's what you mean.'

'I do mean that, Mrs Adams.' Sir Humphrey looked as if he was beginning to like Chinese Lady. 'It's true, isn't it, that you and your family were the only people Miss Chivers went to tea with?'

'I never knew of her going to visit anyone else.'

'During these many pleasant occasions at your tea table, did the accused ever say anything or do anything that made you feel she was capable of committing violence?'

'What a question,' said Chinese Lady, visibly bridling.

'However you regard it, Mrs Adams,' said the judge at his kindest, 'you must answer it.'

'I want to answer it, Your Worship,' said Chinese Lady firmly. 'I want to say Miss Chivers always made me feel she was the gentlest lady alive.'

'Thank you, Mrs Adams,' said Sir Humphrey.

Mr Braithwaite took his turn, and I saw Chinese Lady tense herself. Mr Braithwaite saw it too, and smiled at her.

'Mrs Adams, for all that the accused never discussed her mother with you, did you feel that their relationship was not what it might have been – or should have been?'

'What their relationship was was their business, not mine,' said Chinese Lady. 'I know what my relationship with my children is, but I don't expect other people to nose into it. There wouldn't be no wars if politicians—'

'It isn't politicians who are on trial here, Mrs Adams—'

'Well, they ought to be,' said Chinese Lady.

The judge coughed and regarded her gently. She turned pink.

'You need only answer the questions, Mrs Adams,' he said.

'Yes, sir,' she said, and faced up to Mr Braithwaite.

Mr Braithwaite said, 'Despite it not being your business, Mrs Adams, did you feel Mrs Chivers put the accused under considerable strain?'

'No. Whatever she put up with, she put up with like a lady.'

'Whatever she put up with? Come, Mrs Adams, you've lived for ten years in the same street as the accused and her mother. Do you expect the court to believe you were only vaguely aware that their relationship was disagreeable?'

Chinese Lady had an inspired moment.

'That's not relevant,' she said.

There was laughter in court. The judge lifted his bewigged head. The laughter subsided. Mr Braithwaite smiled.

'What isn't relevant, Mrs Adams?' he asked.

'It don't matter what I think their relationship was,' she said, 'and it don't matter what Mrs Chivers thought of her daughter. In my opinion—' She looked at the judge, silently enquiring whether it was legal to give her opinion, or at least allowable. He nodded. 'In my opinion, what does matter is that Miss Chivers looked after her mother, and cared for her. She spent all the time she could looking after her, never going out anywhere, except to us once a month. If her mother was disagreeable or difficult, Miss Chivers never said so.'

'You expect the jury to believe that in all the hours the accused spent with you, she never once implied or indicated resentment of her mother?'

'Yes, I do expect,' said Chinese Lady, 'I expect everyone here to believe me. I swore on the Bible to tell the truth. If you don't believe I am, you better do what you should an' charge me with – with—'

Sir Humphrey helped her out from the counsel's bench by murmuring, 'Perjury.'

'Yes, perjury,' said Chinese Lady. 'The jury can charge me as well, if it's legal they should.'

Sir Humphrey passed a hand over his mouth. Mr Braithwaite bowed to Chinese Lady.

'I yield,' he said. 'Thank you, Mrs Adams.'

Chinese Lady stood there, obviously not quite sure whether her ordeal was over or not.

The judge, with a perceptible smile, said, 'You may stand down, Mrs Adams.'

'Thank you, Your Worship,' said Chinese Lady.

'Thank you,' said the judge.

Chinese Lady stepped down and was ushered to a seat at the back of the court.

Mr Edwin Finch was called. I'd never known his name was Edwin. I thought the 'E' on his letters stood for Ernest or Edward. Lizzy would have said Edwin was posh. The Army lads would have said it was cissy.

Mr Finch seemed calm, assured and even imperturbable. He was asked by Sir Humphrey, if, as our lodger, he had come into close contact with the accused. He replied the contact had been sociable rather than close. Nevertheless, did he consider himself her friend? He replied yes, certainly. How long had he been a river pilot? Nearly ten years, as his certificate would show. How long had he known the accused? Eight years.

It was matter-of-fact stuff at the moment. Miss Chivers still seemed quite detached, her eyes on the gloves in her lap. Mr Finch's imperturbable front was as intriguing to me as her detached air. But they had always been like that on the Sunday tea occasions. They had always maintained a formal note. But I felt they had both suffered frustration because of the Witch. We had all wished Miss Chivers to be free of malignant maternalism. She was now. But the gallows yawned.

Mr Finch had left our house very early that terrible morning, when everything was still in darkness. If he had—

Jesus, no.

'Mr Finch, you knew the accused as well as Mrs Adams and her family did?'

'Yes.'

'What is your impression of her?'

'A very gentle and kind lady.'

304

'It appears she said nothing to Mrs Adams and her family about her mother. Did she ever say anything to you?'

'Never. She's an extremely reserved lady.' Mr Finch spoke very well, as he always did, and as if he liked the English language. That was why everyone liked to listen to him.

'You had many conversations with her?'

'Many. All in company with Mrs Adams and her family. The conversations were always general. I was inclined to monopolise the talk sometimes, with stories about my years as a merchant seaman, a first mate. Miss Chivers and the Adams family made a very tolerant audience.'

'Can you recall any time when the accused seemed depressed or unhappy or resentful?'

'She always seemed to be extremely happy to be in company. I never knew her depressed or resentful.'

'There was no occasion when you felt her nerves might have been on edge?'

'None that I can remember.'

'It has been suggested, Mr Finch, that there were times when the accused might have been close to losing control of herself. It is accepted by the defence that the deceased was critical of her daughter. In your opinion, was the accused capable of losing control of herself?'

'I always found her a remarkably equable person, very gentle and very pleasant.'

'Thank you, Mr Finch,' said Sir Humphrey, and made way for Mr Braithwaite, who rose and squared up formidably to Mr Finch.

'Mr Finch, what are your feelings towards the accused?'

'In her present plight? Incredulity that she is the accused.'

'I meant your feelings towards her as a friend?'

'The only word I can think of is paternal,' said Mr Finch.

'Paternal?'

'Quite so,' said Mr Finch.

'Do you consider her attractive?'

305

'She is attractive.'

'You are forty-two?'

'Yes.'

'You're hardly old enough to be her father, are you?'

'I'm old enough to have paternal feelings.'

'Despite one witness stating that Mrs Chivers discouraged the accused from associating with men, she had a relationship with you, did she not?'

'Objection to relationship, m'lud,' said Sir Humphrey.

'Mr Braithwaite,' said the judge, 'you must define the relationship you have in mind.'

'Will friendly relationship do?' asked Mr Braithwaite.

'That's correct,' said Mr Finch, 'as long as it's made clear it did not extend beyond the monthly occasions when we were in company with the Adams family.'

'Ah,' said Mr Braithwaite, and regarded the ceiling thoughtfully. 'But how are we to know that?'

'You have my word,' said Mr Finch, and I thought, of course, of the teashop in the Strand, and how he and Miss Chivers had eyes only for each other.

'In your paternal feelings for the accused, did you ever talk to her about the strains and stresses she suffered from her mother's suspicions of her?'

'Suspicions?'

'Of her conduct with men.'

'In my opinion, Miss Chivers has the reserve of a lady who knows little of men. And no, she never said anything to me about strains and stresses. I was never alone with her, in any case.'

'At these many gatherings in Mrs Adams's parlour,' said Mr Braithwaite, 'did the accused play the piano after tea?'

'She did,' said Mr Finch.

'Who turned the music sheets for her?'

'I did.'

'So had you whispered together, no one would have heard you?'

'Since the Adams family liked to sing, I'd have had to shout, not whisper.'

'Mr Braithwaite,' said the judge, 'in what direction are you heading?'

'M'Lord, I'm trying to establish the possibility that the witness, the only known man friend of the accused, may know a great deal more than other people about her real attitude towards her mother. The prosecution can't accept that she confided in no one.'

'Mr Braithwaite, whether you can accept that or not, I think you've arrived at a brick wall,' said the judge. 'Kindly discontinue this line of questioning.'

'Very well,' said Mr Braithwaite, not discomfited. 'Mr Finch, on the day of the murder, what time did you leave for your work in the morning?'

'Six-fifteen,' said Mr Finch, and the cold lump hit my stomach again.

'How long does it usually take you to reach the London dock from which you operate?'

'It averages thirty minutes.'

'What time did you sign in that morning?'

'Four minutes to seven. I was due to board my craft at seven.'

'It took you eleven minutes longer than usual?'

'On occasions,' said Mr Finch, 'the time I take can be a little less or a little more than thirty minutes, depending on circumstances which always have some effect on travel. On this occasion, it was more.'

'Eleven minutes more,' said Mr Braithwaite.

'It happens,' said Mr Finch, who had not looked once at Miss Chivers.

'How did it happen on this occasion?'

'Slow trams, late omnibuses.'

'To the extent of taking forty-one minutes on a journey of thirty minutes or even less?'

Sir Humphrey looked at the judge and said, 'What is the relevance of this, m'lud?'

'What is the relevance, Mr Braithwaite?' asked the judge.

'Collusion?' suggested Mr Braithwaite boldly.

'Objection,' said Sir Humphrey. 'Prosecution has established no grounds for implying collusion.'

'No, Mr Braithwaite, you have not,' said the judge, whom I thought kindly disposed towards the defence.

'We have no doubt the accused is guilty, m'Lord,' said Mr Braithwaite, 'but would like to try to account for the disappearance of the weapon and of the jewellery said to be missing. Collusion could account for that. However, may I ask you, Mr Finch, if you share the opinion of other neighbours that the accused is a kind and gentle woman?'

'I do,' said Mr Finch, quite the most imperturbable of witnesses.

'It's been established that the deceased met her death between six-thirty and seven-thirty that morning, and that the accused left her house at twenty-five to eight. That means her mother was dead before she left. That also means she must have known it. Yet she proceeded to her work. Do you think that the action of a kind and gentle woman, even allowing for the unlikely possibility that she did not commit the murder herself?'

'That, I think, means the law may have made a mistake,' said Mr Finch, standing as squarely in the box as he probably had on the bridge of a ship.

'A mistake?'

'Has no one considered the possibility that someone entered the house the moment Miss Chivers was out of sight? Someone who meant to burgle the house and who murdered Mrs Chivers to keep her quiet, and who saw Miss Chivers place the doorkey under her step mat?'

'How very imaginative, Mr Finch,' said Mr Braithwaite, looming very large as he hooked his thumbs inside his gown and thrust his chest out. 'Someone who just happened to be there at that precise moment, someone who would have had to break the door down had it not been for that highly convenient key. No more questions.'

Mr Braithwaite sat down, and the jury sat up, eyeing Mr Finch with a great deal of curiosity. It worried me.

Mrs Enid Pullen was next. Mrs Pullen was a firm-bodied

woman and a good neighbour. She advanced bravely through life, although she and her husband were so poor they squeezed in two lodgers. She did, however, have a little bit of a temper.

She answered Sir Humphrey's questions loudly and clearly. No, she did not think the relationship between mother and daughter was a happy one, but it still wasn't the kind to make the accused take a knife to her mother. Miss Chivers was a perfectly nice woman and quite able to cope with the ups and downs of the relationship. I felt Sir Humphrey all along had been making a very good attempt to show the jury that whoever murdered Mrs Chivers, it could not have been her inoffensive and kind-hearted daughter.

Mr Braithwaite looked on almost indulgently. The Crown was basing its case on one incontestable fact, that death took place between six-thirty and seven-thirty, with Miss Chivers the only other person in the house – unless there had been an accomplice. That could not have occurred to the police, or they would have investigated Mr Finch, he being the only man friend Miss Chivers had.

Sir Humphrey was not long in relinquishing Mrs Pullen to the prosecution, and Mr Braithwaite took over.

'Mrs Pullen, did you feel Mrs Chivers was justified in being so critical of the accused?'

'I beg yer pardon?' said Mrs Pullen aggressively.

'You didn't hear the question?'

'I 'eard it,' said Mrs Pullen, 'but I didn't like it.'

'Nevertheless, please answer it.'

'She didn't 'ave no justification.'

'Mrs Chivers was quite wrong, in your opinion, in making life difficult for the accused?'

'A spiteful body, that's what she was.'

'You're speaking, Mrs Pullen, of a lady who met a terrible end.'

'Yer can't make a saint out of someone just because she's a corpse, unless yer don't mind bein' 'ypocritical. That woman was an 'oly terror. She even screamed blue murder at the kids in the street.'

'You wouldn't have put up with a mother like her?'

'No, I wouldn't, I'd 'ave—' Mrs Pullen compressed her mouth.

'Do you think the accused might also have?'

''Ave what?' said Mrs Pullen shortly.

'What you had in mind.'

'I didn't say nothing about what I 'ad in mind.'

'Well, I'm asking you to say something now.'

'What I 'ad in mind is my own business.'

'Answer the question.'

'Objection,' said Sir Humphrey, showing pain. 'What the witness had in mind is irrelevant, m'lud. Prosecution is attempting to relate the witness's feelings to those of the accused. It won't stand up, m'lud.'

'It won't,' said the judge equably. 'No more of it, Mr Braithwaite. Jury will disregard the irrelevance.'

'No further questions, Mrs Pullen, thank you,' said Mr Braithwaite, who had obviously attempted to establish, through Mrs Pullen's touch of temper, that Mrs Chivers had got what she had asked for from her daughter.

A Mr Edward Burns was next to take the stand. Mr Burns was like me when I was in civvies, I thought, a clerkly-looking person, except that he wore glasses and was a lot older. Questions elicited the fact that he was a colleague of Miss Chivers, and had been so for fourteen years, ever since she had been taken on by the Admiralty. Sir Humphrey asked no questions about the nature of his work or hers, which I supposed was because the country was at war. He went after a character reference, and Mr Burns gave a very precise description of her sterling qualities, and also paid a handsome tribute to the equability she showed under all pressures and difficulties. Sir Humphrey got what he wanted, a testimonial, which I thought was what the prosecution expected and showed no interest in, for Mr Braithwaite waived his privilege of cross-examination.

The judge called for a lunch adjournment.

I went out with Chinese Lady, Mr Finch and Mrs Pullen,

the latter still bridling over the nature of Mr Braithwaite's questions. Mr Lawrence, the solicitor, came striding through the hall, his expression changing from the serious to the reassuring as he caught sight of us.

'I'll see you all later,' he said, and walked on.

I went after him and caught him up outside.

'Mr Lawrence—'

'Not now, Mr Adams.'

'Yes, now,' I said, and put myself in his way. He frowned. 'Mr Lawrence, what's the opinion?'

'That it's going to be touch and go.'

'That's because no one can rock the prosecution on the assumption that Miss Chivers must have been in the house when the murder was committed. Mr Lawrence, I saw her that morning. I rode on the tram with her as far as Stamford Street, Blackfriars. I spoke to her. Don't you think that if she'd just murdered her mother, it would have shown? Well, it didn't. She was completely normal, believe me. She chatted. She wasn't silent or staring-eyed. She was conversational. I'd like to go into the witness-box. Look, you can see her during lunch, can't you? If so, ask her about the tram ride and how we talked together.'

Mr Lawrence peered at me.

'You'd swear she gave no sign at all of being in the least disturbed or distraught, that she really was her normal self?'

'I'd swear she wasn't a woman who'd just murdered her own mother.'

'Why haven't you come forward before?' asked the solicitor.

'I've been in the Army for the last four months or so. My mother did suggest to you I should be a witness, but you told her it wasn't necessary.'

'Were you questioned by the police at all?'

'My mother was. I was there at the time. They didn't question me. I didn't think about that tram ride at the time, I didn't know about the time of death. No one did then. I'll willingly go into the witness-box after lunch.'

'Good, good,' said Mr Lawrence. 'Wait in the witnesses' room until you're called. I must speak to Sir Humphrey, we must see our client.' He turned about and went back into the building.

CHAPTER TWENTY-FOUR

'You are Robert Adams?'

'Yes, sir.'

'At present serving with a training battalion of the West Kent Regiment?'

'Yes,' I said, and noticed that Miss Chivers had her glasses on and was staring at me.

'You are waiting to be posted to France for active service?'

'Yes.'

'You're on leave at the moment?'

'Yes.'

'Thank you, Mr Adams, for being with us today.' Sir Humphrey was most courteous, most encouraging.

'I'm actually Private Adams.'

'Yes,' said Sir Humphrey, 'and the country is grateful for what that means, I'm sure. You're the eldest son of Mrs Adams, a previous witness?'

'I am.'

'Then, like the rest of your family and your lodger, Mr Finch, you know the accused as a friend?'

'Yes.'

'Would you please tell the court how events came to concern you on the morning of the murder?'

People sat up, the jury sat up and Miss Chivers bent her head.

'I opened the door of our house at twenty-five to eight, my usual time for starting my journey to the firm I worked for at Blackfriars. As I opened the door, Miss Chivers passed by. Since the beginning of the war she had had to go to her work earlier than before, and our times of departure

313

from our houses often coincided. She gave me a smile as she passed—'

'She gave you a smile?'

'Yes. She always did. I waited for a little while before following her.'

'Why did you do that?' asked Sir Humphrey, 'with singular interest'.

'Because as a male person in long trousers, I counted in her mother's eyes as a dangerous man, with designs on her daughter, and I knew Miss Chivers preferred me not to provoke her mother by walking up the street with her.'

Murmurs from the crowded court arrived in my ear. Mr Braithwaite rose.

'Objection, m'Lord,' he said bruisingly. 'Witness can't possibly know how he counted in the mind of the deceased.'

'Sir Humphrey?' said the judge enquiringly.

'If the witness might continue, m'lud?' said Sir Humphrey.

'It will remove the objection?'

'I'm sure it will,' said Sir Humphrey, and gave me a nod.

'Mrs Chivers once spoke to me when I was cleaning the windows of her house,' I said. 'I was in my last year of school at the time, and in long trousers. Miss Chivers had given me sixpence to do the job. While I was up the ladder, Mrs Chivers opened her bedroom window and accused me of having lustful inclinations towards her daughter. I was staggered by the accusation and the words she used. And her actions shook me, for she tried to push me off the ladder. I lost my footing, I slid down the ladder and landed on my back on the pavement. There was a witness to this, by the way. The girl who lives next door to us, Emily Castle.'

There were more murmurs. I felt hot inside my uniform, and the palms of my hands were sweaty. Miss Chivers still had her head bowed.

'Continue, Mr Adams,' said Sir Humphrey.

'As I said, Miss Chivers passed our house at twenty-five

to eight that morning. She looked nicely dressed, as usual, wearing a hat and a grey raincoat, and was carrying her handbag and a shopping bag.'

Sir Humphrey's eyes flickered, and I knew I'd made a mistake. I hadn't mentioned the shopping bag when I talked with Mr Lawrence towards the end of the lunch adjournment. I'd been more concerned about emphasising how normal Miss Chivers had been. I knew that in mentioning it now, I had almost certainly put into the minds of the prosecution and jury the thought that a shopping bag could conveniently contain a carving-knife – and jewellery. I drew a breath and continued.

'I waited a little while, as I said, then walked up the street, and when I turned into Browning Street, I saw Miss Chivers ahead of me. I crossed Walworth Road and caught her up at the tram stop, where she was waiting with other people.'

I saw the large, lounging figure of Mr Braithwaite, I saw him regarding me indulgently, and I knew he was waiting to spring. The shopping bag was a hideous thing in my mind. I should never have mentioned it, but I had never thought about it in suspicious terms. It was going to weaken the effect of my declaration that Miss Chivers behaved absolutely normally. Wait – there was something.

'Miss Chivers gave me another smile, and I said to her, "Glad to see you're wearing your glasses."'

'Her glasses?' said Sir Humphrey, looking as if he regretted having called me to the stand.

'Oh, she knew it was only said as a joke. Her mother always called after her when she left for her work in the mornings – well, almost always, as neighbours will confirm. Mrs Chivers would put her head out of her bedroom window and call, "Elsie, have you got your glasses on?" Or, "Elsie, are you wearing your glasses?" I'm afraid she was a woman who preferred her daughter to look unattractive, and glasses aren't considered very appealing – well, it's my opinion she preferred it that way.'

Sir Humphrey's eyes levelled with mine.

'Mr Adams, why did you make that joking remark to the accused?'

'It was a silly habit of mine, and the joke was against her mother, not her. I didn't make it every time I saw Miss Chivers, just every now and again.' Now and again couldn't have been more than once or twice, but I had a deep furrow to plough. 'I suppose it could have been irritating, but if it was, Miss Chivers didn't show it. She gave me another smile when I made the joke that morning.'

The judge laid solemn eyes on me. The prosecution laid sharp eyes on me. Miss Chivers lifted her head.

'Mr Adams,' said Sir Humphrey, 'was it out of habit that you made the joke on that occasion?'

'I suppose so. Well, her mother had called after her, as usual—'

'Mr Adams?' said Sir Humphrey, blandness cracking.

'Yes, while I was waiting, as usual, for Miss Chivers to get well ahead of me for the reason I've stated.'

The court buzzed. The prosecution was in startled conference. The judge's eyes never left me. My palms were sweatier. Miss Chivers seemed to be gazing in myopic wonderment at the top of the dock. Sir Humphrey's expression was one of intense curiosity. He was thinking, of course, that this was something else I hadn't mentioned during my talk with Mr Lawrence.

'Mr Adams,' he said slowly, 'you heard Mrs Chivers call out that morning?'

'Yes, of course. You could rarely fail to hear her if you were out of your house. And at that particular time, the street was very quiet, the factory workers hadn't begun to arrive and the schoolkids would only have just been getting up. There was nothing to stop me hearing Mrs Chivers very clearly. She called, "Elsie, have you got your glasses on?" Sometimes Miss Chivers would reply, sometimes she didn't. I could understand that, because it was a stupid question – she always had her glasses on when she left for work. She didn't reply that morning. Anyway, on our tram ride to work, she—'

'Mr Adams.' Sir Humphrey quietly interrupted me. 'I'd like the court to be absolutely clear about this, and I'd like you to be absolutely sure. Let me ask you, was it on that particular morning, the morning of the murder, when the time was twenty-five to eight, that the accused's mother called out to her?'

'Well, yes, as she always did. There must have been very few times when she didn't, as anybody in our street will tell you. I'd have thought it odd if she hadn't on that occasion. I'd have probably asked Miss Chivers if her mother was feeling ill when I caught her up. As it was, I said, "Glad to see you're wearing your glasses." It was just my joke.'

At the time, of course, I'd said it because I hadn't heard her mother ask the eternal question.

'Thank you, Mr Adams,' said Sir Humphrey. 'Will you tell the court why you haven't made this known until today?'

'I've spent the last four months or so training for active service with the Army. I joined up only a few days after the murder. I was at home when the police called to ask questions of my mother. They didn't ask me any, and as I didn't know what time the murder had been committed or that Miss Chivers was under suspicion, I never gave any thought to the early morning moments. I simply thought someone had broken into Miss Chivers's house, that that someone was responsible. When I heard later on that she'd been arrested, I still didn't give any real thought to the early morning. It's only since the trial's been on that I've heard about the estimated time of death. It didn't make sense to me. I remembered how normal Miss Chivers was on our tram ride to work together. Well, she would have been, of course, because she knew her mother was still alive when she left the house.'

'Do you think, Mr Adams, that the estimated time of death was inaccurate?'

'I don't think, sir, I'd better give any opinions on that.'

'M'lud,' said Sir Humphrey, 'I'd like at this stage to recall Dr Edwards.'

'I should like that myself,' said the judge. 'The witness may stand down for a few moments.'

I went and sat with Chinese Lady and Mr Finch. Chinese Lady was shaking. She gave my hand a quivery pat. Miss Chivers bowed her head again as Sir Humphrey questioned the recalled Dr Edwards. I was sweating all over. I heard Dr Edwards agree that it was not impossible for death to have taken place after seven-thirty, although he preferred the original estimate and would dispute any time later than seven-forty-five.

'But you would go along with an extra fifteen minutes?' said Sir Humphrey.

'Yes, just about.'

'The accused left home at twenty-five to eight. The key was under the step mat for your convenience. At that time, with the morning still not light, someone might have used the key unobserved. It need not have taken very long for an intruder to go up to the bedroom, go to the dressing-table drawer, be disturbed by the victim waking up and cut her throat with a sharp knife or similar weapon?'

'It need not have taken longer than a minute.'

'Thank you, Dr Edwards. Your witness.'

'No questions,' said Mr Braithwaite, 'but I'd like to cross-examine the previous witness.'

I took the stand again, the judge reminding me I was still under oath.

'Mr Adams,' said Mr Braithwaite, 'what was it you said Mrs Chivers called out that morning?'

'"Elsie, have you got your glasses on?"'

Mr Braithwaite's smile was cynical.

'But the accused did not reply?'

'No. She sometimes didn't, as I said. If my mother called after me every morning to ask me a question that was always the same, like had I cleaned my teeth, I'd get into a state where I'd never answer at all.'

'You seem a very talkative young man,' said Mr Braithwaite, 'but if I want you to make observations, I'll ask you for them. Otherwise, just answer my questions.

318

Perhaps, Mr Adams, on this particular occasion, the accused didn't hear her mother?'

'Yes, that's possible, sir. She had gone a little way then, while I hadn't yet left our doorstep.'

'I mean she didn't hear simply because her mother didn't ask the question.'

'But her mother always asked. I'm not saying there were people who heard her every morning, but any time anyone was in the street when Miss Chivers left for her work, her mother would certainly be heard. Before the war, when I was at school, Miss Chivers mostly left home at about twenty-five to nine, and those of us on our way to school—'

'Yes, yes,' said Mr Braithwaite, waving a large hand about, 'you've made your point a dozen times. What I'm suggesting, Mr Adams, is that the accused didn't hear because her mother was incapable of getting to the window or uttering a single word. She was incapable because she was dead.'

'She wasn't dead then,' I said, and I could only hope, for the sake of my soul, that perhaps she hadn't been.

Mr Braithwaite regarded me witheringly.

'Are you sure you aren't being led astray by wishful thinking?' he asked.

'I don't understand what you're getting at. I've told you that a little while after Miss Chivers passed by, I heard her mother call out—'

'Yes, we've had all that.'

'Mr Braithwaite,' said the judge, 'I think the witness is entitled to enlarge on his answer. Please allow him to.'

I went on. 'I didn't hear any reply from Miss Chivers, as I've also said. On the tram we boarded together, she was absolutely normal. If her mother hadn't called out, I'd have probably asked her why, and if she'd left her mother with her throat cut, I don't believe she could have behaved in her normal way or faced up to her day's work without showing some strain. She'd not only have had the ghastly thing on her mind, she'd have had the nasty ordeal in front

319

of her – the police, the questions and everything else. You could ask her colleague, Mr Burns, what she was like at her job that day. What I'm trying to say is that Miss Chivers simply couldn't have known her mother was dead – she couldn't have been her normal self if she had known.'

I saw Sir Humphrey relax. I saw the judge make a note.

'I suggest, Mr Adams, that you could still be guilty of wishful thinking,' said Mr Braithwaite, 'wishful thinking brought about by your close friendship with the accused. I ask you, are you in love with her? You're at the age when a young man can become disastrously infatuated.'

'I like Miss Chivers very much,' I said. 'I don't know anyone who doesn't like her. But I'm not infatuated, I don't look at her romantically. I've got a girl.'

'Really?' Mr Braithwaite was caustic.

'Yes.' It was very odd, because I didn't say Rosie Harris, daughter of my drill sergeant, I said, 'Emily Castle, the girl who lives next door. I'm taking her out on Saturday. I'm on leave until next Monday.'

The heads of some members of the jury were together. Miss Chivers's head was lifted, her expression soft. Mr Braithwaite took a note from a colleague.

'Mr Adams,' he said, 'the shopping bag you said the accused was carrying. What did she do with it on the tram?'

'Placed it on her lap.'

'Was it a linen bag?'

'Yes, a brown one of thick linen, with leather handles and a leather base.'

'Was it folded?'

'No. It lay over her lap, with her handbag on top of it.'

'Was it empty?'

'It looked empty.'

'But it may not have been quite empty?'

'I don't know. I didn't give it all that much attention. It was just a shopping bag.'

'What was the size of it?'

'The size of a usual shopping bag.'

'It could have contained a knife, then, a carving-knife, without it being noticed?'

'Well, I didn't notice anything like that, sir, certainly.'

'The bag wasn't folded, you say?'

'No.'

'I see. Not folded. Her handbag was placed on it to keep it secure on her lap?'

'Her handbag was on it – I don't know whether that was to keep it secure.'

'If there was a carving-knife in it, the accused would not have wanted to be careless with it.'

Sir Humphrey murmured, 'My learned friend is tilting at windmills.'

'Are you raising an objection, Sir Humphrey, or making a comment?' said the judge. 'If a comment—?'

'I withdraw, m'lud,' said Sir Humphrey, 'with apologies.'

Mr Braithwaite said, 'You mentioned Miss Chivers was quite normal in her manner, Mr Adams. What did you talk about on the tram?'

'About the war, and about my sister's fiancé and how he was intending to join the Army in response to Lord Kitchener's appeal. I mentioned that my sister was very cut up about it. Miss Chivers was very sympathetic.'

'A paragon,' said Mr Braithwaite drily.

'I don't know about that, I only know she was the same as she always is – very nice to talk to, very pleasant in her manner and a little shy.'

'Shy?'

'Yes. I like her for it. I think shyness in the fair sex is rather nice.'

'The accused is thirty-one years old, Mr Adams.'

'She's still a shy person.'

The faintest smile showed on Sir Humphrey's face. Miss Chivers had her head bent again, as if even a blurred court was too much for her. I thought the atmosphere in the court was lighter. I thought the King's uniform was helping me. People liked the look of a uniform these days. I thought it had helped me to commit perjury more convincingly than if I'd taken the stand merely looking clerkly.

Mr Braithwaite said abruptly, 'No further questions.'

He did not recall Miss Chivers's office colleague. Nor did Sir Humphrey ask Miss Chivers to take the stand. I returned to sit with Chinese Lady and Mr Finch. Chinese Lady looked dizzy. Mr Finch gave me a grave smile.

The summing-up by both sides was brief. But I hardly heard anything, my mind being full of buzzing fog that smothered voices and my thoughts. I was only vaguely aware of Mr Braithwaite trying to cast doubt on my evidence and on my credibility, and of Sir Humphrey sounding confident in his assertion that the Crown's case had fallen apart. The judge made his address to the jury. He was brief too. Because of the state of my mind, his voice came and went, but I did hear him tell the jury that if they were to find the prisoner guilty, they could only do so if they were sure beyond any shadow of doubt that the prosecution had proved she was. They were to bear in mind that the prosecution had insisted the crime was committed while she was still in the house, and they were therefore to weigh up very carefully the evidence of the last witness, Private Robert Adams.

The jury retired. A terrible fingernail-biting began.

'Boots—?'

'What?'

'Are you falling asleep at a time like this?' whispered Chinese Lady. 'D'you want to come out for a cup of tea somewhere? People are sayin' you've give the jury something to talk about, that it'll take hours.'

'I don't want anything. I just want to sit here. You go.'

'It's all right.' Chinese Lady patted my hand. 'Mr Finch and me just thought you might like a cup of tea.'

'I'll wait.'

The jury, in fact, was out for only forty minutes. Everyone came back into court, including the prisoner and the judge. You could have heard a pin drop when the clerk rose to ask the jury foreman if they had reached a verdict. The foreman said yes.

'Do you find the prisoner guilty or not guilty?'

'Not guilty.'

The court erupted and reporters rushed out. The judge got a little stern about the noise, and not until the place had quietened down completely did he address Miss Chivers.

Majestically, he discharged her.

'Oh, Boots,' breathed Chinese Lady, 'you done it, you done it proper on the prosecution.'

Mr Finch leaned across her, gripped my hand hard and shook it.

'An unforgettable day,' he said, and I wondered if he meant this one or the other one. His eyes were darkly grey. I think he knew I'd lied. Chinese Lady had no idea, of course. When the judge had disappeared, Mrs Pullen squeezed herself into view and gave me an ample bussing. People began streaming out. Mr Lawrence arrived and shook my hand.

'You were splendid,' he said.

Miss Chivers appeared when the court was almost empty. She was in company with Sir Humphrey Dunbar. They came up to us, Miss Chivers pale but calm.

'Mr Adams,' said Sir Humphrey, 'I think we must say you arrived in the nick of time, like a knight in khaki armour.'

'Frankly, sir,' I said, 'I feel as if I fell off the horse.'

Miss Chivers put out a hand and lightly touched my arm.

'Thank you, Boots, for remembering. You were right, I didn't hear my mother that morning. My mind was on my work. We were so harassed at the Admiralty. Boots, my dear friend, thank you, thank you.' She kissed my cheek, and she smiled. Her glasses were on, her eyes clear. I thought her beautiful.

'I'm only too glad it's all over,' I said.

'We won, perhaps, by a matter of minutes,' said Sir Humphrey, 'when Dr Edwards conceded those minutes.' Again his eyes levelled with mine. 'Mr Adams, your memory is excellent, and your performance was faultless.'

323

'Oh, he was very upstanding,' said Chinese Lady, not questioning Sir Humphrey's use of the word performance.

Mr Finch, hovering unobtrusively, said, 'I'm going to find a cab or a taxi. There may be all kinds of people outside, waiting to get a look at Miss Chivers. When I've got something that'll carry us away, I'll let you know, Miss Chivers, and Boots and I will hustle you through.'

'Thank you,' said Miss Chivers quietly, and Mr Finch left. Miss Chivers turned to Sir Humphrey. 'And thank you again, Sir Humphrey.' Her smile was sweet. 'Your performance too was faultless.' At which, Sir Humphrey raised an eyebrow. 'I'm really quite free to go now?' she said.

'Quite free,' he said.

'I'm so grateful,' she said, and put out a hand. Sir Humphrey shook it.

'It was touch and go until Mr Adams took the stand,' he said. 'Mr Adams?' And he shook my hand too, his grip surprisingly firm. 'Don't soldier too recklessly in France, for you should have quite a future in front of you when the war is over.'

Sir Humphrey, I knew, had his doubts about me.

When Mr Finch returned, he and I rushed Miss Chivers through the mob outside. Not that the mob was hostile. Far from it. It was a cheering mob. Mr Finch elbowed a reporter aside, and behind us Mrs Pullen bumped another out of the way with a vigorous buffet from a broad hip. Press cameras took photographs.

We went all the way home in a motor taxi, and Chinese Lady at once made a pot of tea, a victory pot. Miss Chivers shared it with us. She drank it while it was still very hot, and it brought a little colour back to her cheeks. Chinese Lady talked as if the victory had intoxicated her, repeating herself so much that she sounded as if her tongue was on an unstoppable merry-go-round. It sustained the atmosphere of glad and wild relief. Mr Finch said hardly a word, though there was a smile on his face as he listened to Chinese Lady, while Miss Chivers, accepting a second cup of tea, seemed gently happy to let her do all the talking. When the pot was empty, Miss Chivers rose.

'You will excuse me?' she said. 'I'd like to go home now.'

It was beyond Chinese Lady to understand how anyone could want to go back to that house of murder, more especially Miss Chivers herself, but she didn't argue. She said she was sure Miss Chivers needed rest and quiet, but that she was to say if she needed any help or any company at any time. And she was to come to tea on Sunday.

'What can I say but thank you so much?' said Miss Chivers. 'Mrs Adams, you will never know how dear you and your family are to me, and Mr Finch will never know just how grateful I am for his friendship and support.'

'It was given willingly,' said Mr Finch, 'by all of us.'

They were not looking at each other. Her eyes were cast down, his were on the empty teapot.

'Boots?' said Miss Chivers. Her hand touched my shoulder. 'Thank you.'

She left then.

CHAPTER TWENTY-FIVE

Lizzy and Emily gobbled up all the details later. Emily was already primed. After seeing placards referring to a sensational verdict at the murder trial, she'd been unable to resist splashing out on an evening paper.

'Oh, crikey,' she said breathlessly, green eyes shining, 'I just couldn't believe Boots being in the paper like he was. It said 'is evidence was a sensation, and it was on the front page, would yer believe.'

'He pushed the war news out of the way, would you believe *that*,' said Lizzy.

'I hope it's all going to calm down,' said Chinese Lady, hat still on, 'I don't like being in the papers.'

'Oh, Mrs Adams, you got an 'ero in the family,' said Emily. 'Imagine you saying I was your girl, Boots. It got me in the paper as well.'

'Sorry if I took your name in vain, Em,' I said.

'Oh, that's all right,' said Emily, basking in the general glow of happy relief, 'you had to think of something when they was goin' on at you about bein' in love with Miss Chivers. That was shameful. I mean, Miss Chivers is nice, but awf'lly old.'

'Old?' said Chinese Lady. 'Well, if Miss Chivers is old, I don't know what that makes me, Em'ly Castle – near to me grave, I should think.'

Emily, who held our mum in much respect, blushed to her roots.

'Oh, Mrs Adams, I didn't mean you was old at all, really I didn't,' she said. 'I was only meaning it was shameful that prosecutor tryin' to make out Boots was bearing false witness because he was in love with Miss Chivers, and her years older than him.'

'Bearing false witness?' said Lizzy. 'You read that somewhere, Em'ly?'

'Oh, you read it in books,' said Emily. 'But the prosecutor was tryin' it on with Boots, don't you think so, Mrs Adams?'

'Boots was one too many for him,' said Chinese Lady, almost sounding proud, 'he just stood up and spoke what he knew was right.'

'It was right all right,' said Lizzy, and gave me a little smile.

'Me mum an' dad said Boots'll go a long way in life,' said Emily.

'If he don't get his head blown off by the Germans,' said Chinese Lady tersely.

'He's not saying much,' said Lizzy.

'A good thing,' said our mum, 'I don't like people blowing their trumpets.'

'Still, heroes shouldn't be too silent,' said Lizzy, 'they ought to beat their chests a little bit.'

'I said it all in court,' I said, 'I'm taking a rest now.'

We had a noisy evening. Neighbours kept calling, Emily's mum and dad among them. Emily's mum was getting very fat, and her dad had the kind of paunch that put a strain on his trousers and braces. It was all the beer they drank. It was a common sight to see Mrs Castle wobbling a careful way home from the jug and bottle counter of the Browning Street pub, a jarful in her hand. That was the cheapest way of buying beer. Neither she nor Mr Castle looked as if they ever spent much on clothes. Nobody spent a great deal, when food and rent had a prior claim on threadbare purses, but the Castles seemed to spend even less. But they were a good-natured pair, and highly pleased that Emily was giving them three shillings a week out of her new wages. It meant Mrs Castle could take her pitcher more often to the well.

They both came in wearing carpet slippers, their shiny

327

faces beery and amiable, and Mrs Castle's untidy hair full of hairpins that were of no help at all. Mr Castle gave me a huge slap on the shoulder, and Mrs Castle gave me a loving cuddle with her arms and her overflowing bosom.

'Ain't yer gettin' 'andsome, Boots, ain't yer growin' up a fine soldier like yer dad, and ain't yer been a real 'ero to Miss Chivers?'

'Good on yer, Boots lad,' said Mr Castle, 'Em'ly's that proud of yer she's been dancin' 'er 'ead orf.'

Mr Finch was talking quietly with some of the men. Chinese Lady, hatted, moved about amid people coming and going. She looked very upright, giving the impression she could hold her head very high, even if she was still frequently in and out of the pawn. Pots of tea kept appearing, and Sammy earned himself a penny by keeping a flow of washed-up cups and saucers available. Emily and Lizzy handed fresh tea round, and constant was the imbibing of this Walworth nectar.

Tommy, who had regarded with awe the family's involvement in the trial and Miss Chivers's release as an act of wondrous mystification, spoiled things a little by suddenly shouting, 'Mum, there ain't no more sugar.'

That pained Chinese Lady. One could hold one's head up however much one was in pawn, but to run out of sugar when the place was full of neighbours was a sickening blow to one's pride.

Mr Finch came to the rescue in his understanding way.

'I've still the best part of the pound you lent me, Mrs Adams,' he said. 'It's in my little larder.'

From the scullery, Sammy put his head in.

'I'll go up an' get it, Mr Finch,' he said, 'I'll only charge yer a ha'p'ny.'

'How good of you, Sammy,' said Mr Finch, 'but I'll get it – no trouble.' He got it himself. It was his own, of course. Chinese Lady hadn't lent him any. It was like him to help her keep her pride intact.

I spent most of the evening listening to people telling me what a good job I'd done for Miss Chivers. I was right, they said, about the Witch calling out every morning, and it should have been mentioned before, by other witnesses. They hadn't heard her themselves that morning, but all their doors and windows had been shut, of course, and most of them were still in bed or only just getting up. What a bit of luck for Miss Chivers, what a stroke of rare good fortune that I'd been on my doorstep when that mother of hers had called after her. What a mercy it had been that I'd been able to get home from the Army and give my evidence, Miss Chivers might have had to swing otherwise.

I responded diffidently to all these neighbourly comments.

'Now don't 'ide yer light, Boots lad,' said Mr Castle. 'Yer mum an' Mr Finch 'as been sayin' yer stood up like a real trooper to them lawyers, yer never let 'em shake yer once. Yer don't need to be so modest. Good on yer, that's what I say.'

Lizzy got me alone in the passage when everyone had finally gone.

'You never once said you heard Mrs Chivers call out that morning,' she murmured.

'No, well, why should I have? Anyway, I've spent most of the time away, in the Army and on the training square, where all that goes on in the outside world is drowned by the clump of boots.'

'You got the real gift of the gab, you have,' said Lizzy, 'and more of it since you joined up. Still, I can't think why you never mentioned before about that morning.'

'I never had any idea about the time of death, that's why.'

'Oh, you must have,' said Lizzy.

'Well, I didn't, sis.'

Lizzy gave me a long look, and then a smile.

'Good old Boots,' she said.

'What d'you mean?'

'Nothing,' she said. 'Anyway, don't you see? We all know she couldn't have done it, and that's what counts, don't it? Come on, we better help Chinese Lady get the kitchen cleaned up.'

As we went back into the kitchen, the front door shook to a loud knocking, followed by a voice hollering through the letterbox.

'Telegram! Come an' get it!'

Chinese Lady paled. We'd never had a telegram, for which she had been thankful. Telegrams always meant death or disaster.

'Oh, lor',' breathed Chinese Lady.

'Telegram for Miss Eliza Adams?' hollered the cheerful voice. 'Come an' get it.'

Lizzy blanched. Her eyes dilated, and I knew she was thinking it could only mean something terrible had happened to Ned.

'You get it, Boots,' she whispered. Sammy and Tommy were both too awestruck to offer.

The time was almost ten o'clock. It had to be bad news at that hour.

The telegraph boy, bike propped against his hip, handed me the flimsy buff envelope, addressed to Lizzy, but by the name of Eliza. That definitely meant it had come from Ned or his parents.

'Any answer?' asked the telegraph boy.

'I don't know. I'll see.'

I took the telegram to Lizzy. Lizzy, quite the young woman though she was now, retreated in alarm as I offered it to her.

'No, I can't,' she gasped, 'you do it for me, you read it.'

Emily, who was still with us, put an arm around her shoulder. I opened the telegram and read it.

'DARLING ELIZA JUST SEEN EVENING PAPER STOP HOORAY FOR ELSIE CHIVERS STOP TELL BOOTS WELL DONE STOP LOVE TO ALL STOP AM DELIGHTED FOR MY NEW FAMILY TO BE STOP ELIZA IS MY DARLING STOP LOVE NED.'

Lizzy shook.

'You're making it up,' she gasped, 'let me see it.' I gave her the telegram and she read it for herself. 'Oh,' she said, and drew a long breath. But she was still shaking, and

Emily gave her shoulders a squeeze. There they were, the two of them, fast friends for years, even when the incidence of headlice might have separated them. Lizzy, flushed and misty-eyed, was lovely, Emily quite smart in her still-cherished bottle green costume, which she took as much care of as Lizzy did of her plum-coloured winter coat, and which she had put on in celebration of victory. The jacket, however, did not button up quite so perfectly, for Emily, nearly seventeen, had very firm and pouting breasts. Extraordinary. It was a great pity she still looked so plain beside Lizzy. She deserved some prettiness. Perhaps her fine, firm mouth and her big green eyes represented all the prettiness life was going to bestow on her. I was glad she had this boy Arthur. She had become a credit to her mum and dad, and it was another pity they weren't more of a credit to her. She was remarkably loyal to them, and I knew her to be exceptionally fond of her beery, hearty dad.

She did have another fine feature, of course. Her auburn hair was beautiful.

'There, yer see, Lizzy,' she said affectionately, 'it's a nice telegram, ain't – isn't it?'

'It's one you can frame, Lizzy,' I said.

'All the money it must have cost him,' said Lizzy, eyes overbright, 'the wasteful extravagance.'

'Not wasteful,' I said.

'Oh, gosh, no,' said Emily, 'I'd kick me legs up if I got a telegram like that.'

'It must have cost him over three shillings,' said Lizzy. 'Three shillings.'

'And really just for two words only,' I said.

'What two words?' asked Lizzy.

'Darling Eliza,' I said, and she blushed, and I thought how nice that was, my sister blushing. 'Any answer?'

'Oh, I can't think of one now, I'll send him a letter,' said Lizzy, so I gave the telegraph boy tuppence for bringing a cheerful message instead of a death notice. He rode off whistling into the darkness.

I saw Emily to the front door a little later.

'Lizzy's got wet eyes,' she said.

'Oh, well, young love,' I said.

'No, it ain't.' Emily was quick with her retort. 'It's a lot more than that. It's old an' tried love, that's what.'

'Old and tried?'

'Yes. Ain't you never seen that? Lizzy wants Ned.'

'I know she's sick he's away in the Army.'

'Lizzy's all grown up. She wants Ned, she wants him with her. She's not ever going to feel like a woman should till he's out of the Army an' married to her. So the two of you better help to get the war over quick.'

'Right, I'll go charging in as soon as our West Kents get to France.'

'I don't mean you're supposed to do anything as silly as that. There's enough soldiers gettin' killed without you joining them.' Emily sounded quite short. She sounded almost angry. 'Talkin' like that – no wonder your mum gets shirty with you. You got to think about your family an' people that's fond of you. You shouldn't talk so silly.'

'All right, Em – sorry.'

'Oh, I didn't mean to – I'm being interfering – it's not any of my business – don't take any notice. Boots, your mum said you did so good at the court, you stood up fine an' fearless, she said.'

'I didn't feel fearless, take it from me. I can tell you our mum was the one who was that, she looked a proud and upright widow woman, and Mr Finch was the calmest person in the court, except for the judge.'

'Boots,' said Emily, 'you sure you don't have a girl?'

'Girls are something to think seriously about when the war's over.'

'You don't really have to take me out Saturday.'

'Why don't I? We're all going. You, Mum, Lizzy and Tommy. Sammy's not keen, so I'm giving him sixpence instead.'

'Oh, he does jobs up the Lane on Saturday evenings, anyway,' said Emily. 'He helps to clear up the stalls, an' the stallholders pay him a penny each.'

'Our youngest kid's making his fortune. Put your glad rags on come Saturday, Em.'

'Could you—' Emily hesitated. 'Could you wear your uniform? Oh, it's not that I don't like yer in a suit, only yer look grand as a soldier, and I never been in company with a soldier. I can swank a bit – oh, yer don't mind if I do that, swank a bit?'

'Well, I can swank a bit myself in company with you and Mum and Lizzy.'

'Oh, yer the grandest bloke,' said Emily, and darted indoors to her parents.

I didn't look at the paper next morning. I let it lie on the table while I got breakfast for the kids and for Lizzy. Chinese Lady was at her town hall work, as usual.

At half-past nine, when I was alone, Miss Chivers called. I opened the door to her knock. She smiled. Without her glasses, she looked as she always did when she left them off, softly and engagingly short-sighted. It gave her attractiveness a sweet appeal. The people in the court would have found her very appealing. So would the jury. In court, her glasses had been off most of the time.

'Hello, Boots,' she said.

'Nice to see you looking refreshed,' I said. 'Come in.'

'Oh, I don't want to disturb you.'

'You won't disturb me,' I said, but she had been disturbing me for ages, even before I had seen her in that black silk nightdress, through which her breasts had roundly peered and glimmered.

I took her through to the kitchen.

'I won't stay,' she said, 'I've some shopping to do and the house to clear up. It's in such a mess after all the police searches. They searched it again, you know, while I was in custody.'

'They were looking for that knife, I suppose.'

'Yes,' she said, and faintly flushed. I noticed then that she was carrying the brown shopping bag, that she was carrying it openly and without guilt, and that was a brave

333

and open thing to do, I thought. I looked her in the eye. I had to do that, I had to find out if there was something there, something that showed she knew her mother hadn't called out that morning. Her eyes met mine without faltering, and there seemed to be nothing there except a melting softness. 'Boots, I've called because I know I never thanked you properly yesterday. I only said thank you. I want to say more than that, much more. I want to say you were brave and wonderful, and that as I listened to you I felt full of sweet and beautiful tears. Do you believe that, Boots, that unshed tears can be sweet and beautiful?'

'The way things were for you in the dock, I believe you could have felt suffering emotional.'

'Yes.' Her voice was soft and warm and sweet. 'I really didn't hear my mother call out that morning, I really didn't. She was in bed when I left. I told Sir Humphrey that. And as she said she was feeling poorly, I suppose that for once I wasn't expecting her to call after me, I suppose I wasn't listening for her call, and I did have my mind on my work. Do you realise how much I owe you for being where you were at the time? Everything else was against me, except that. You know you saved me, don't you?'

She was so earnest, so intense. Had it been someone else, then, someone who would have known about the key or made a guess, someone who had slipped unnoticed into the house as soon as we were both out of sight?

'I only know that all the time I was in court, I couldn't think why you were in the dock. I'm only too glad I remembered everything about that morning.'

'I shall be forever grateful that you did.' She smiled again then, and looked beautiful. It was easy to understand why she never wore her glasses except when she had to, at her office, for instance. They did diminish her good looks to some extent, but to me she was always attractive.

'Have you thought about the fact that you're free now?' I asked.

'Oh, that was something that was unbelievable at first.'

'I mean free of your other prison.'

That seemed to puzzle her, startle her and sadden her, all in turn.

'I haven't given it much thought at all,' she said. 'I'm aware of what you mean, but it's a freedom no one could have asked for at such a terrible cost.'

'No,' I said, 'but it's there. You can do what you like now, go where you like and meet who you like.'

'I shall be happy first of all to take up my job again at the Admiralty. I know it will help me to forget the awfulness of these last months. Boots?' Her smile came, and it was gently teasing. 'Boots, do you really think me shy, even at my age?'

'I've always thought so, yes, but I like you for it. You're going back to the Admiralty, then?'

'They've been very understanding. I received a telegram from my chief this morning. I shall be going back on Monday. I'm grateful for their generosity, but it's you I owe most to.'

She was close to me, and I wasn't sure how she had arrived within chesting distance. Her handbag and shopping bag were on the table, her hands resting lightly on my shoulders.

'Miss Chivers—'

'Dear Boots, we're both shy about gratitude, perhaps, but I can't go without showing you just how much I feel in debt to you.' And she lifted her face and kissed me on the mouth, warmly and sweetly. Her bosom cushioned me. 'Thank you, Boots.'

'You can make a habit of that, if you like,' I said.

'Oh, I—' She stopped, she smiled again. 'Yes, I'm free, aren't I?' she said.

I saw her out, I saw her on her way up the street, walking in her graceful way. A neighbour said good morning to her. I heard her respond. 'Good morning, Mrs Higgins.' Mrs Higgins said, 'I was goin' to come and—' 'Come tomorrow for a cup of tea, Mrs Higgins.' Her voice sounded as if there was a lilt to it.

When Sammy and Tommy came home from school in

the afternoon, I sent them along to Miss Chivers to ask if there was anything they could do to help her get her house straight. I imagined the police had turned it inside-out not once, but several times. The kids didn't come back, except for their tea interval, and it seemed Miss Chivers was paying them handsomely for their help. They had, among other things, taken a bedstead to pieces and stored it ready for collection by the old-iron man when he next came round. It was the Witch's bedstead. The kids were unconcerned that murder had been done on it.

On Saturday afternoon, I took Emily up West, together with Chinese Lady, Lizzy and Tommy. We took in the wartime atmosphere of the West End, with lots of servicemen out with their girls and the theatres running Saturday matinees. Emily walked beside me. It was quite a warm April day, and she wore a dress and a boater and looked very nice. I told her so.

'Oh, I would've worn me green costume,' she said, 'only the jacket – well, it's begun to be a bit tight. Mum took the costume to the dyers an' cleaners, an' the jacket must've shrunk a bit. D'you think your mum could let it out for me? She's ever so good at that sort of thing – oh, Boots, look at that sailor – he's drunk, would yer believe, at this time of day.'

'He's got his own rum, I expect.'

'Would yer ask your mum for me? Only the costume's me favourite outfit – it's the one – well, it's just me favourite. Only the jacket's got tight an' it notices, like.'

'Well, of course it notices,' I said. 'You're a growing girl, Em. It's nothing to do with the jacket shrinking, and you know it.'

'Oh, you don't mind me growing, do you?' she said.

I laughed. Emily was very comical at times.

'Why should I mind?'

'In case I got fat. I'd rather be like I am, a bit skinny, than all fat.'

'You're not skinny all over, Emily,' I said, 'not when your jacket won't button up.'

336

'Oh, you cheeky bugger,' said Emily in one of her impulsive rushes. Then she turned pink, of course, amid the crowds in Regent Street, with Chinese Lady, Lizzy and Tommy ahead of us.

'You'll get locked up, Em, if you talk like that in the West End.'

'Oh – sorry – I didn't mean it – oh, ain't I awful? You won't tell your mum, will you? She wouldn't like it if she knew I said a thing like that. Boots, while we got time, would yer come into a store with me and help me buy a new dress? I brought some money with me—'

'Not on your life,' I said, enjoying the stroll and the windows we stopped to inspect every so often. 'I've had some of that. I'll end up looking at things. Ask Arthur.'

'Arthur? I ain't – I'm not takin' him shopping with me.'

'You took me. Twice. Why should Arthur be spared?'

'Well, he's not here, is he? Oh, you come an' help me choose, won't yer?'

'All right, let's all find a store. Mum and Lizzy will be tickled. Tommy will think it's purgatory.'

'Oh, I don't know why you're so good to me,' said Emily.

'I'm not being good. I'm being dragged.'

We all helped Emily choose a lovely light summer dress of turquoise, and she paid for it out of a purse stuffed with savings. Emily had a good head on her, and the acumen of a girl wise enough to save and buy the kind of clothes that offset her plainness. She had made her decision a couple of years ago, I think. She had decided she wasn't going to be a ragbag like her mum. I felt Emily was always going to look nicely dressed, even if never a beauty. She was going to buy good clothes that would last. There was sound economical sense in that.

We went into a Lyons teashop, enjoyed a high tea and then went on to music hall at the Alhambra. It was my treat, out of my saved Army pay. The seats in the back stalls were a shilling each. Chinese Lady hadn't been to a music hall since our dad had been courting her. Emily had been twice with her mum and dad, Lizzy and I once, up in a gallery. Tommy had never been at all. He was smitten by the splendour of the Alhambra, and Lizzy, Emily and Chinese Lady were thrilled by the variety of the turns. Tears came to their eyes at the rendering of the heart-tugging ballad, 'My Old Dutch'. Different tears rolled as they laughed themselves into fits at the comedy of Dan Leno and others. Dan Leno shared the top billing with Marie Lloyd, a tremendous turn, and they both brought the house down, the house being packed.

We took a tram home. The fried fish shop in Walworth Road was still open, offering rock salmon or skate at tuppence a piece, chips a penny, and salt and vinegar free. There was talk of prices going up because of the war and fish getting short, but it hadn't happened yet.

'Who's for fish and chips?' I asked, when we got off the tram.

'Oh, yummy,' said Lizzy.

'Boots, you spent enough,' said Chinese Lady, but fish and chips were a joy to her.

'Oh, let me pay,' said Emily, 'you all been so good to me, an' I got plenty of money.'

'No, let Boots,' said Lizzy, 'it's his week, Em'ly, his big week.'

Tommy went across to the shop to get the order, while we walked home. Sammy was still up. We caught him counting his money. He began to shovel it all back into a painted wooden box with a sliding lid.

'Well, look at that pile of spondulicks,' said Emily.

'It's me capital,' said Sammy, 'for when I start a pawnshop. Boots, do yer need a 'stificate to be a pawnbroker?'

'No, just a bit of capital and a stony heart,' I said.

'Oh, that's all right, then,' said Sammy, unscrupulous where Tommy was honest.

'Tommy's bringing fish an' chips for everyone,' said Chinese Lady. 'You too.'

'Oh, bless yer cotton socks, Mum,' said Sammy, 'ain't yer 'eavenly?'

338

'Boots is paying,' said Lizzy.

'Stone the jackdaws,' said Sammy, who had an affinity with those acquisitive birds.

'Yours will cost you thruppence,' I said.

'Oh, yer skinflint,' said Sammy. He frowned. 'Well, I'll 'ave to owe yer. Me resources is a bit strained.'

'He's pulling your leg, love,' said Chinese Lady. 'I'll put the kettle on for some tea.'

I sat down to loosen my puttees and to slip my Army boots off.

'Oh, I'll do it for yer, Boots,' said Emily, impulsive again, and knelt down to unwind my puttees.

Chinese Lady, on her way to the scullery, stopped in shock.

'Em'ly Castle, get up this minute – what d'you think you're doing?'

Emily crimsoned.

'Oh, I just thought – well, he's give us such a treat – '

'Well, we can all thank him for it,' said Chinese Lady, 'but I won't have no one be his servant. It's not my place to tell you what's right and what's wrong, but I can give you a bit of sound advice, which is don't do anything for a young man that he can do for hisself. Young men is conceited enough as it is, and lazy too, some of 'em, without girls making them so swollen-headed they can't get their hats on. Neither don't it do to make them think they're lords and masters. They're all of 'em only too ready to think they are. The best thing girls can do for young men is to help 'em grow into proper men. It don't help to take their boots off for them.'

Emily, red-faced and crestfallen, got to her feet.

'That's more than a bit of advice, Mum,' I said, 'that's a bookful.'

'Mum, she was only trying to be nice to Boots for taking us out,' said Lizzy, always loyal to Emily.

'Yes, that's it, my girl,' said Chinese Lady, 'that's when we're at our weakest, when some man has been nice to us for a change, that's when we start runnin' around for them.'

339

'I don't see it's weak to be loving when someone's been nice to us,' said Lizzy. 'Em'ly was only being naturally loving to Boots because he give us a good time.'

Emily turned redder. Tommy arrived with the wrapped fish and chips then, creating a diversion that was an obvious relief to her. Chinese Lady put the kettle on, and Lizzy piled plates with the fish and chips.

Sammy, watching the doling out of the hot chips with luminously hungry eyes, said, 'Some blokes from a newspaper come to see Boots. They knocked at Miss Chivers's door as well. Miss Chivers come 'ere afterwards an' told me to tell Boots they want 'im to give 'em 'is story. They wanted 'er to tell 'ers too, but she sent 'em away. Is that mine, Lizzy? You ain't give me as many chips as you give Tommy.'

'Well, Tommy went and fetched them,' said Lizzy. 'Are you telling the truth?'

'Course I am. Miss Chivers said they'll pay Boots an 'undred quid for 'is story. It's that Sunday newspaper—'

'Boots don't want money earned like that,' said Emily.

'It's an 'undred quid,' said Sammy, tucking in. 'An 'undred quid. They said they'd come back tomorrer, Sunday.'

'It's blood money,' said Emily, looking upset. 'Boots don't want blood money, do yer, Boots?'

'Whether he wants it or not,' said Chinese Lady, arriving with the teapot and seating herself, 'he's not going to get it. I'm not having this family in that Sunday newspaper, and he knows it.'

'I wonder how much they offered Miss Chivers for her story?' I said, parting the succulent flesh of my rock salmon. 'Something like five hundred, I should think.'

'Oh, Boots, yer wouldn't tell, would yer?' said Emily, very upset. 'Yer wouldn't tell about her as well, would yer?'

'No, he wouldn't,' said Chinese Lady, 'his dad 'ud turn in his unknown grave, and I'd be that ashamed I'd put me head in the oven.'

Lizzy laughed. Chinese Lady gave her a stern look.

'Oh, Mum,' said Lizzy, 'you're so funny at times.'

'I don't think it's funny,' said Tommy, 'Mum with 'er 'ead in the gas oven.'

'I'm going out tomorrow,' I said. 'Let's all go for a tram ride to Abbey Wood and take a picnic with us, and have dinner in the evening.'

'Sometimes,' said Chinese Lady, 'you sound as if you might have a bit of your dad's sense.' She sighed. 'I'll never understand why he got hisself done to death so careless.'

Our mum missed our dad.

'D'you want to come with us, Emily?' I asked.

'Abbey Wood an' a picnic?' said Emily, green eyes glowing. 'Oh, could I? Would it be all right if I come with you, Mrs Adams?'

'We'll be pleasured, Em'ly.'

'Oh, ain't life grand?' said Emily.

'For some,' said Lizzy, and her eyes took on their faraway look.

Our Lizzy missed her Ned.

We had a rousing, open-air day at Abbey Wood, the April weather very kind. Miss Chivers, whom Chinese Lady had invited to Sunday tea, asked to be excused, as she was going to Brighton for the day and had no idea what time she'd get back. Mr Finch, invited to join us for our excursion, also asked to be excused. He had to work in the afternoon. Sunday duties were becoming frequent for him, because of the war.

When we arrived back from our day out, Chinese Lady said Emily could stay and have evening dinner with us because she'd missed Sunday dinner at home. Everyone set to work preparing the meal. Chinese Lady hadn't been able to get a joint, only some mutton chops, but at least these didn't take so long to cook.

It seemed only right to go to the front door with Emily when she finally left.

'It's been me best weekend ever,' she said. 'You got a real

lovely fam'ly, Boots, I like all of you ever so. It's been lovely being with all of you.'

Emily, an only child, must have had moments of loneliness, and she had long stopped taking friends into her house. I knew that was because her mum had long stopped taking any pride in the state of it. Emily had become a very sweet girl, even if she did have an odd inclination to take me into ladies' wear departments at times.

'It was nice to have you with us, Em. By the way, you can bring the jacket of your costume along sometime. Mum'll let it out for you.'

'Oh, tell her thanks ever so.' Emily edged out of the door onto the step, whispering, 'D'you think it's scary for Miss Chivers being all alone in her house? I'd run a mile, I'd feel it was all haunted, wouldn't you?'

'Only if I didn't have a clear conscience,' I said.

'It 'ud still give me the shivers. Today's been real swell, honest. So was yesterday. We'll all miss you when you go back to the Army tomorrer. Boots, can I – can I kiss yer for being so nice to me?'

'I'll kiss you,' I said, 'as long as you don't tell Arthur.'

I kissed her. On her very nice mouth.

'Oh, you'll take care in the Army, won't you?' she said, and went.

About to close the door, I held it open. Mr Finch was back. He came in briskly, looking healthy from his hours on the river on this balmy April day.

'Hello, Boots,' he said.

'Hello,' I said.

'It's a little late,' he said, 'but have you time to come up and have a glass of beer with me, since you're leaving tomorrow?'

I went up and had a glass of beer with him. He was much more his old self, with the light of alert life in his eyes. We talked very easily together, about the war, about the Army and about the trial. He said my evidence had prevented a great miscarriage of justice.

342

'I suppose I'd like to think that,' I said. 'You'll be keeping an eye on Miss Chivers?'

'I'm sure your mother will, and the neighbours,' he said, 'so why do you ask me, Boots?'

'Well, I think life might get difficult for her. Everyone's welcomed her back, everyone's being friendly, but there's still the fact of the murder and the fact that it hasn't been solved. When all the excitement of Miss Chivers's release has died down, I think there's going to be new talk, I think everyone's going to start looking at everyone else, wondering if someone round here did it. It'll be the kind of talk that won't ever completely die down until the police find the murderer, and I suppose if the police want to go through her house again, the law will allow them to do so. I know she can't be tried again, of course, but there could be times when she'll need someone, someone strong and kind.'

'Boots, you've got a very thinking head on you.' Mr Finch pulled on his pipe. He was a handsome man in his vigour and his maturity. I imagined some women would find him very attractive. It was strange he hadn't married, that he preferred this kind of existence, stuck in two rooms in a house in Walworth, when he was so worldly and mixed so well. But there were many lodgers in the houses of Walworth, and not a few of them were characters, with their own ways and their own secrets. Some were recluses, some eccentrics, some had come down in the world and some were such penurious and hopeless drunkards that they'd drink themselves blind on twopennyworth of methylated spirits. Mr Finch gladdened Chinese Lady by being an upright and gentlemanly lodger. 'You know, Boots,' he said musingly, 'Miss Chivers is a very reserved woman, and a man must be careful not to intrude on her. I'll do what I can whenever it's necessary to offer her help, but I think she's a little stronger and more resolute than we give her credit for.'

'She must be, to have come back here to live,' I said. 'I think I'd have wanted to move as far away as possible.'

'You're forgetting, my fine young soldier friend, that here is where her friends are. You and I know what her problems were, how she was denied friendship, but she did manage a very close friendship with you and your family. It's a friendship that's dear to her, I'm sure. But what about your own life, now that you've committed it?'

'Committed it?'

'To the risk of battle, Boots. Soldiering in wartime is total committal. You now have very little control over your own destiny until the war's over. It's a damnable war, Boots, and so hard on people like your mother and your sister. So don't be too brave or too reckless.'

'I must remember to duck, as Emily's dad said.'

Mr Finch smiled and the light in his eyes became a warm one.

'All my good wishes go with you,' he said. 'You deserve a future.'

'Goodbye, Mr Finch.'

We shook hands, and he was very sober then. He looked intently at me, and I wondered if there wasn't the same kind of curiosity about him as Sir Humphrey Dunbar had shown.

Last thing that night, I gave Chinese Lady all that was left of my Army pay except for a few bob. She didn't want to take it, but I knew she was hard up and I insisted. I told her she could use some of it to redeem a few of the articles that were in pawn again.

Look after yourself, she said.

CHAPTER TWENTY-SIX

Back with the training battalion, all was at sixes and sevens with our lot. There was a new lot on the square. Our lot was crumbling away as the different platoons were broken up and the men posted to their permanent companies. I might have been more of a sensation than I was, since the men who knew me as a member of C Platoon disappeared to their new companies as soon as they got back from leave. Except for three or four, which included Freddy Parks and me. It was a relief to have just a few men wanting me to tell them all about the trial, which had made the front pages of every newspaper.

Postings among other platoons happened each day, and I wondered where I would end up. Sergeant Harris said not a word to me about the trial. He and Corporal Purvis were no longer on the square. They were in charge of what was left of our lot. They gave us rifle practice on the range and bayonet practice on the dummies. Corporal Purvis was loudly blasphemous, Sergeant Harris silently impassive, except when range targets were hopelessly missed or a dummy was merely tickled. Then he would close his eyes and wince. He sought me out on Friday, the day before I was due to meet his vivacious daughter again.

'Star witness, were you?' he said, breaking his silence at last.

'That trial, you mean?' I said.

'I'm wondering what you're going to mean for the West Kents. Bloody bad luck, I should think. Any man who knackers his leave by spending it at a murder trial must be bad luck for himself and his regiment. Here, this is for you.'

He produced a letter in a plain envelope and gave it to me.

345

'Is this my posting, Sarge?'

'You don't get it in a letter,' he said, and walked away.

I opened the letter. It was from Rosie.

Dear Bert, Sorry I can't meet you Saturday, like we said. I've got work to do for Grandma, and you know what she'll be like if I try to dodge it. I'll let you know about another day sometime, if you like. I saw you in the papers. Rosie.

I couldn't imagine her grandma being as difficult as that, but I could imagine her dad being sure he didn't want me to have too much to do with his daughter and his family. It would interfere with discipline, and he was iron-hard on discipline. He had obviously told Rosie to drop me or else. Pity, really. Rosie was a lively girl and full of fun. I could have got very fond of Rosie.

However, I still went into town on Saturday afternoon. It was more civilised than the barracks, and was good for a wander, a stroll and an evening beer. I took my comrade, Freddy Parks, with me. Freddy was keen to pick up a pair of smiling eyes. I said that if he managed it, I'd leave him to his frolics and not get in the way.

'Ta,' said Freddy, as we wandered. 'Well, it's a bit of a bleeder, getting nothing out of being in uniform except the kiss of death from Jerry.'

'Where'd you get that stuff from?'

'They've been pulverising us since Mons, mate – ain't yer twigged that yet? And when our lot gets out there, it'll be our turn. What I fancy before it all happens is probably approximately hereabouts, if only I could lay me eyes on her.'

'I'm willing to help,' I said. 'Did you see the one we've just passed?'

'I'm looking for a little bit of heaven, not someone who looks like my aunt.'

There was really no shortage of girls in the busy streets of Maidstone, but Freddy, of course, was thinking ambitiously. He probably had Gladys Cooper or Fay Compton on his mind.

'I don't think you've got time to be too fussy,' I said, as we strolled along a shopping street. 'How about that one? There, across the road, driving a baker's van.'

Freddy looked. The young lady in question was buxom and healthy-looking. She was trotting the horse.

'What do I do with that?' he said. 'Run after it and ask her to sell me a crusty cottage?'

'No, just ask her the time. She'll know what you're after.'

'Any more jokers where you come from?' Freddy eyed passing people. He eyed girls who were window-shopping. He eyed a vivacious-looking girl coming towards us. She was on the arm of a tall, muscular and handsome corporal. She was smiling up at him.

'Hello, Rosie,' I said.

Rosie's smile vanished and her face screwed up. I walked on, with Freddy glancing back at her.

'Who's she?' he asked.

'She was my girl once. Just for a couple of weekends. Then she met a corporal.'

'Hard luck,' said Freddy.

Someone came running up behind me, and a hand touched my arm. I stopped. Freddy walked tactfully on.

'Come on, what did you give me a look for?' asked Rosie.

'It's all right, no hard feelings.'

'A girl's only young once, you know. It wasn't my fault you went on leave and I met Stan.' Rosie was cross, probably because I'd found her out. 'Anyway, you told me you didn't have a girl, but you said you did at that trial. It was in the papers. Gracious me, you at that trial, I could hardly believe—'

'Yes, I see what you mean.'

'You never said a thing about that trial. You're a cool one, you are. Are you angry with me?'

'No, of course not. Not now I see what you mean. So long, Rosie.'

'Oh, blow,' said Rosie, and went back to her corporal.

Freddy had found a girl, a girl with shy eyes, a girl who wanted a soldier friend and was happily grateful that Freddy had had the courage to speak to her. I wished him luck and they went off together.

I didn't feel too heartbroken about Rosie.

Emily wrote.

'*Dear Boots, I hope you don't mind me writing again, only your mum said soldiers like to get letters, and so did Lizzy. I told Arthur you took me out and he didn't mind, I said your family came too. He was more interested in the trial, what with my name being in the papers with yours and because of what you said about me being your girl, I told him you only said that to do them in the eye. Well, I'll give you all the news, your mum said she hadn't had time to write herself yet, but she's going to make a bread pudding for you and send it to you in a tin. My dad's been off work with a nasty tummy but says it's only something Mum must have put in the stew on Tuesday, he'll be right as rain soon. He says he wishes he was young enough to be soldiering with you as it would be a change from mucking out drains for the council. Mum's a bit harassed having to make milk puddings for him which he's not fond of anyway.*

'*Miss Chivers looks fine though a bit sad sometimes, well who wouldn't be with what she's been through, and she pops in quite a lot. In your house, I mean, she likes having a cup of tea with your mum and a little talk of an evening, and she always asks after you, I expect you're her hero and she would like to marry you if she was years younger. People from that Sunday newspaper still keep worrying her, but she won't talk to them. Mr Finch is working all hours piloting ships up and down the river, and he don't like hearing about the Germans sinking them. He shakes his head and says oh Emily it's a sad thing to make war on ships, he's such a nice man and Mum says it's a shame he don't have a good woman to build a home with. He gives Miss Chivers kind advice, she comes to*

Sunday tea just like she used to and your mum always asks me too, I do love your mum and going to tea Sundays and she lets me bake a cake to take in, but you can't get dried fruit so easy.

'Lizzy's thinking of getting a new job in a war factory where she'll get more money than at Gamages, it's to save for when she gets married, only your mum and me don't think she ought to work in any factory, not when she's getting to be a real lady. She speaks so nice now just like a real ladies' wear assistant, you've got a lovely sister, she could go on the stage with her looks. She still misses Ned though, she told me so, she said she'd never forgive Lord Kitchener for making young men like you and Ned go to the war. Would you believe, he's an officer now, and Lizzy is scared she won't be able to live up to him, but I told her he knows when he's well off, and anyone would be well off having Lizzy for his very own. But she said she'd die if Ned walked in one day and caught her looking like something our cat had left on the mat. Love is awful painful.

'Well that's all except that Arthur's still nice to me, I don't know how long it'll last, me not being any oil painting. I haven't brought him home yet, I'd better do some tidying up in the parlour first, Mum don't seem to get time to. We all hope you're as well as it leaves us and Dad says to be remembered to you and you did give me a swell time when you came on leave, have you found a nice girl yet, you ought to have by now, yours faithfully Emily.'

'Private Adams.'

'Sergeant?'

'You seen today's orders?'

'No, Sergeant.'

'They've just been posted. You're leaving. Tomorrow. Nine-thirty. Full kit and rifle. You and the rest of the left-legged remnants.'

'Which battalion, Sergeant?'

'The Third. And you can look forward to embarkation in a couple of months, after field training has at least made half a soldier of you.'

'What happens to the other half, Sergeant? Does it stay behind?'

'Jesus,' said Sergeant Harris, eyeing me as if I was one of Lord Kitchener's few mistakes.

'Is it all right to say goodbye to you?' I asked.

'Don't cry your eyes out,' he said. 'You'll be in A Company, of which I'll be Sergeant-Major.'

'I'll write and tell my mother, Sergeant.'

'Very touching,' he said. 'By the way, that wallpapering job you did.'

'It's all fallen off?'

'No, but don't go in for house decorating after the war. Buy yourself a bike and be an insurance man. Have you learned your lesson?'

'What lesson?'

'I told you you were out of your class, didn't I?'

'*September, 1915.*

'*Dear Mum and All. Well, here I am again, your family idiot, although I can't say where here is. But we're out of the line and resting. We're not far from a town, we're billeted in barns, a nice change from the trenches. I'm a full corporal now. Last time I wrote I was a lance-corporal. Now I've got two stripes. I'm afraid that means Corporal Saunders has gone to his rest. I've got charge of the platoon at the moment, what's left of it. Freddy Parks is still with us, I'm pleased to say, and his Maidstone girl is probably just as pleased. He wrote and popped the question and they'll get married when he gets Blighty leave. We're expecting replacements before our rest period is up. We had a bit of bad luck last week, the Jerries saw us coming.*'

I scrubbed that out to save Lieutenant Marsh, our company censor, the job.

'*It's not a bad billet, the barns are big and give us plenty of room for our kip at night. But you're not missing anything by not being here, as the mice come out when it's dark to say hello, and I know you're not partial to them. I'm fit and well, though I fancy one of your mutton stews with dumplings. The lads are perky, as there are some friendly mademoiselles in the town, and some cheerful estaminets where you can have a drink and sing Blighty songs. There are always some blokes with mouth organs.*

'My French is getting quite passable, which is useful whenever I want to ask a mademoiselle if she'd like to waltz. It impresses the lads who spend their time parley-vooing and only get blank looks. I met a fine strapping ambulance driver last night. Her name's Lily Cartwright-Forbes, or Forbes-Cartwright, whose dad owns most of Berkshire. She likes to be one of the boys, and you should hear her rendering of "Any Old Iron". She sang it sitting on my lap.'

I crossed that out.

'She's very chummy, and she's promised to bring other ambulance drivers tomorrow night, all lady ones. She said she'd try to bring one for every Tommy, she said every Tommy was entitled to an off-duty female ambulance driver.' (I paused for thought. It was a temptation among all the blokes to deal in fact, not fiction, when writing home. It was a temptation to let families know there was a sickening amount of blood and spilled guts about, and some odoriferous smells as well. To say nothing of some compulsive fornicating if the chance was there. But company censors scored out everything that wasn't nice or wasn't allowed. I ended my pause for thought.) *'To sing a duet with,'* I wrote.

Chinese Lady wouldn't take too kindly to other suggestions. Nor did I think she'd like to know that Lily Cartwright-Forbes had helped me acquire carnal knowledge. I was still trying to believe it had actually happened.

'Where's your billet, ducky?' the lady had asked when we left the estaminet.

'Freyere Farm,' I said.

'I know it. We'll find a field of French clover, shall we? French clover is lucky.'

'I thought that was Irish clover.'

'You'll change your mind after tonight. Dearie, did you say you never had?'

351

'Yes, I did say that.'

'Well, that's sweet. Isn't that sweet? It makes me lucky already. And as it's a lovely warm night, that makes you lucky.'

I think she meant because she didn't mind taking all her clothes off. It hurt my eyes a bit, seeing her turn into a moonlit Juno, but I didn't feel it was anything to complain about. I discovered, with her help and guidance, that everything which was always a burning curiosity in the minds of the uninitiated, resolved into something quite beautiful. After the second time, actually even better than the first, I thanked her for being lovely.

'And if I get wounded,' I said, 'I hope I'll end up in your ambulance.'

'Aren't you sweet?' she said. 'By the way, what's your name, ducky?'

She was like that, lovably casual.

I couldn't tell Chinese Lady about her. Chinese Lady didn't care for that kind of casualness, lovable or not. I asked her to let me know how she and the family were coping with things, and whether Sammy had yet become a war profiteer. I told her to give my love to Lizzy, and to remember me to Emily, whom I'd written to now and again, and that I hoped Arthur was still being nice to her. Had her dad got over his tummy upset?

There was a letter from Chinese Lady the very next day. She wrote to say Ned was home, but in hospital and badly wounded, in the chest and leg. Lizzy had taken it very hard, and hadn't been to work at all. She was visiting the hospital every day, although it was miles away in Middlesex. What the war was doing to young men like Ned and nice girls like Lizzy was criminal, and it ought to be stopped. Ned was seriously ill and Lizzy was out of her mind with grief. Emily was proving a comfort and a godsend, going with her to the hospital Saturdays and Sundays, and St John's church was offering up prayers for the wounded loved ones of its parishioners. Ned had been mentioned as a loved one of the Adams family, but whether it would do any good only the Lord knew.

Chinese Lady went on to warn me not to get myself into the same dreadful mess as Ned, or she'd wish I'd never been born. She said one thing was for sure, if I ever came home with a lot of medals but no legs, she'd go round to the War Office and make Lord Kitchener wish he'd never been born, either. And don't think I won't, she said.

The family had met Emily's boy, Arthur, she said. Emily had brought him to Sunday tea at the family's invitation, as Emily's mum didn't go in much for Sunday tea and Mr Castle's stomach was still a bit discomfortable. Arthur was a very nice boy, he'd brought his stamp album for everyone to look at, and treated Emily as if he was very fond of her. It was Chinese Lady's opinion that Emily deserved someone a bit more manly, however, but Emily had said a girl had got to take what she could get, especially these days, when so many young men were going to the war and not coming back. What Lizzy in her present state was saying was unmentionable. Miss Chivers was very upset for Lizzy, but hadn't said anything about Lord Kitchener being shamefully responsible, and Chinese Lady supposed that as she worked at the Admiralty she wasn't allowed to say anything at all about the war and the people running it.

Tommy had got a job. Jobs were easier to come by now, what with lots of men leaving to join up, and Tommy was a packer at a war factory in Bermondsey. Oh, and the latest was that the police had come and told Miss Chivers they were doing a new investigation. They'd been very polite, they'd asked if they could go over her house again just to see if they could find anything which would help to show someone really had got into the house that morning. They said if only they could find that knife it might have fingerprints on it. Miss Chivers turned the house over to them while she went to work, but they hadn't let her know if they'd found anything.

Chinese Lady closed by saying all the family were upset about Ned, and that while it was always nice to hear from me, I didn't have to make it sound as if the soldiers were having a picnic because Ned certainly hadn't had one himself. It would be better for my health, she said, if I packed up and came home.

On our way up to the line again, I thought about Miss Chivers and a carving-knife and her warm, kissing mouth. Once we were back in the trenches again, I thought about Chinese Lady's suggestion to pack up and go home. I wondered if she had an inkling about exactly what it was like here, how hideous the trenches could get with their mud, their rats, their filth and their smells, or how nerve-shattering the trench warfare was, with wounded men sometimes left hanging on barbed wire if the stretcher-bearers couldn't get to them. One wasn't allowed to write home about how the German guns could blow men into sticky bits and leave the survivors numbed, shaking and face down in funk-holes. I was allowed to say I was bearing up and that Company Sergeant-Major Harris was now Captain Harris. I wasn't allowed to say his promotion had come about because of the high casualty rate among combat officers. I could say he made a fine officer, but I couldn't say he wished and we wished that the generals and their staffs would try going over the top just once to let them see what a howling nightmare it all was.

I wouldn't have been surprised if Chinese Lady didn't wish the same thing too.

'Everything all right, Corporal Adams?'

'Well, it's quiet at the moment, sir. I suppose you could say that's all right.'

'And would you say that's a complaint?' asked Captain Harris, bleaker than ever beneath his tin hat.

'No, just a comment, sir.' I was standing on the firestep. No-man's-land was shrouded in the grey gloom of twilight. Everything was grey, the earth, the trenches, the sandbags, the timbers, the faces and the tin hats. 'Things all right with you, sir?'

'I won't treat that as a serious question.' He fished out a packet of Players Navy Cut from the pocket of his trench coat. He opened it and tapped it. A couple of fags popped up. Silently, he offered me one. I took it. He put one into his own mouth. We stooped and I struck a match. We lit up. He inhaled deeply. 'Well?' he said.

'Yes, thank you, sir, a fag's always welcome. Any chance of Blighty leave, sir?'

'Ask the Major. It's his turn to die laughing.' He peered out over no-man's-land. The distant German lines were lost in the deepening grey. 'The buggers are sitting there cooking their sauerkraut.'

'Smells like rotten cabbage to me, sir.'

'Same thing,' he said.

'Yes, sir.'

He was silent for a while, an impassive, grey looking man. Well, we were all that colour. Then he said, 'The teashop door's going to be painted light blue.'

'That'll be nice, sir,' I said. 'By Rosie, sir?'

'With the help of a sailor.'

'What's a sailor doing in the wilds of Kent, sir?'

'I don't know, you don't know, and I don't suppose he does, either. Carry on, Corporal Adams.'

I think he almost had a ghost of a smile on his face as he moved on through the trench.

CHAPTER TWENTY-SEVEN

I received a letter from Ned early in December. Lizzy and Chinese Lady had both exaggerated the extent of his wounds. They'd been serious enough, a bursting shell having deposited a collection of splinters in his chest and thigh, but after operations to pick them out he had made a fine recovery and was due to be discharged any moment. He wrote to tell me so, and to say his chest looked like a map of Flanders canal systems. He also told me there was to be a wedding. Eliza, he said, had issued an ultimatum. Not later than March, or it was all off. And in between she was going to spend Sundays looking for a little house with a garden, in one of the nice roads off Denmark Hill. She had some useful savings and he had lots of unspent Army pay, and they could easily put down a deposit. Ned had said yes, of course, and Eliza had said it was nice to make a man see sense for once. Then, he said, there was uproar in the ward, for he kissed Eliza from his bed several times, despite Eliza saying oh, not here. She was going to see the vicar of St John's and arrange for the wedding to take place on the last Saturday in March, by which time he hoped he'd be a hale and hearty bridegroom without a limp to his leg.

Ned closed with a few soldierly comments and by wishing me a merry Christmas.

It was hardly merry. It was bitterly cold and I froze in my greatcoat, balaclava, tin hat and gloves. Emily had knitted the gloves for me, and also a thick pair of grey socks. The trenches were slippery with ice and no-man's-land was a ghostly carpet of grey-white frost. But at least the guns were quiet.

'Dear Boots everyone's so proud you're now a sergeant, my mum says what a fine soldier you must be to have got to be a sergeant so quick, although my dad shook his head for some reason which he wouldn't say. Oh can't you come home for Lizzy's wedding? I said I'd write and ask, I hope you don't mind, only Lizzy wants you there, can't you get special leave? Your mum said she hoped you're not getting too set on blowing off the heads of German boys who all had mothers the same as you, but she didn't mean it in an unkind way, it's just you've been away so long and it is your sister's wedding. Everyone's coming, well everyone Lizzy wants to come, including Miss Chivers and Mr Finch, Miss Chivers is so thrilled for Lizzy and is going to give her a lovely brass companion set for her hearth. The police haven't been to her house any more, so she's not got any more worries thank goodness. Ned come out of hospital limping a bit in convalescent blues, and Lizzy took him to see a house she saw, it's in Red Post Hill and so pretty though it's been empty years and wants a bit done to it, its garden is all overgrown but they don't mind that. Ned thinks he'll have to go back to his unit after the wedding, and oh would you believe Lizzy asked me to be a bridesmaid – me, would you believe, I hope I can do myself up a bit and not look too bad. She asked me if I'd like Arthur to be invited, but he don't really know Lizzy too well, he's only met her once, and he don't know Ned at all, so I don't suppose it'll be his cup of tea, he likes doing his foreign stamps best. Mr Finch, as you can imagine, is very happy for Lizzy, loving her like a daughter I think and Lizzy as fond of him as if he was her dad, don't you think? My dad's not very good, he's got ever so thin and his work's an effort for him, but he doesn't grumble, he just says there's plenty worse off than him, specially the soldiers. The vicar's son has been blinded and the Chinese laundryman's son has come home crippled. We don't like reading about all the battles, it makes your family worry about you, and your mum said she hoped she wasn't going to suffer two careless men in her family.

357

'Can't you come home, Boots, can't you talk to your officer, he ought to do something for you now you're a sergeant having done your bit and it is your only sister who's getting married. Your mum and family send their very best, and my mum and dad said keep your pecker up, yours faithfully Emily.'

'Do I look like Father Christmas?' said Major Harris, now the officer commanding the Company.

'We've had Christmas, sir,' I said. I stood before him in his shored-up earth warren. He was blue of chin and drawn of face.

'Repeat what you just said, Sergeant Adams. The bit before Christmas came up.'

'My sister's getting married on the last Saturday of this month, sir. I'd like to be there. Could I have some leave?'

'Jesus Christ,' said Major Harris.

'I'm overdue, sir.'

'You'd better see a doctor, then, hadn't you?'

'Not that kind of overdue, sir.'

'Nothing would surprise me,' he said. 'Well, don't just stand there. Make a written application, stating the reasons. If I like the reasons, I might approve it. Put down that your sister's got consumption.'

'Right, sir.'

'Boots!' Lizzy flung her arms around my neck as I walked into the kitchen on a cold Friday night in late March. 'Oh, why didn't you write and say you were coming?'

'Didn't have time. Didn't think it was going to happen. You look good.'

Lizzy was all shining brown eyes.

'Oh, ain't yer a sport for coming?' she said in perky cockney.

'Where's Chinese Lady?'

'Out. Buying herself a new hat.' The shops always stayed open late on Friday nights. 'She's got everything

358

else, except a new hat. Aunt Victoria gave her a lovely dress, nearly new it was. Oh, I'm glad you're here, and look at you, a sergeant and all. Here.' She helped me off with my greatcoat and hung it on the doorpeg for me. 'Drink a nice glass of port, Boots. We've got port, six bottles. Mr Finch gave them, for the wedding. He said they fell off a ship. Drink a large glass.'

'Why?'

'Well, before Chinese Lady sees you.' Lizzy's buoyancy had a guarded note. 'I mean, you look a bit thin, like, and – oh, I know about it. Ned looked like that in hospital, only worse, of course. Drink some port, it'll give you a warm look. I'll pour some for you.' She pulled a bottle of port out of a large cardboard box by the dresser. She opened the bottle, filled a cup and handed it to me. 'You've come all the way from France, so you need it, anyway.'

I drank it down. Lizzy poured some more. I drank that too. The rich port warmed my cockles.

'That's not half bad stuff, sis.'

'Well, Mr Finch wouldn't let anything but the best port fall off a ship, and you look better already. Wait till Em'ly finds out you're home.'

'She ought to have let you invite Arthur. I'd have liked to meet him. Where are the kids?'

'Sammy's up the Lane, Tommy's out with his pals.' Lizzy laughed. Excitement and animation danced. She was a young woman, taller by an inch or two, her figure blooming and her colour healthy.

'How's Ned?'

'Oh, isn't it marvellous he got over his wounds so well? Of course, he's rather lame, but that's almost a blessing. Boots, you look as if you could do with a good sleep.'

'I can do with a good sleep.'

'It's rotten over there, ain't it?' she said. 'They're talking about when Ned can rejoin his regiment, but what with him being lame they can't have him, can they? Lord Kitchener will have to do without him.' Lizzy's smile was suddenly overbright. She knew and I knew that his

359

regiment would grab him back if he became fit enough. 'Oh, never mind, you're home. Em'ly's comin' in soon to help me do things with my hair for tomorrow. Boots, you'll give me away, won't you? Now you're—'

'Coo-eee! Lizzy!' That was Emily's voice, clear and ringing, as she opened the front door by the latchcord and entered the passage. She came dancing into the kitchen, but not in the way she used to, all sharp jostling elbows and jerking legs. She stopped when she saw me warming my behind at the fire. Her green eyes opened wide and her mouth gaped. She was an inch or so taller too, and that made her look even slenderer, except around her bosom. Her chin pointed, her nose pointed, and her neck was very thin, but with her swimming green eyes and abundance of auburn hair, one could forget she didn't compare with Lizzy.

'Who's this lady?' I asked my sister.

'Oh, crikey,' said Emily faintly.

'Well, you said I ought to be here for Lizzy's big day tomorrow.'

'Oh, I didn't think – I can't believe—' Emily bent her head and looked at her buttoned shoes. Her hair burned darkly.

'I've only just arrived,' I said. 'I've had some port and now I fancy hot tea. You girls like a cup? I'll put the kettle on—'

'Oh, I'll do it,' said Emily breathlessly, and dashed into the scullery, forgetting to take the kettle with her. I lifted it off the range hob and took it out to her. She turned her back on me. I lit the gas and put the warm kettle on.

'There you are, Em.'

She didn't say a word. I went back to Lizzy.

'I think Chinese Lady's back,' said Lizzy.

'What's up with Emily?' I asked.

'Don't be daft,' said Lizzy, and Chinese Lady came in. She had a cardboard box in her hand, and was wearing her black coat and hat. She regarded me as if she was suffering a slight shock. Then she gave me an approving nod.

'Nice you remembered it was your sister's wedding,' she said.

I gave her a peck on the cheek. She never encouraged more than that. She had a cold, tingly and faintly fruity smell, like cider apples picked in frosty October.

'Nice to be here, Mum,' I said.

'Mum, it's so good he managed it,' said Lizzy.

'I thought he wasn't coming, I thought he was too busy earning medals,' said Chinese Lady, pulling off the shiny, shabby kid gloves Aunt Victoria had given her years ago.

'Well, I know you're not keen on medals, so I gave them a rest, old girl.'

'Old girl?' Chinese Lady quivered. 'I hope we don't hear too much of that. It's bad enough the Army don't feed you proper. Your bones are showing.' She eyed me critically. 'You're all flushed – have you been drinkin'?'

Lizzy laughed.

'I give him a drop of port, Mum, that's all, to warm him up,' she said.

'Well, it's nice he didn't forget to come, I'll say that much,' said Chinese Lady. 'Who's that in the scullery?'

'Emily,' I said. 'She's making some tea.'

'That girl's a saving grace. I could just do with a nice cup. I expect your dad would like it you're a sergeant. Well, I'll go and try my hat on.'

'Try it on in here,' I said. 'Let's see it.'

'I'll put it on in my room first. It's nice you got here.' She gave my arm a pat and disappeared with her cardboard box.

Emily brought the teapot in and placed it carefully on the table. Lizzy put out cups and saucers.

'Imagine you actually being 'ome,' said Emily to the teapot.

'Touch and go, Em,' I said, and put an arm around her and gave her a cuddle. She went stiffer than a frozen sentry suffering the bitterness of icy dawn.

'Oh, I—' She hurriedly detached herself. 'I forgot the milk.' She went and fetched it. She began to milk the cups.

'We didn't think you'd get here – well, it's tomorrer – oh, ain't it grand he managed it, Lizzy?'

'Mum's pleased,' said Lizzy. 'She's gone to blow her nose as well as put her new hat on.'

Emily poured the tea. She pushed a cup across the table to me. Her hands, I noticed, looked well-kept.

Chinese Lady reappeared, wearing a glossy hat trimmed with feathers. Lizzy at once declared it lovely, Emily declared it was just like what Queen Mary wore, and I declared it a treat.

'You sure?' said Chinese Lady.

'It'll do for Sundays,' I said.

'Oh, it's really something, Mrs Adams,' said Emily, and Chinese Lady sat down with a little bit of a flourish.

'That reminds me,' I said, and opened up my kitbag. I brought out some parcels, two of them wrapped and ribboned with dainty French artistry by a shop in Calais. I'd had quite a time in that shop in consultation with a young lady assistant, French. She convinced me it simply wouldn't do to say I'd have that and that. Who was I buying them for, if you please, and what was their size and colouring and so on. 'Let's see – that's for you, Mum, and that's for you, Lizzy, as it's your wedding – and that's for you, Emily, as you're like one of the family – only don't tell Arthur.'

Lizzy began an excited unwrapping. Chinese Lady began a methodical unwrapping. Emily just stared at her own parcel.

'Me? It's for me?' she said.

'Well, you've got a liking for things,' I said.

Lizzy, discovering her present, a black silk nightdress, shrieked with delight.

'Boots – oh, you love – Em'ly, look, it's real French silk – there's a French label too – oh, I never seen anything more special. Look, Mum.'

Chinese Lady made a startled inspection of the nightdress, coughed, drank some tea to clear her throat, gave me a look and then bestowed a smile on Lizzy.

'It's sweet, lovey, it being your wedding time and all,' she said. She uncovered what I'd bought for her, a white broderie anglaise blouse. Her almond eyes began to shine.

Emily, slightly flushed, undid her own present. A pink satin concoction dropped into place as she held it against her. Lacy hems fluttered.

'Em'ly!' Lizzy shrieked again. 'Boots – oh, you wicked thing.'

Chinese Lady, caressing her blouse, stared at the satin garment.

'What's that?' she asked.

'Just something French,' I said.

Emily looked down at herself, at the shimmering satin and lacy hems. Her colour began to rise.

'Oh, Boots!' Lizzy was riotous with giggles. 'French camiknickers, that's what they are, Mum.'

'I can see that now.' Chinese Lady was stiff. 'I'm not all that blind.'

'They're comin' in as the latest French fashion,' said Lizzy, 'but you never did go in the shop and buy them yourself, Boots.'

'Why not? They were very helpful. And Emily likes those kind of things.'

'I don't know how you know that,' said Chinese Lady sharply, and Emily's colour rushed into scarlet. 'I don't think I want to know, neither.'

'Oh, Mrs Adams, I—' Emily was lost in confusion.

'That's not nice, Mum,' I said. 'Emily's a young lady, she's bound to like silks and satins. That's all I know.'

'Well, that's some relief,' said Chinese Lady. 'But giving a respectable girl like Em'ly things like them? It's shameless. Em'ly, give them back.'

'Oh, Mrs Adams, must I?' gasped Emily, clutching the satin possessively to her. 'They're so pretty – I do like them – oh, please let me keep them.'

Chinese Lady became motherly.

'Em'ly love, you know you can't let a young man give you intimate things, even if you have grown up together.

You know it's not proper. Think what your mum'll say. She'll be shocked.'

'Oh, her mum won't mind, I bet,' said Lizzy, cuddling her nightdress. 'Mum, Boots has done us proud. Em'ly will look really swish—'

'That's right, encourage your brother in his iniquity,' said Chinese Lady. 'Look at him, all smug and smirkin', expecting Em'ly to do a turn in them like some low chorus girl, never mind she'll freeze to death in them. And what would her Arthur say, I'd like to know.'

'Oh, I won't tell him, really I won't,' said Emily. 'He don't talk about – about ladies' things, anyway.'

'I should hope he wouldn't,' said Chinese Lady. 'Just because I've got a son who's a disgrace don't mean Arthur's mum has. Em'ly, stop flaunting them.'

'But, Mrs Adams,' said Emily pleadingly, 'it's just that Boots brought them all the way from France, and they're so pretty, really, and Boots don't mean to be a disgrace, I'm sure. I mean, look what he's give us all, he's got such good taste, don't you think so?' Emily, grown up, was still so ingenuous that Lizzy and I exchanged a smile. 'I don't mind if they don't keep me warm – well, I could just wear them in summer, couldn't I?' Emily looked at Chinese Lady with her swimming eyes, and Chinese Lady visibly softened.

'Em'ly, you sure you don't feel outraged by Boots being so disrespectable?'

'Oh, no, Mrs Adams, really I don't. Just imagine him takin' all that trouble, going into Paris shops all by himself to buy these things—'

'Calais,' I said.

'Better there than Paris,' said Chinese Lady, who had every respectable woman's suspicion that Paris lacked righteousness. She gave Emily a motherly look. 'Well, all right, Em'ly love, but only if your mum don't mind, and for goodness sake make sure she don't tell our neighbours.'

'Oh, Mrs Adams, thank you,' said Emily, and impulsively stooped and hugged our mum, which turned our mum pink, especially as the camiknickers dropped on her lap.

Tommy and Sammy appeared later, when Emily was helping Lizzy to do things to her hair. They had both grown. Tommy was sturdier and tidier, Sammy the scruffiest Walworth urchin. I told him he didn't have to go around looking ragged and poor. He said yes he did, he said the stallholders sometimes gave you tuppence instead of a penny if you looked ragged and poor. He also said, in his frank way, that I looked as if I could do with some of our mum's nourishing bread pudding. Then he and Tommy wanted to know about the war. Since Chinese Lady was present, I told the boys some Flanders fairy tales, which they gobbled up as if they were gospel.

Emily came from the bedroom to heat a curling fork in the fire. I asked her how her dad was. She said he was still poorly.

'I'll pop in and talk to him, if you like,' I said. I'd thought about having a chat with Mr Finch, but he wasn't in yet. 'Shall I do that, Em?'

'Oh, would yer, Boots?' Her eyes shone with gratitude. 'He's up in his bed. Mum's out at her sister's in Camberwell. I'd have stayed in, only I promised to do Lizzy's hair, and Dad said I should. I'll be in soon, but I know he'd like to see you. He hasn't been at work again lately, but the doctor's give him some medicine, and he goes to let the hospital look at him once a week.'

Mr Castle lay in his bed in the upstairs front bedroom. A candle in its holder was alight on his bedside table. A glass held a small amount of pink medicine. His head and shoulders rested on heaped pillows. He had lost a desperate amount of flesh, and was grey, gaunt and hollow-eyed. He grinned when he saw me.

'So there y'ar, Boots, yer got 'ome fer Lizzy's weddin'.'

'Yes, I managed to manage it. What's happened to you – did you fall down a hole or something?'

He grinned again, but his face was lined with pain.

'Feels like I did,' he said. 'Yer gonner sit down fer a bit, Boots?'

I sat down. We talked. He asked about the trenches.

'You don't want to hear all that,' I said.

'Yus, I do. I ain't so simple I believe all they say in the papers. I bet it's bleedin' murder.'

'Oh, some good days, some not so good. You've got some medicine, I see. Is that in place of beer, or as well as?'

'Nah yer talkin',' he said. 'Yer might find a bottle in the kitchen.'

'Or what about a nip of the best medicine?' I said, and pulled a half-bottle of whisky from the inside of my khaki jacket. Major Harris had introduced me to the fiery comfort of Scotch, from a flask, after a soul-blasting German assault had nearly succeeded in overrunning our position and left me with a bullet in my arm. An overworked medico had taken it out at a casualty station.

Mr Castle's sunken eyes lit up.

'Yer got a drop of the real stuff there, Boots,' he said.

'Your doctor hasn't said you can't have it?'

'That he ain't. Bring two glasses, eh, Boots?'

I went downstairs. The kitchen didn't look too messy. It was quite tidy, in fact. I felt it had Emily's touch more than her mother's. I found two glasses, went back to Mr Castle and poured generous tots for both of us.

'All right?' I said, noting him sipping with relish.

'Yer can lay to that, Boots,' he said, 'it's me grub I can't keep down. But I tell yer, I'll be up fer Lizzy's weddin', yer bet I will. I ain't missin' Lizzy's big do. Your mum's brought up a fine 'un in Lizzy. Ain't she a real May queen? Em'ly's that 'appy fer yer sister, an' that grateful Lizzy wanted 'er fer a bridesmaid.'

'She doesn't have to be grateful. She's Lizzy best friend.'

'Well, Em ain't a girl who expects.' Mr Castle took more relishing whisky. 'Yer know, the missus an' me ain't really give our Em what we should of be rights. We ain't give 'er the right attention at times, we been slipshod with our Em. The missus sometimes ain't found time like she should of to keep 'er in clean clothes. 'Ere, don't say I said so. It's me own blame as well.'

'What are you worrying about that for? We were all

scruffy ragamuffins when we were kids. Sammy still is. Besides, look at Emily now. She's the best-dressed girl in Walworth. She's a credit to you.'

'It's 'er own doing, not ourn.' Mr Castle rubbed his chest and burped. 'That's better. That's what a drop of the real stuff can do fer yer. Em's got character, Boots. She 'as, yer know. Only I wish she wouldn't call 'erself Ugly Mug.'

'I've never heard her.'

'Course you ain't. Missus an' me 'ave, though. But she ain't such a bad-looker now, yer reckon, Boots?'

'Not with eyes like she's got, and that auburn hair. And she's got a decent boy now, this Arthur bloke.'

'Oh, 'im.' Mr Castle burped again, then winced. ''E's all right, but 'e ain't got much go. If Em marries 'im, she'll spend 'er life draggin' 'im into the land of the livin' year in, year out.'

'She might like that.'

'She might, but I'll lay she won't.' Mr Castle finished his whisky and burped again. 'Does that to me, whatever bleedin' thing goes down. Ah, yer a sport, Boots,' he said, as I gave him another tot. 'Still, it could be worse. I gotter do that wall.' He nodded at the far wall. 'I gotter do all Em's bedroom walls. We got bugs now, would yer believe. I borrered a blow lamp, an' I'll burn the buggers out.'

Bugs were hideous. They could live and multiply under old wallpaper, they could crawl out at night, climb up bedsteads and get into bed with you. I'd seen the red circular marks of bug bites on the necks of kids.

'I'll do it for you,' I said.

'No, yer won't,' said Mr Castle, 'yer can't spend yer Blighty leave doing what's my job.'

'I'll do it. I'm home for a week. I'll have plenty of time. I'll fry 'em with the blow lamp, bloody hell I will.' The trouble was that Emily's parents had never been houseproud. Dirt and neglect issued their smell from decaying wallpaper. Other people would have got on to the landlord to change it. Emily's parents had never bothered. 'I'll do it on Monday.'

367

'I ain't keen on yer wastin' yer leave like that, Boots, but all right, I won't say no.' Mr Castle sounded painfully relieved. 'I oughter try to git back to work Monday, anyway. It's good of yer, Boots. Always thought a lot of yer, me an' the missus did. Yer mum's been a real Christian lately, too, an' that nice Miss Chivers. She brought me some 'ot soup after she got 'ome from work yesterday, the missus 'aving 'ad to go out. A real lady, she is. Pity the police ain't found the bloke what done 'er mother in. It makes some people look at 'er an' talk about 'er. The missus don't like it, but yer know what some people is fer a bit of scandalising. She'll 'ave to move, I reckon.'

Mr Castle, tired, lay back. I reached to take the glass from his hand, but he gave me a faint grin and shook his head.

'Oh, well, people talk,' I said. 'You take it easy finishing your whisky while I go and look at Emily's bedroom walls. She said she'll be in soon, by the way.'

'There's bugs there all right,' he said with a sigh.

I went into the back bedroom. I struck a match and lit the gas mantle. The front bedroom, even in the small light of a candle, had looked a mess. Emily's room was clean and tidy. The bed, I noticed, had been pulled clear of the walls. Over it lay a pink dress. A bridesmaid's dress, carefully spread. I examined the wallpaper. It was old and stained, cracked and musty. I knocked at a spot with my knuckles. It brought a bug out. It crawled slowly from a crack. I killed it.

'What you doing?'

I turned. Emily stood in the open doorway, expression stiff and tense.

'I'm going to burn them out, Em. On Monday. Your dad's too sick to do it himself.'

'Go away,' said Emily fiercely.

'It's got to be done,' I said.

'You got no right comin' into my bedroom – you got no right.' Her face was burning, her eyes angry. 'Go away an' mind yer own business.'

'We're neighbours, Em.'

'You're shamin' me. What d'you mean, burn them out?'

'The bugs,' I said.

'Oh!' Emily shook in her distress. 'You pleased you found we got bugs, you pleased?'

'No, I'm not. But everyone's got some.'

'You ain't got any. Go away.'

'I'm coming back Monday. I promised your dad. Em, it's got to be done.'

Emily's auburn head dropped.

'Oh, ain't it shamin', though?' she said unhappily. 'I cleaned an' cleaned, I put carbolic in the water – oh, yer won't tell yer fam'ly, will yer? Lizzy's so particular, and yer mum hates vermin. Oh, don't tell 'em.'

'I'll just say I'm helping your dad to strip off his wallpaper. You'll need new paper, in here and the other bedroom.'

'Oh, I'll pay for it, out of me savings.'

'Go round to the landlord first and tell him. He knows the town hall sanitary inspector will make him responsible for the cost, so you make sure he lets you deduct it from the rent.'

'Yes,' said Emily. 'Yes, I'll do that.'

'Well, you get the wallpaper you want, and if the landlord says his workmen are too busy to hang it yet, which he will, I'll hang it for you before my leave's up.'

Emily lifted her head, her face still burning.

'Oh, your leave and all,' she said, 'Dad wouldn't want you to—'

'It's all right, we fixed it between us. Stop worrying.'

'Oh, yer a lovely man, Boots, an' special to us – to me mum an' dad, an' yer brought me this all the way from France.' She held up her little parcel. 'Oh, imagine me with satin camiknickers from Paris—'

'Calais.'

'No, they got Paris on the label,' said Emily, bright-eyed. 'Boots, d'you think I – I mean, d'you think it would be all right to wear them with me bridesmaid's frock tomorrer?'

'Is that it on the bed?'

'Yes. Do yer like it, Boots?'

'It's pink,' I said.

'Oh, that's right — so's me camiknickers,' she said in a little burst of delight.

'Be a pink bridesmaid,' I said.

'I can wear them? You don't mind? Lizzy said now you've got here you'll take charge an' order everyone about — but only to make sure everything's done right, of course.'

'She said I'd boss everyone about?'

'Oh, I don't mind you ordering people about, it's what a proper man should do,' said Emily. 'Boots—' She hesitated a moment. 'Boots, you got awful thin — is it bad in France?'

'It's better here. I'll just say goodnight to your dad, then I think I'll get some kip myself.'

'Dad's not too good, is he?' Emily's eyes were sad. She liked her beery, easy-going dad.

'No, he's not very well, Em, but he says he'll be at the wedding.'

I heard her mum come in then. Emily went quickly down the stairs. I heard her say a little fiercely, 'Mum, where you been? Leaving Dad all this time — you wasn't in when I got home from work and you knew I promised to help Lizzy with her hair. Mum, it's not right.'

'Now don't you take on like that,' said Mrs Castle, 'I been 'aving to talk to your Aunt Mabel a lot lately. Me and 'er's got to talk about things, we got to see if we can come to an arrangement fer us to live with 'er when your poor dad—'

'Don't you say it!' Emily's voice was a fierce whisper. 'Dad only wants a bit of decent care an' nursing — you've got to look after him better. It's not right when I come home an' find him all by himself. You left him all alone — it's not right!'

'Em'ly Castle, don't you talk to yer mum like that — '

I went into the front bedroom, had a few more words

with Mr Castle about giving the bugs hell on Monday, and said goodnight to him. He'd finished the whisky, and had a little flush that made his grin seem less painful. I went down the stairs to the front door. Emily and her mum were in the kitchen by then, and I called a loud goodnight and left. Last thing before I went up to my bed, Chinese Lady told me she supposed I realised I was to give the bride away. Uncle Tom had said he'd do it if I didn't turn up. Well, I had turned up, thankfully, so I was to give the bride away like I should.

'Be a pleasure, Mum,' I said. 'I'll wear my suit.'

Chinese Lady gave me a straight look.

'No, you won't,' she said. 'You're a soldier now. You'll wear your uniform. Your dad wouldn't want you dressed in no suit. Well, it's nice you come – get a good night's sleep now.'

I lay in my own comfortable bed, with Tommy and Sammy as sound as usual in the other, but I woke up at midnight beleaguered by the ghosts of the living, as well as the dead. I began to toss and turn and silently swear. I thought of recruits who had drilled on the square with me, recruits who were now dead ghosts. I thought of Freddy Parks, still a miraculously living one, like me. Nurse Wharton of Guy's. Where was she now? Mr Castle, grey and wasted. Germans, twisted, stiff and dead. Men in muddy shellholes, faces pale and sweaty. Miss Chivers, soft and floating. Mr Finch, vigorous and self-assured. Ambulance drivers, stretcher-bearers, Chinese Lady, a waitress in a teashop, Rosie and Rosie's martial dad. None of them lingered. They all flitted in and out. I slept, awoke, slept and awoke. The Witch appeared, and glared. Her throat was cut. She glared, but was dead.

I slept.

CHAPTER TWENTY-EIGHT

The marriage service began in St John's Church, Larcom Street, at two in the afternoon. The March day was crisp and fine. Lizzy drew a full house. It was a wartime marriage of a girl to a soldier, and everyone was there who could be there. Old school friends, new friends and neighbours. Miss Chivers was there, bravely composed and bravely arrayed. She had been wearing black for her mother, but for Lizzy's wedding she had on a lovely coat of silver-grey and a white hat. Mr Finch was also there, in dark grey, but with a very dressy tie of pale grey. Aunt Victoria was there, so were her husband, Uncle Tom, and her daughter Vi. So was Mr Castle, who had dragged himself there on his wife's plump arm. So was the church choir. Ned and Lizzy had both wanted a choral service.

Lizzy was in virgin white. She was beautiful. She was not quite eighteen, but she was beautiful. I walked slowly up the aisle with her to the music of the organ, and felt her trembling a little. I saw Ned, out of hospital blues and in the uniform of a captain. Promotion could happen quickly on the Western Front. He looked very lean, and when he turned his head to watch the approach of our Lizzy, his face looked very lean too, but his smile was unnervously broad. Lizzy trembled quite violently, and her arm tightened through mine. Ned moved from the front pew to take his place beside her, and I relinquished my sister to him. I heard him whisper, 'You darling.'

The bridesmaids, Emily and Ned's sister, Anne, were in pink. Emily, I thought, looked tall and slender and very proud, proud not of herself but our Lizzy. She could have been proud of herself. Emily, I realised, had painstakingly modelled herself on Lizzy. She was as upright as Lizzy.

Chinese Lady, with Tommy on her left and Sammy on her right, held her head high throughout the service, except when she knelt in prayer. In the adjacent pew, Ned's parents were in smiling approval of their son's choice. I gave Lizzy away without regret, though I knew home wouldn't be the same without her. Lizzy had always known what she wanted from the time she first met Ned when she was thirteen. It had taken me a long time to understand that even at only thirteen, a girl can fall into lasting and faithful love. Her dreams had taken a bitter hammering once, and she had reacted with bravado, but the dreams had never changed.

'I now pronounce you man and wife.'

Lizzy lifted her veil and they kissed.

I saw Chinese Lady blink in a rare moment of weakness. I saw Miss Chivers smile, and I saw Mr Finch smile too, as if Lizzy's happiness was precious to him.

The newly-weds were to live in a little old house in Red Post Hill, a house with a garden, a house which Chinese Lady had told me was near to falling down, and so Ned got it at a bargain price of two hundred pounds. Ned had engaged workmen, and the house was ready for occupation. Sammy had been a knowing middleman in respect of furnishing the house. He had pointed Lizzy and Ned in the direction of furniture that saved them pounds. He worked on commission, of course.

The bride and groom were not going away, for Ned still had to see the doctors twice a week. They were to honeymoon in their new home.

Back they came from the church, riding not in a motor limousine, the kind one could now hire for weddings, but on a horse and cart belonging to Mr Greenberg, the rag and bone man. He had groomed his horse until it looked glossy, and cleaned the green cart until it shone. He had decorated both horse and cart with ribbons, under the supervision of Sammy, who was getting his cut of the five bob hire fee, since he had suggested it and arranged it. Guests walked alongside the cart, showering confetti, and if Lizzy looked flushed and rapturous, Ned looked as if the horse and cart, and its attendant procession, had to be the merriest summit of Sammy's imagination. Passers-by stopped to cheer, and to gaze on the spectacle of a Walworth girl showing herself as the bride of an Army captain.

The house burst at the seams, and hilarious pandemonium reigned. Chinese Lady, Emily and Tommy, up at six in the morning, had spent until ten o'clock preparing the wedding breakfast for fifty and more people. God knows how Chinese Lady had paid for all the food. I asked her. She'd had to borrow from Sammy, she said, but he was charging hardly any interest at all, seeing it was his sister's wedding. I'd gone out with Tommy, Sammy and Mr Finch at eleven, and we'd brought back crates of beer, mineral waters and two bottles of whisky. And Ned's firm had donated two cases of wine, twelve bottles in each case, and had delivered them.

Ned's best man made a speech. Ned made a speech. The best man's speech, a toast to the bridesmaids, wandered about. Ned's speech was brief but funny, and brought the house down. But he did honour his parents and he also honoured Chinese Lady, now his mother-in-law, and that made her look embarrassed under the feathered hat.

He didn't seem to have any limp, and when we managed a few words together in the scullery, I asked him if his leg was now as good as new.

'Eliza's been talking, has she?' he said.

'She said you still had a limp.'

His smile was wry.

'Difficult,' he said.

'Difficult?'

'Well, what can you say to someone who wants you to have a limp?'

'Oh, I see.'

'They'll sign a form next week,' he said, 'that'll pass me

as fit to return to active service. If the honeymoon lasts as long as a fortnight, I'll be surprised.'

'Lizzy'll kill them.'

'She won't like me very much, either. Bloody hell, Boots.'

'Let's have a whisky. I've got a bottle out here for emergencies.'

We had a stiff whisky each.

'Survival, Boots,' said Ned, and we drank to that.

'If your mother-in-law catches us,' I said, 'tell her it's sherry.'

'My who? Oh, yes.' Ned laughed. 'You're too young for this stuff, are you?'

'She'll think we both are.'

'Ned?' Emily, flushed from being busy and excited, put her head round the door. 'Ned, you've got to come and meet Lizzy's aunt and uncle.'

'I've met them,' said Ned.

'I mean talk to them,' said Emily, who, because of the occasion and her part in it had been striving to please Chinese Lady, as she often did, by speaking as proper as she could. 'Lizzy thought you ought – just a little chat so's they'll have kind thoughts of you, she said.'

'Lead on, me love,' said Ned, and disappeared with her. I rejoined the throng in the kitchen, and saw Emily's dad manfully trying to rise above his weakness amid a pack of noisy neighbours. I drew him out. He looked grey with exhaustation.

'What say we beat a retreat?' I said. 'There's a couple of chairs in the scullery, and some Scotch. Could you take a tot?'

'I ain't none the worse fer what yer give me last night,' he said. 'Yer got a man's way of twistin' me arm, Boots.'

'Well, you and me both, we need a sit down. I had a lousy kip last night. Come on.'

I liked the old geezer, I liked it that Emily liked him, and I liked him for standing up to what was killing him. We closeted ourselves quietly in the scullery and I poured the whisky. He accepted his gratefully. Its fire warmed his exhausted-looking face. We chatted. Someone looked in. It was Emily again, her expression strange, her eyes moist.

'There y'ar, Em, yer look grand,' said Mr Castle.

'We're just taking a bit of time off, me and your dad,' I said, 'but if I'm wanted, I'll come.'

'It's all right,' said Emily quietly. 'Everyone's made themselves at home now, and Tommy's being a great help. We're seeing to anything people want.' She gave her dad a bright smile. 'All right, Dad?'

'Boots 'as give me a tot of the best,' he said, 'and a chair as well. I'm fine now me plates of meat is restin'.'

'You got the nicest chair in the house, Dad,' said Emily, and went back to the milling guests.

'She's a good girl, yer know,' said Mr Castle, and took down more smooth fire. He used to down a jar of ale in great draughts. He used to be boozy, fat and happy, with his shirt undone and his brawny throat exposed. He was dressed in his Sunday suit today, and it sagged on him. 'Em's come up trumps, I reckon.'

'I told you that last night.'

'She likes it when yer like a big brother to 'er, Boots. She oughter 'ave 'ad some brothers, like yer Lizzy. Given 'er a real family, it would of. Ain't yer Lizzy a corker today? I never seen no girl look a more picture bride. An' she's picked a good 'un in Ned, 'e ain't got a bit of side. I 'ope they don't—' Mr Castle grimaced.

'Send him back to France?' I said.

'Bleedin' shame if they do,' he said. 'Ain't right. Once yer copped it like 'e copped it, it ain't right. Yer gimme a real tot, Boots, that yer 'ave.'

'Plenty more in the bottle,' I said.

The door opened and Miss Chivers stood there. She looked warm, charming and stylish in a brocaded dress of cream. She had worn her glasses during the ceremony, but they were off now, and so her eyes had that soft peering look which I found fascinating, although I knew some people might have said, 'For God's sake, put your glasses on, woman, or you'll walk over a cliff.' But we're all a bit vain. We all use mirrors.

'Boots?' Miss Chivers smiled.

'Yes, I'm over here and Mr Castle's over there.'

'I'm not as blind as that,' she said. 'Mr Castle, how are you today?'

'All the better fer seein' Lizzy churched, and fer 'aving Boots warm me cockles,' he said, and received another tot with obvious pleasure, a large one. I didn't know what the whisky would do to his suffering stomach, but it seemed to make things less painful for him.

'Yes, isn't it wonderful that Boots managed to get here?' Miss Chivers pressed my hand.

'And it's not a bad thing, as the bride's brother, to have the privilege of kissing the lady guests,' I said, and kissed her on the mouth. It startled her, but did not seem to offend her.

'That's the stuff,' said Mr Castle, and sank a mouthful of whisky. 'It ain't much of a weddin' if yer can't do some kissin' after givin' yer sister away.' He burped. In front of Miss Chivers, it embarrassed him. 'Beggin' yer pardon, Miss Chivers, it catches me that sudden, like.'

'Emily told me to tell you that if you want to go home now, she'll take you,' said Miss Chivers gently.

'Sounds like it could be restful,' said Mr Castle, 'but I got me tot and I'd like to 'ang on a bit longer an' see Lizzy dressed up fer goin' away.'

'That won't be long now,' I said, 'she and Ned are leaving at five-thirty. There's a motor taxi coming for them.'

'I'll 'ang on,' said Mr Castle.

'This'll keep you company,' I said, and topped him up from the bottle.

'Kind of yer, Boots,' he said.

'I'll sit with him, Boots,' said Miss Chivers, 'you go and show yourself to the girls here.'

She was still gentle in her manner, but her release from maternal possessiveness had made her much less diffident in her approach to people.

Emily reappeared.

377

'Still all right, Dad?' she asked brightly. 'Or d'you want to go indoors? Mum says you're not to tire yourself.'

'I'm 'anging on fer Lizzy's going-away,' he said. The whisky was putting quite a rosy glow on his grey cheeks.

'Well, can I take Boots for just a few minutes?' she asked. 'Ned's sister is after him, would you believe. Come on, Boots, I think she's gone on you.'

'Yes, take him, Emily,' said Miss Chivers, 'I'll talk to your dad.'

Emily dragged me through the crowd.

'Must you?' I asked.

'Yes,' said Emily quite firmly. 'You got to face up to girls sometime. It's silly you don't have your own girl yet, and you a sergeant. You ain't – you're not shy, are you?'

She was dragging me through the crowded passage.

'I was quite happy talking to your dad.'

'I know.' Her hand squeezed my arm. 'But you ought to talk to Anne. She can't think why you're hidin' yourself. There she is.'

Ned's sister was at the end of the passage, standing by the open front door, which was letting in some pale March sunshine. She was dark, round-faced and plumply pretty, her bridesmaid's outfit as pink as Emily's. Sitting on the stairs were young people, and the parlour was packed. Anne smiled.

'Here he is,' said Emily. 'He said he's sorry he's been a bit invisible, but when I told you you were dyin' to talk to him—'

'I'm not actually dying,' said Anne, 'it's just it's the first time we've met. Pleased to know you, Boots.'

'I'll leave you to it,' said Emily.

I gave her a slight scowl. Emily smiled brightly and struggled back to the kitchen. The house was full of voices, of shrieks of laughter and the sound of glasses. I talked to Anne. She was pert and eye-peeping, flirtatious and bubbly, and reminded me of Rosie. She took the conversation over. We stood at the open door together. The afternoon sunshine was welcome, but there was a faintly

378

sooty smell about it. I supposed I could call it a homely smell. It was preferable to other smells, smells that stuck to your khaki and your boots and your hands. Anne talked on, looking very pretty. It was a mystery to me why I didn't feel interested in her or in any other pretty girls I knew. Miss Chivers alone excited me, and she was hardly a girl.

Mr Finch, who had been playing as helpful a part as Emily in looking after guests, suddenly appeared and clapped a warm hand on my shoulder. Having already been introduced to Ned's sister, he joined the conversation, making his own kind of contribution. I thought he might have used the occasion to socialise with Miss Chivers on a perfectly reasonable basis. But they had made no attempt to get close to each other.

A complete diversion happened. Lizzy suddenly emerged from the passage bedroom in her going-away outfit, a new chestnut brown costume with a cream blouse, and a brown and cream hat. Our Lizzy looked all of a lady. Our Lizzy was leaving Walworth, to live in a house with a garden. Mr Finch's eye caught mine, and he smiled.

With perfect timing, a motor taxi drew up outside the front door.

Lizzy and Ned made their way to it amid a fanfare of cheers, confetti and farewells. Lizzy kissed Chinese Lady. She kissed the kids. She kissed Emily. She kissed Mr Finch. She kissed me.

'I'm so happy you came, Boots – love you for it,' she said, and her eyes were wet. 'Take care.'

'Good luck, sis, be happy. So long, Ned.'

'Survival, old lad, don't forget,' he said, and we shook hands.

Last thing before the taxi moved off, surrounded by the street kids, Lizzy tossed her bridal bouquet. She seemed to toss it in laughing carelessness, but it sailed straight at Emily, who caught it and looked stunned.

'Em'ly's next, Em'ly's next!' shrieked girls, and Lizzy's final smile was for Emily, and Emily, I saw, was full of tears because her years with Lizzy were over. They would remain friends, but there would be no more sorties into the park together, no more laughs and giggles together, no more moments when they would talk together in Lizzy's room. It was now Lizzy and Ned, not Lizzy and Emily.

Miss Chivers had brought Emily's dad out to see Lizzy depart, and Emily took him home a few minutes later. The poor old devil had made his effort, including an attempt to give Chinese Lady a hearty and grateful goodbye cuddle. A cuddle was not something Chinese Lady encouraged, but on this occasion she lent her help to it. Emily was very tender with her dad, calling to her mum that she'd see to him. Since he looked exhausted, I went with her, giving her dad my arm. One good thing the Scotch had done for him was to make him sleepy. I helped him up the stairs, Emily leading the way in a frothy shower of pink, but despite his weakness and his drowsiness, not by any means would he let her undress him. He managed that himself, and then Emily came in to see he was comfortably tucked up. He gave her a slow, slightly drunken grin.

'Reg'lar fusspot, you are,' he said, 'ain't she, Boots?'

'Blessed are our daughters,' I said.

'Eh?' said Mr Castle.

'Oh, that's Boots – he talks like that,' said Emily. 'All right now, Dad?'

'Been a treat of a day,' he said, his eyes closing.

Emily and I waited a few minutes, and Emily looked glad when we realised he really was deeply asleep. On the way down the stairs, she said, 'You been so good to him, lookin' after him like you have. You could have been havin' a swell time with the girls, but you sat with him. Boots, I'm ever so grateful.'

'He's an uncomplaining old dad,' I said.

'Your mum said it could all be a party now, but I'll pop in and look at him in between.'

Emily cared very much about her dad.

No one wanted to go home, except Aunt Victoria and Uncle Tom, who were taking their Vi to another social event, a birthday party. Before they left, however, Aunt

Victoria told Chinese Lady it had been a lovely wedding and that Lizzy had done far better than anyone could have expected. Uncle Tom nodded in agreement, as he usually did, and Cousin Vi smiled pleasantly but vaguely, as she always did.

The evening became very festive, for in response to eager requests, Miss Chivers played the piano and the house rang with music hall choruses. I thought her magnificently resilient under all her diffidence. The Witch had departed this life in a welter of blood, and Miss Chivers had stood trial for her murder. She had endured all the trauma and risen above the sensationalism. I wasn't surprised, however, that some people had begun to gossip. But she was enduring that too. At the piano, she seemed almost tranquil, like a woman who knew she was loved. She played everything the guests asked for, and was serene in her sociability. Mr Finch stood apart from her, smiling at the enjoyment the people of Walworth took in rousing song.

Far into the evening, with the stock of drink running low, the inevitable happened. The hilarious request had to come, and did, and Miss Chivers played the refrain that enabled the guests to do 'Knees Up, Mother Brown'. I watched in company with Chinese Lady and Mr Finch. In the parlour, in the passage and on the stairs, everyone else participated joyously.

'*Knees up, Mother Brown, knees up, Mother Brown,*
Under the table you must go,
Ee-i-ee-i-addy-oh,
If I catch you bending, I'll saw your legs right off,
Don't get the breeze up,
Just get your knees up,
Knees up, Mother Brown.'

It went on and on. Skirts were lifted, petticoats were flying. And there were the two bridesmaids, Emily and Anne, pink frocks high, stockinged legs kicking, Emily flushed and ecstatic, Anne shiny-faced and exuberant.

'Oh, lawks,' said Chinese Lady, 'look at that Em'ly.'

'Emily has become delicious,' said Mr Finch.

'She's been drinkin' for sure,' said Chinese Lady.

'No, no, she's in joy,' said Mr Finch.

Emily's frothy pink and lacy petticoat were swirling. Her legs, which had been so skinny, were long, slender and silk-stockinged. How well Emily made the most of her savings and her better features. She had splashed out on those silk stockings, expensively prohibitive to Walworth females, and in doing so had made her legs a wonder to behold.

Ned's sister, highly charged, induced her parents to participate, then kicked a leg at me.

'Come on,' she cried, 'come on!'

'Go on, join in,' said Chinese Lady.

Anne dragged at me, Emily pulled at me. I joined in. 'Knees Up, Mother Brown' never failed to be riotously infectious, and no true cockney could stand permanently aside. Chinese Lady was eventually sucked in, and even Mr Finch, not a cockney, could not resist when Emily rushed, took him by the hand and drew him into the jig. At the piano, Miss Chivers was in such tune with the infectious atmosphere that she repeated the refrain endlessly, and she was actually laughing. Knees were up in the parlour, on the stairs, along the passage, at the open front door and out in the street.

Only exhaustion brought a finish to it. It was late, but Mr Somers, Ned's dad, asked if there could possibly be one more song. Miss Chivers said she was willing. What was the song to be?

'For Mrs Adams, who's opened her house to all of us,' said Mr Somers, 'and given us a wonderful day.'

So we all sang 'For She's a Jolly Good Fellow.' It was sung rousingly, and Chinese Lady covered her embarrassment by taking hold of Sammy and combing his untidy hair with her fingers.

We managed to get rid of everyone by midnight, except for Emily and Miss Chivers, who sat with us around the kitchen table and shared our pot of tea. Mr Finch was there too, Tommy and Sammy in bed. Mr Finch and Miss Chivers were friendly to each other, but that was all, and I wondered now if their meeting in that Strand teashop had ever meant anything. We all talked about the wedding, about Lizzy and Ned, and the occasion as a whole. No one talked about the war.

Emily said, 'Lizzy was rapturous you gave her away, Boots.'

'We were all rapturous,' said Miss Chivers, smiling softly at me.

Emily said, 'Lizzy told me last week that if Lord Kitchener kept Boots away from her wedding after all he'd done to get Ned blown to pieces, she'd throw a bomb at him.'

'Oh, dear,' said Miss Chivers.

'A pity Lizzy and Ned didn't stay for the Mother Brown knees-up,' I said.

'I agree,' said Mr Finch, 'Emily alone was worth the price of a seat.'

'Sweet,' smiled Miss Chivers.

'Em'ly, them legs you showed,' said Chinese Lady, 'dear goodness.'

'Oh, 'elp,' breathed Emily, and blushed.

'All the boys lookin' and seeing,' said Chinese Lady, actually teasing the girl. 'It's the drink that does it.'

'Oh, Mrs Adams, I didn't have any drink, not drink,' said Emily earnestly. Nearly eighteen, she could still be girlishly earnest before Chinese Lady. 'I only had some lemonade and two glasses of port. It was just that everything was so exciting – I never enjoyed myself so much ever.'

'It's all right, lovey,' said Chinese Lady, who still had her glossy wedding hat on. 'Me and Lizzy's dad did the knees-up more than once at our own wedding. Your dad liked the knees-up when he was one over, Boots.'

'You didn't let him get one over at your wedding, did you?' I said.

Mr Finch laughed. Emily put a hand over her mouth. Miss Chivers smiled.

'I don't know how I come to bring up a comedian,' said Chinese Lady.

'Oh, he don't mean it, Mrs Adams,' said Emily, 'he was ever so nice to me dad, and Ned's sister's gone on him.'

'A charming girl who may like comedians,' said Mr Finch gravely.

'Well, it's certainly time he had a girl and thought about the future,' said Chinese Lady.

'But how sad that the war stands in the way,' said Miss Chivers.

That remark turned the kitchen quiet. Emily looked into her empty cup.

'I better go now,' she said. 'Thank you ever so much for the best day ever, Mrs Adams.'

'I must go too,' said Miss Chivers.

Mr Finch said politely, 'Shall I see you to your door?'

'Thank you, but it's really not necessary.'

I saw Emily out after Miss Chivers had gone. Emily lingered on the doorstep.

'I didn't want it to end, did you?' she said.

'Not the knees-up, no. I never knew you had legs like that.'

'Oh, don't you start,' said Emily. 'What d'you mean, like that?'

'Well, what does Arthur say about them?'

'Arthur?' The street was dark and Emily was shrouded in shadowed pink. 'What d'you mean? Oh, are you saying I go and show him my legs?'

'No, of course not.'

'Doing the knees-up is different.'

'Lots of fun, Em.'

'Oh, wasn't it just?'

'You've been a lovely bridesmaid. Your dad was proud of you.'

'I ain't lovely, you know I'm not.'

'You're lovely, Em, in all kinds of ways.'

'I'd rather be – oh, well, never mind. But I didn't look common, did I, showing my legs and everything?'

'Legs and everything aren't common, Em, they're a treat.'

Still lingering, Emily said, 'Oh, yer do say nice things sometimes. Only I wouldn't like Chinese Lady—' She stopped.

'You know what we call our mum, do you?'

'Yes, course I do, but – oh, I'm sorry, it's fam'ly, its private.'

'Well, you're as private as we are.'

'Ain't she got lovely eyes, though?' said Emily sighingly.

'Chinese colour,' I said.

'She's been a good mum to you all, specially since your dad went and—' Emily didn't finish that. She said, hesitantly, 'I know we all had the swellest time today, but you got to go back to France next week, and I know it's awful for yer there, I just know. And it shows.'

'Shows?'

'Like it was haunting you every so often. Boots, you got to take special care, you got to come back. Now Lizzy's married, your mum'll need you more. You don't mind if I still go in and see your fam'ly, even though Lizzy won't be there? I'm comin' in tomorrer to help clear up.'

'Good on yer, Em, you're a real godsend. By the way, don't forget to tell Arthur you caught Lizzy's bridal bouquet. It might make him speak his piece.'

'Me a bride myself?' Emily shook her head. 'That's a laugh.'

'It might not be to Arthur. Goodnight, Em, and thanks for being a tower of strength today.'

'Oh, I like helping your mum all I can. I been thinking. She's right – we don't want you to go in for winning medals and being a hero—'

'I don't and I'm not. Goodnight, Em.' I kissed her pointed nose.

She flitted away, ghostly-pink in the darkness.

I burned the bugs on Monday. I burned the wallpaper off in the Castles' bedrooms and the bugs with it. They

385

were just coming out of winter hibernation and looking forward to a warm spring and hot summer. I burned them and their nests in the cracked plaster. I nearly set a door lintel alight. Mr Castle was up, but not at work. He sat in the kitchen with Mrs Castle, while I did the deed of fiery purification. When Emily came home in the evening, she brought rolls of new wallpaper with her. She had rushed round to see the landlord during her midday break at the factory, and engaged in a furious argument with him before he consented to letting her go to his builders' yard after she finished work. There she had selected rolls for one room. She was going to pick up the rest tomorrow evening. She viewed the scorched bedroom walls with wide eyes.

'Oh, you got it all off, Boots, you burned every bit away. You make me so proud we live next door to you.'

Emily never kept her emotions to herself.

On Tuesday, I filled in the many cracks in the plaster. On Wednesday, I repapered both bedrooms. Chinese Lady said even if the Army wasn't improving me, I still knew how to do right by my neighbours. Being a good neighbour, she said, was more important than trying to win medals. It was her opinion that wars were fought to glorify the look of men's chests.

'I suppose you could say women's chests don't need glorifying,' I said.

Chinese Lady's proud bosom stiffened.

'Are you trying to say more than you should?' she said.

'Not really, old girl.'

'I'm not old girl. And you're not a man, not yet. You're not a man till you're twenty-one. Soldiering might have made you look like one – yes, you look near to thirty sometimes – but you're still not old enough to take women in vain. Yes, I know what you mean. And what you soldiers get up to with them loose French women might make you feel you're learning things, but that's not what life's all about, as you'll find out.'

'Is that what you told our dad?'

386

'Your dad didn't have to be told. Well, never mind, we'll have a nice pot of hot tea, shall we?'

'That's what life's all about — hot tea?'

'No, it's not.' Chinese Lady, on her feet, gave me a little pat. 'Just don't think I don't know what you been going through over there, that's all.'

I had some conversational moments with Mr Finch most evenings. On one occasion we discussed the mystery of the murder quite frankly. It was his opinion the police hadn't closed their files on it. He agreed Miss Chivers might have to move because there would always be some people around who would look at her and whisper about her until the murder was solved. He did not hint in any way that he would be pleased to move with her, or that it would grieve him to see her go.

He did not ask me what it was like in the trenches. The war seemed a sad and painful thing to him.

On Thursday, a telegram arrived. I took it from the boy, since I was the only one in the house at the time. It was addressed to Mr Finch. I placed it on his table, then wondered whether or not I should open it. It might be urgent, and in need of a reply. I could go out, find a post office with a telephone, and get through to the docks, either to talk to him or leave a message. I hesitated, then decided telegrams were mostly more urgent than private. I opened the table drawer in which he kept his small supply of cutlery, thinking of slitting the telegram with a knife. At one side of the drawer, in a long narrow compartment, he kept his carving-knife. It was there. It had a worn, shiny wooden handle. With it, was another, with a bone handle. I'd only ever seen him use the former. I'd never laid eyes on the latter. I closed the drawer and left the telegram unopened. I felt very disturbed for a while, then shook myself. There was no reason why he shouldn't own two carving-knives. We had two ourselves, one very worn and the other hardly ever used. It had a magnificent carved ivory handle, and had been picked up by our dad in Africa, during the Boer War. Chinese Lady cherished it, and the pawnbroker admired it so much he willingly advanced her a shilling on it from time to time.

I went upstairs to see Mr Finch in the evening.

'There was a telegram,' I said. 'Anything I can do?'

He turned brooding eyes to me.

'No, Boots. It's simply sad news.' He pointed to the telegram, lying open on the table. I read it.

'REGRET AUNT TRUDY PASSED AWAY THIS MORNING.'

That was all. He sounded almost harsh, as if the news angered him more than it distressed him.

'How old was she?'

'How old?' He seemed at odds with the question. 'Oh, yes, how old. She kept that to herself, in the fashion of a woman, but she must have been over seventy. Well, I must go to her funeral.'

'At Chatsford?'

'Yes, I imagine so,' he said.

'I'll say goodbye – I'm off tomorrow.'

He came out of his dark mood and shook my hand in his vigorous way. He smiled.

'Always remember, Boots, that whatever I had from my demanding aunt—'

'Demanding?'

'Fondly demanding.' He smiled again. 'Whatever I had from her, nothing can equal what I've had from you and your family. Take great care of yourself. I've said that before, but it has to be said again. You're haunted, aren't you?'

Emily had said that. I didn't like the fact that it showed.

'It's all that bloody barbed wire,' I said.

'It's waiting for a lot of us, Boots.'

I came out of Emily's house not long after ten o'clock, having said goodbye to her and her parents, and having left her sick dad with what was left of three bottles of whisky I'd brought home in my kitbag.

It was dark. It was early April, and it was dark. As I turned right out of the railed gate, a solid hammer blow caught me between my shoulder blades. The ferocity of it, and the unexpectedness, sent me pitching. I struck the pavement. The impact robbed me of breath. I heard a hideous cackle of laughter. The ice pierced my spine and I froze.

'Gotcher, yer bugger – 'old that.'

The toe of a boot thudded into my ribs. I rolled over, sucked in air and scrambled to my feet.

'You silly old cow,' I said in relief.

The looming, bruising bulk, swaying drunkenly on the pavement, was that of a woman, Mrs Percival, whose incurable animosity towards men had been caused by her husband running off to Australia with her sister. She was the one who brawled with men outside pubs after closing time. She little knew what a relief she was to me. For a few paralysing seconds I'd actually thought the Witch had risen up from her grave.

'Yer bleeder, I'll kick yer guts in,' said Mrs Percival, and lurched towards me. I placed the flat of my hand against her huge, swaying bosom and gently pushed. She staggered back, floundered about, lost her balance and sat down, her heavy bottom giving the pavement a solid thump. She put her feet in the gutter, her elbows on her knees and her hands to her head. She moaned. 'Oh, yer bugger,' she said.

'Have a fag,' I said, and sat down with her. I offered her a cigarette. She pawed about for it. I stuck it into her mouth for her. I lit it for her, and lit one for myself. 'We've all got troubles,' I said.

'Poop off,' said Mrs Percival.

She was better five minutes later, after she'd been sick.

CHAPTER TWENTY-NINE

The 7th West Kents were on the move. The generals were planning a new offensive. There was the usual clampdown on everything that might have given the Jerries a hint of what we were up to on our side. From the cryptic look that Major Harris wore, I knew what he was thinking. That even if the pall of silence blanketed the whole of France and Flanders, once the PBI went over the top, Jerry would be waiting for us and few of our generals would know what the others were up to. The local commanders would be left to sort it out.

I had a letter from Chinese Lady the second week in May. It was brief and bitter. Ned had been sent back to active service a fortnight after the wedding. He had been pitched, with his unit, straight into a battle in Flanders, and had lost a leg. Not content with having had the Germans almost cripple him for life before, the Army had seen to it that the Germans made a better job of it this time. Ned, his left leg off, was chronically ill. Lizzy was heartbroken.

I wrote to Lizzy from somewhere in France.

Our battalion was up to full strength. The troop trains were crowded, fifty men packed into every waggon built for twenty horses. Tommies were on the move from sector to sector. It wasn't the best way of seeing France, but while the build-up lasted it was better than mouldering in the trenches.

It was at Albert, while the battalion was waiting to entrain again at the end of the first week in June, 1916, that I learned Lord Kitchener, the mighty and far-seeing warlord, had gone down in the North Sea with the cruiser *Hampshire*. He'd been on his way to Russia. Some clever and undetected mine-laying by the German Navy was responsible, blowing huge holes in the cruiser. The *Hampshire* and Kitchener were sunk without trace, along with hundreds of sailors.

I wondered what Lizzy would say. Kitchener had been responsible for the recruitment of hundreds of thousands of men, including Ned. She hadn't liked that. Ned losing his leg wouldn't have improved her outlook.

Some mail caught up with us before we left Albert, and I received letters from Chinese Lady, Emily, Lizzy and Uncle Tom. Uncle Tom's letter was gentle and kind. Lizzy's letter was a relief. She thanked me for mine and for what I'd said in it. Yes, she understood. Yes, there was a consolation. And she was going to pull Ned through, even if she had to haunt the hospital. Afterwards, she'd have him to herself. Lord Kitchener had had as much of him as he could. What was left was hers. (Her letter had been written before Kitchener was sunk). She was going to have a baby, she said. And her baby was going to have a dad. We hadn't had a dad ourselves, except when we were very young, so she was going to make sure her infant did. Other wives were widows, and that was something to make her realise how lucky she was herself.

Chinese Lady's letter was very family. She referred to Ned improving very slow and Lizzy bearing up wonderful, which was a blessing considering she was expecting. Tommy was well and growing to look like our dad, and Sammy wasn't looking like anybody except a dellirick. (She meant derelict.) Oh, Cousin Vi had got tonsillitis. Mr Finch was over the death of his aunt and kinder than ever. The rickety state of the stair banisters had been worrying, and Mr Finch himself had talked very firm to the rent man, telling him that unless the landlord had them seen to she'd be entitled to hold back the rent. So the banisters had been seen to. Miss Chivers was working long hours at the Admiralty, Mr Finch's hours were irregular, Tommy was doing overtime and zeppelins were still coming over.

Chinese Lady said I'd be upset to hear Emily's dad had died. They'd taken him to hospital to give him an operation, but he had still died. Emily was grievous. There was talk that she and her mum would go and live with one of her aunts in Camberwell. Well, look after yourself, said Chinese Lady.

Emily began her letter by saying it was nice I never minded her writing to me. She was sorry to say her dad had died. Her mum was bearing up, like Lizzy was over Ned, but Emily hoped they wouldn't have to go and live with Aunt Mabel as she liked it best where they were. Our mum had rallied round and been a blessing, she said.

'It's awful about Ned, but Lizzy told me she'd rather have him with no leg than not have him at all. Imagine, she's going to have a baby, that's what they call a silver lining to a dark cloud, don't they? I'm glad Dad saw her married, he didn't want to miss that, specially with me a bridesmaid. He enjoyed seeing you, he was so grateful really about the wallpaper and everything, I know he wasn't perfect but he wasn't bad either, he liked his beer but never got drunk or troublesome, just jolly. He was a nice old dad really, he never laid a hand on me not even when he should have, I'd have been better I expect if he'd walloped me just once, but I'm glad he didn't. I don't want to be all mournful in this letter, I expect things are bad enough for you as it is, but Dad thought a lot of you and you did him a real bit of good giving him that whisky at the wedding, he had such a lovely long sleep that night which he hadn't been having at all.

'I didn't really thank you proper for the lovely present you give me, the satin camiknicks. I didn't tell your mum I wore them at the wedding, I thought I'd better not, but I did tell Lizzy, and said they really did feel swish. Lizzy said she bet it was a Frenchified swish. It's all right telling

392

you I hope, I didn't say anything to Arthur, except I did tell him how the bridal bouquet landed in my arms and Arthur said did I put the flowers in a vase to make them last. It didn't make him speak his piece like you thought it might. Mum said you looked a real soldier at the wedding and much older, oh only in a manly way she meant. Wasn't it sad about Lord Kitchener, we just seen the news in the paper.

'Well, I do hope and pray you and all the other soldiers aren't having it too bad, I never know what to say as I'm sure I don't really know half of it, but everyone hopes it'll come to an end soon, please look after yourself, yours faithfully Emily.'

Everyone in the Company said it was going to be the bleeding Somme, and the Somme it was. Major Harris looked as bleak as Dartmoor granite. The weather was wet, and he knew, and we knew, what the going would be like in the Somme terrain. Everyone makes jokes about English weather. No one, as far as we were aware, had ever made jokes about French or Belgian weather. No wonder. The Somme was going to be a floundering curse. On top of that, and despite the pall of hush, we all knew the Jerries would be ready for us.

Freddy Parks, my platoon corporal, kept cleaning his fingernails with the point of his bayonet. Some men took a rabbit's foot or a lucky sixpenny bit over the top with them as a good luck charm. Freddy always took clean fingernails. Lieutenant Olby, twenty years old and our platoon officer, grew a moustache to take.

Our guns opened up early on the morning of July 1st, and the assault on the German trenches began a little after 7 o'clock.

It was murderous, and it went on for days. The Germans took a hell of a battering, the kind that made them concede a hundred yards here, a hundred yards there, and that amount of ground was always chronicled as a great victory. Every British unit involved in the slogging, soggy assaults suffered horrendous casualties. Major Harris bore a charmed life, as if even the most inimical elements of war were reluctant to take out a soldier of his like. I had a deadly feeling that my own luck was going to run out at last. Freddy Parks's good fortune stayed with him, for he collared a lovely Blighty one from a bullet that wrecked his right kneecap. I began to keep my fingernails clean. Almost at once, a bullet hit my left shoulder. There was a lot of hopeful blood at first, but it proved only a nick, and when a field dressing had been applied, I wasn't rated a casualty. It turned me blasphemous. In a shattered German trench we were occupying, Major Harris appeared and shoved in beside me. He asked what the hell I was blinding about. I began an obscene recitation. Major Harris, grey, haggard and bloodshot of eye, split his mouth in a savage grin and told me to shut up. I shut up. We shared a fag.

On July 13th, the West Kents were ordered to advance through Trones Wood, just west of the village of Guillemont, what was left of it. Trones Wood was stuffed with Germans, most of them living and breathing – and waiting. The 7th Buffs had attacked and taken the enemy strongpoint in the wood, only to be forced out by a violent counter-attack. Our orders were to enter the wood from the south, help the Buffs retake the strongpoint, and then clear the place completely of Jerries. Orders were always orders, and although obedience had cost us dear many times, we went in. I don't think women would have been so daft. I think they'd have packed up on both sides and gone sensibly home.

We were all filthy, our uniforms full of sweat, and after nearly two weeks of shot and shell, we were fed up with all the trouble resulting from German counter-attacks. They were buggers at that, and Trones Wood was one more trouble. They were also diabolical at laying into us from positions of defence. They hit us not long after we entered the shattered wood. It became a yard by yard advance, a German machine-gun giving us particularly objectionable problems. Lieutenant Olby, twenty yards to the right of Major Harris, rose up from cover, fired a brace of shots from his revolver, and made a dash. Rifle fire caught him and down he went. I jerked up from my knees. Major Harris, scrambling from cover to cover, swung his arm to bring us on, and ran into a burst from the machine-gun. I saw him fall as if his legs had been taken from under him.

I went berserk. Major Harris was a great, enduring, bitter soldier, and among the last of his kind, the kind who, like my dad, soldiered to keep the peace. He had been at Mons. The German machine-gun had blasted him. I glimpsed him, flat on his back beside a tree. Upright, my rage was as sickening as wormwood and bile, and I ran. The machine-gun clattered. A comrade hurled a Mills bomb. It dropped well short, but the explosion was enough to make the machine-gunner duck and take his finger off the trigger. I ran on. Behind me, Tommies were cursing and diving for safety from rifle fire. I fell over Lieutenant Olby, who had gone down seconds before the Major, and was already a corpse. I scrambled on, bent double.

Major Harris lay at the foot of a bare, leafless and war-torn tree. Both legs were hit, inches above his knees, and blood was swamping his trousers. He lay very quietly, but his lips were drawn back in a grimace of frustration, his strong white teeth showing. Hell and the devil were his company. The machine-gun opened up again, and I flattened myself beside Rosie's dad.

'Oh, Christ,' I said, and lifted my head. The West Kents were fanning, peeling and falling.

'Get up.' The Major spoke quietly. 'Take that machine-gun out.'

'Let it bloody wait. You need tourniquets.' I came up on my knees to get at his field dressing.

He looked up at me, his face filmed with sweat, his grey eyes as bleak as ever.

'Don't arse about,' he said, 'get that machine-gun.'

A German stick grenade, lobbed by an unseen hand, struck the nearby ground and exploded. I was conscious of a fiery, blinding flash. And that was all.

CHAPTER THIRTY

Chinese Lady said, 'I thought it wasn't your own writing in that letter. No wonder it wasn't. And whoever wrote it for you didn't say nothing about your eyes.'

'A nurse wrote it.'

'It's all right, I'm not reproaching you.' A hand lightly patted mine. 'Still, I hope it don't mean you're not going to be able to see.'

'Well, I can't at the moment.'

'No, you got all them bandages round your head at the moment. I mean afterwards.'

'We'll have to see, won't we?'

'Is that supposed to be a joke?' she asked.

'I've gone past all that.'

'Well, that's something to be thankful for. What with poor Ned and now you, we don't want no more music hall comedy. You've grown up very flippant, Boots. I've noticed you being like it with friends and neighbours, specially with Em'ly, who's been a saving grace since the war. Still, I won't go on about it, but I do think you might of remembered her birthday when she was eighteen. You could of at least sent a card.' Chinese Lady, of course, was going on because that was her way when she was upset. 'You and Em'ly grew up together, and that Arthur, d'you know what he give her for a birthday present? A stamp album, so's she could start collecting stamps.'

'Not a bad hobby, and I suppose it would give them a common interest. I'll buy Emily a packet of mixed foreign ones to help her get that start.'

'There you go again, being a comedian. Em'ly don't

397

want to collect stamps, she wants to be — well, whatever she wants to be, she don't want to sit in corners sticking stamps in books. That's not what a woman's for, a woman's a lot more use to God's world than that. Anyway, you got to be serious for once. I asked some nurses about you, and they said be of good cheer or something, and I said I supposed that meant live in hope. We better do that, Boots, live in hope. I don't want you to be bedridden, and I don't suppose you do, neither.'

'Bedridden? I'm not legless, old girl. I'm not in bed now, am I? I think I'm sitting in a chair in the sun. Is it a lovely day where you are?'

'Where I am? Now what you talking about? Oh, I see. Yes, it's lovely an' sunny. What I mean is, you got nurses here to look after you and guide you about. What's going to happen when you come home? I'll have to get Tommy and Sammy to move your bed downstairs, for a start. You can sleep in the parlour. Then you won't have to go up and down the stairs.'

'No, I don't think we'll do that, Mum. I think I'd better go up and down the stairs.'

I sensed Chinese Lady giving thought to that. I heard the murmur of bees at work, gathering the nectar of late summer. There must have been flowering shrubs nearby.

'Yes, you might be right, Boots, I can see what you mean. I'll think about it. But I don't want you being proud and tryin' to do things you shouldn't for a while, I don't want to hear you falling about. You wouldn't like that, nor would I, nor your brothers. Just as long as you understand that. Have they give you a medal?'

'No, just a couple of operations.'

'Oh, they'll give you a medal all right. It's so you won't ask for money as well. Our country's always been full of good and willing men ready to soldier for us in war, but we never had any Government that treated our soldiers right once a war was over, except if you were a general. We had a fine general once, the Duke of Marlborough, and he was so disgusted with what the Government paid his crippled soldiers, he came right out and said so.'

'How do you know that?' I asked. I liked Chinese Lady for the little surprises she often treated us to.

'I do know. Your dad told me. Your dad was self-learned, he always carried books in his kitbag. He liked being historical. Well, never mind about medals, Boots.' Again a hand lightly patted mine. 'Your dad would of been proud of you. That's better than a hundred medals. But he'd of been a bit upset the way you got yourself blinded.'

'I'm not blinded. I just can't see at the moment, that's all.'

'Well, we'll live in hope, that's the best, so don't worry. Tommy an' Sammy will be helpful, and you'll get a few shillings pension. We'll be a bit hard up, but we'll make do. You'll be all right. It's not as if you don't know where everything is in the house. Lizzy'll come and see you, and Ned too when he gets fitted with his artificial leg. Lizzy's bearing up very good, specially with her baby due just after Christmas.'

'I'll enjoy seeing Lizzy. Anyway, the eye surgeon is quite hearty about me.'

'Hearty?'

'Every time he takes a look at me, he says, "Fine, fine, but don't go kicking footballs about."'

'I should think not. Don't you go doing things like that.' Chinese Lady was taking things well. 'D'you want Em'ly to come and see you? She could come on Sunday and bring Arthur with her.'

'I can't wait to see Arthur and his stamp collection, but no, I don't think so. I shan't be here much longer. They'll be sending me home in a few days, and I'll have to attend some eye hospital two or three times a week. Well, that's the way they're talking.'

'We can go on the tram. You feeling well enough for me to talk to you, Boots? Only there's something on my mind.'

399

'Talk away.' Homeliness was spreading its light over depression.

'It sent me dizzy, what happened. Mr Finch didn't come home at all one day last week, nor since. All his stuff's there, nice and tidy, but we haven't seen him for six days. And two gentlemen come three days ago, on Monday.'

'Police?' I suffered a sinking feeling, and a return of depression. As much as anything, I was depressed about the fact that Major Harris had bled to death in Trones Wood. It was no help to think again about a carving-knife and the re-entry of police.

'No, they wasn't policemen,' said Chinese Lady out of the warm air, 'they were well-dressed gentlemen, they said they was actin' for some Navy department or other. They asked me a hundred questions about Mr Finch, and I had to tell them everything I knew, but of course there was nothing I knew that was unkind or anything. I said he'd never give me a moment's trouble, that he was the most thoughtful lodger anyone could wish for, and a kind friend. Boots, they asked me if I knew anything about his movements the week before June the 5th.'

'June the 5th?'

'They didn't say why.'

'On June the 5th, Lord Kitchener went down with the *Hampshire*.'

'Was it then? The date didn't mean nothing to me. I said I only knew that Mr Finch went to his work and come home from his work, and went to church on the Sunday, with Em'ly, and had a quiet afternoon and tea with us. Boots, Lord Kitchener's drowning couldn't of had nothing to do with Mr Finch.'

'Just the date – that had everything to do with it, or they wouldn't have mentioned it.'

'Oh, don't talk like that, you'll make me worry. It's all on my mind, as it is. You'll hardly believe it, but Miss Chivers, she's disappeared too. The Saturday before the two gentlemen come, she never got back from her morning work at the Admiralty. No one's seen her since. They asked me questions about her too, then they went into her house. They got the door open with some key they had, and they went in. They was there quite a time, then they come to see me again, and asked me to let them know if anything happened, if Miss Chivers or Mr Finch turned up again. They told me it was my serious duty to give them any information I could, and they said what had passed between them and me was confidential, and I wasn't to say nothing to anyone. Well, it's different talkin' to you about it, you're my only oldest son.'

'God Almighty,' I said, 'Miss Chivers worked at the Admiralty.'

'You shouldn't take the Lord's name in vain.'

'I'm not. I mean it. The Admiralty, for God's sake. And she's disappeared. With Mr Finch.'

'They didn't say she'd done that.'

It was terrifying. The Admiralty, where the movements of every naval vessel would be charted, where they'd know the course the *Hampshire* was steering. Lord Kitchener had been on his way to Russia. He was a power in the war. The Germans, in grateful receipt of the right information, wouldn't have turned down the chance to sink him.

'There's no one listening to us, is there?' I asked. I couldn't get used to being always in the dark. And I hadn't miraculously acquired an advanced sense of hearing. That would come gradually, a nurse had told me. I'd said I wasn't desperate, I was quite satisfied with my hearing as it was, and all I'd like was to get my sight back. She tut-tutted at my irritation. But I was like that, I had bursts of chronic irritation. 'There's no one near us, is there, Mum?'

'There's people – patients, like, and nurses, but they're not near us, Boots, or I wouldn't of spoken my worries to you, specially as they're confidential. And I don't know as I should of, anyway, seeing you got your own worries.'

'You had to share this with someone, or it would have

sent you grey. But stiffen yourself, old girl. Did you tell those two men about Mr Finch's Aunt Trudy?'

'Yes, course I did.'

'Well, I don't think there ever was an Aunt Trudy, not after what you've just told me.'

'Boots, of course there was. Mr Finch used to write to her, and go and see her, and he had a telegram when she died.'

'Well, don't let's think about it.'

'I couldn't tell those men where she lived, of course, because I didn't know. When they searched his rooms, perhaps they found the address. Oh, I can't bear thinking he's done something wrong, and Miss Chivers too.'

'Forget about it, Mum. Leave it alone, and don't – did those men tell you to telephone them if anything happened?'

'Yes.'

'I wouldn't bother, if I were you, old girl.'

'Not me. I can't bear them infernal instruments, anyway, they're not natural.' Chinese Lady, instinctive in her defence of Mr Finch and Miss Chivers, spoke emphatically. I was worried. It sounded to me as if Chinese Lady had been visited by Naval Intelligence. Had they been policemen, I'd have thought they were re-investigating the murder. Naval Intelligence would be after Mr Finch and Miss Chivers for something very different. 'Well, I won't burden you any more, Boots,' said Chinese Lady, 'but it's been a relief talkin' to you. I better be on my way now.' I heard her rise from her chair, I heard her garments rustle and I felt the light touch of her hand on my shoulder. 'You done your bit for your country. We'll manage. Here's a nurse coming.'

'Sergeant, would you like to see your mother out?' That was the voice of the nurse who had tut-tutted.

'Yes, why not?' I said.

'Take her along the path and round to the front. It'll be a little walk for you. I'll give you five minutes, then come and collect you.'

So I saw Chinese Lady out with my hand on her shoulder. She walked slowly and carefully. She walked upright.

'There, you're managing fine,' she said, 'I thought you would.'

'Why did you think I would?'

'Well, you're not always just a comedian,' said Chinese Lady.

CHAPTER THIRTY-ONE

'All right, Sergeant?' said the driver of the military ambulance, having seen me to my front door.

'Yes, all right. Thanks.'

'Good luck.'

I heard him clump back to his vehicle. I heard the hum of the factories. The afternoon sun of September was warm on my back as I groped for the latchcord. Finding it, I pulled it. The door opened. The sound brought Chinese Lady from the kitchen. I'd sent a card from the hospital, written by the nurse, and my arrival was expected.

'Nice they brought you, Boots,' said Chinese Lady, and gave me a pat. 'Come and sit in the parlour, in a comfy armchair, and I'll put the kettle on. Sammy'll be home from school soon. Come on.'

She was brisk. I groped and felt my way. She didn't interfere, but I knew she was watching me. I was watching myself, aware of my impatience and my quick irritations. It was a swine, being in our own house, but still having to blindly feel my way. My right shoulder brushed the parlour door frame.

'Where's the nearest armchair?' I asked.

'Straight ahead, by the fireplace,' she said, and I heard her move something out of the way. People said that. Straight ahead, they said, but there's always a feeling something's going to materialise out of the black void and clout you silly. I moved forward and my toe stubbed into the fireplace rug.

'Clumsy cow,' I muttered.

'What's that you said? There, you're all right – that's it, that's the armchair, the one you like.'

My hand found it and explored it. I eased my way to its front and sat down. I was finding out that when you can't see you're limited to sitting around or fumbling around. You can eat and drink, of course, and you can talk and use the lav, but you can't do much else, so you keep asking yourself what sort of a life you're going to have. You have long periods of feeling sorry for yourself, and you have soberer moments when you think of born soldiers like Major Harris lying beside a war-shattered tree with both legs full of machine-gun bullets and bleeding to death amid shot and shell.

'All right, a nice cup of tea, Mum.'

'Yes, I'll put the kettle on – but what's the doctor said?' I told her he had said it was going to take time. I didn't tell her he had said it was fifty-fifty. 'How much time?' she asked.

'A year or so. They've been scorched. They'll take time to heal.'

'Well, that's not so bad. I'll make a nice pot. Em'ly might pop in soon, she's come home early from her work, knowing you was getting here today. Now don't say flippant things to her. She's had to grieve for her dad, then for Lizzy an' Ned, and I don't suppose she's too happy about what the Army's done to you.'

'The German Army.'

'Same thing, can't you see that?' said Chinese Lady, and silence descended as she returned to the kitchen. The house seemed to advance into a period of respectful quiet, as if in tribute to its departed lodger. Was he with Miss Chivers? And if so, where were they? With Naval Intelligence after them, they'd find England a very small place. On the other hand, there was a lot of water about, and Mr Finch knew the river and the sea as well as he knew the land.

I pulled out a packet of Players, opened it, fumbled and drew out a cigarette, which I immediately dropped. Bugger it, I thought. I got up, bent down and ran my hand over the old but still serviceable rug, which Sammy would always

405

beat in the back yard for a penny. I searched for the cigarette. It was a bit of a fillip when I found it. I heard the front door open. I straightened up and hit my head on the corner of the mantelshelf.

'Sod it,' I said.

I heard a gasp, a rush of skirts, and felt the impact of a warm body against mine, and the straining embrace of strong, slender arms.

'Oh, Boots!' It was Emily.

'Steady,' I said.

'Boots – oh, let me come an' take care of you.' Emily sounded in pain. 'Let me come an' live with you – I couldn't live at Aunt Mabel's, not now you – oh, it won't matter I'm no ornament, not now you can't see.' Her arms wound tighter, and her face was against my shoulder. 'Let me come an' live 'ere – I won't be no trouble – I'll help your mum look after you – '

'That's nice of you, Emily, but you've got your own life to live, and I'm not going to be permanently blind.' My fingers were crossed. 'The specialist said it would take a year or so for my mince pies to heal. They were scorched, but not too badly, he said. When these bandages come off, I'll have to go around in black glasses, but I won't need looking after, so don't get so worked up.'

'Oh,' said Emily, and her straining body withdrew. She was silent for a moment, then said quietly, 'I'm sorry – that was silly of me. I don't have any more sense sometimes than when I was a schoolkid. I'll come in again later, when you've had time to settle in a bit. I'm sorry.'

I heard her footsteps in quick retreat, and I heard the front door close on her. I sat down again and lit my cigarette. I'd mastered the art of that without burning my nose off. After a few minutes, Chinese Lady brought a cup of tea in.

'Did I hear someone?' she asked.

'Emily popped in.'

'Why didn't she stay? She could of had a cup of tea with

you. Boots, I hope you didn't act casual and ungrateful.'

'Ungrateful?'

'Em'ly's a girl blessed with giving. Mind, she wants to better herself a bit. She's trying to find evening classes where they teach people to speak nicer. Here.' Chinese Lady took the cigarette from me and got rid of it. She placed the cup and saucer carefully in my hand.

'Emily's doing what?'

'Well, Arthur speaks quite nice, like you do. I wish Tommy an' Sammy took more trouble. Sammy fairly gabbles sometimes. Em'ly said she don't want to speak posh, just not so common. Lizzy's talk has improved remarkable.'

'Yes, she decided she was going to be a lady from the moment she met Ned.' I tried the tea. It was hot and satisfying.

'Some people think wantin' to speak nice means you want to be toffee-nosed, but it needn't mean that at all.'

'Emily's not common,' I said, 'she's a cockney. We're all cockneys. Some of us sound our aitches, and some don't. Emily can sound hers very clearly. It's only when she's excited that she drops them. Who cares?'

'You used to tick Sammy and Tommy off something chronic,' said Chinese Lady. 'Anyway, I can't think why Em'ly didn't stay and have a cup of tea with you, unless she got a bit upset seeing you in them eye bandages. Now, you'll be all right while I start gettin' the meal ready? I managed to buy some scrag end of mutton for a stew with dumplings. The gravy's going to be nice and thick, I put some barley in it. Drink your tea up before it gets cold.'

She left me to it. I drank it and placed the cup and saucer carefully down on the linoleum floor. Sammy came in from school. I heard his usual exuberant entry into the house. Then silence. The parlour door was obviously open, and I guessed he'd seen me. I heard him come in.

'Boots?'

'Hello, Sammy.'

'Sorry yer got nobbled,' he said.

'It's not for ever,' I said, 'I'll be fine in a year or so.'

'That's all right, then,' said Sammy, now fourteen. 'We brought yer bed down in 'ere, me an' Tommy. Chinese Lady said never mind what you said, yer'll be better down 'ere for a bit, she said.' I heard his feet shuffle. 'It ain't worth arguin' with 'er, Boots, it's best to do what she says. We'll take yer bed back upstairs later on, when yer got used to things more. I'll tie yer laces for yer, if yer like, an' on Sundays me an' Tommy can walk yer up the park. Chinese Lady said we got to see yer get out an' about fer yer own good. Yer can't argue with 'er, Boots.'

'Good on yer, me lad,' I said. 'Made yer fortune yet?'

'Well, no, not a fortune, not yet, but I got quite a bit.' His feet shuffled again. 'If yer got to 'ave more operations, I can loan yer a few bob so yer can pay something to the Lady Almoner.'

'The government's supposed to take care of that, but if they don't, and if you loaned me a bit, you wouldn't ask for security?' I thought I might fox him with that word.

'Oh, I wouldn't ask no security from you, Boots,' he said. He knew the jargon all right. 'Not after yer done yer bit like yer 'ave. I might not charge no interest, neither. Are yer still gettin' yer sergeant's pay?'

'Until I'm officially kicked out, yes.'

'Still, all the same,' said Sammy, and paused. Then he said generously, 'All the same, I won't charge yer no interest.'

'God bless yer, mate,' I said. 'Listen, do me a favour. Go and ask Emily if she'll come and see me. She's just been in, but tell her I'd like to see her again.'

'All right,' said Sammy, and went, asking nothing for going. He returned after a couple of minutes. 'She's comin',' he said, and I heard him go through the passage to the kitchen.

Emily came back. I heard her enter slowly, as if she was nervous, embarrassed and wounded.

'Emily?' I said, and stood up. My foot collided with the cup and saucer I'd placed on the floor. The cup rattled and clinked. 'Damn, have I broken it?'

'No.' Her skirts whispered. The cup rattled again as she picked it up with the saucer and placed them on the table. 'It's all right.' Her voice sounded subdued.

'Emily, I've been thinking about what you said. If your mum doesn't mind, yes, why shouldn't you come and live with us?'

'What?' said Emily on a gasp.

'Having had time to think, it seems a very good idea to me. Are you still in favour?'

'Am I! Oh, am I!' The words burst out. 'Oh, yer don't know how good yer being to offer – oh, yer mean it, don't yer? I—' She quietened herself down and spoke nicer. 'Oh, you see, I don't want to go and live with Aunt Mabel, and Mum won't mind a bit if I live here instead. It would make it easier for Aunt Mabel, and I couldn't leave here, not now you – not now you—'

'Not now I'm bandaged up? I'm not thinking about that, Em.'

'No,' she said, and I heard her swallow. 'I mustn't be silly. Only you all been so good to me, you got such a nice fam'ly. I could lodge with you, couldn't I, now Mr Finch – oh, can you believe him disappearing without taking his things, and Miss Chivers too, almost like as if they'd eloped?'

'No, I can't believe it, Em.'

'It's made people start talkin' all over again – oh, you know.' Emily sounded breathless. 'But I expect after the awful trying time Miss Chivers went through, I expect she and Mr Finch just wanted to – to—'

'Quietly vanish?'

'Yes. Don't you? They probably went to some place

where no one knew them. D'you think they were in love?'

'Yes, Em, and I don't think they'll come back.'

'Then—' I heard her swallow again. 'Then would it be all right if I had Mr Finch's bedroom and paid your mum rent out of me wages? That would be a kind of proper arrangement, wouldn't it? I could help your mum with the work, and I could go an' do shopping for you whenever you wanted anything particular – oh, only if you asked, of course. You don't have Lizzy now, and I wouldn't mind being a sister to you and the boys, really I wouldn't.'

'The boys might want another sister. I don't.'

'Oh. I'm sorry, I keep saying all the wrong things.' Her voice became anxious. 'It's just that – please, you do mean it, don't you? I can come and live with all of you – like a lodger? I won't be interfering—'

'Don't you think it would be better if you married me? Have you ever thought about getting married, Em?'

There was total silence. I couldn't even hear her breathing. Then she said, in a painful whisper, 'You're joking.'

'I'm probably not very good at this, but do people joke about getting married?'

'You are joking,' she breathed.

'No, I'm not.'

'But you could marry someone pretty – hundreds of nice girls would fall over themselves if you asked.'

'I'm not going to ask hundreds of girls to fall over themselves. I haven't noticed hundreds of girls. I've noticed you, though. You're the best girl in Walworth, and you're a treasure to this family.'

She was all of that. She was steadfast, loyal and kind, as much of a true comrade as all those I'd known in the West Kents, the dead as well as the living.

'Boots, what're you saying?' she asked huskily.

'There's Arthur, of course. I'd forgotten him. But that doesn't alter what I feel about you. You've got a houseful of love inside you, Emily Castle, and I'd like the best part of it, before Arthur gets it. And why should I be proud? Anyone can see I need you far more than Arthur does. Let him marry his stamp album.'

'Boots,' she said faintly, 'you sure you know what you're saying?'

'Well, what am I saying? I'm saying I love you.'

'Oh!' It was a gasp. Then there was a new impact, and the feel of a warm, shaking body and winding arms. 'Oh, I didn't ever think – Boots – oh, yer don't know what yer doing to me.'

'Is it hurting, then?'

'Yes – oh, yer don't know. I've got a pain all over. I never thought you'd – oh, I just can't believe what's 'appening. Did yer – did you really say you loved me, that you'd marry me?'

'Yes, I did say that.'

She smothered herself against me, and her body spread its warmth.

'Boots, I know I'm not the best-lookin' girl in the world, but – but I'm nice underneath, I know I am. I got a good figure – look, you'll like me here, won't you?' She took my hand and brought it to her bosom, which felt as if warm jersey wool was shaping it. She drew a breath as I made a feeling survey of a firm curve. 'D'you like me there?'

'Yes, and the other one too.'

'Oh, yer cheeky man – Boots – oh, yer got a lovely touch—'

'Well, that's something.'

'It won't matter I'm not too pretty if I got a pleasing figure, will it?' she said. 'And Lizzy said I got good legs. Is that going to be nice for you too, if I got good legs?'

'I know you've got good legs. You did a flying knees-up, remember. Yes, it's going to be very nice, Em. Pity I won't be able to see them for a while.'

'Oh, but if you wanted to, you could feel—' Emily stopped. I think she was blushing. 'I mean, if we're really going to be married – well, I wouldn't mind you finding

411

out if you liked them, just so you'd know it makes up for me not being no oil paintin'.'

'Look, I don't care what you think you see in your mirror, I know what I've seen, and that's the best girl I know.'

'Could I – could I have a kiss, then?'

That didn't prove difficult. She gave me lots of help. She was very kissable.

'How was that?'

'Oh, yer lovely to me, Boots.'

'All right, we'd better get married, then, but there are going to be problems. I don't know what kind of a job I'm good for while I'm like this. I'll be—' A warm hand stopped my mouth.

'We don't want any talk like that,' said Emily, sounding just like Chinese Lady. 'You been spared to us, that's what counts. All the bad days I've had, thinkin' you might never come back. You're not to worry. I'll be earning wages, and your mum said only yesterday you'd get a disabled pension. We'll manage, you see – oh, yer've made me so happy – yer don't know. We'll all be a nice fam'ly together, won't we?'

'Wouldn't you like a little garden, Em?'

'Oh, when we're older, if you like. We've got our nice home here now, and a back yard, and your mum and everything. D'you think she'll mind you marrying me?'

'She'll love it. She'll treat you as a godsend.'

'I love your mum,' she said. And because she was Emily, she added, 'Wouldn't my dad 'ave been pleased? Well, he still will be, I know he will. He'll be dancing in heaven, don't yer think so?'

'If I know your dad, he'll be doing a larky knees-up with some larky lady angels.'

Emily laughed and hugged me.

'What's going on?' That was Chinese Lady. I felt Emily turn in my arms and hastily disengage.

'Oh, Mrs Adams, I—' She sounded emotional. 'Boots

412

and me – he's asked – oh, would yer believe, he's asked me if—'

'Now it's nothing to cry about, Em'ly love. He'd have wanted his brains testing if he'd asked anyone else. Still, it's nice he's woken up at last. You can be an Easter bride come the spring. An Easter bride's lovely.'

'If it's all the same to you,' I said, 'don't let's wait for the spring. I'd like her for Christmas.'

CHAPTER THIRTY-TWO

I lay awake that night in my bed in the parlour. Night was the same as day to me in one way. Parrots were funny birds. Throw a blanket over the cage of a parrot in the middle of the day, and it thought night had descended. It went to sleep. Lucky old parrot.

They were still fighting on the Somme. The French, British and Germans were still being fed into the gigantic mincing machine. I thought of Rosie's dad, Major Harris. He'd been a natural soldier, a regular, and had never minded facing up to the risks of war. But he had minded men being turned into cannon fodder. That had never been his idea of soldiering.

I thought of Emily. Emily, eighteen, with what was it she'd said? Yes, a pleasing figure. And she was sure her legs weren't bad, either. Imagine if it turned out I was never going to see them. Seeing was more believable than feeling.

The house was silent, the street was silent. I lay in the silence, and the darkness, and was sleepless. I thought of Miss Chivers, and the Admiralty, and the sinking of the *Hampshire* and Lord Kitchener. I thought of a cottage in Chatsford, and the studious-looking man who answered the door and told me Mr Finch's Aunt Trudy had gone away for a while. A woman had been there, a woman who might have been the man's wife. She might have answered to the name of Mrs Gertrude Livingstone, but she could not have been Mr Finch's aged aunt.

The silence stirred. Very quietly, the front door opened. I heard it. Very quietly, someone entered the passage, someone who knew our front door could be opened by a latchcord and was never bolted. The petty crooks of Walworth did not burgle their own people. The passage returned to soundlessness. Someone was there, standing and listening. I lay unmoving. Then I heard the lightest of noises. Someone was cautiously climbing the stairs. Tommy and Sammy would not wake up. They always slept like logs. The little sounds ceased. Someone had reached the landing. Everything became silent again. I eased myself out of the bed, very carefully, and tried to decide exactly where I was in relation to the open parlour door. Chinese Lady had insisted on leaving it open in case I did something silly and needed to make myself heard.

I moved forward, hands stretched out, and felt a draught of warm night air. The front door had been left open. That was to allow a quick, silent exit. I waited. I heard movement on the stairs quite soon, then the soft sound of rubber soles over the passage linoleum.

'Come in, Mr Finch,' I whispered.

He drew a sudden breath, and I felt him brush me as he came into the parlour.

'Boots?' he murmured softly.

'I can't see you. My eyes are bandaged. They might be all right in a year. Well, that's what the man said. Would you like to talk to me, or are you in too much of a hurry? We can talk quietly, without disturbing anyone.'

'Dear old Boots,' murmured Mr Finch, and I heard him close the door. 'What happened?'

'The Somme. A grenade. No shrapnel, but a lot of fiery light. Shall we sit down?'

'Here, Boots.' I felt him take my arm, and he sat me down in an armchair. 'I'm sorry, old man, about your eyes and my situation. Yes, I'll tell you. It's *verboten*, but who'll care now?' He was silent for a few moments, listening. 'Now. I was born in Frankfurt, joined the German Navy out of university and entered German Intelligence when I was twenty-four. I spent a year as an agent in Russia, when I was then required to prepare myself for years in England. With others. For the purpose of acquiring useful information concerning the British Navy. I spoke English, and perfected it by sailing the seas for several years aboard British merchant ships, with forged papers and forged passport in the name of Edwin Finch. It was a fine and vigorous way of perfecting my English, with no questions asked about what little accent I had in the first place, and a very practical way of anglicising me. I eventually settled down in England at the age of thirty-one, and was accepted as an English seaman who had left the merchant navy. I learned many things, Boots. I learned how difficult it was not to become more English than the English. I learned how one's loyalties can become divided, how hard it is to work against a people when one lives among them as one of them. I lived in Portsmouth first, then here. The difficulties become very real when one becomes attached to individuals, but can be bearable while there is peace. To be more English than the English, to begin to admire their culture, their institutions and their resilience, isn't too disturbing in peacetime. One tells oneself that war is the unlikeliest thing to happen, and therefore information acquired and transmitted is only something that will gather dust on a file. One can't stand apart from people, one must identify with them and become one of them. To stand apart, to live alone, is to be a recluse, to arouse curiosity and then suspicion. But to make friends, as one can't help doing, is a worry, old man, for one can't escape the possibility of betraying every friend, every friendship. You realise I'm a German spy, of course.'

'Yes,' I said.

'Will it offend you if I refer to my friendship with you and your family?'

'No.'

'Thank you. I've loved your family. I've seen your family survive many hardships, I've seen the endurance of your fine mother, and I've seen you become a soldier and a man. But there it is, there's my own country, my Fatherland.'

'And no Aunt Trudy?'

'No Aunt Trudy, Boots. Only colleagues and their little

wireless station in an English village. You had a moment of suspicion there?'

'Not really.'

'In all these years, I've had only two really bad days – the day England declared war on Germany, although I knew it was coming, and the day of the telegram. The telegram was a coded message informing me my present role was at an end, that my not too dangerous existence as a gatherer of useful data was over and something far more difficult and risky was required of me. I had to contact our pre-eminent man in London. I was informed I'd been chosen because of special circumstances.'

'Meaning you were a very close friend of someone working at the Admiralty?'

He did not answer that. He said, in his murmurous voice, 'I'm sorry to say, Boots, that the result was the sinking of the *Hampshire* and the drowning of Lord Kitchener. At first, we thought it was going to be your new Prime Minister, Lloyd George, for it was originally proposed that he should go to confer with the Tsar of Russia. He decided against it, however, and Lord Kitchener was sent instead. We didn't mind. Kitchener, a brilliant man, was a military target and therefore a more moralistic one.'

'And Miss Chivers gave you all the information you needed about the *Hampshire*?'

'Ah.' Mr Finch sighed. 'Miss Chivers thought about Lizzy and Ned, and about all the young men Kitchener had recruited to fight and die. And when Ned lost a leg, she was most upset.'

'Upset?'

'It cost her her peace of mind, Boots.'

'You mean she joined forces with you to destroy our warlord,' I said. 'That would have cost anyone their peace of mind. Do you love her?'

I heard him sigh again.

'I left Portsmouth not because it became too hot for me, but to escape an emotional involvement that was proving

417

difficult. The lady wished marriage. I'd denied myself any real love affair, because in my trade it's fatal to let a woman get as close as that, and a wife would be even closer. And one has to draw the line somewhere in one's role. That's what you say, Boots, draw the line?'

'Yes, that's what we say,' I said.

'After leaving Portsmouth, and after my references had secured me work as a river pilot – a useful occupation, that – I thought to live a comfortable, quiet and safe existence here as your lodger, while continuing my work for the Fatherland. Such work didn't keep me operative every day, but London did prove excellent for making contact with a certain type of people prepared to sell naval secrets. That seemed my only diversion, my espionage work, until a few years ago when Miss Chivers first began to come to Sunday tea. You'll never know how fascinating I found the ritual of English Sunday tea as served and supervised by your mother. Bread and butter first – before jam or cake could be eaten. Endearing, Boots, really. Miss Chivers, of course, began to entrance me. I knew her, naturally, although I'd never formally met her. Our paths crossed in the street sometimes, when I would raise my hat and she would murmur good morning or good afternoon with her head bent. Meeting her here at Sunday tea was to me not unlike Adam meeting Eve in the Garden of Eden.'

'Garden of Eden? You're pushing your fancies a bit, aren't you?'

'A little, perhaps. But I found myself far more emotionally involved than I'd ever been in Portsmouth. I knew I ought to move again, but I was trapped, Boots. I was trapped by a deep affection for your family, and my love for Miss Chivers. And Miss Chivers was trapped by a deep need.'

'A need of what?'

'Oh, I say, old man.' There was a hint of amusement in his voice at his use of that very English phrase. 'Must I answer that? A healthy woman, a normal woman, dominated, suffocated and repressed by her mother?'

'She could have got what she needed from other men, from someone at her office, couldn't she?'

'With a fellow clerk? She could, perhaps, but didn't. She chose me. We reached the ultimate in mutual committal, so much so that all secrets were confided. That meant there came a time when she had to make a heartbreaking choice between my country and her own. Our boats are burned, Boots, and we have to swim for dear life. She's consented to leave England with me for a neutral country, where we shall marry. We'll be gone in two days. I can't give you the details, for I don't want to burden you with information you'd have to pass on. Your people are after us, of course.'

'I know. They've been here.'

'Yes, I know.' Again he sighed. 'I'm sorry for the shock that must have given your mother. I'm not going to insult you by asking you to forgive us, but I am going to ask you to believe we shall always hold your family in love and affection. If that sounds hypocritical, or even absurd, it can't be helped. If you feel bitterness, I understand. I've told you what I should have told no one, because in my love for your family I owe you that much at least. The war, in which I've played my own very small part for Germany, has left you blinded, and that gives me grief.'

'Mr Finch, who murdered the Witch, you or Miss Chivers?'

'I shan't answer that, Boots, but I will say Mrs Chivers was in a position to make things distinctly awkward. She found out, I'm afraid.'

'About you and Miss Chivers?'

'And about the fact that I came from Frankfurt.'

'Yes?'

'She'd still be alive otherwise, although she would still have lost her daughter.' Mr Finch sighed yet again. 'I think I must go, Boots.'

'I think you still owe me a little more.'

'Yes, you're right, I do,' he said. 'Yes. Well, I was in their house once, once only, late on a Sunday night. Miss Chivers had let me quietly in some time after her mother

419

had gone to bed. I made a little mistake, probably because after making love we were both in a reckless mood concerning the desperate steps needed to ensure our future together. Miss Chivers wanted me to stay in England for the rest of my life and to give up my espionage work. She was ready at last to defy her mother and to marry me. I explained that no Intelligence agent could hand in his notice in wartime, especially when operating in the country of an enemy. It would mean that she and I would both be disposed of. We could hide, she said, we could go to a place where we would not be discovered. I said we'd have to give it long and serious thought. We had forgotten, in our mood of deep committal to each other, that although her mother was upstairs in her bed, and had apparently been asleep when Miss Chivers looked in on her before letting me in, she was always quite capable of getting up and stealing silently about the house. Instinctively, however, we had been talking very quietly. As I opened the parlour door to let myself out, Miss Chivers spoke her final words of the evening. She said, "Wherever we went, no one would know you weren't English, that you'd been born in Frankfurt."'

'That was Miss Chivers's mistake, not yours.'

'No. Her voice was still very low. The mistake, Boots, was in my opening of the parlour door before we'd really finished our conversation. Had it not been for that, the devilish old woman, lurking down the passage, wouldn't have heard those words. She'd have seen me go, which I did immediately, without knowing she was there, but Miss Chivers would only have had to face an inquisition about what I'd been doing there. In which case, she was in the mood to defy her mother for once. As it was, she was subjected to foul abuse about what had been going on, and to frightening questions about my real identity. Miss Chivers protested her mother had misheard her, and in her desperation took the offensive. This actually reduced her mother to a mumbling whine. Her mother went back to her bed, but turned at the top of the stairs and said, "We'll

see, we'll see, you disgusting creature – wait, just wait."
Miss Chivers informed me of this the next day. I won't say
what her mood was. I asked which person her mother was
most likely to talk to. Her doctor, Miss Chivers said. Her
doctor was the only person with whom she had regular
contact. He was due to call in two days time. When he did
call, Boots, Mrs Chivers was dead.'

'But why didn't you kill her at night, when you could
have arranged for Miss Chivers to be out, and so given her
an alibi?'

He was silent then. I sensed him frowning and thinking.

'It's of no importance now,' he said.

'You know I lied at the trial, don't you?'

'Yes. You loved Elsie too.'

'I thought I did. By the way, I think there's a carving-
knife in your table drawer that belongs to Miss Chivers.'

'No, I don't think so, Boots,' he said softly. 'When the
police hear Miss Chivers and I are being investigated by
your Naval Intelligence, as they may, I imagine they'll
come back to this street yet again. I hope they won't turn
your house inside-out, for it'll do them no good and will
distress your mother. Incidentally, Boots, even if you
hadn't lied, Miss Chivers wouldn't have hanged.'

'You'd have made a confession?'

He didn't answer that, he only said, 'Shall we say
goodbye now?'

'Yes. Leave the front door open. You can't close it
without making some sort of noise.'

'Yes.'

I felt him take hold of my hand and shake it firmly and
strongly.

'Loyalties opposed to love, Boots, put our
responsibilities in desperate conflict with our hearts at
times. I'm sorry, very sorry, about the Somme.'

He made hardly a sound as he left. I rose from the
armchair and began a familiar groping. I found my way
into the passage and very carefully mounted the stairs to
the landing. The darkness of night was no different from

the darkness of day. Using my hands, I kept in contact with things I knew. I managed to enter Mr Finch's room without hitting anything. With my arms extended, I made sweeping searches until I connected with his table. I fumbled my way around it and opened a drawer. I felt inside the long knife compartment. My fingers closed around the handle of a carving-knife, a wooden handle. That was his own carver. There was no other. There was just the one. I knew then why he had taken the risk of coming back. On the morning when he had departed for good from our house, he had not known it was for good. His contact must have warned him during the day. Or perhaps Miss Chivers had been able to let him know that questions were being asked. The Naval Intelligence men had subsequently searched his room for papers, for anything that might relate to his espionage work. They would not have been interested in a carving-knife. In coming back for it, he had ensured it was kept out of the hands of the police. He was a German spy. She was an English traitor. They knew that might become known, one way or another. They did not want it also known that he or she, or both of them, had been responsible for the murder of her mother.

He or she, or both? No. She had done it. He would not have let her stand trial if he had been guilty in any way. He had said she informed him of what her mother overheard, that she had informed him the next day, Monday. But not until Wednesday had the doctor called. That meant he and Miss Chivers had risked giving her mother three days in all in which to reveal what she knew of his real nationality. For all her dislike and distrust of people, for all her hermit-like existence, the Witch wasn't a woman to wait three days before telling someone that Mr Finch had been born in Frankfurt, that he belonged to a country we were at war with.

Three days. Monday, Tuesday, Wednesday. I'd asked him why Mrs Chivers hadn't been killed in a way that would have given her daughter an alibi. Three days would have given them plenty of time to concoct a murder far tidier and less messy.

There hadn't been three days. Never. It had been Tuesday night when the Witch found them out. Out of protective love for Miss Chivers, Mr Finch had given me his version of events, not the true one. He had given me the truth about himself, but not about the murder. Deliberately, he had left me confused, so that I would never be able to say definitely yes, it was her.

But it was her. She had done it. On the morning after the night before. Suffering the torments of many years of viperish harassment, she had been faced with the certainty that her mother's tongue would destroy her lover, and herself too, for she was already one with him in his espionage work. Only when one realised Miss Chivers had hidden depths could one accept she would betray her country and commit murder for love of a man. She had kissed me, two or three times. Each time, her fires had been burning, and I could imagine her passion in the arms of a man as masculine and mature as Mr Finch.

In an uncontrollable moment of revenge for all the repressed years, and in mind-shattering desperation at what might happen to her and her lover if her mother was not silenced, Miss Chivers had struck. If anything was true at all, if anything was more certain in my mind than all else, it was the fact that Mr Finch would not have let her stand trial had he either committed the murder himself or been partner to it.

After the deed, whatever her distraught state, she had given herself time to think. She had removed the jewels, of course, and taken them to work with her. The jewels – and the carving-knife – had been in that shopping bag. I had known it, I think, the moment I mentioned the bag in court. She had probably cleaned the knife, but it had also probably haunted her and worried her.

Only after the murder had she spoken to Mr Finch. She would have had to, and she no doubt had her way of contacting him. They had met somewhere, probably at lunchtime, and Miss Chivers had placed the jewels and the knife in his keeping. And while disposal of the jewels might have been no problem, he was a man who would have been careful about disposing of a carving-knife. The docks were always busy. He could not drop it into the river without the risk of being seen, nor when piloting a vessel. So he had simply brought it back to his lodgings, where no one would have suspected its presence. The only time he was in any trouble was when the prosecution had hinted at collusion, and that had been derided. Neither Mr Braithwaite nor Sir Humphrey had mentioned it in their final address to the jury, and the judge had ignored it when summing up.

I wondered how she had looked when telling her lover she had murdered her mother. During that tram ride with me, she had only looked a little faraway once or twice. I wondered what Mr Finch had said to her. Whatever it was, he had not rejected her or failed her. Coming back to the house tonight had been a brave act of love and protection. She would never return to England, but he had still not wanted her to be remembered as the slayer of her own mother. If he had left the knife in his cutlery drawer, and the police had subsequently discovered it, the law might have pointed its accusing finger at him, but everyone would have known he could not have entered the house and murdered the Witch without Miss Chivers's collusion.

He obviously hadn't said to her it didn't matter now what the people of Caulfield Place thought or remembered. To her, it had mattered. Wherever she was, wherever she was going, she had loved Chinese Lady, adored Lizzy and found pleasure in Emily. I felt she simply could not bear them thinking her a matricide as well as a traitor. As for the latter, who was going to think that? If neither she nor Mr Finch were caught, if the State was unable to put either of them on trial, they could not be denounced or condemned. They were innocent until proved guilty. Perhaps she had thought of that. Perhaps they both had. And so, perhaps, she had said to him please go and get that knife, then I shall be remembered only as a mystery.

Would she have said that? Would she have cared about it as much as that? I felt she might. What would she say when Mr Finch told her of his confession to me? They would talk about the fact that I knew of their secrets and their collusion. But Mr Finch, of course, had made his confession knowing I was unlikely to tell Chinese Lady. Chinese Lady had already shut out what was an unbearable suspicion. She would want to remember Miss Chivers as a lady and Mr Finch as a gentleman. But except for that, how could I be sure I was right about anything? I'd been a clerk for a little while, and I'd done some soldiering, but I did not have Mr Finch's years, I did not have his maturity or his comprehensive knowledge of life and people. In life, I was still a beginner. I could only make guesses, and all of them might have been wrong.

I made a slow, careful way downstairs, one hand on the banisters, the other in touch with the wall. I groped my way back into the parlour. No one had been disturbed. Upstairs, Tommy and Sammy were sound alseep. In her downstairs room, Chinese Lady slept on.

Where was I? Suddenly disoriented. The parlour was all around me, but where was I pointing myself? Sod it, I thought. The irritation was as bitter as rising acid.

Someone had been disturbed, after all. Someone had got out of bed. I heard the soft sound of bare feet on the passage linoleum, and the cautious entry of someone into the parlour.

'Boots? Oh, you're up.' It was a whisper from Emily. 'Your front door's open – can't you sleep, neither? Oh, you ain't been out in the street, have you?'

'Emily, for God's sake, it must be two in the morning.'

'I—'

'Don't wake Chinese Lady.'

'Oh, no, I don't want to do that.' She breathed the words. 'I'm sorry, but I just couldn't get to sleep – and

425

what're you doing out of bed? Boots?' A warm hand took mine, and she gently turned me and led me forward. My knees touched the bed. I sat down on it. Shyly she whispered, 'Is it your eyes? Do they hurt?'

'No, they don't hurt, Em.' I had a mind to tell her everything was just bleeding dark, that was all, but it was hardly her fault.

'But you couldn't go to sleep?' she whispered. I felt the bed sink a little as she sat down beside me. 'Oh, nor could I. I kept thinkin' of you and me – it's been like a fever, like – oh, like it couldn't be 'appening. I ain't never—' Rushing her words, she steadied herself. I heard her draw breath, and perhaps she told herself she was eighteen, not thirteen, and that Chinese Lady would expect her to talk more proper. 'Boots, I never felt like this before, like all my dreams have come true. I been sitting in our kitchen. I got up to make myself some tea, you see. Then a few minutes ago, I thought how selfish I'd been, how I acted as if Christmas had come, talkin' nineteen to the dozen to your mum and the boys, and I remembered Tommy giving me a funny look. Now I know why he did, he was thinkin' what's she going on like that for when Boots has come home blinded? Oh, I didn't mean to be so selfish – yer won't think badly of me, will yer?' She was rushing again. 'I just 'ad to come in, I just 'ad to come an' see yer.'

'You thought you'd like a chat with me in the middle of the night?'

'Oh, no.' I felt her hand take hold of mine and grip it tightly. 'I wasn't going to wake you up, really I wasn't, I was just going to sit beside your bed and do penitence.'

'Penitence?'

'Yes, because I'd only been thinking about myself, about being so happy I couldn't believe it, I didn't think about how awful everything is for you. I didn't even tell yer—' Both her hands clasped mine. 'Boots, I do love yer – oh, you don't know – and I never even said so. I'd let yer walk over me if it would help you to see, honest I would.'

'I've never heard that treading one's future wife into the

ground can do wonders for the eyes. But I'll mention it to the next eye specialist I see.'

'No, don't joke, not when I've been so unthinking,' she whispered earnestly. 'It was even worse than that, because when I couldn't sleep, when I went down to the kitchen, I – I walked about in vanity and conceit.'

'You did what?' I was as wide-awake as Emily, if for a different reason. Even so, I was beginning to feel that if anything could cure the disastrous state of my mind, it was Emily's whimsicality. 'You did what, Em?'

'You see – you see—' Again she drew a breath. 'You see, I came down wearing just the satin camiknickers you give me, and I – I paraded about in them.'

'In your kitchen?'

'Yes, and with the light on.' Emily, breathlessly confessional, sounded lovable. 'Oh, what Chinese Lady would've said if she'd seen me flaunting myself, I can't bear to think.'

'What I can't bear to think is that I missed it all.'

'Boots?'

'Well, you must have been worth a look.'

'Oh, you're bliss to a girl, you are. But then the kettle boiled and I made the tea, and it was when I was drinkin' it that it come to me how selfish I'd been, and that what I'd been doing, parading about, was vanity and conceit.'

'God help us both. But wasn't it exciting as well? I mean, you must have looked exciting, and I don't suppose even the vicar minds a little bit of natural vanity.'

'Yes, but not when my fiancé's just come home suffering like you – oh, yer don't mind me saying you're my fiancé, do you? I'll make up for being selfish, really I will. I don't want you to stop loving me, I do know how awful things must be for you, but I'll be a good wife, I promise, I won't go in for vanity and conceit, I'll just be thankful.'

It didn't seem possible. It was all going on over there, the slaughter in the mud, and the world was looking on and doing nothing. It made the whole world a mess, and yet in that mess Emily existed in unbelievable innocence and humility.

427

I put an arm around her, and squeezed her. Her body felt very lightly clad. I felt her turn swiftly, I felt her arms wind around me.

'Em—'

'Oh, ain't this nice, Boots? You're so good for a girl.'

Do you have any idea of what Emily would ask for, Boots? I think Emily would ask only to be cuddled.

'Emily, you haven't said. Was it exciting, parading about like that?'

She hesitated before confessing.

'Oh, yes,' she whispered. 'I was thinkin' of you, and our wedding and our honeymoon – oh, you know – loving and all. It wasn't wicked of me, was it?'

'It might have been wicked to Arthur. It's not wicked to me. Emily, what are you wearing now?'

'Oh, I do like you in pyjamas,' she said.

'Come on, I asked you – what are you wearing now?'

'I – oh, just my camiknickers.'

I laughed out loud.

The sound woke Chinese Lady up.

Emily fled.

THE END

OUR EMILY
by Mary Jane Staples

Emily had been a quite horrible child. Pushy, rough, and none too clean (for it must have been Emily who passed on her head-lice to the Adams family), she had been the bane of Mrs Adams and her children who lived next door, and especially she had been a trial to Boots, who had avoided her whenever he could.

But Emily grown-up was a different matter. She was still a cockney girl, but now she had a certain elegance, a style. The fighting toughness was still there – and she needed it. For Boots, back from the trenches, was blind, and Emily was to prove the mainstay, the breadwinner, and the love of his life.

Here again is the Adams family from *Down Lambeth Way* – Chinese Lady determined more than ever to be respectable, Tommy facing unemployment, and Sammy well on the way to becoming a street market tycoon. And above all here is *Our Emily*.

0 552 13444 9

KING OF CAMBERWELL
by Mary Jane Staples

Sammy was the sharp one of the Adams family. Since he was nine-years-old – when he'd charged his mother interest on a loan to make up the rent money – he'd been busy setting up deals and expanding the family business – a china stall in East Street market. But as his mighty empire grew – two shops and a factory in Shoreditch – so did the determination of his assistant, Susie Brown.

Susie adored Sammy – although she thought he needed a bit of work done on him, a few rough spots knocked off – and she had decided, quite early on, that Sammy was going to marry her. But Sammy, rapidly becoming the King of Camberwell, and dreading that marriage was going to cost him money, decided to put up a fight. It was a battle he hadn't a hope of winning – especially when all the rest of the Adams family were on Susie's side.

Here again are all the magnificent characters from *Down Lambeth Way* and *Our Emily* – Chinese Lady, keeping her family in order and contemplating matrimony for the second time. Emily and Boots, facing a serious rift in their marriage – a rift not helped by the hovering Polly Sims. Tommy, daring to woo Cousin Vi when he 'wasn't quite good enough for her', and Sammy, pulling his wonderful Walworth family into the good times at last.

0 552 13573 9

ON MOTHER BROWN'S DOORSTEP
by Mary Jane Staples

The big event of the Walworth year was to be the wedding of Sammy Adams, King of Camberwell, to Miss Susie Brown. Everyone was looking forward to it, and Susie was particularly overjoyed when her soldier brother suddenly turned up on leave from service in India in time for the approaching 'knees-up'. The reason for Will's extended leave wasn't so good, for bad health had struck him and he didn't know how long the army would keep him, or how he could find a civvy job in the slump of the 20s. When he – literally – picked Annie Ford up off the pavement in King and Queen Street, his worries were compounded, for Annie was a bright, brave, personable young woman and Will knew that if he wasn't careful he'd find himself falling in love.

And over Walworth hung a greater anxiety – the mystery of three young girls missing from their homes – a mystery that was to draw closer and closer to the Adams and Brown families, and finally culminate – along with Will's personal problems – on the night of the wedding.

Here again is the Adams family from *Down Lambeth Way*, *Our Emily* and *King of Camberwell*.

0 552 13975 0

A SELECTED LIST OF FINE NOVELS
AVAILABLE FROM CORGI BOOKS

THE PRICES SHOWN BELOW WERE CORRECT AT THE TIME OF GOING
TO PRESS. HOWEVER TRANSWORLD PUBLISHERS RESERVE THE RIGHT
TO SHOW NEW RETAIL PRICES ON COVERS WHICH MAY DIFFER FROM
THOSE PREVIOUSLY ADVERTISED IN THE TEXT OR ELSEWHERE.

☐	14060 0	MERSEY BLUES	Lyn Andrews	£4.99
☐	12887 2	SHAKE DOWN THE STARS	Frances Donnelly	£5.99
☐	14442 8	JUST LIKE A WOMAN	Jill Gascoine	£5.99
☐	14096 1	THE WILD SEED	Iris Gower	£5.99
☐	14537 8	APPLE BLOSSOM TIME	Kathryn Haig	£5.99
☐	14385 5	THE BELLS OF SCOTLAND ROAD	Ruth Hamilton	£5.99
☐	14535 1	THE HELMINGHAM ROSE	Joan Hessayon	£5.99
☐	14332 4	THE WINTER HOUSE	Judith Lennox	£5.99
☐	13910 6	BLUEBIRDS	Margaret Mayhew	£5.99
☐	13904 1	VOICES OF SUMMER	Diane Pearson	£4.99
☐	14125 9	CORONATION SUMMER	Margaret Pemberton	£5.99
☐	14400 2	THE MOUNTAIN	Elvi Rhodes	£5.99
☐	14466 5	TOUCHED BY ANGELS	Susan Sallis	£5.99
☐	13951 3	SERGEANT JOE	Mary Jane Staples	£3.99
☐	13845 2	RISING SUMMER	Mary Jane Staples	£3.99
☐	13573 9	KING OF CAMBERWELL	Mary Jane Staples	£4.99
☐	13444 9	OUR EMILY	Mary Jane Staples	£5.99
☐	13635 2	TWO FOR THREE FARTHINGS	Mary Jane Staples	£4.99
☐	13856 8	THE PEARLY QUEEN	Mary Jane Staples	£3.99
☐	13975 0	ON MOTHER BROWN'S DOORSTEP	Mary Jane Staples	£3.99
☐	14106 2	THE TRAP	Mary Jane Staples	£4.99
☐	14154 2	A FAMILY AFFAIR	Mary Jane Staples	£4.99
☐	14230 1	MISSING PERSON	Mary Jane Staples	£4.99
☐	14291 3	PRIDE OF WALWORTH	Mary Jane Staples	£4.99
☐	14375 8	ECHOES OF YESTERDAY	Mary Jane Staples	£4.99
☐	14418 5	THE YOUNG ONES	Mary Jane Staples	£4.99
☐	14469 X	THE CAMBERWELL RAID	Mary Jane Staples	£4.99
☐	14513 0	THE LAST SUMMER	Mary Jane Staples	£4.99
☐	14548 3	THE GHOST OF WHITECHAPEL	Mary Jane Staples	£5.99
☐	14118 6	THE HUNGRY TIDE	Valerie Wood	£4.99

All Transworld titles are available by post from:

Book Service By Post, P.O. Box 29, Douglas, Isle of Man IM99 1BQ

Credit cards accepted. Please telephone 01624 675137,
fax 01624 670923, Internet http://www.bookpost.co.uk or
e-mail: bookshop@enterprise.net for details.

Free postage and packing in the UK. Overseas customers allow
£1 per book (paperbacks) and £3 per book (hardbacks).